Spoon Knife 3:
Incursions

Edited by Nick Walker
and Andrew M. Reichart

Weird Books for Weird People

Autonomous Press is an independent publisher focusing on works about neurodivergence, queerness, and the various ways they can intersect with each other and with other aspects of identity and lived experience. We are a partnership including writers, poets, artists, musicians, community scholars, and professors. Each partner takes on a share of the work of managing the press and production, and all of our workers are co-owners.

ISBN-10: 978-1-945955
ISBN-13: 978-1-945955-14-3

Cover art by Adrian Scharfetter
(http://www.machineelf.net).

Contents

Gouging Away: An Introduction to the Use of the Spoon Knife

Nick Walker

A spoon knife is a woodworking tool used for carving out those bowl-like concavities in the heads of wooden spoons. It's a sharp little implement with a nasty hook to it. The spoon knife is not intended for use on human flesh, though it's difficult to hold it in one's hand without vividly imagining the possibilities. Or maybe there's just something wrong with me.

One does not jab or thrust with a spoon knife. One *gouges,* dragging the hooked blade back toward oneself in exactly the way one is taught never to do with a regular knife. Gouging away, carving out a hollow in the unyielding wood, one small cut at a time.

The *Spoon Knife* anthology series, of which this is the third volume, features short fiction, memoir, and poetry by queer and neurodivergent authors. While each volume has its own specific theme, the series overall emphasizes the theme of *resistance.* There's an analogy to be drawn between the use of the spoon knife and the ways in which queer and neurodivergent individuals, and all sincere human beings with the fire of poetry in their souls, resist a world that brutally punishes any deviation from the soul-deadening dominant norms. The world gouges away at us, one cut at a time, trying to hollow us out and carve the spark of beautiful weirdness out of us.

And we, in turn, gouge away at the world, one cut at a time, trying to carve out some space in which we can be our true selves, some little hollow in which we can keep the spark alive.

For this volume, I invited my esteemed collaborator Andrew M. Reichart to come on board as co-editor. Andrew and I are the co-creators of the *Weird Luck* saga, an ever-growing body of interconnected stories and comics which includes the stories that he and I contributed to this volume of *Spoon Knife* and the previous volume. The *Weird Luck* saga features an agency called the Reality Patrol that deals with situations in which the boundaries between alternate realities have become compromised. The Reality Patrol refers to these situations as *incursions,* and our constant immersion in writing about such things probably contributed to our decision to make *incursions* the theme for this volume.

The theme of *incursions* can serve as yet another way of framing the struggles of creatively divergent souls. The dominant normative culture treats our presence as an incursion, and, in response, makes incursions into our lives to force normativity upon us or to crush us if we won't comply. We, in turn, resist those incursions and make incursions of our own, subverting the dominant culture where we can. Gouging away, because it's what we need to do to survive, and because it's our sacred duty. Because, in the words of Dr. Martin Luther King, "Human salvation lies in the hands of the creatively maladjusted."

Rather than say anything here about the stories in this volume, I've written a brief introductory note at the beginning of each piece. This practice of introducing each individual piece in an anthology is a practice I've loved ever since I was twelve years old and first read Harlan Ellison's introductory notes to the stories in the groundbreaking *Dangerous Visions* and *Again, Dangerous Visions* anthologies—anthologies that, in their time, helped to carve out more space for weirdness in the field of speculative fiction. If this volume of *Spoon Knife* can also help to carve out more space for weirdness in the world in some small way, I'll be satisfied that my co-editor and I, and all the extraordinary authors who graced us with their contributions, have done our jobs well.

So... ready for some stories?

Let the gouging commence.

Nick Walker
March 2018

Our first story, "The Bob Show," is a fun and delightfully understated piece of speculative fiction from Jeff Baker. The incursion here is a leak of information *between realities. Seems harmless enough, but this sort of thing can have far-reaching consequences, and someone really ought to report it to the Reality Patrol.*

The Bob Show

Jeff Baker

The bunker my brother built outside Wichita, Kansas seemed like a pretty good place to spend the summer, especially a summer where I had several warrants out for my arrest. And that was where I first saw The Bob Show.

Little brother Gordie had tunneled underground a couple of stories for his concrete-reinforced basement and sub-basement, but had a nice (but expansive) farmhouse as his first floor on the ground. Front porch, rocking chairs, living room, kitchen, second floor with bedroom windows that looked out on the prairie and the distant highway. All looking like it had been built about 120 years ago, but built only about four years ago. The retro look. Hey, he had cable, air-conditioning and a microwave so I didn't gripe. And he didn't turn me in to the cops when they came by, which I really appreciated. After that, I spent most of my days in the reinforced lower levels. It had all the amenities, several bedrooms, Gordie's library and computer and a couple of working bathrooms. A kitchen with a load of supplies (no beer) and even a weight room. And just off the library was the TV room.

Let me, the Older Brother, explain about my Younger Brother, Mr. Gordon Jacks. Gordie was genius level in High School and was still on the track and baseball teams. Got a track scholarship to a major university, where he studied science, biology and every math course he could get his hands on. Gordie swung through a bunch of high-level positions before he got the one he now had, which enabled him to build the house, bunker and all and to afford to be away most of the time.

Me, Big Brother Danny, didn't do so bad in school either. There were girls and football and soccer, and I did get a scholarship to go to college (not the one Gordie went to!). I went a year-and-a-half and then I realized I was making more money on my own than I could if I went ahead and got my business degree.

So, Danny Jacks bailed and hit New York. That led me to L.A. And to make a long story short, it led me to my brother's hospitality. And a lot of boredom as I paced around the Bunker (as he called it) and tried to figure out what I was going to do when a bunch of people wanted me in their custody for, as a mentor of mine once put it, "stretching the law."

Underground, despite the lights set to fake sunrises and sunsets, you lose track of time, and it didn't help that I was sleeping a lot, so I wasn't that sure even what day or time it was when I opened the door at the far end of Gordie's main office (the one he'd asked me not to, I picked the locks, all three of them) and found out that what he was doing was watching the ultimate big-screen TV.

The room was simple, the TV dominated it as it does a lot of rooms (I remember begging my Dad when I was a kid, to let me have the black and white TV he was going to throw out for my and Gordie's bedroom.) but instead of an armchair in a living room there was a table, and a long, flat bench, knee-high, partly covered with spiral-bound notebooks with plastic covers on the front. Lying on the table was what I gathered to be the remote. I couldn't make heads or tails of it. I looked at the notebooks. The covers had dates like "July-August" and "2017, Wednesday." Some of the notebooks were on the shelf on the wall, some on the couch in front of the TV.

I looked over at the darkened screen of the TV and grabbed the remote. That's when I noticed the thin notebook under the table. I recognized Gordie's handwriting on the cover: "How To Use The I-3 40."

I smiled. Smartest guy in the world I knew and he'd always had to write notes to himself about day-to-day-stuff. I opened the notebook. Should be easy to figure out.

About a half-hour later I'd used the remote to turn the TV, on which displayed the current time: July 17, 1:55 a.m. Like having a time channel. Then there was a static noise and the screen went blank for a moment. Then the screen showed some black-and-white scene of a flowerpot, full of blooms while a bunch of closing credits rolled by.

I ducked out to grab a soda from Gordie's fridge, realizing that the next show was coming on and I was bored so what the hell.

The screen went black for a moment, and then I saw a black-and-white stage curtain, with a superimposed caricature of a smiling face, balding head and a pointy nose, all done as one line. At the same time, I heard an announcer, who said: "From Hollywood, it's the Robert Benchley Show, starring America's master of mirth, Mister Robert Benchley!" The applause, which sounded canned, began as the show's title replaced the caricature. Then a picture of a bag of coffee filled the screen.

"Brought to you by the maker's of Rounder's Coffee, the coffee America chooses."

The bag faded from the screen, replaced by the same curtain as before. The announcer went on.

"And now, get ready to laugh! Here's Bob!"

The applause was high on the treble and really fake, I thought, as the scene cut to a tall man, with grey hair fringing a balding head walking along the curtain and acknowledging the nonexistent applause. He was the man in the caricature, and I tried to remember where I'd heard his name. He turned to the camera, the applause immediately cut, and began to speak.

"Thank you. You know, during the war, you do remember the war, don't you? Well I heard about the need to plant gardens, and so here is a short film about an ordinary man who tries to plant an ordinary garden. And I hope it grows on you!"

The short movie was obviously of the same man Benchley, years younger, as a guy with a wife house and job trying to plant a backyard garden. And while a lot of things got in his way I realized quickly that he was his own biggest problem. I was laughing so hard that I had to lie down on the sofa and was grateful for the commercial break so I could have a breather. And I realized that I really hadn't laughed in a while. After the short film ended, and they aired a few more commercials, Benchley was back in front of the curtain.

"When our brave boys came home from the war, it was my privilege to travel from base to base to entertain them as best as I could. And what better entertainment than showing them life on the home front. Oh, this was filmed at three separate shows, so my tie changes a couple of times in mid-scene. Don't be alarmed."

This one was different, clearly filmed on a makeshift stage, I could see some grinning young men sitting on the ground just at the edge of the stage and the backs of a few heads at the front of the stage. There was a small counter with a row of shelves behind it at the far end of the stage, but when Benchley walked in, wearing suit, overcoat and hat, there were laughs and applause from the crowd.

I was a lot sleepier than I thought and dozed through part of it where Benchley was trying to see where he could exchange some book of coupons, and after finally narrowing it down to the counter and sales clerk he was talking to, the clerk cooed "Sorry, can't use those. War's over." This brought another roar from the crowd and an exasperated look from Benchley.

And I was all but asleep, glimpsing the closing credits for the Benchley show and seeing the opening credits start again. It must've been around two-thirty in the morning I realized. Then I was asleep again, only waking up during the last part of the second of the shows, hearing Benchley introduce "a bit of foolishness for which I became famous early on, and someone decided to film it. We were very young then. This is called 'The Treasurer's Report.'"

The clip began. After a few moments of set up, Benchley walked up to a podium and began fumbling through a speech which made me laugh again, and his efforts to get through it made me laugh all the harder. When the speech ended and the commercial came on, I stretched out on the couch and dozed off, waking up about a half-hour later seeing some game show on TV. In color this time. I fumbled for the fancy remote, found the off switch and headed for bed. I didn't know when Gordie was coming back and I didn't want him to catch me in a room he'd had locked.

I didn't think about The Bob Show or anything on TV at all for much of the next week. Then, having bummed my way through some of Gordie's books and checked out what was on the computer until I was certain I could come up with something better myself, I went back to the TV room late one afternoon and picked the locks again. I sat down and reached for the remote but Gordie's notebooks caught my eye and I started thumbing through them. One of them, labeled "Current Schedule" was just that: a handwritten TV schedule, the sort of thing he and I would have done while we were in grade school. Pages of it. I flipped through it until a familiar name caught my eye.

2:00 a.m. The Robert Benchley Show (comedy)
2:30 a.m. The Robert Benchley Show (comedy)
3:00 a.m. I've Got It! (game, repeat of afternoon show)
3:30 a.m. The Man Upstairs (comedy)

There were more pages like this, about a week's worth, and then at the back of the notebook several pagefulls of my Brother's handwriting:

"Robert Benchley Show. Aired apparently early 1950's, not sure of the year, can't quite make out roman numerals in the old kinescope. My guess, show made between 1952 and '54. (!!!)"

Below this was a long rambling explanation of the game show that followed Benchley, "I've Got It!" which my Brother was apparently hooked on. Me, I'd never liked game shows that much.

I set the notebook back on the pile and then it hit me that I'd better put everything back where I'd found it. I didn't want Gordie to be too furious when he got back and if he didn't know I was breaking into his office and watching his private TV we'd both be better off. I got everything put back the way I remembered it from last week, and locked the door behind me as I left. Good thing I did because there was a message on the answering machine upstairs, which didn't mention my name, but was Gordie saying he'd be back in town sometime next afternoon.

It was early that morning when I decided to check the computer. I knew I'd heard the name of the guy on The Bob Show before. And after sifting through results like "Buy Benchley Here!" I finally saw something promising and clicked on it. The entry was much like I'd expected:

> *Robert Benchley (1889-1945). American humorist, writer and actor. Wrote reviews and columns for various New York City papers in the 1920s and '30s. Appeared on radio and in films, many of which he wrote. See Round Table, Algonquin.*

That didn't tell me a lot, and it didn't mention the TV show. I searched for "The Robert Benchley Show" and then "Robert Benchley Show" with no results. I sat and tried to remember what the listing had said about the Bob Show. I considered breaking in again and bringing the notebooks upstairs to the computer, but that would probably have been as bad as my going up to the ground level and sitting out on the front porch drinking beer, daring the authorities to find me.

I was microwaving a pizza, wondering when Gordie was going to show up when something I'd seen in the last couple of days hit me. I went back to the computer, searched again and again. Every entry for Robert Benchley said he'd died in 1945. The notebook had said he was on TV in the early 1950s, hadn't it?

I wondered about that as I ate the pizza. It could be a misprint or the sloppy research the internet was famous for, but not on so many different websites. I went down to Gordie's big-screen TV again and found the notebook I'd looked at earlier. No doubt Gordie had felt the show had been made in the early 1950s. But Benchley had died years earlier, hadn't he? I was back at the computer again a few minutes later, searching for Benchley. Something had occurred to me and after a few minutes I found it; a couple of clips on a video site. I clicked on the site and hit 'play.'

In one of the clips, which must have dated from the 1930s, Benchley was a researcher explaining about getting a good night's sleep, while on the screen he was shown attempting to follow the advice. I laughed and replayed the clip several times. The other video was the one I'd seen on the TV show of Benchley trying to tend to his garden.

I was downstairs in the TV room, leafing through the notebooks when Gordie walked in. Like I'd expected he was mad but not to surprised. He was more relieved when he asked if I'd tried to record anything off that TV and I told him I hadn't.

"I barely figured out how to turn this thing on."

"Good," Gordie said bending down to examine the small metal box beside the TV. His slacks, jacket, and white button-down short sleeved shirt were wrinkled and his tie was just draped around his neck. I didn't have to ask if he'd slept in them. He stood up with a half satisfied, half relieved expression on his face and let out a long breath.

"Sorry if I got all touchy," he said.

"S'okay," I replied. "I know how it is when you miss your favorite program."

He nodded, staring at the black screen.

"Hey, where'd you buy this thing, anyway?" I asked. Gordie smiled.

"Didn't buy it," he said. "We built it."

"You built it?" I said. "Then this is a new model that nobody else has?"

"A few other people have ones like it," he said. "That's where I've been. We were checking the," he paused, "reception in various parts of the country." Then he started talking about the days when he and I were growing up and had to show Dad our report cards or he'd take the TV out of our bedroom. Gordie had changed the subject and he was pretty good at that. It should have made me suspicious right there but I was just so glad he hadn't brought up my picking the lock on the door I was happy to let it drop.

Gordie took a shower and exchanged his suit and tie for sweatshirt and jogging shorts as he puttered around the kitchen putting stuff together for dinner. He'd told me once that his first marriage had fallen apart because he was always at work so he'd learned to fend for himself pretty well.

"Besides, I really can't have a housekeeper, not here," he said.

That was when something in my head clicked and I realized that my hiding out at Gordie's wasn't the only thing out of whack. Why did he need a damn bunker? I should have asked a bunch of questions right there; the whole thing was sounding a lot more suspicious than just hiding his brother from the law. But I was his guest so instead I asked him about The Bob Show.

"Oh, yeah, he's funny!" Gordie said, busily chopping up a couple of carrots. "I took a bunch of notes on that. I'm still a compulsive note taker."

Gordie'd always kept a notebook with him even when we were kids. He'd kept one in his car and when he was in High School a girl had walked out on him at the drive-in because she caught him scrawling a few notes to himself when she came back from the restroom and accused him of 'comparing how all the girls do.'

"Dad had a book of Benchley's stuff that had been Granddad's when we were kids," Gordie went on. "I only looked at the drawings in it when we were younger. I didn't ever read it."

Me either. I was never much into books. The internet was another matter.

"I checked on the computer. The DVD of the Benchley show isn't out yet," I said.

Gordie looked thoughtful for a moment.

"Maybe there's a lot of copyright problems," he said. Then he turned the conversation over to our Dad's books and how we probably shouldn't have been so quick to sell a lot of his stuff after he died. I'd honestly needed the money back then. Hell, I probably needed it right now! We continued the conversation over dinner and over a couple of beers (from the six-pack he'd bought in town) on the back porch. It was dark by then and we figured we could hear if a car drove up and I could duck into the house. Besides, sitting outdoors in the night breeze did me good.

From Gordie's back porch I could see for miles. He told me he owned a lot of acreage. Off in the distance I could make out what I assumed to be a wheat field. I'd seen a silo in the distance out of one of the upper windows. Sitting there I couldn't believe how much I'd wanted to get away from the Midwest when I was young. Now I thought it was all so peaceful. I was leaned back in my chair watching the stars when Gordie finished his beer, looked at his watch and said that he had to "go do some work" in his office. I nodded as he got up and went back inside. I could tell he wasn't that crazy about my hiding out there but we both knew I had nowhere else to go except probably jail or an unmarked grave in a landfill somewhere.

After a little while I went inside, taking care to lock the door behind me. I checked the fridge, got another beer and wandered downstairs and heard voices from Gordie's office, the TV room. The door was partly open so I looked in. Gordie was sitting at the table writing in one of the notebooks, with a couple of other pens beside him on the table. He looked back and forth from the notebook to the TV, which was showing the game show that I recognized as following The Bob Show early in the morning.

Gordie didn't notice me standing in the doorway. I figured at that moment he wouldn't have noticed anything. I'd been hooked on football, but never on game shows. I heard applause from the TV and then the host's voice.

"For 600 points, cite the formula that solved the Unified Field Theory."

As the contestant rattled off a long set of numbers I edged in to where I could see the screen and the green light on the box beside the screen. The player was on, Gordie was watching one of the shows from earlier. I remembered from one of the notebooks that the game show was on in the afternoon and early in the morning, but wasn't on right then. I turned my attention back to the game show where the host was talking about some scientist I'd never heard of. That didn't mean much, I knew about Einstein and Hawking, but this was something different.

"And is best known for solving the problem of negative effects of weightlessness on astronauts. For 250 points, exactly how did he do this?"

One of the contestants began answering and Gordie began scribbling again. He reached for the remote and rewound the show to the point where the contestant gave her answer and began scribbling in the notebook, scratching out a word. He put the show on pause and that was when he looked up and noticed me.

"You've been watching?" he asked, pointing to the TV.

"Yeah," I said. "That's not local cable is it?"

Gordie shook his head.

"You've got one of those dishes?"

"Sort of." Gordie said. "This signal is coming from out-of-state."

I glanced over at the pile of notebooks. "You're being paid to watch this stuff, aren't you?" Gordie nodded and smiled.

"And you're not paying for it, right?"

"Right," he said. "This is all new. All experimental. The company I work for has shelled out billions for these TV's. But the thing is, you pick up different stations or no station depending on your location."

"Like regular broadcast TV." I said. "When we were kids."

"Yeah," Gordie said. "It's like that."

"I'll tell you, Bro," I said starting to laugh, "that game show is beyond me."

"It's beyond everybody." Gordie said. "At least right now."

"Is this stuff coming in from, like Canada?" I asked.

"No. It's from here. At least from the U.S. Just a little different version."

Gordie and I talked for a little more, then I went back to my room and went to bed. But a few hours later I got up and wandered back to the TV room. The door was still open and I looked in, and this time Gordie didn't see me, he was staring at a news broadcast. I recognized the newscaster but the only thing the show got right was the date. They got the President's name wrong and then started a story about a U.S. moon base. I thought it might have been a movie but then they showed something about a strike that I knew was still going on. I got a glass of water and went back to bed.

A couple of days later when Gordie was gone I went into town to buy some beer. I guess I got careless and cocky and imagined my luck could hold out for a while. It didn't. I got picked up by a couple of cops who recognized me from my picture. In jail I used my one phone call to apologize to Gordie's answering machine. I didn't hear from him then or when I got sent to the penitentiary for a few years. At least not directly.

One day, in my cell, someone passed me a newspaper which had a picture of Gordie accepting an award for his discovery of something called the Unified Field Theory while working "for a government research agency." It hit me that I'd heard that on the game show. Everybody knows that already, I thought.

"Bro," I muttered, "you've got yourself one hell of a good scam going."

Like all the best dystopian satire, Alyssa Gonzalez's story "Future Dive" takes a hilariously over-the-top approach to an all-too-real problem: the ways in which an ever-more-exploitive socioeconomic system makes incursions into the quality of our lives, and the way in which many people continue to accept an increasingly nightmarish and unlivable status quo as "normal" rather than recognizing the incursions for what they are.

Future Dive

Alyssa Gonzalez

We always picked the Crawlspace. Nobody really liked the Crawlspace. Some of the roof is strapped to the half-dead chestnut tree whose roots are damaging the sidewalk outside, and the constant drip in that part of the bar was used to water a bamboo that no one dared call lucky. At least one bar stool was half of a barber's chair that the owners never bothered to unbolt from the floor after buying Crabbie's Cuts, and it still smelled like old hair. We were pretty sure that the combination of fluids that over the years made the light brown stain at the far corner swell to take up half of the floor would make a health inspector blanch, but the last health inspector who looked at the Crawlspace did an about-face at the door while reciting "NOPE" under his breath, so, that hasn't been a problem.

A young white woman in a gray sweater and red skirt resting her head on her hand and holding a large mug of beer in a bar.

It is never this nice in the Crawlspace.

I usually got there early. I liked to get my order in before the rush, and arriving early meant I got first dibs on Barb. The other bar stools had cushions stuffed with human hair and shredded fast-fashion clothing too worn to be used as automotive insulation, so Barb was an important part of my day. My Crawlburger™, salad harvested from between the sidewalk cracks outside, and water were already in front of Barb by the time I raised my hand to get Gina's attention. Gina returned to cleaning the coffee machines with her usual dead-eyed smile.

I envied that smile. It said, "Sometimes, when I go out to eat, it's not Crawlburgers™."

Ashley arrived next. She was still in her all-black ensemble from her own server gig, and looked like she'd had a rough shift. Shaking the dust from her leggings, she took the seat to my left and immediately removed her high heels.

"One of those egg and sausage sandwich things, please," Ashley directed at Gina.

"One Biscuitcreep™, coming right up," Gina answered, disappearing into the kitchen.

"Still having breakfast for dinner?" I asked Ashley, half a smile on my face.

"It's how I deal with not having time for breakfast at breakfast," she answered, putting her head in her hands. "Has that jar of olives always been there?"

I leaned toward the jar of olives at the other end of the counter. It appeared to have fused with the bar varnish, and I couldn't move it. "Probably."

"I don't remember olives here." Ashley seemed unnerved. "We go through them so fast at Skoti's, I hardly notice them at all."

Our next thoughts were interrupted by Jennifer's phone notification noise. We could hear hers before she even entered the bar, because she used the loudest setting she could and each web site that sent her notifications had a different movie-monster sound effect. The Godzilla roar just now meant that someone was soliciting her services on TaskRabbit. She pushed through the front door, holding it open with one arm and typing out a message with her other hand. She took the other seat next to me, and kept typing for another minute while Gina brought Ashley her Biscuitcreep™. I picked up my Crawlburger™ and took a big bite. Jennifer's phone rang, and she answered on the first note. Her nigh-delirious excitement soon waned, and she eventually turned down the gig.

"They're always farther than I can get to between shifts," she sighed darkly. "Doesn't seem to matter what distance I set in the system."

"Mine are always 'didn't read the ad, can you do this thing you can't do?'" I responded, "Or 'can you do it for half your rate?'"

All three of us sighed. Jennifer took most of my weed salad from my plate and started munching. I didn't stop her. We all looked up in time to watch Nazreen collapse into the chair next to Ashley, without us noticing her come in. She stayed there, arms down and head thrown back, for a few minutes, while Jennifer's and my phones alerted us to inquiries about our services on the Internet.

"It's over," Nazreen intoned, leaning up and then putting her head on her folded arms on the bar. "I just sold the last thing my ex left behind when he took off. That's it. There's nothing after this. I can't make rent after this."

Ashley put her arm around Nazreen.

"I'm supposed to be better than this," Nazreen squeezed out, voice cracking. "I trained to be so much better than this."

"We all did," I added. On my phone, I scrolled through a mix of multi-level marketing offers and contract positions that capped out at about three hours a week as long as absolutely nothing else was making firm claims on one's time, and felt inspired.

"Gina," I called, "four of whatever the opposite of your finest scotch is."

"Sure thing," Gina answered, pouring each of us a glass of Klaus's Peaty Armpit from a bottle whose label depicted a kilt-clad Santa Claus playing bagpipes on the Giant's Causeway, and then pouring herself one. It smelled the way falling off a bicycle into a muddy ditch feels.

"If this is how it ends," I began, holding up my glass, let it end drunkenly."

The five of us clinked our glasses and took long sips.

"Remember when it wasn't like this?" Gina asked, checking her watch to make sure she had time to get ready for her shift as an overnight stocking clerk at the nearby grocery. "Remember unions? Remember when those were a thing?"

"Remember full-time hours?" Ashley added, putting her glass down. "Remember needing only one job to make ends sort of meet?"

"And doing work and then getting paid for the work you did!" Nazreen added, sipping a bit more.

"And having health insurance!" I continued, reminiscing bitterly.

"And being able to occasionally not work for at least a few conscious hours at a time!" Jennifer contributed, acknowledging pings from various contract sites without looking down from her glass.

"Those were the days," Gina mused.

"None of that ever happened," a much younger voice chimed in from behind us. He sniffed and took a long snort from his Starbucks-brand Cocacchino. Ashley swallowed the rest of her drink while the rest of us raised eyebrows at our visitor. He adjusted the stack of readings he was carrying for his Master of Science in Being a Barista. "You're making things up," he insisted, looking like he might doze off where he stood. After another Cocacchino snort, he continued, "there's no way it's ever not been like this." The five of us sighed, and turned back to our drinks. The visitor looked at his watch again, panicked, muttered "shitshitshit, too much studying, gonna be late for job number seven!" and ran out of the Crawlspace.

"Maybe we did imagine all of that," Nazreen thought out loud. "If we'd ever had it, how could it fall apart so fast?"

Outside, it started to rain. The bamboo's tray swelled.

Eliza Redwood's poem "9-5" is another, less light-hearted take on the way corporate culture and unfulfilling jobs constitute soul-crushing incursions into our lives.

9-5

Eliza Redwood

I watch the seasons pass from inside my cubicle.
Well, that's not quite right.
I don't get any natural light from inside my cubicle,
So

I watch as the company-provided calendar
Switches from snowy mountaintops
To budding weeping willows
To a rocky shoreline bathed in sun.
All while I struggle to remember
What happiness feels like.

When the lightbulb above my cubicle flickers out,
I don't get it changed for a month.
When they ask me why I waited so long,
I can't answer.
I hadn't even noticed it was out.

Every morning
I exchange pleasantries,

As though something has changed.
Tomorrow someone is bringing in bagels—
I force a smile because
In a time loop, tomorrow never comes.

During a holiday
I get gifted a plant,
A pathetically sallow thing
That's supposed to remind me of something.
When the stem begins to curl
Around the filing cabinet,
I forget to water it. And it dies.

On a Saturday when the calendar shows a snowy mountaintop,
I find myself at my cubicle accidentally.
I'd forgotten what day it was.
I immediately turn around and drive home,
But lying in bed, I'm still back in my cubicle,
Hollow and empty.

And at night when I dream,
I dream that I have dreams,
Not just specters of a life unled.
I can almost hear a faint ticking in the distance,
When my alarm clock rings
And the dawning slips away.

Our next piece, "A Twentieth-Century Comedy of Manners," is a true story, a brief reminiscence from a now-retired autistic software engineer who goes by the handle Old Cutter John. Like "Future Dive" and "9-5," "A Twentieth-Century Comedy of Manners" addresses the invasive demands of corporate culture. But instead of being overwhelmed by the incursions of the system, Old Cutter John is himself an incursion, innocently disrupting the hierarchal mindset and banal typecasting on which the system and its enforcers thrive.

A Twentieth-Century Comedy of Manners

Old Cutter John

Ronald Reagan was starting his second term in the White House and I was working for a computer software company in New Jersey. I'd been with them almost twenty years. My job title was *Senior Staff Consultant,* and I reported to a corporate vice president, which put me at the same level as a product manager—a person who had responsibility for development, support, and documentation of a major software package. The vice president who supervised me was Dave. He was a drunken, sexist neurotypical who put pathological stock in the pecking order. He disapproved of me as much as I disapproved of him, for reciprocal reasons, but he recognized my value and let me do pretty much what I wanted. I designed software, I did the most difficult programming tasks, I was troubleshooter of last resort, and I managed the company's Los Angeles support center (mostly from afar, but occasionally I visited).

The company was headquartered in a three-story building. The lowest level housed a few corporate offices (including the president's), the order-fulfillment department, and shipping and receiving. The middle level housed more corporate offices and the marketing and sales staff. The notorious third floor housed the development and support staffs, including me. People who didn't work on the third floor were warned not to go there—not as a matter of policy, but by folklore: The people on the third floor were crazy.

I lived four miles from the building, and I didn't own a car. By choice. We had one until Labor Day of 1981, but it was destroyed when my wife and I fell asleep at the same time at fifty-five miles an hour on the New Jersey Turnpike while returning home from an orgy, and we didn't replace it until 1989, when we'd already moved to Las Vegas. I walked to and from work every day, even in the worst of weather. Some of the walk was through the woods, which I really enjoyed. I had (and still have) appropriate footwear and an arctic-expedition-grade parka, among other paraphernalia, so it wasn't as bad as it might sound, and it kept me in shape. Among my fellows on the third floor, I was widely rumored to live in the woods without electricity. I wore hiking or mountaineering boots at the office every day. Usually I also wore blue Wrangler jeans and a blue chambray work shirt. While thinking about technical problems, I was in the habit of wandering the halls of all three levels of the building. Not surprisingly, most people on the two lower levels thought I was the janitor. The ones who knew the janitor thought I was his assistant.

When designing software, I had a preference for making diagrams on quadrille pads—pads of white paper, eight and a half by eleven inches, ruled horizontally and vertically, four lines per inch. One day

I found myself running low, and I went to the supply room to get more. The supply room was on the second level, and it had always been unattended; but when I got there, I discovered that some woman had been hired as Keeper of the Supplies, and part of the supply room had become her office. I walked in and she asked me what I wanted. I told her I'd come to get a pack of quadrille pads, politely averting my eyes as I spoke. (I'm autistic, after all. Except at those orgies I mentioned, I didn't do eye contact. Still don't!) She asked me what I wanted them for. I told her I use them in my work, to make diagrams. She asked me to bring her a sample of my usage to show her. I told her she wouldn't understand what she was looking at, but okay, I'd do it. She asked me my name and the name of my supervisor. I told her. Then I left, went back to my office, grabbed a recent design diagram, took it to the copy machine, and copied it.

Obviously, no neurotypical of my position in the company would have responded as I did. But I'm autistic. And my approach to life has always been, *Buy the ticket, take the ride.* I'm sure that's not universal among autistics, but it's me: I'm not real self-important, I don't care about the pecking order, and what the Keeper of the Supplies asked of me was no great hardship. I had set out to take a break from the more demanding aspects of my job, and doing what she asked was as good a break as any.

As might be expected, but unbeknownst to me, the Keeper of the Supplies called Dave while I was copying my design diagram. Luckily for her (and I don't know this either), she didn't get Dave. Instead she got Sandy, Dave's secretary. She explained the situation as she saw it, still not knowing Dave's position in the company but imagining he must be the facilities manager; and Sandy, realizing what Dave would do to the poor woman if he found out, gasped and told her what she'd just got herself into.

I returned to the supply room and proffered the requested copy of my design diagram.

"Oh, you don't have to give me that! Here!"

And she handed me a stack of quadrille pads. I thanked her and went my way, never letting on that I understood what had happened in my absence. We autistics never seem to understand, do we?

Two weeks later the Keeper of the Supplies was gone. Self-destructed. Couldn't handle it. Maybe it was the stress of waiting for the other shoe to drop, which of course it never would; or maybe the disorientation of realizing she was in an environment where the familiar cues fail badly. I know it had something to do with her interaction with me, and I know she mentioned it in her exit interview, because when another two weeks had gone by, a memo was distributed to everyone on the third floor, advising us that thenceforth we'd have to go through our secretaries to get supplies. The folks in personnel didn't want to be burning through Keepers of the Supplies at the rate of one a month. The system protects itself.

Judy Grahn is one of the distinguished elders of queer literature. When one is putting together an anthology of queer and neurodivergent literature and one receives a submission from Judy Grahn, it's hard to keep thinking like an editor and not just dissolve into a gushing fanboy. We would have been more than honored if she'd just offered us a brief poem she had laying around, but when it turned out she was giving us an original 9000-word short story... well, I'd like to think I maintained an outward veneer of professional composure, but I may have made some "Squeee" noises. Did I mention this piece is from Judy Grahn? "Only Strawberries Don't Have Fathers" is a beautiful and delicately complex story about how family systems and the individuals within them respond to newcomers and other changes, as related by a neurodivergent narrator who's also dealing with a different sort of incursion.

Only Strawberries Don't Have Fathers

Judy Grahn

I've had to make my own jobs up ever since I got out of the hospital, the sixth floor ward, psych ward to be exact, so I wasn't surprised that nobody would hire me. That was ok, or at least it was familiar, "be resourceful" I said, and collected scrap metal around town and took it over to the junk yard down on second street, that's how you stay in cheese and bread. They had a dog there among the discarded car parts and cans, a supplement to the barbed wire on top of the fence, a Rottweiler who looked half starved so I shared my food. This worked out ok until one day the dog just went nuts, reminded me of my dad, and chewed on my arm, then it looked like a flute from wrist to elbow. Amazing regular red holes!

After a couple days my arm started to feel like it wanted to leave the material realm, well, I didn't want to go back to the hospital for anything, fortunately someone I knew on the street, my friend Hayscoop, told me about Dr. Darby, that she would treat poor people on the spot so to speak, so I hung out in front of her clinic for a few hours and after a while there she was. Noticing me. Tender eyes. Took a short look at my flute and invited me to her house; we got into her car together. Turned out she not only cleaned everything up and gave me a shot, she listened and then told me I could sleep in a little cottage in the back of her house while she took me through a course of rabies vaccinations in case I needed, even though I wouldn't tell her where the dog lived. Her house was a neat three-bedroom rowhouse on a 150 foot long lot, with one of those delicious-looking two-story tumble down cottages in back, built in the 1930s. Perfect for me, even a crawl space underneath stuffed with wild crabgrass where I could hide whenever necessary. First thing, I met her wife, Sarah, and their cat Morgan. Sarah held my flute arm just so while the doctor bandaged me.

To repay this ultra spectacular kindness I became their gardener that very moment. Told Dr. Darby I could raise all the vegetables and fruits she and her wife Sarah could eat. They went inside their house to talk this over, which I could hear through the open window, and while they did I changed my name to Clovis. My dad would never find me with a name like that. Sarah said I could stay for a trial period if I would take a shower, comb my hair, and allow them to buy me some new clothes. Ho, I wasn't ready for all that but said I would do some of it if they would let me go get my cat Marmalade as I was missing her, and the not-always-reliable Hayscoop was keeping her on the street while I was in the hospital. So, more confab inside the house while I counted the different food garden spaces they were wasting with landscape plants, and decided where the compost pile should go.

I had a prescription and a bottle of meds from my last stay—in the hospital—but after a few weeks I just had a problem with those meds. Here is what I love to do: get to know creatures and plants, get the dirt wet with buckets of water and put my hands in it to stir it up, come upon a little tangle of earthworms down underneath, and look at their dark and bright red stripes like Scandinavian Tee shirts. Then listen to the wind talking to me, especially at night. With these meds no matter how small I cut the pill, I felt dull, you can't feel dull in a garden, it begins to dislike you. You have to dance with the plants! And the wind lately wasn't saying anything interesting, as I kept forgetting to ask the questions. Lonely times like these, I stop taking anything, don't even eat, and it works out better. Until my dad comes after me and I need to hide.

It was during one of these times that Dr. Darby came back to the cottage yard to find me. By now I was sometimes calling her Dr. D., to myself. More intimate, don't you think? She peered at me under the house where I was curled into the crab grass, had been there for a couple of days. She stretched out on the ground so we were on the same level. "What's up?" She picked a blade of flat onion top and sucked on it.

"My dad again," I said. "He came by on the street in his black pickup truck earlier. I know he's looking for me. He goes round and round the block. Until."

She moved the grass to the other side of her mouth. "I don't think your dad could drive all the way from Kentucky to this exact street, and find you," she said.

"Oh yes, I saw him. I've seen him lots of times."

"Well, we won't—Sarah and I would never let him take you. I hope you know that. And I will be on the watch for him. Now come on out."

I rolled out. Crabgrass, I had noticed, was crawling up through the floorboards on its way into my kitchen. Dismantling a house from the floor upwards. How creative!

"What's that blood on your arms and face?" Dr. D. asked, "Did you cut yourself?"

I licked my arm. "Strawberry!" I said. I had rolled right through my own carefully planted strawberry bed, and some were already fruited out. When I first planted the bed Dr. Darby had come out and read the plants' life story to me from the *Good Neighbors Gardening Newsletter*, delivered free twice a month:

"Strawberries don't have fathers. The strawberry plant, clumped with integrity into a short cylindrical body (the 'crown') seated on roots and enfolded by small, neatly defined deep green leaves, is a matriarchy. Though producing flowers which then convert to the luscious pointed fruits so dear to lovers of the sweetmeats of earth, the seeds are irrelevant to strawberry reproduction. Instead of mating and matching, the strawberry plant sends out root runners with probing tips which plant themselves and grow daughter plants complete in themselves, continuing the process until the strawberry bed is a dense matrix of parthenogenesis."

Strawberries don't have fathers but cats definitely do. Cats are matriarchal too as far as I can tell, and the way Morgan and her daughter incorporated fathers into their family is what I want to tell you about. Making a comparison of Dr. Darby's lesbian family with Morgan's cat family makes sense given that in both cases the question is, what is the experience of two mothers raising a baby who wish to turn its care at least partially over to a male of their choice? Because it turned out by the time I moved in, Dr. D. was pregnant.

♦ ♦ ♦

Morgan had to be the smallest grown cat anyone has ever seen, jet black with yellow eyes, thin and vivacious. We became soul mates on first sight, and soon I had stolen her heart away from the women in the front house. She was about ten months old when she came to live with me, and soon she went into heat for her first time, when boy friends galore showed up to posture with each other in the back yard. She chose only one: Papa Cat, a small muscular guy who had the pretty orange, brown, and black markings of a Burmese. She loved him so much she brought him inside the big house to have sex under the big shiny dining room table. No one else being home, I followed them in and watched. As he pulled out, she shrieked and slapped him across the face, yet obviously she enjoyed herself and soon they were back at it. Later I learned that Nature—the strangest person I know—had set it up this way; his penis has a hook that scratches and causes her to release her eggs. For this alone I don't want to be a cat. Except sometimes.

I must say that dining room table came in for some multiple uses. That's where I had sat while Dr. D. swabbed out my arm, and that's where Sarah set the table with two lasagna steaming plates for the two of them, and green cloth napkins. She loved cooking and food of all kinds, and she also loved to lay naked out on that dining room table while Dr. D. sat in a chair between her legs. I found this entertaining to hear while I puttered in the fern bed under the window, where I had planted garlic and onion bulbs, and have to say I love orgasms myself. I won't tell you where I get them from, though I will say it has to do with water. Anyhow, to get back to Morgan and Papa Cat, he stayed with her for weeks, sat with her on the back steps of the big house, ate inside my little cottage by her invitation, and left before she swelled all the way up. Then weeks later he returned for a short visit and she brought him into the cottage downstairs bedroom where she allowed him to see the babies.

The cat family became the Dynasty of Morgan as soon as I kept one of her daughters from that first litter. Leah (Leah-pard) was rabbit brown and spotted like a leopard, with the deep apricot apron of her Burmese father, Papa Cat. Like him she had the feral fur of wild animals, each hair genetically painted with three colors, casting lights and shadings of camouflage across her body. She always looked as though she was tensely crouched in dappled sunlight falling through dense foliage. Her ears were sharply pointed with long spikes of black fur at the ends, like a lynx or a bobcat. Her personality was calm and removed, and unlike me who is always on watch she paid little overt attention to human beings. Her central focus was her tiny black mother.

My central focus is in case that truck comes to get me. My dad says that I am the kind of creature God does not like, and that everything bad that happens is all my fault. So naturally I have felt closer all my life to other creatures God does not like. Number one is earthworms. My dad hates them, says they are little snakes and a snake ruined life in the First Great Garden. But I know that no garden does well without worms, they make the plants prosper, and besides they outnumber human beings by a buzillion to one. So if the garden loves them, I love them.

I love them even more now that I have learned they are androgynous, they aren't men or women, each one is both, yet they don't mate with themselves, instead fall in love with each other and mate for the longest time you can imagine, hours and hours, think about this in worm time: days, even years, of continual bliss. I love them so much for this! I just wanted to be near them so crept out quiet about midnight where I found two of them in the ground cover, on their honeymoon, slick with mucous, shiny and perfect. They were facing opposite directions, each one balanced in the saddle of the other. I have never even imagined such perfectly executed love. So I covered my eyes with a bandana, in honor of them not having eyes, and laid down as close as I could without bothering them.

I was lying out there like that one night on my back, feet splayed out, as still as a dead rabbit when suddenly I heard, "Clovis, what are you doing?" and sat up in a whirl. There was Sarah with a flashlight, gave me such a start, at first I thought my dad had surely found me. But right away I had to reassure her that I was ok because I guess lying on the ground at night was strange to her.

"You can c-c-come out Clovis, it's Sarah," she said, as I had rolled under the cottage into the crab grass cave. "I know," I said, "everything's fine." Hoped I hadn't crushed any of the baby spiders.

"I came to tell you that D-D-Darby and I are going to the hospital now, she's h-h-having contractions."

"Oh all right," I answered. She went on. "We might not be back by morning so you will need to bring the trash cans in from the street after the—um, you know, the g-g-garbage trucks come by at six."

"Oh yes," I said, not sure what else to say. "Bring a nice baby back" might not say what I meant.

They did bring a nice baby back and named him Jeremy.

For a long while the Mothers, as I called Sarah and Darby, almost completely disappeared from my life, so transfixed were they on raising their new baby. Lucky for me as they never did really miss their cat Morgan. Time went fast as Dr. D. had given me a new assignment: plant fruit trees in the big rear yard. The rear yard was like a meadow except for the crabgrass overgrow, so wild a wild goose landed there one year to rest for a while. I dug, using a pitchfork and small sharp shovel to drive through the dense clay. Tore the crabgrass loose again and again until it fell back in discouragement. Lowered those young trees into the holes prepared with compost, water and mulch. Huge reward when the sapling trees quickly took root, made new leaves and smiled at me. No, they did!

Six months went by, a year, then more months. One morning I heard Sarah and Darby talking about wanting the biodad to become a real father, a companion father, for Jeremy when I went in their kitchen to pick up some eggshells to feed my worms. There were twelve half shells right there on the counter, as though earlier they had made an omelet for themselves and a visitor.

"Worms eat egg-eggshells"? Sarah was covering her mouth, laughing. "How do they do that when they don't have teeth?"

I appreciated that she was attempting to relate to me. Resisted snapping my fingers to fix her attention. Looking at the wall to the right side of her face I said, "The eggshells *are* their teeth. They have gizzards, like chickens, and need some grit to chew stuff with."

"Oh!" Sarah now fell all over herself to praise me for being so much smarter (for a minute) than her, and kept moving her head around trying to meet my eyes. I quick grabbed the shells with both hands and ran out the back door. Sometimes living with them is like being in a theater piece. And Sarah had once been an actress, so maybe that explains it.

But before all that happened I heard Dr. Darby say, "He needs a real father, a caretaking father, not just a bio dad. So let's try and see what happens, shall we?" Sarah sounded tense when she answered, "Hmmmm.....maybe. Of course I agree a father figure could be good for him. But I-I-I want to—um, you know—t-t-take it slow at first."

♦ ♦ ♦

Adopting someone into the family can be tricky, though it didn't seem difficult for the cat family. The Ladies, as I called the mother-daughter pair of them, decided who belonged in the family and who did not. That included me.

One night I got up without turning on any lights to go to the bathroom and as I came out of that room I had the odd sensation of being bumped in the knee. Then again. Then again. Though I could barely see, I soon recognized that the bumper was Morgan. That tiny black cat was literally throwing herself at my legs, hitting her head and shoulders against me. Sleepily, I tried to go around her, and the bumping increased. I stopped. I decided not to negate her actions but to float along with them and see what was happening. Following the directions given by her bumping, I soon found myself across the dining room headed for the kitchen. She wants a midnight snack, I thought, somewhat annoyed. But she blocked my way to that room, switched legs, and bumped more emphatically.

"In here?" I said, unable to imagine why she wanted me to go into the little room, an extra tiny bedroom that was filled—you're not surprised—with seedlings planted in egg cartons. I turned on the light. Indulge her, I thought. Be scientific. I turned on the light. Looking me in the face, she trotted to the closet, and when I followed, found Morgan's second litter, black and brown, squirmy, cute as baby eggplants. Felt quite proud to have been invited to attend the grand event. Felt quite thick-headed to have assumed that Morgan was interested only in food. Thus was I invited into their family. And I was not the only one.

One day a young white cat about sixteen weeks old, same as Leah/pard, showed up on the sidewalk in front. Leah brought him into the back yard where I was weeding with Morgan, who was chasing dirt clods around helping me out in her own way. The new cat sat nearby while Leah, very excited, raced between him and her mother, as though to say, "Can we keep him, huh, huh, please Mom?" After a few of these displays, Morgan leaned over toward the new friend and licked him on the head. From then on, he was her son. He took this literally. I called him Willie.

As he grew, his long white body was a leviathan among the tiny Burmese and black babes nursing at her row of spigots. She tolerated him pushing the littler ones aside to claim his nipple; tolerated his superhunger in the kitchen when she provided food for all; and even tolerated him pushing her off any chair he wanted for his own, his huge body squeezing her small one out, over my outraged protests.

The night ward nurse on the sixth floor, the only one I liked even a miniscule amount, had a habit of snapping her fingers when she wanted us to pay attention to what she was saying. For some reason, it worked, mostly, unless we were all bombed on thorazine. So I snapped my fingers at Willie when he took the chair away from his mother Morgan, his true mother.

"She's the one who loves you now, who gets food for you and everything," I told him. Snap. But it didn't help. He always got the chair he wanted. And then he went outside to sit at the curb wailing, as though for his original mother to come get him.

♦ ♦ ♦

What could be more natural than to put a small boulder of lava rock in the fern bed? My friend Hayscoop, who is huge, helped me do this late on a Saturday night when no one would notice us taking it from a nearby park and putting it in Hayscoop's little red wagon. Now I had a great perch under Sarah and Darby's dining room window to hear a lot of their business because the Mothers say it to each other on Sunday mornings when the clinic is closed and again on Wednesday afternoon when Dr. D. stays home. Sarah calls it "processing the week." I know it's going to happen whenever I hear the gurgle of coffee draining from the glass pot into Dr. D.'s coffee cup and the light clink of Sarah's tea cup brushing the saucer or clattering as she is getting more nervous. I don't use saucers myself, and prefer to eat and drink everything from my forest cup, that

Hayscoop stole one time and gave me. It's made of ceramic, creamy colored on the inside, then on the outside it's green and has a little enamel picture, blue sky with a tiny forest painting, looks like a window to the earth, and under this the words "Washington State Fair" in gold and brown. I like to imagine I could crawl through that window and come out in deep green trees, this takes my breath away. I know it's possible.

I spend a lot of time underneath the other window, the one in Sarah and Dr. D.'s dining room. Taking my time planting onions and carrots, listening to them talk across their table. Yes, that table. So one Sunday I learned a lot about the biodad, Vern.

Sarah was saying, "You went to school with him, what is he like? Why is he so distant most of the time and then blam!—right in your face?"

Darby used her smooth as a cucumber doctor voice, "Vern's relation to his own father is problematic—his father was a professor at a prominent University, a successful, ambitious man, a golden boy, who was afraid his career would be held back if he gave too much attention to his children. Vern is a hungry son. His father loves him but won't let him in, won't be vulnerable to him—this is my concern, that Vern will emulate his own father, that he has the potential to be short-tempered, critical and competitive."

Sarah's voice was bumpier, with rough panels like a stalk of asparagus: "Well, your own background was somewhat similar to Vern's; you had a mother who by and large abandoned motherhood."

"Yeah, well Vern's mother gave herself permission to be weak and unable to function well. But my own mother could be tough with me, like, making me sit for an hour with a mouthful of Brussels sprouts which I did not want to swallow, but other times so neglecting kitchen duties that I would come home from school, go into the kitchen and peel a stick of butter to eat as a snack, not knowing any better!" Darby chewing a stick of butter with great gusto was so funny I nearly laughed out loud, and slipped on the stone, feeling the pale yellow lichens grip the stone tight as my toes skidded over them.

Sarah laughed. "Well, at least you had the butter to eat, but that's ghastly—think of your poor young intestines!" Sarah laughed again and bit down on something crunchy. "Makes me want to go cook you something right now."

"Here, have some marmalade. Bitter orange, your fave. Thanks to living with you I am much better taken care of since my butter days—and healed inside too. Vern hasn't had that advantage."

Sarah said, "I noticed he was sharp-tongued with Jeremy over the Star Wars toys."

"Vern has envy because Jeremy gets more attention than he does."

Sarah talked around something in her mouth, "You mean like Vern's disdainful tone when he tells me that Jeremy has too many toys, or he thinks the toy is 'too fancy'?"

"Yes, and also it comes out in Vern not wanting Jeremy to be spoiled. He expects Jeremy to be tough, as he had to be tough." She set her coffee pot down with a thump. "I've had to intervene with him twice lately when he's with Jeremy. The last one was I had to get in the middle of a power struggle between Vern and Jeremy over who was to sit in a particular chair. Can you imagine? The baby was just asserting that this was his house and he has the right to sit where he wants, and Vern was doing this competitive thing, as though, no one in the world—not even a child—has the right to tell him where he can and cannot sit."

I slid backwards right off the rock at this point and had to quick slip away before they could look out the window and see me. I had just learned all about Morgan and Willie—why she gave him even the chair she was sitting in, because he was now her child. He was her big dopey son she would do anything for.

They have their own ways, and those are family ways. I had found Morgan's behavior with her family incomprehensible. Thin and smaller than anyone except the children, that little mother cat solicited food from me relentlessly, as her brood grew in number. Seeing how thin she was, and how constantly entreating me, I assumed she was starving. I would set heaping bowls in front of her, only to watch as members of her family, including the grown ones, rushed past her and devoured everything, while she continued to solicit.

Furious at what I saw as their rude "animal greed," I pushed them aside, scolded and held back their thundering tide so the Great Mama could eat. But she wouldn't eat, and it took me a while to realize that this was her choice. This was her behavior. And this was her power. She, not I, was feeding them, by contracting for lots of goodies from me. I was the warehouse, she was the grocer. I was nature, she was culture. And she always ate last, after everyone else had their fill and had gone away. Thus did the matriarch grandmother rule her family. Thus did the caretaker reign supreme.

When I finally understood this about her I was moved to humility, and bowed three times to her, touching the top of my hair to the floor. Thus did the caretaker reign over me, as well.

♦ ♦ ♦

Sunday morning again, the Mothers were processing about—who else?—Vern and Jeremy, father and son. And I was up on my rock, learning.

"Why did you choose Vern as the donor?" Sarah sounded irritated.

"Well, for one thing he's smart, and also small, so I knew it would be an easy birth. And also it was for certain warrior characteristics."

Sarah snorted. "He's a skinny vegetarian who mixes music on soundboards for a living! You on the other hand, you ran an AIDS clinic in defiance of a city ordinance. You're the warrior!"

"No, no, I mean that Vern can finish what he starts, he can go all the way with something and achieve a goal. I know, I can do that too. But at the same time he has a delicate aesthetic, which I know you will agree I just don't have."

Sarah sounded worried as she replied, "Vern is just not easy or joyful with Jeremy. He focuses on perils of every environment, health concerns and fears, possible speech defects, and on and on. He even fusses about the compost heap and Clovis living in the cottage!"

"Yes, he is very particular."

"Speaking of that, what about food? He can go all day eating only bagels. He's very thin, and he thinks he is 'too fat'. He is a strict vegetarian."

Darby snorted this time, "Well, not so strict—he eats nothing 'with a face or that ever had a face.'" Then she softened her tone, "Sarah, you darling. We're lucky that because of you, Jeremy loves food. For Vern, food is something to resist through strength of will.

Thanks to you, Jeremy is a little boy who loves broccoli and celery."

"You know I think food is love," Sarah says. "I take cooking very seriously, and I take it personally if it's rejected."

"Is that why the tears this morning?"

"Oh I know it's s-s-silly, but Jeremy didn't want any of his oatmeal."

Darby had her most reassuring tone, "Well, for me, I can step outside this feeling state and ask, what is the bigger question, what is the child really asking for?" At the end she raised the volume of her voice so Sarah must have gone into the kitchen as Darby continued, "For myself, I get upset when he throws things at me or makes other physically aggressive gestures. And in those situations, it's you who stands outside, calmly, and can ask, what is the real question here?" She cleared her throat. Sarah's chair squealed as she returned.

Darby resumed in a normal tone, "I want to tell about something that happened one Wednesday afternoon a few weeks ago, while you were out shopping. It's when I said 'no' to Jeremy for the first time. He had scraped my face with his nails. I said 'No,' and then watched him try out the various limits of the no—he touched my face tenderly and I said, ok; then he curled his fingers next to my cheek and I said that's still ok; then he scraped my face again and I said 'No!' So he wasn't afraid of me, he could explore the whole range of the word 'no' and judge for himself what it was made of."

These last words faded in volume and I knew they had left the room. So I left mine, thinking about Dr. Darby's courage not only with the AIDS clinic, but also bringing me home here to live, even knowing that my dad might show up with his black pickup and wreck everything for everyone before I could even warn them.

♦ ♦ ♦

The cat mothers were warriors too. Once I witnessed what Morgan and Leah did with an interloper who came into the big house kitchen one day when no one else was there, and I had gone in to make them come out before the Mothers came home from work. The poor bumpkin was a sort of shapeless long-haired bluish-grey and white cat twice their size without much sense who wandered in thinking to claim turf and then ran into the back bedroom in terror when the Ladies gave chase. The mother-daughter team trapped him up on top of the window on the drapes, which collapsed under their combined weight as they climbed up the cloth, knives in hand, to slash him to bits. Their voices swirling around his ears in a hurricane of hate made him fall, the material wrapping him in a protective shroud as he hit the floor rolling over and over. Gleefully screaming, they mounted and rode him around the room like a bronco, shredding him through the cloth while he bucked and shrieked. I intervened, dragging the whole package to the front door and his blessed release.

The Mothers were upset that an intruder cat had pulled down their drapes. I didn't mention he was chased by the Ladies. When Sarah asked me why on earth a strange cat would climb the floor to ceiling drapes in an inner room, let alone leave the fabric with big puncture marks and threads hanging loose—she looked at me with a such a puzzled expression as though I might have changed size and run up there myself to scare him. Sarah did not believe that female cats were capable of what she called "violence."

I already knew their fearlessness as earlier that year, before Leah had her first family, I looked out the front window just in time to witness the two of them as they approached a wandering Doberman pincer, their whining voices threatening to tear her canine face off, and sent her fleeing full speed down the block with them on her heels, literally, since even bounding at a dead run they were only as high as her ankles.

Where did they get this courage in the face of a ferocious dog? Perhaps it's inherited, but also perhaps it runs in family lines and they learn it. One afternoon, I looked down to see Morgan, Leah, and Morgan's five tiny apricot and black kitties in a single file line, going somewhere in a very focused manner. I followed the line down the fence, and around, along the side of the neighbor's fence, and up to a spot near the neighbor's house. This yard was the daily home of a lonely, bored, noisy terrier mix, a cat-killing dog who earlier that year had destroyed a small wandering feline that fell off the fence into his territory.

The dog was now barking ferociously at the little gathered family, sticking his nose through a hole in the boards in this part of his container, enraged that he couldn't reach them. He had a long, bony nose. Morgan stepped up to the fence just beyond his snarling teeth, lifted her right front paw and smacked the top of his nose six or seven times. Then she sat back. Her daughter Leah came forward, and she too flailed at his nose while he yipped and snarled. She sat back. Then one by one every one of their little kittens stepped up and practiced smacking the snarling dog's nose with their tiny paws. I just bent over laughing.

Maybe I needed some claws too. Lately I'd been seeing the black truck, more than once. So I sharpened the shears that were for trimming, then practiced stabbing the blades deep into the clay ground. Unfortunately Dr. D saw me doing this, and became unusually upset, she who practiced calmness as a way of life. "Clovis," she said sternly, "you have *got* to take your medicine." I tried, really, I did. I took half doses and quarter doses and full doses and no doses. I occupied myself with the garden and the cats, and with learning about Vern's progress as a caretaker dad. I started reading scripture again, thinking it might calm me down.

♦ ♦ ♦

The cat family too, had incorporated a caretaking dad. And it wasn't Papa Cat, though with Morgan's blessing, he became her daughter's mate too. Chosen not only for his steadfast character; he was also gorgeously muscled and the smallest of the males who came to ask. But he went away soon after the mating.

Leah/Pard's first litter was born in the kitchen, in an open box, and so I got to watch. She had delivered the number one baby with some difficulty, and was noticeably panting. Her mother stayed nearby, but not interfering. Then, to my surprise, her stepbrother Willie got into the box and curled his big body around one corner of the box, cradling her. He put one paw on her belly, as though helping with her contractions. He leaned over to lick the newborn, washing the translucent amniotic sac from its mouth and nose to give it air, while Leah rested. The newborn meowed, and Willie answered. He stayed through two more births. His tired sister rested her head against his shoulder for a few moments, and then he stepped out of the box, and left the room. Though not a biodad and never would be

(Sarah and I had taken him to the vet to get him neutered soon after he arrived) Willie was sure seeming to be a caretaking dad. Just what the human mothers were looking for.

Leah/Pard's first-born daughter was a gorgeous swirl of black and orange, rabbit and apricot, very red in contrast to her black grandmother and brown spotted Burmese looking mother. Their faces were narrow, while she had an impish broad face. I decided to keep her, assuming the three would become a triumvirate of fierce Ladies. But they fooled me again. Morgan and Leah continued to be a tight inseparable pair, and when Rossie, as I called the young lady of the third generation, was twelve weeks old, they gave her to someone else to raise.

They gave her to Willie Weeper, her step-uncle. I was already calling him "weeper" because despite the many ministrations of his step-family he missed someone or something terribly and spent the better part of his life out on the front sidewalk calling in a high pitch like a monotonous bagpipe note.

I was lucky enough to be present on the afternoon when the Ladies turned Rossie over to Willie. I sat on a chair against the north kitchen wall, quiet as a lizard, observing. Morgan and Leah were lined up on the west side of the kitchen, facing inward, each in sphinx position, and with barely open, slitted eyes. In the center of the room, Rossie, twelve weeks old, small and gregarious, was lying on her back under Uncle Willie's big white body. They were wrestling. She would shriek and wiggle and he would reach down to bite her. But his teeth never touched her skin. On every motion he made to engage with her body, both mothers began a deep-throated seriously-threatening growling that made him halt, raise his chin and roll his green eyes in their direction. Rossie continued to wiggle, nip and paw him, shrieking continuously in her baby voice, while he clasped her between his paws, his mouth open, lunging and halting, his ears back listening to the instructions of the mothers. This lesson—which astonished me more than I can say—continued through the afternoon, until the grown females seemed assured that he knew how to be intimate with their baby without hurting her.

From then on, Rossie was Willie's responsibility to raise. During this time he was devoted to her, and spent much less time on the front sidewalk wailing. They were two inseparable chums, usually outdoors romping and exploring. Rossie developed some of Willie's tradition, which differed from Morgan's. Morgan was a great mouser, and Leah was too, she did everything her mom did. I never saw either of them stalk a bird, not even in play. But Willie was a bird hunter, and so was Rossie. The day the two of them slaughtered the block's only mockingbird I scolded them all morning, fruitlessly. They two bird bandits were clearly pleased with the pile of feathers to which they had reduced the mockingbird. I was so mad I kicked the fence and nearly broke my big toe.

Willie and Rossie not only hunted differently, they ate differently. Morgan and Leah both ate brewer's yeast, Leah/Pard so avidly she would steal a two pound package off the table and break the plastic open for her babies; I would find yellow powder strewn in deep lines across the kitchen floor, and little rabbit colored babies standing on the package, their whiskers and faces coated with the golden pollen.

Leah also loved cantaloupe, so much so that once, having followed me to the field portion of my garden, she picked one herself. I was raising little French cantaloupes in the cool summers of the coast. About the size of an orange, they were the only melon that would ripen. I had picked two of them. When I looked back, Leah/Pard was trotting on the path behind, head lifted high on her slender neck to account for the third cantaloupe, clutched in her teeth. She presented it to her litter, who were romping on the back steps, and I opened it for them, enjoying how they fell on the cantaloupe as though it was an antelope and they a pride of lions.

In contrast to these habits, Willie and Rossie never ate either brewer's yeast or cantaloupe. And unlike the others, Willie made a snuffling, slurpy noise when he ate, which Rossie took up as well, so that I could tell who was eating just by the sounds emanating from the kitchen. When Rossie grew up she frequently sat with her mother and grandmother, and the three of them occasionally took an herb bath. They would gather together in the herb bed, each vigorously chewing leaves of oregano, marjoram, and thyme plants, until a bubbly white froth appeared on the leaves. They applied this to their cheeks, necks and chests, making a lovely perfume and probably flea deterrent. A family bubble bath.

"Are these cats *rabid*?" Sarah's tone of horror jolted me. She had come down the back steps of her house, which overlooked the herb garden I had planted in a hard clay patch last year. I tried to see what she saw: they did all have bubbly white beards. I explained some of what they were doing but she laughed it away. "I doubt *that*," meaning they weren't smart enough to use plants as medicine. "There must be some catnip in there."

"No," I said. She cleared her throat. "Well, at least it isn't rabies." She shifted her hips uncomfortably as I went silent, my eyes on the wall behind her. "Well," she finished, and went back upstairs.

Through all this the cats continued calmly making froth.

This is how Sarah was with the cat family, always speaking from her fantasies and fears about them. One day the beautiful Marmalade turned her green eyes up to Sarah's face. "Meow," she said very politely. Sarah looked down at her.

"I'm not going to-to-to *feed* you," she scolded.

"Marmalade just said 'hello,'" I explained.

"We can't afford all these cats," Sarah continued as if I hadn't spoken. But I knew that Marmalade was such a good hunter, she never asked for food. She even brought a moth she had caught into my cottage as a present for the baby kittens, setting the insect body down in front of them as they played in the kitchen.

On the occasion of Rossie's coming of age party, a dozen boy suitors showed up, none of them Papa Cat. The Ladies tore madly around the yard, day after day, chasing them off her. Finally Papa Cat arrived, greeted with affection by the Ladies; he promptly fathered Rossie's litter. Hung out with the family for a couple of weeks as they sat, each on a step, eyes closed, sphinx position, dreaming together I guess. Rossie was a grown-up, and Willie Weeper took up patrol again on the front walk, moaning his deep sorrows.

♦ ♦ ♦

On a Sunday morning I was near the front of the big house when Sarah swept gracefully up the steps with a sack of what I knew were bakery sweet rolls. They never had shared any of these delectables with me, but I loved to smell the doughy fragrance laced with cinnamon, eating them with my nose so to speak. So I hopped up on my stone under the window, inhaling and almost accidentally listening. As usual, Vern was their subject.

"You seem so much easier with him lately," Darby said.

"Well, it's been a little bit of a bumpy road, uh because your relationship with Vern is very different from mine, I, I don't know him as well and—uh—it was—uh—hard for me not to feel resentful of, of, Vern at first, because he was not participating as much as I thought he should—huh! and I didn't have the buffer of being an old close friend of his that you have." Darby made a sound like a kind of moan.

Sarah continued, "But I see now, with your help, that Vern and Jeremy had to work out their own way of being together, and their own relationship, those were the people that we were given, eh, y'know, it was up to them to sort things out, and not up to me to say how they should be, and now that I have stopped grousing about it and, and am, just letting things develop it's became very pleasurable to have Vern around, and, and, uh, I have started liking Vern a lot better. He and Jeremy get on a lot better; I see them forming a relationship more strongly after, now that Jeremy is verbal, because his dad didn't know how to handle an infant, at least it didn't seem like that to me. Of course—huh! I didn't have any experience in that area either but of course, it, it, came, it came a little more naturally to me than I think to him. Uh—I guess I had a little bit of a competitive thing with him but that has completely—eh—diminished. But, uh, I see that Jeremy finds something with his dad that he can only get from him. It's sort of indefinable. I can't know exactly what it is but I know it's important. The other day," she was laughing, "Jeremy and I were playing a rhyming game and I was very impressed because he just volunteered that *store*—he said, we were talking about going to the store and he said *store* rhymes with *poor*, and I said yeah, it does, and then I said it rhymes with *door*, and *floor*, and a bunch of other things, and I said what rhymes with *day*, and he said *flay*! and oh some other things, I don't know where he came up with *flay*, I don't even think he knows that it's a word—and we were going on and on playing this rhyming game and he said *daddy* rhymes with *penis*!"

She laughed.

"Which about says it, y'know. And whatever it is that males understand about each other, around that, they have—"

Sarah broke in, "and I respect it and I like it. I like Vern a lot better now that he has a love in his life, he has a girlfriend now, that has also opened him up enormously, and he's much more warm and giving, and his, his..."

"He's always had a problem with his self image," Dr. D. finished. I could almost see her licking chocolate doughnut frosting off her fingers, meticulously, taking her time one finger after another, not slobbering the way some do. Me, for example. Dr. D. ate quietly, and I would guess held her head down, her bright eyes flicking up to Sarah's face now and then.

Sarah kept on it, "Every time that Jeremy would cry he would take it personally, but he's grown past that and knows better now, and I think he feels better about himself and so I feel better about everything."

From my rock outside I was thinking, if there is one thing I would want to do if I could not be a gardener it would be to work in that bakery where Sarah goes every Sunday morning. Why? Because those little live yeast cells are so appealing, I feel like they are related to me—

bubbling and swelling up with good feelings when everything is warm and moist, and then busting down to something hard and grey, then up again. Smelling so great, you always know their little yeast bodies have been there, floating in your air.

I was preoccupied with this when something Sarah said clicked in my head. I realized she was a different person than she had been. She'd been saying this:

"Um. Well I, I, yeah, I think after a while he could see that Jeremy was likely to cry for us too, and—he saw us dealing with Jeremy's situations with equanimity and it, it, made him realize that kids are kids and they cry and get cranky with all their parents."

"Yes, and that we honor Vern's place in Jeremy's life I think has made him feel much better about himself."

Sarah kept on, "And uh—I'd love to see, I'd love to see them be more together. Cause I think that what happened is that, is that, uh, Vern in some sense felt parented too, I think parenting does help the parent, I feel parented in the situation."

"Yeah," Darby agreed, "I understand my own parents much better, and I see a lot about myself in my own development that I couldn't have known in any other way."

Sarah kept on, "Now I think only in terms of encouraging him more, to spend more time with him. Last year I sometimes I would almost fib, to say, 'Well Jeremy really is looking forward to your coming over,' and actually there were times that Jeremy said he didn't like daddy."

"Yeah, I remember. I think that was because Vern was not very forthcoming and not very giving, he was defended, and held back a lot, and Jeremy picked that up right away."

Sarah continued, "And uh, there was a time that Jeremy didn't really want to invest the child effort, y'know this incredible effort that children make, to bond, to relate, they really put themselves out and they, they, try everything, to be sure that they, they, *have* you, and I think there was a time he didn't think daddy was worth all that." She laughed. "'No, I don't like daddy,' he would say, and that was during the time we especially wanted them to have time together because we figured that that would help them sort of meet each other half way."

"And it did," Darby affirmed.

Sarah continued, "I think the only thing we did in the way of steering how things went w-was to invite him around a lot more, just to be sure that, uh—and I have to say I, I, didn't enjoy Vern's company in those old days, I really didn't, he was very self-centered, he would come plowing into the kitchen and say, 'Oh I've got a terrible cold,' and 'Oh I haven't gotten any sleep,' and 'Oh I'm having problems with my, y'know—*job*,' and he was going to come in and tell us all about his life. But that too has, um, changed a little bit, I think just continued exposure to each other and continued willingness to try and make the situation grow h-has helped all of us."

Darby sounded ready to stop, "Uhuh."

Sarah had one more point, "It really has helped all of us I mean I had my narcissistic streak, still do, that sometimes, uh, takes me away from...uh, uh, situations or, or, makes me not optimal in it, y'know, so I recognize that, I recognize myself in Vern, and sometimes I, I, would resent that I had no choice but to overcome my narcissism, and, and, do all the stuff that you have to do for a kid, you know, you just have to drop everything, and I wanted him to know some of that too and in a mean kind of way but the funny thing is, the funny thing is that when you make those sacrifices, and they're really rather small in the scheme of things, you feel good."

So there was Sarah comparing herself to Vern. I went away from under the window feeling better about her, as well as being full from the doughnut smells. Yet for some reason in the next few days I kept getting mad at everything. Maybe it was because I was trying to tell them: "And another angel came out of the altar, which had power over fire, and cried a loud cry to him that had a sharp sickle, saying Thrust in thy sharp sickle, and gather the clusters of the vine of the earth, for her grapes are fully ripe." I hand wrote this on a piece of paper, added "Rev. 14: 18" and slid it under their back door. A minute later the door opened and Sarah stood there with the paper in hand, looking distracted. Instead of responding to my message, Sarah asked me why I was rubbing my eye with my knuckles. I did not want to tell her that I was practicing washing my face like a cat. Getting ready. So when she suggested "allergies?" I nodded, and afterwards was grumpy at myself, because it was a lie.

One day sitting on the top of the back steps drinking coffee from the beautiful and may I say magical cup Hayscoop had stolen for me, which I don't usually drink, but Sarah had left some in their kitchen so I sneaked it but then I got so mad, I stood up and threw the cup at the sidewalk by the hedge, as hard as I could. The cup hit the cement but instead of a satisfying shatter, it bounced straight up in the air for about twenty feet, and then vanished. I mean vanished. I looked everywhere, all through the hedge, the neighbor's yard, the garden on that side. Nothing.

So I'm thinking did it go into a different dimension? Were things better there, as cup lives go? Did it, at the top of its arc, just step off the material planet, without so much as a crack or flash? And given that it bounced straight up without shattering, had the molecules that named it "ceramic" fused into something else before it even landed? Were the molecules fired by the rage that flamed in my launching hand, and did the cup change into something that could get into the mind of everything?

The behavior of Morgan and Leah on the afternoon they instructed Willie how to be gentle with their daughter left me with other questions: how did they decide, together, to turn Rossie's education over to Willie Weeper? By what means did they communicate this possibility, desire, and decision, to each other? How did they know what method would work to effect the transfer? How did he know to listen to them? It's like they too had a window to a forest where they all lived in their minds together. I wanted to live there with them!

Everything was going well with the cat family, and for Sarah and Darby's family, they were getting closer. Everything was going pretty well for me too, so I knew it was time to worry. Garden was flourishing. My nine corn plants had grown tall—the red kind, chattering together in a double row. Corn is talkative, always rustling. The long green tomato horn worms that I borrowed from a garden the next street over, had turned into enormous charcoal grey moths the size of bats. I went out at night to see them hanging on the side of the fence, so graceful, waiting for their next step.

Last night I dreamed the end of everything. My dad's black truck had arrived, parked in front of Dr. Darby's house. All kinds of people were lined up down the block, and I lined up too, so did Sarah, Dr. D. came, carrying Jeremy, who was looking backwards over her shoulder.

My hands were full of plants and lumps of earth, and as I got closer to the open door of the truck red worms wriggled out of my hands and fled; strawberries were running down my arms like little red mice and getting away. But I wasn't, so I began to shake, felt sure I was about to get in. Knew this was a very bad idea. Hung in that moment of knowing. Then it happened, I stepped into the truck. The whole inside was liquid with flames. Beautiful yellow, red, and blue fire, just melting everything. Metal and plastic parts of the truck dissolving. I took a breath. Even knowing better I had climbed into that truck. Snap!

In RL Mosswood's short story "Stag," the incursion is erotic in nature—not just erotic in the sexual sense (though it certainly is that!), but also in the sense that it's an incursion by the Eros, the joyous and untamed life instinct. Sometimes an incursion can be just what we need to wake us up to life's potentials.

Stag

RL Mosswood

The faucet was dripping.

Or maybe it was the gutter, outside the single pane window. Something was always dripping here, this time of year.

Hugh's elbows were heavy on the well-worn tabletop, the grain raised into a barren, windswept landscape by decades of thrice-daily wiping. The coarse knit of his sweater was biting into his skin at the points of contact, but he couldn't quite work up the motivation to reposition himself.

The mug of tea he was cradling tried to brighten the mood with its relentless cozy warmth and inviting waft of bergamot, but his attention was elsewhere.

Outside the window, it seemed everything *loomed.* The trees, doug fir and leafless alder, were dark and cheerless in the late afternoon light. They seemed to threaten to engulf the cabin entirely, if given the chance. The clouds above them created a uniform, slatey backdrop. Even the small birds, pecking avidly through the forest duff for overlooked seeds, seemed more desperate than gay in this setting.

He had told everyone he was going on a retreat. The words were true, but he knew that the way he presented it left them envisioning something rather more spa-like. This was a retreat in the literal sense: withdrawal—from work, from life, from the very fact of who he was, if he could manage it.

The blankness he felt was almost a relief. A tiny sentinel of his fully functioning mind tried to raise an alarm, to alert the rest of him to the fact that this void was not quite right; but no other part of him had the wherewithal to do anything about it.

He'd always had a fondness for the word anhedonia, and he wondered idly if this was the state of mind to which the word referred. It seemed right. No pleasure, but no pain either, so he'd take it.

He stared vacantly at the peeling floral paper on the kitchen wall until his emptiness was broached by the unmistakable feeling of being watched.

On first glance, there was nothing outside the window to explain the sensation. With time though, the stamp of a cloven hoof on the mossy ground brought his attention to a large stag standing among the trees only yards from the window and seeming, against all odds, to be making direct eye contact with him.

The beast held itself with divine confidence, bearing the weight of its massive rack like a crown. Even its gaze was imperious, and Hugh felt a prickle of annoyance. Didn't the thing know it was a prey animal? What gave it the right to stare him down in his own kitchen?

He chastised himself for being ridiculous, but the stag's stare continued, unwavering. Hugh stared back. It felt as if something significant hung in the air between them.

Just as he was about to force himself to tear his eyes away, the stag tossed its magnificent head and turned to stride off nonchalantly through the woods.

Hugh was halfway down the front hall before he could make a conscious decision to follow, a thick lined flannel shirt in one hand. His own reflection in the mirror over the coat rack startled him as he passed. The deep receding widows peak and steely gray at his temples was nothing new, but the rest of his face seemed ten years older than it should be. His very skin must be sagging under the weight of his depression, falling now into heavy folds around his eyes and mouth. Not that it mattered. There was no one to care what his face looked like, why should he?

Hugh shrugged on the flannel as the door of the cabin slammed behind him.

The air outside was cool, and sharp with smells of moss and mushrooms, leaf mould and lichen. The scent zinged to some primal part of his brain, awakening memories of such days in the woods all the way back to childhood and perhaps earlier—into past lives or the collective unconscious of human history.

He remembered a cologne he'd been given once as a gift, called *November in the Temperate Deciduous Rainforest*. He'd been ecstatic when he read the label, imagining a fragrance that would allow him to carry that treasured wildness with him through his day-to-day, but on his skin it had dried down to a musty sameness, redolent of a grandmother's powder room more than any ancestral woodlands. He'd worn it anyway, trying to convince himself that it was close enough.

He strode around the cabin and off into the woods with rather more purpose than he'd felt in weeks.

Game trails criss-crossed the woods, and Hugh set off along the one nearest to where he had last seen the buck. A raven croaked up in the canopy, and the mud of the path was squelching up to wet his feet through the seams of his boots, but he pressed on until a fork in the path forced him to pause and listen.

The crack of a branch drew his attention off to the left, so he headed that way, doing his inept best to keep his footsteps quiet on the densely littered forest floor.

As the underbrush opened up into a small clearing beneath the sweeping branches of a cedar tree, Hugh stumbled face to face not with the stag, but with a man.

The man was standing in the middle of the open space, alert and wary, as if he'd been listening for Hugh's approach. His clothes were unusual, some sort of hide from head to toe, assembled with visible and wandering stitches in heavy thread. Probably one of those hipster kids from the organic farm down the valley. They all fancied themselves some sort of hybrid of Davy Crockett and the Buddha as far as he could tell.

"You, uh... looking for that stag?" Hugh's voice came out thinner and reedier than he'd expected as it tried to fill the damp expanse of the forest.

The man said nothing, continuing to stare at him with what was becoming an unnerving degree of focus.

"I just... I came this way because I heard, I thought—"

With two long strides, the man was upon him. Hugh had only a fraction of a second to decide if he was being attacked; but as the man's fingers went coursing through the hair at the back of Hugh's neck, raising goosebumps all over his body with a possessive clutch, it became clear that his intent was not violent.

The man's lips bore down on his, and Hugh tried, weakly, to protest. "I'm sorry, I don't—" but the man was not dissuaded, and when his kiss landed, filling Hugh's mouth with the taste of fresh snow and wild berries, he was forced to admit that he very much did, actually.

Body several steps ahead of his mind, Hugh found his hands roving frantically over the solid planes of the other man's back, then grasping his ass through the supple hides to pull their hardening cocks into close contact. Hugh moaned at the sensation, so long forgotten but so perfectly familiar.

In this moment, it was impossible to dredge up the reasons that this was a very bad idea, was in fact the very thing he had come here to the woods to flee. For now, he was consumed by the hot press of this vital, muscular form, the scent of cedar and sweat, the untamed virility that was swiftly dragging him to new heights of arousal. Hugh clung to the man, and met and redoubled his kiss, pressing their lips together with a desperate hunger to consume the wildness that was being offered to him.

The kiss ended abruptly, and Hugh found heavy hands bearing down on his shoulders, forcing him to kneel in the soggy moss. He knew what was being asked of him, and obliged with wanton enthusiasm, pulling the man's trousers from his hips and greedily filling his mouth with the impatiently erect member that presented itself.

Hugh knew, on some level, that this should be degrading. He, an established professional, a responsible adult, down on his knees for an anonymous woodland tryst with a man who could likely pass for his son, stagnant rainwater seeping through the knees of his expensive wool slacks. In actuality though, he felt only a kind of defiant pride. The forest had conspired to bring him here, seemed now to be looking on with approval; what right did civilization have to enforce its judgment on this moment that was entirely outside its jurisdiction?

He applied himself, reverentially, to the cock before him, attempting to absorb with every stroke of his lips and tongue a little of the primal rightness that exuded from his partner. A glance upwards found the man gazing into the naked treetops, neck slack with pleasure until, as if feeling Hugh's eyes on him, he looked abruptly down, nearly paralyzing Hugh with his expression of feral passion.

Those same strong hands on his shoulders pried Hugh away from his work and brought him to his feet, simultaneously driving him back against the sturdy trunk of the cedar. It seemed that the man would kiss him again, but instead he held himself at arms length and stared as if seeking to communicate something silently across the space. Hugh was mesmerized by the leaping pulse of the man's throat, the cedar boughs reflected in his eyes, and with sudden clarity he reached down to open his fly and bare himself to the knees, turning to press his face and chest against against the craggy bark, presenting himself as an offering.

With little warning, the man's cock, still slick with Hugh's saliva, was delving between his buttocks and pressing insistently at his entrance. This sort of rough and dirty treatment roused murky memories of back rooms and public toilets from his misspent youth, but it was impossible to attribute that same meaninglessness to what was happening here. Hugh did what he could to open himself, and the man entered him with bold and driving thrusts, the discomfort a willingly paid penance softened by the promise of sanctification.

The mighty root found a point of pleasure deep within and pounded at it with the relentlessness that allows water to pierce stone. With each percussion, ripples of sensation compounded themselves until the mounting chaos resolved into a single cresting wave. As it crashed, Hugh felt ferns unfurl in his heart, rainwater course through his veins, and succulent green saplings spring forth from his fingertips. The man slipped away, and Hugh fell to his knees, consciousness receding. A thinning in the high overcast temporarily brightened the clearing, and he swore as he slid down to rest in the loam that his shadowed silhouette wore antlers of its own.

◆ ◆ ◆

Hugh was alone and the woods were silent with the growing dark when he awoke under the cedar tree. An exploratory hand to his head found only his tousled hair, but he could still feel the wildness coursing through him, out of sight.

When he returned to the cabin, the warmth was oppressive, more cloying than cozy. He stripped naked and threw open all the windows, rejoicing in the zinging constellations of goosebumps that rose on his hide as he stretched shamelessly in the middle of the kitchen and a wandering breeze reached out to offer its caress.

A sense of vibrant animality prompted him to consider his physical form. He ran his hands down his ribs and over his flanks as he took stock. His body was lean and able. Maybe not a particularly impressive figure, but he could feel his muscles singing with strength beneath his skin. Perhaps he carried a little paunch, but that was just proof of his body's ability to handle itself, preparing to see through adversity and emerge worn but victorious on the other side. There could be no shame in that.

It occurred to him how little there really should be shame in, how little he really needed the things that had so vexed him when he fled to the woods. What was respectability? Could you eat it? Use it for shelter? If living as came naturally would cause a scandal, maybe the problem was with the company he kept, rather than with himself.

He would stay here, not to hide, but to live. Maybe what he needed was not so much a retreat as a rewilding.

Short as it is, B. Allen's childhood memoir "Life on Mars" is packed with all manner of incursions: the cruel negative statements that children hear about themselves from adults and internalize, the traumatic incursions of illness and unempathic medical treatment, the mysterious incursion of a sudden vision from elsewhere, and the kind of incursion that can save one's life.

Life on Mars

B. Allen

Because I am burdensome, I got sick.

I got better, then I got sick again.

And again.

When the pills didn't make me better, I got the shot.

When the shot stopped working, I got bigger pills that seemed to glue themselves to my tongue as I tried to swallow, filling my nose with their yeasty stench.

As I gagged, my mother cried that I wasn't even trying to get better; that I wanted to be sick. I felt too sick to argue the point.

Because I am manipulative, I still got sick again.

This time, Dr. Platt talked past me in that way adults do when they're tired of addressing children like people. I was familiar with the far away look adults get when they are certain real information is too complex for a mere child to understand. There would be an injection today and pills for the next two weeks.

Panic began to rise from my empty stomach to the icy, choking pit in my chest. My throat already swollen and infected went from being hard to swallow to impossible, and the harder it got, the more I kept trying to swallow, then gasping for air. I sat humiliated by my lack of control until I saw that no one noticed. I was irrelevant in their discussions. After all, I was only a problem to be dealt with. The real issue was how the problem impacted the adults around me.

I closed my eyes and let the words turn to meaningless buzzing. I remembered to keep my breathing shallow, keeping my mouth open and taking only tiny breaths that wouldn't force my throat closed. My heart stopped pounding. I was dizzy but calm, focused on nothing but my own breathing.

I sat still, lightly sleeping until startled by the clang of metal as the nurse set a tray on the exam room counter. My eyes locked onto two syringes large enough that they had to be placed on the tray at a diagonal to fit. No one had said there would be *two* shots. The nurse scolded me, saying that if I wasn't so skinny, they wouldn't have needed to break the medicine into two shots.

I heard the screams before I realized they were coming from my own mouth. I could not stop screaming any more than I could stop my body from pushing and kicking the nurse away. I knew I was only making it worse. I knew I couldn't stop the shots, but I also couldn't bring myself to be still and cooperate.

My mother was quick to agree to the suggestion that she wait outside. In the end, it took three nurses to hold me face down on the exam table while the doctor administered the shots. The paper exam sheet dissolved in my mouth and muffled my screams. As he pulled down my pants, Dr. Platt told me to stop fighting because I wasn't in charge here.

Some weeks passed, but I knew I'd get sick again. I would let everyone down again. It seemed clear that Sister Margaret, my teacher, was correct in assessing me an unnatural, sinful thing. What she said rang true because everything I learned about sin made no sense to me. I couldn't understand how actions that harmed no one were as bad as actions that inflicted suffering. No matter how hard I tried, I would never be a good person because my soul, to its core, was inherently bad. My intentions were irrelevant. I only made life worse for everyone I loved. The only kind thing I could do was to go away.

I was seven, and I was done.

Two days before, I took a plastic garbage bag from the kitchen and put it under my bed. Although he was loathe to actually wear them, my father had an extensive collection of neckties and was happy to show me how to tie them. He let me keep my favorite, sea foam green and pearl white paisley on a pale blue background.

Then it was only a matter of waiting for my mother to leave me home alone. School had been out for a week, and the only thing my mother enjoyed less than teaching was being cooped up at home. When she left to run errands, I was ready.

I left a note on my nightstand that read, "Please, play Life on Mars." It seemed a way to explain myself enough to anyone who might care to understand my actions while affording distance to anyone else.

Although it was almost noon, I was still wearing my blue nightgown because it made me look like a girl. I wanted to spare my parents the embarrassment they felt when strangers called me a boy. I played with Rosie because she was the best dog, and I didn't want to leave her, but leaving was better for everyone.

I was the problem only I could fix. I put the bag over my head and tightened the necktie around my neck. When the air became stale, I started to panic, but I didn't want to give up. I was tired of failure. I laid down on the floor and concentrated on shallow breaths, just like when I was sick. In a few seconds everything just fell away.

I could see the whole den as if I was almost above it, but more apart from it. I saw my body unmoving and was struck by how frail and small it looked, much smaller than it ever felt from within. The dog, usually sedate and affectionate, pawed at my head in an agitated manner. I wanted to tell her I was sorry, to comfort her, but I was too far away now.

I found myself looking at the playroom where I never played, its pink walls battling the avocado green play kitchen. I finally understood this room was never mine. It belonged to a fictional version of me trotted out when my mother wanted to socialize with other mothers. The guilt over hating that room and everything in it melted.

Outside my home and high above it, the uniform grid of cookie cutter houses and lawns was disrupted. The house behind my home was gone, replaced by a crater deeper than any basement. Green grass grew in a ring around charred dirt and debris. This was not the neighborhood of now, but of when?

I felt pain and panic, sorrow and loss, but these feelings were not my own and belonged to a future past. I wondered, where is the baby, but I didn't know who the baby was or how I knew about him. At the same time, I knew the baby was no more, and I felt sad.

Suddenly, I am back on the floor.

Air stings my lungs like shards of glass. Rosie is pawing at my face, ripping the plastic bag. Drenched in sweat, I rip the bag off and gasp for air amidst a flurry of doggie kisses.

I lie there, basking in the unconditional love of this wonderful dog, and I am happy to have failed.

Sean Craven's memoir "Black Dogs, Night Terrors, and Lights in the Sky" explores the question of how to navigate one's life when one's reality is subject to constant incursions of the weird.

Black Dogs, Night Terrors, and Lights in the Sky

Sean Craven

I have a friend who's superficially the exact opposite of me but the moment we were in proximity to one another we knew we were the same basic person. She treated me to lunch one afternoon and in the course of the conversation asked, casually, "So what do you do when ghosts come through the room?"

I backed out of the conversation, hands flapping. "I have no idea what you could be talking about, etc., etc." It was a really shitty thing to do. I had no idea how to gracefully maneuver the intersection between public and private realities. I'm close enough to crazy to have to worry about crossing that line. I did not have the confidence to tell her the truth.

Because with me? It's not ghosts. It's monsters.

I am writing about how I cope with an experience of life that radically diverges from the norm. I'm going to explain what happens when strange things come through the room, what do I do about them, why do I do the things I do, and my best guess as to what's really happening.

(Please understand that while this essay may take on a tone of authority? That authority is spurious. I do not have a degree. Any knowledge I have is self-acquired and thus subject to doubt, as are any and all of my conclusions.)

I've been diagnosed with post-traumatic stress disorder, obsessive-compulsive disorder, mixed-state bipolar disorder, and just a mother's kiss of fetal alcohol syndrome. I am prone to hallucinations and emotional extremes relating to stress and fatigue. My anxiety expresses itself somatically—if I get too unhappy I become physically ill and have displayed symptoms that have been interpreted as everything from colon polyps to an exotic fungal infection. This is regarded as a life-threatening condition. I've been repeatedly told I need to behave as if it were diabetes or a bad heart. I'm also prone to compulsive ideation and pattern-making. If I were less intellectually rigorous I'd be a religious fanatic or conspiracy theorist. But I've been lucky enough to channel all this into art.

At times I've strayed from the mainstream of human thought to a dangerously alienating degree. I am in danger of being incapacitated rather than just having to deal with issues. The difference seems to lie in my intellectual stance. There's a concept I picked up from the works of Robert Anton Wilson—the reality tunnel. The world presents us with so much information that we can't possibly deal with all of it at once. So we ignore most of what we take in and perceive reality through psychological tunnel vision. Knowing that you live in a reality tunnel doesn't keep you from living in a tunnel. But it lets you realize your tunnel is malleable.

This isn't comfortable, though. Things like religious or political beliefs, basically any form of zealotry limits the information we allow ourselves to perceive. And this is something that's useful in daily life. It's only possible to make meaningful choices when your choices are limited. Living in a perpetual state of existential crisis has done me few favors.

Reality is a hallucination. This is something verifiable. As an example we do not see with our eyes. If we did we would see the world upside-down—that is the way the lens of the eye casts an image on the retina. All of our sensory inputs are similarly compromised by their nature as physical objects. We perceive—turn these jagged random impulses into something coherent and meaningful—with our minds which are primarily generated by our brains.

As with reality, the notion of a singular, unified mind is an illusion. I've always been strongly aware that the I-that-says-I isn't really representative of who or what I am. As a child I used the term 'rogue sub-personalities' to describe the maze of conflicted desires and compelling antipathies I must negotiate.

The most dramatic expression of this principle I've experienced centered around my left hand. I was switched from left- to right-handed in kindergarten. When I encountered combination locks I found there were times I'd try and unlock one for as long as twenty minutes or half an hour, resorting to written copies of the combination, before realizing I was working the combination counter-wise with my left hand. In high school I was part of a study on learning disabilities and was strongly encouraged to try and maintain as much bilateral symmetry as possible.

My left hand did not like this. At one point I had a job that involved making note pads. The paper cutter was a monstrosity from the eighteen hundreds and its handle was an iron rod a yard long. If you let it drop, its weight alone was enough to shear the blade through two reams of paper. Once or twice a week as my right hand was straightening stacks of paper, my left hand would sneak up and pull the safety stop. The handle would swing down, the blade would drop toward my right wrist, and at the last second tragedy would turn to comedy as the iron rod bopped the top of my head, stopping the blade's descent. KABONG!

Detente was reached one afternoon when my brother and I were walking and he noticed that my right arm swung while my left arm stayed stock-still. "Fuck it," I said. "I'm done with bilateral symmetry. Let Lefty do whatever the fuck he wants." After a few steps? My left arm, slowly, creakily, began to swing. Off-time with the right arm but it's the thought that counts.

As an adult I see those experiences reflected in the current theory of the mind. The brain is a physically divided organ. Any repeated pattern of thought forms an organized group of brain cells. (The jargon is, "If neurons fire together, they wire together.") It's not unreasonable to view the brain as an ecosystem and the habits and beliefs that shape our reality tunnels as organisms competing for resources. That's why it's so hard to change. Habits fight for their lives.

The flexibility of that hallucinated reality is, again, verifiable. In court eyewitnesses are worse than no witnesses because different people experience reality differently—one person sees red hair, another sees black. The most vivid example of this I've experienced happened at the grocery store. There was a woman I found attractive and you know how it is—you don't follow people around but you do notice when you run across them. "Oh, there she is again. How lovely." When I saw her in the produce section she stopped her cart square in the middle of a four-way intersection and pulled out her cell phone to place a call.

As she placed the call her face melted from cute to crude right in front of me, features changing in exactly the fashion of a character in a movie morphing. Flesh made putty. It would have affected the way I'd have described her in court. You can only spot the flaws in so-called reality if you're looking for them. Otherwise they're so normal, so boring, you'd never notice.

I most frequently hallucinate as a response to boredom. The objects in my vision are transformed to shifting panes of undifferentiated color and another set of panes in a non- or un-color something like an X-ray. This is a common response to psychedelic drugs as well and has its roots in the nature of vision—we perceive color and shading with two separate physical structures in the brain. Our mind normally combines them. In the state I describe you perceive them as the disconnected perceptions they actually are. This is one of the most common visual effects of psychedelics—the first time I did mushrooms and had that experience I was greatly relieved to find the things I saw in school and church and other intolerably boring situations were just hallucinations.

Psychedelics don't make most people hallucinate. But if you have visionary tendencies they can bring them out. The physical mechanism by which they work mimics the effects of extreme fatigue on the brain. (I cannot stress enough how much fatigue has to do with my experiences. Insomnia, agitation, and lack of appetite are fuels for weirdness.)

I've gotten good use out of psychedelics. An Indian holy man once had a dose laid on him by some hippies back in the day. "Nice," he said. "You've got a pill that can turn someone into a guru. You got one that can turn them into a mechanic?" Well, guess what. If someone taking acid were a student of mechanics it might help make them a better mechanic. (I'll describe an example of this later.)

The chemicals in the brain that allow one brain cell to communicate with another are called neurotransmitters. In order to keep the brain from being randomly stimulated by stray signals, neurotransmitters are reabsorbed or counteracted by other chemicals in the brain. In extreme states of fatigue those chemicals become depleted. This state allows areas of the brain that normally exist in isolation to interact with one another. Psychedelics block neurotransmitter uplift to much the same effect.

The second most frequent type of hallucination I have is pareidolia. This is what happens when you look at a scorched tortilla and see Jesus. One of the functions of the human mind is pattern recognition which leads to pattern making—we like to see patterns in everything. In my case poor eyesight, visual training, and a keen imagination make life interesting at times—I once saw a discarded push up-style ice cream bar sitting in the gutter. It had the Crest logo on it. I've spent the rest of my life thinking about cool creamy toothpaste-flavored push-up popsicles. I've done a series of prints that made heavy use of pareidolia—the compositions included faces I saw in rocks, landscapes I saw in inkblots, and so on.

The passage in and out of sleep is the time when I most frequently experience what I perceive as spiritual or mystical phenomena. According to some psychiatrists my hypnogogic and hypnopompic visions qualify as hallucinations. It usually takes around an hour to fall asleep. First I have to still my obsessive thoughts. At this point I usually experience a series of brief vivid flashes of scenes of extreme violence, injury, and mutilation. These are full-sensory experiences that take me entirely out of conventional reality for a second or so.

My return is marked by a physical sensation as if I've been dropped a foot or so and when I come to I'm in an agitated state, sweating, heart racing, short of breath… "You'd think that was the PTSD but it's actually the OCD," one psychiatrist told me. While I always experience them while going to sleep these visions can hit me any time I'm distracted. Honestly? They feel like memories from other lives. Many of them are of US military personnel in a jungle environment. In all likelihood they're a response to being around Viet Nam veterans in childhood.

After that state passes it is time for a trip to another world. There are a number of scenes or locations I return to over and over that have consistent geography and architecture—the garden on the seaside cliff, the docks, the underground… but over the past few years things have changed radically. I'll discuss those changes at the appropriate spot in the narrative. But when I begin to see elaborate visions of fantasy I know I'm finally, finally going to sleep.

The hallucinations I specifically associate with exhaustion come in two forms. My vision becomes wiggly, as though I'm looking through jelly lenses, and I see dark shapes flickering at the periphery of my vision. They look like the chromosomes of cells undergoing mitosis. These conditions are both persistent for as long as I'm at a certain level of exhaustion. And for brief moments, fractions of a second, I may see something vivid and strange, say a brown shape something like a tarp and something like a bat, fluttering down to envelop me.

Finally there are those hallucinations that seem as if they are real. Full-blown extended experiences that are contrary to conventional reality. Strange creatures, lights in the sky, visions of God— that kind of stuff.

Because so many of my experiences of life have been bizarre I chose atheistic materialism as my primary reality tunnel. I consciously choose to reject any notion of supernatural forces having any external reality and place great faith in science. The idea of existence as something planned and purposeful seems aggressively deleterious to any attempt at understanding the workings of the universe, which I hope may be ultimately explicable.

I can maintain this perspective consciously, it is supported by a large community, and it has more credibility and internal consistency than any other reality tunnel to which I have been exposed. It is also convenient for accessing dopey old conventional reality. That it contradicts my routine experience of life is a source of comfort.

Let me expand on the statement 'faith in science.' While I'm a lot more knowledgeable about the sciences than most folks I'm still just a layman. There are vast areas of scientific knowledge I cannot understand, mostly due to ignorance of mathematics. But in-between my knowledge and my ignorance are areas where I sort of get it. So when I look at the sciences and I see there are things I have to take on faith? That faith is bolstered by an informed, intuitive sense of the shape of things, the way the world works, that draws from what I see as the best of the human tradition. It's not just a matter of accepting received authority. Science is almost certainly at least a little wrong about everything but it is a system intended to analyze information—

any time we can get reliable information the scientific method will give us the most reliable results from analysis.

Of course I don't have an academic background. I'm probably nowhere near as scientific as I like to pretend. Who knows? It's not like there's litmus paper for this stuff. Rational thought is sophisticated, imperfect, and difficult. It is an unusual skill.

And when you get people to open up, almost everyone has had some kind of strangeness in their life, some breach of conventional reality. I may not believe in Bigfoot-the-North-American-Hominid but I believe people see Bigfoot.

(While I have investigated traditional religious scriptures I have found their dogmas problematic when questioning the nature of reality. Forgive me. I cannot help reading them as folk literature.)

As a counter to worship of science I had the good or bad luck to be exposed to the thinking of Charles Fort early on. I've never been able to penetrate his prose and recently, reluctantly, passed his collected works on to a second-hand bookstore. But the passages from his work quoted in various books on the paranormal I have read make it plain that he treated reality not just as a hallucination but also a game. He played it by going to the library and systematically poring over every newspaper he could get his hands on in search of every report of a rain of frogs and lights in the sky he could find. He then constructed surreal (they were more Dada, actually) hypotheses explaining how these things might happen if one disregarded conventionalities such as the shape of the world or the extent of the atmosphere.

More useful has been the previously-mentioned Robert Anton Wilson. His skepticism was Fortean in style but closer to the spirit of science than Fort's gleeful intellectual anarchy. Wilson felt much of science was dogma and the blanket opposition to the investigation of mysticism and paranormal phenomena on any but a hostile basis was actually unscientific. One example he used was a study that seemed to support one particular aspect of astrology. It had been denied publication on the basis of the results rather than the experiment that produced them. He himself practiced astrology and while skeptical regarding the objective reality of his work, he found his readings frequently seemed meaningful. This is consistent with my own experiences with psychic readings and so on. I suspect the human capacity for pattern-making is at work here—that any kind of random data can be turned into a meaningful story by a capable person.

I didn't start having strange experiences until I was a teenager. As a child I found the world too small, too limited, so I went searching for magic. I found it in the library at the low end of the Dewey Decimal System in books by people like John Keel and Ivan T. Sanderson, books that spoke of mothmen, archeological images of spaceships, and academic research into psychic powers.

In elementary school I assumed all the mysteries I read about had some tangible basis. The media loves to present this stuff in an uncritical fashion and I wasn't a skeptical child. My fear of monsters lurking in the dark conflated with my readings. Horror fiction rarely frightened me but reports from people claiming to have had real experiences did. I felt there were things watching me. Worse, I was afraid I might actually see one of them and that act of observation would gain its attention. Aliens and monsters had been seen everywhere, at every period in history. There was no reason to believe my world would be an exception.

But after a lifetime of research I've found that most of the paranormal has been adequately explained and the remaining mysteries don't make me think popular mythology is real. Popular mythology is a form of folk culture. In other words, semi-formalized nonsense.

The issue of fashion in the world of strangeness is a topic in itself. In the eighteen hundreds the fascination with spirituality and enlightenment gave us such cultural movements as Transcendentalism and Theosophy. Theosophy was a religion started by a marvelous fraud who called herself Madame Blavatsky. Its central document, The Book of Dyzan, was a startling piece of imaginary writing that, along with the novel Gulliver of Mars, directly inspired Edgar Rice Burroughs' adventure fiction, starting with A Princess of Mars. These novels in turn inspired the pulp writer Robert E. Howard. Howard is best known for his creation of the character Conan but a more obscure story featured a conspiracy of shape-shifting non-humans called the Serpent-Men of Valusia. They in turn inspired the shape-shifting reptilian invaders of the television show V. There was no UFO lore involving shape-shifting reptilian invaders before that show.

So there is a direct line of influence running from Madam Blavatsky to modern-day conspiracy theorists like David Icke. That it runs through the genre fiction I loved as a child gratifies me obscurely but it's good to keep in mind that these kinds of connections are everywhere. Magic and make-believe cannot be definitively separated. In fact most of the time magic (and I do include religion under that rubric) is make-believe taken seriously enough to become real.

My early dreams consisted of the fear of monsters without the release of seeing the monster. On waking from such dreams I was terrified of the dark. Going to the bathroom at night was a trial. Even though I knew it was nonsense I was viscerally convinced that the sound of a flushing toilet was something angry rushing up through the pipes.

There were a handful of specific creatures over which I obsessed. Mothman, the famous West Virginia phantom, came to me with the iridescent green wings of a gargantuan Luna moth, glowing multifaceted eyes surrounded by coarse hair and a disturbing coiled proboscis. On what did it feed?

There are claims that in February of 1855, one night a track anywhere from forty to a hundred miles long appeared in the English counties of Devon and Dorset. Small hoof-prints ran single file across rooftops, walls, even haystacks, making it seem as though whatever made them had been capable of flight or great leaps. I thought of something crawling out of the sea, a man-sized caterpillar with hoofed legs arranged single-file along its belly, one unblinking eye a foot across at the top of a centaur-like extrusion of grubflesh and a pair of crab-like pincers, imagined it jumping onto the roof outside the window of my bedroom, staring at me in the night.

Worst of all was a creature that I saw in my one really vivid dream from that time, the one dream with color and motion and physical sensations. It was shaped like a bowling pin, bulging at the base, a smaller bulge at the top, and one joint in its neck. Its wet amphibian skin was glossy black and it was without eyes or other features. What made it horrid was the way it moved, as though it had a two-boned skeleton made of flexible cartilage. It quivered nervously, clung to walls as if it had a suction cup at its base, then bounced impatiently and sprang like a piece of living rubber.

At that time my brother Duncan and I shared a bed. We had two beds in our room but we slept together out of animal companionability. Unfortunately Duncan was a bed-wetter and sleep-walker. At one point he began to routinely pee behind our dresser in his sleep. At first I was horrified and disgusted but after a few months I was used to the stink and decided it couldn't hurt if I did that myself rather than risk an encounter with the Toilet Monster.

When my father found out he made us move the furniture and tear up the rug while he stood over us, his anger something I felt with my skin. I expected a beating but he said, "If I laid a finger on you, I'd kill you." I believed him. Duncan later told me Dad had asked, "I understand why Sean would do something like that because he's crazy but why did you do it?" That really bothered me. Duncan had started it! (Also, that was the first time I was told I was crazy...)

My sister became involved as well. One night she burst into the room I shared with Duncan, sobbing in fear. She'd had a nightmare about what she called 'mush-faced rabbits.' It was only the first. The mush-faced rabbits were furry creatures with faces made out of some doughy, clay-like substance who let themselves down from the moon on extensible tails. One of them, Fred, could talk and his manner was threatening. He made it plain that at some point the mush-faced rabbits were going to do something bad to my sister.

I played into it, insisted on performing magic rituals to keep them away. It got out of hand—at one point Duncan and I sat down and discussed the mush-faced rabbits, mutually admitting while we knew they weren't real we kind of believed them anyway.

This ended when my sister burst into angry tears and said, "They didn't come from that movie!" It turned out that the night she'd had the initiating nightmare she'd seen the movie Harvey on TV. The movie is about a lovable drunk played by Jimmy Stewart who claims his best friend is a pooka, a type of Irish goblin, who took the form of a seven-foot tall invisible rabbit.

That was my first taste of skepticism but my easy belief in strange phenomena took a more serious blow on a trip to visit my relatives in Oregon. On the way, we stopped at a Goodwill store where I purchased a paperback from the fifties on flying saucers. The cover was a black-and-white photo taken by George Adamski showing the underside of a saucer with three balls that looked like landing gear. It's a popular image. You can find it on the net.

On the farm owned by some relatives on my father's side of the family I was given the opportunity to play with some chicks. When I picked up the chick brooder, a round metal gadget with a light bulb in it that kept the chicks warm, its underside was the flying saucer on my paperback. It dawned on me I was wading in murky waters and just because a book wasn't shelved with the fiction? Didn't mean it was truth.

But what exactly were they lying about? While I don't believe we're being visited by aliens—given our current knowledge, the laws of physics overwhelmingly oppose interstellar travel—there are strange things in the sky. When I was about nine I had been babysitting on a stormy night and was being driven home. While passing my elementary school, the driver and I saw three luminous balls swirling around each other as they drifted toward the ground. Their motion was like that of falling leaves and they were connected by a nimbus of lightning-like filaments. As they vanished behind the school there was a flash of light.

I strongly suspect this was a freak of weather. The next time I saw something strange it was during the day. I was in a crowd of whale-watchers looking out over the Pacific near Bodega Bay. Bodega is the town where Hitchcock filmed The Birds and was part of my extended family's territory when I was a kid. As a child I always got along better with adults than other children and it was accepted that I'd spend time with them. A couple of such friends had graciously invited me to go spend the weekend with them. As we stood on the cliff, pressed against the railing, it soon became obvious I couldn't see anything the people around me claimed to be spotting.

But I couldn't miss the object that passed directly in front of us at a speed that seemed far too slow for a flying object. It looked like an old-fashioned science fiction rocket ship, an aluminum cylinder with tail fins and a red nose cone. It had an odd shimmy as it moved and I had the impression it was following the edge of the water as the waves washed against the beach below us.

"They're testing a cruise missile," one of my friends said. He was an inventor and engineer and knew what he was talking about.

That night as I fell asleep on my friends' couch, their black dog Misery was licking my left arm. When I woke up my arm was bald and pink. It stayed that way for six months or so, much longer than seemed proper. My family doesn't remember me talking about the cruise missile but my weird bald pink arm is still regarded as a family mystery. Again, I don't believe in saucermen but it was an odd coincidence. And there will be more on the subject of black dogs before we are done.

During the year I attended UC Santa Cruz I had two more peculiar experiences. At that time I'd been experimenting with psychedelics. Although I was completely sober for both of these events I would not be at all surprised if drug use had exacerbated my natural tendency to hallucinate. I was also experimenting with meditation, Crowley-inspired rituals, studying tarot, and lucid dreaming. Going through my mystic phase.

Meditation is one of those things that gets recommended without thought, as though every person in the world could benefit from this lovely practice. I have found it impossible and the attempt unpleasant. My mind is too busy. There are always gears grinding away, level after level of them, so my experience of sitting meditation is a churning maelstrom of anxiety. But when I learned art I found certain passages in the production of a finished piece that provide me with a state of egoless awareness that seems much like that sought by practitioners of Zen. The need to spend hours consciously focused on a repetitive mechanical process is the key. My mind becomes focused on the physical act of producing art and I go away and the only thing in the world is graphite or ink touching paper.

As the best-known practitioner of the modern era, Aleister Crowley is hard to avoid if you get serious about magic. Crowley is about results. But he's problematic. He gives every impression of having been a genuinely bad man. You can learn things from his work that you can get no place else but it is like carving nuggets from roadkill. On one hand, his couplet, "We place no reliance on virgin or pigeon/Our method is science, our aim is religion," is magnificently inspirational. On the other? He called his memoirs an 'autohagiography,' or autobiography of a saint, and that was typical of the man.

There are two aspects to his work I think worth communicating. The first is that the act of breaching conventional reality in order to achieve one's goals is strenuous and demanding work. His position was that one should have an artistic practice and an athletic practice thoroughly under one's belt before attempting to perform magick. (His spelling.) I think there is much to be said for this. The way I've repeatedly gotten in over my head has a lot to do with not being sufficiently developed as a human being.

The main concept he delivered to me was the creation and execution of ritual. A ritual is an artistic production conducted in order to produce a result in real life through unconventional means. They can be curiously effective—while I believe they act by allowing the practitioner to organize their minds toward a particular end and directly access intuitive thought, the actual results frequently feel like magic.

Which would be the point. A ritual might involve chanting, the rendering of diagrams, a series of mathematical calculations, dance, ritual sex, beating drums—a series of directed mental and physical activities that act by focusing the mind on a particular end while inducing the type of fatigue of which I've spoken, the point at which the mind begins to disintegrate. Entering into these kinds of states with conscious purpose can be a genuinely transformative experience. These concepts co-exist harmoniously with Timothy Leary's dictum that the way to have a good psychedelic trip is to determine your mindset and physical setting in advance. I'll give a specific example later.

The ultimate goal of this kind of activity is to achieve what the psychologist Abraham Maslow referred to as a peak experience. There is a myth that we only use ten percent of our brain and that if we could access our entire brain we would become superhuman. That is not how the brain works. Different parts of the brain are used for different purposes and when we use the brain those parts of the brain appropriate to the use light up. You know what makes the entire brain light up? Complex mental activities. If you can trigger an emotion and a sensory perception and either evokes a memory? The brain lights up like a pinball machine. Storytelling is a perfect example of a genuinely complex mental activity. Art provides peak experiences.

A peak experience positively engages us on as many levels as we are capable of consciously perceiving and more. We think, we feel, we remember, we are aware—all at the same time. Our brain forms new connections, fresh ways of relating to the world. Happy people have peak experiences on a regular basis.

As an artist my work is extremely controlled and deliberate, based on multiple layers of organization. There is a tremendous amount of unseen labor in my work. And one of those organizational principles is that of ritual. Every one of my major works is done with a hidden intention.

Lucid dreaming is the ability to recognize dreams as dreams while experiencing them and to be able to control the dream. Learning the skill involves keeping a dream diary and engaging in directed meditation. To be honest I was hoping for sexual gratification which did not occur—to this day I have had only a handful of erotic dreams, mostly unpleasant—but as a result of this course of study my dreams took on color and motion and began to display fantastic imagery. I found myself dreaming with all senses, smell, taste, motion, balance, and touch combining with sight and sound. My dreams became a significant second life. I have a strong intuition this triggered what happened to me next.

I'd become close friends with the preceptors of the student apartments where I lived at the time, a married couple who were both seriously involved in the New Age. The New Age belief system—which emerged in the eighteen hundreds alongside Transcendentalism and Theosophy—is a very loose spiritual practice whose dogma consists of anything that appeals to the individual, with an emphasis on exotic weirdness and relentlessly positive thinking. Psychic powers, Indigo Children, reincarnation, Biblical miracles, and of course, alien visitors are blended into one indiscriminate mess of theological pulp fiction. More damning in my squinty little eyes is the New Age fondness for crystals, elixirs, workshops, and bells, beads, and trinkets of every variety.

If I seem scornful it is because while I love and respect the New Agers in my life they drive me a little nuts. I find the lack of intellectual rigor and the earnest desire to believe kind of dumb and sappy and lazy—it's like a cake made out of nothing but frosting roses. It can keep people from being willing to look clearly at the world. More to the point, when you are actually messing around with your mind superficiality isn't just tacky. It's dangerous.

(There's a New Age label for me—I'm a 'walk-in,' an alien soul reincarnated in a human body. Basically, it's a way for people to be able to say, "Yeah, I teach clairvoyance for a living but we all know who the real freak is.")

Anyway, Mike the preceptor had an amazing library dealing with everything from sea monsters to Uri Geller to a wide variety of sacred texts. I spent a lot of time devouring his books and listening to him talk about his beliefs. I was trying to take them on as my own with mixed success.

One Friday afternoon I was in my room. The week's classes were over and I decided to do a little recreational reading. But when I lay on my bed I left my body. I drifted up in the air and looked down at myself. The walls seemed to be transparent and I could see the studs and the conduits for the wiring, details I was not familiar with at that time.

And I sensed a presence. Everything in the universe was part of a single object and that object was living and conscious and it was aware of me. I can't use any other word than God to describe that consciousness.

I felt myself picked up, watched my body vanish into the distance as I rose above the Earth, saw the coastline then the shape of the planet. I was pulled away, the Earth diminishing until it vanished into the distance. I didn't come to rest until I was in the void, nothing anywhere near me except God. It was as though I rested in a great hand, was regarded with a mixture of pride and benevolence.

I have never been more frightened. I did not fear for my safety; it was the difference in scale between myself and God that intimidated me. I sensed amused sympathy, then was plunged down as God returned me to Earth, to my body. I was back on my bed. It was dark; the experience had lasted about six hours.

Maybe it was a psychotic break, maybe I had been dosed with a drug. And if it never happens again? It's fine with me. It was devastating and it's not the kind of thing you can talk about comfortably. People think you're crazy if they aren't religious and they think you're bragging if they are. When I tried to tell people about it I got both reactions.

How can someone who's had that experience claim to be an atheist? First off, that sense of holiness, of God's presence? It's built into the human machine. It is possible to trigger this experience in people by the use of focused magnetic fields and it's such a common response to psychedelic drugs as to be their primary characteristic.

My study of the natural world led me away from the notion of purpose in the universe. It is only possible to understand the scientific examinations of observable phenomena that relate to change in the universe—things like evolution or the development of astronomical features—if one abandons the notion of a world shaped by a master will. And the notion that God answers our prayers or determines our fate is one that does not make God look sane or decent by most human standards. Pursuing these lines of thought made my concept of God grow more and more abstract over the years. Eventually I realized that I'd gone from being an agnostic to being an atheist in that God had become a functionally meaningless word for me.

Except when applied to specific personal experiences. I am not without contradictions.

A few weeks after my taste of gnosis I found myself agitated while in conversation with Mike and his wife. They had been communicating with a Breatharian named Wylie Brooks and had arranged for him to do a series of lectures and performances in Santa Cruz. Breatharianism is the belief that it is possible to become so spiritually advanced that you don't have to eat. As vegans subsist on vegetables, breatharians subsist on breath. Brooks was a minor media figure at the time, having made a number of television appearances pitching a diet that would purportedly allow people to make the transition to Breatharianism. That Haagen-Dazs was on the menu says it all.

That afternoon my friends got a call from Brooks' girlfriend who explained that Brooks was a fraud. But he'd seemed to perform some remarkable athletic feats on TV and I found myself obsessing over that incongruency. How had he done that stuff? Had they faked it? What if his fraudulence was concealing something less explicable? My agitation increased until I was uncomfortable to be around so I went for a hike, out into the moonless night.

I went to the Upper Quarry, a spot on the UC Santa Cruz campus where they'd mined limestone to make concrete to rebuild San Francisco after the 1906 earthquake and fire. The Upper Quarry had been converted to an outdoor theater and had much the beauty of a ruin. It was also one of three or four spots on campus that felt as if they were part of my personal territory. I spent some time expending energy lifting rocks and rolling logs and so on. When I'd finally calmed down I sat and stared at the night sky.

What looked like a star was moving, slow enough so I doubted the motion until it dipped below the starline until it was behind a pair of redwoods whose swaying tops alternately concealed and revealed it.

The hair on my arms and neck rose but I felt oddly calm. My calm evaporated when I heard the sound of a rock fall behind me, then one to my left, in front of me, to my right, as though someone were drawing the tip of a stick around me in circles. This happened a few times, the unseen motion accelerating. I felt as if there was a belt around my chest. The darkness at the base of the redwoods gave the impression of a tangible animal and the image of a wolf made of shadow came to mind.

I heard another rock fall to my left, turned to look, and saw a luminous figure in robes. It had four arms folded over its chest and a grasshopper's head. The fear left me; this was a woman and she was guarding me.

The shadow in front of me seemed to retreat. I looked back to the insect woman but she had vanished. I looked at the star dancing behind the tree and it zipped straight up into the sky, its motion fast and purposeful, until it vanished directly overhead.

I went back and told my friends what had happened; interestingly, Mike seemed offended and doubtful. His wife, my best friend at the time, had me tell her the story in detail while she typed it up. Her faith in the subjective reality of my experience helped me adjust to what had happened.

The next day I went back to the upper quarry and saw a number of small black rabbits at the spot where this had all taken place. They didn't act scared of me at all, just hopped around and stayed out of my way.

Soon after, I dreamed I was menaced by a spaceship, an industrial-looking artifact of the sort Chris Foss used to paint. Using a dream-logic technique I was able to mentally reach into the sky, grab the ship, and smash it into the ground. There was a physical sensation as if I were the fulcrum of a lever stretching from the Earth's gravitational center to the spaceship. The act of destruction was profoundly satisfying.

After that my semi-lucid dreams turned into an ongoing hunt for the creatures that had haunted me since childhood. My second life became a festival of slaughter. I was intent on destroying the objects of my fear, whether through dream-magic or bare hands and sharp teeth. I still remember toothed tentacles ripping at my hands and face as I bit into mucus-coated skin and tasted strange blood.

For the next four years I slept for two or three hours a night then awoke paralyzed, unable to move and struggling to cry out, in terror of the creatures that peered in at me from the windows, that listened from the other side of my bedroom door, that waited for a moment of vulnerability. The brain releases a hormone in sleep that inhibits motion in response to dreams and this experience, the classic nightmare, is the result of being conscious while still under its effect. Powerful as I was in my dreams I was helpless when I woke. Afterward? I was too frightened to return to sleep.

This didn't end until I was twenty-three and met my first girlfriend. It was like a fairy tale—all it took was love's first kiss to end the curse. After the night fears faded, the creatures in my dreams began to ask for mercy and became friendly or obsequious.

Years later when I read the book Communion by Whitley Streiber I found a passage where he claimed memories of black animals are associated with so-called alien abductions. The image of those rabbits from the Upper Quarry came into my mind and I curled like a cooked shrimp, burst out weeping, and ran to my spouse for shelter and comfort. Aside from being touched by God, it was the purest, most direct experience of fear I've ever had, as if a button had been punched in my brain. And while not as intense as my reaction to God, there was something ugly and tainted about this fear. I was destroyed for days, especially after I remembered the cruise missile, the black dog, and my pink arm.

It was suggested I get regression therapy to help recover any missing memories I may have had of being abducted. I did a little studying and decided regression therapy sounded a hell of a lot like brainwashing so I said no.

Around this time I'd become more conscious of something I'd experienced my whole life without giving it much attention. In the passage between waking and sleeping, I will occasionally feel an impact as though an animal has jumped on the bed. This has happened in households without pets. I'd come to intuit that these impacts signaled the presence of entities or spirits.

One night I felt something jump on the bed and had an instinctive sense of hostility toward the entity. When it touched me I envisioned myself as a surface consisting entirely of blades in motion and the nasty little brute was caught up and devoured. I felt a sense that I had not dispelled this thing but consumed it utterly. My spouse is a body worker. When I mentioned what had happened to her the next morning she told me that afternoon she'd had a client who had been abused as a child spit up a demon and she'd wondered what happened to it.

At this point I was further from conventional reality than is healthy—I remember in particular seeing an old high school friend and trying to tell him about this stuff and he looked at me as if I'd shaved my eyebrows and taped caterpillars in their place.

I addressed the problem by going through the Feeling Good cognitive therapy books by David D. Burns. Cognitive therapy teaches how to examine one's thoughts critically—essentially it's a course in bullshit detection. I also began to read the works of both Robert Anton Wilson and Colin Wilson in a critical but deep fashion and did a number of exercises in cognitive exploration that they suggested. (I found Robert Anton's Prometheus Rising and Colin's Accessing Inner Worlds the most useful of their books.) Between those two and further reading of Crowley's The Book of Lies I began to understand how to take responsibility for my perceptions of reality.

The infrequent but serious use of psychedelics was also very useful in stabilizing my emotional state and learning deep cognitive skills. Here is an example of how I've used them in a ritual. One of my problems as a visual artist was an inability to summon concrete images in my mind—my work all happened on the paper. So I did a planned trip/ritual intended to push my visual skills. I took what I believe was between four and eight hundred micrograms of acid and focused on visual exploration. I surrounded myself with art books, instruction manuals, portfolios, old sketchbooks, and as I waited for the acid to come on I focused obsessively on artworks.

One of the central concepts I was taught as an artist is that of the picture plane—while objects in reality are solid things with mass and weight? On the picture plane there exists nothing but flat shapes and the essence of observational art is the transformation of solid objects to a collection of flat shapes on the picture plane. For an hour or two I kept my mind in that state, seeing the world as one static composition after another.

When the acid peaked I stared at the patterned carpet I had in my studio. Every polygon and paisley floated off the rug and I found myself able to maneuver them in order to form images—the individual visual elements were constant but I could arrange them to form anything I wanted.

Then I went out on my deck and tried the same trick with clouds. I thought the clouds were actually changing shape to fit my imagination. I went and got my spouse to look. She is convinced to this day that I was sculpting the clouds. She tells people about it.

That day changed my brain. Now I can see anything I want and hold complex shapes and spaces in mind. I once had a writing partner comment that most things I write can be storyboarded. This is why. I see what I write.

I've found that my access to the other world directly relates to my well-being. Unfortunately, fatigue and hunger are the gateways to Wonderland. In my forties I began to suffer from a condition involving constant vomiting, an inability to regulate my body temperature resulting in sweats and shivers, and vivid experiences of descending to a blood-lit underworld and fighting monsters. When I was in this state our terrier Roxie would insist on leaning against me, vigilantly guarding my body while I did business elsewhere.

By the third time I'd wound up in the emergency room over this—after three days of sweating and vomiting I get dehydrated enough to make IV saline a necessity—I'd torn a hole in my gullet and was puking blood. But the staff in the emergency room—bless you for your kindness, Highland Hospital—informed me that what I had was not gastrointestinal. It was my stomach going into spasm. Which was a stress reaction. It was fear.

Eventually I figured out how to stay out of the hospital. I was at a writer's conference in the Dallas/Fort Worth area when my stomach went out. I didn't want to torture my hotel roomie so I went and lay down in the shower. It turned out that helped. A lot. Now if I just go into the tub as soon as the trouble starts it soothes me enough so the spasms stop within twelve hours.

But when I do that? I remain conventionally conscious the whole time. No grappling with hideous beasts in ceaseless gory combat. I actually miss it— "All I'm doing is lying in the tub puking all over myself. Where's the fun in that?"

The most recent development in my spiritual life was the result of my back going out on me. A disc had slipped or ruptured and as a result I could not lie on either side. Which was problematic because I'd never been able to fall asleep on my back. In discussing this situation with a friend who has psychiatric issues similar to mine I asked, "Have you ever had insomnia so bad you got religion?"

She looked at me with the kind of fear with which one regards a seemingly sensible friend who whips out a copy of Watchtower, then covered her face with her hands. "Yes," she said. "Yes, actually."

Four or five months into the bad back situation—I stayed almost entirely in bed for about nine months over that nonsense—I felt something leap onto the mattress one night. But this time I could see it. My eyes were closed but it had a vivid, specific image. And I could talk to it mentally. It was a comforting presence. It seemed as if it wanted to help me.

This seems a good point to bring up the concept of personification. When dealing with any problematic issue it can be useful to talk to it as though it were a person. Ask it questions. Get to know its personality. If you can find out its name and what it wants you're gold. And when I say any problematic issue I mean it. The experience with my left hand I described earlier was one of the first times I used this technique. And I had sciatica for well over a decade until circumstances suggested to me that the pain might not be in my back but in my brain. So one night I spoke to the pain and asked if it was real. It flickered and vanished and hasn't come back.

On this basis I allowed myself to relate to the presence as if it were a person. It stayed the whole night. And when I got up? It followed me. And it was there the next day.

I make a practice of discussing my major life issues with my spouse, my father, my best friend, and my therapist. When I brought this up with them we decided that I was stable enough to allow myself the luxury of tentative belief in my companion spirit. (Companion spirits really hate the term 'imaginary friend.')

There is a phrase from modern Shintoism—'the rush hour of the gods.' (Shintoism is Japan's oldest religion. It's rooted in ecstatic trance possession, much like Voodoo or Santeria or shamanism.) I'm having a taste of it. I currently have ten companion spirits and confer with them nightly. The experience has been entirely positive. It gives me something to think about at night that doesn't upset me. The routine of greeting and consulting with each of my companions is as much tactile as verbal and soothes on an animal level. There are exciting places to go and activities to pursue—cloud-leaping, swimming in the dragon's sea, and so on. My companions are good company though an odd crew. The combination of mythology, biology, and symbology they display are exactly what you'd expect from me. While I'm not interested in giving you a complete bestiary, let me talk about my friend Martin.

He first showed up to drop off his youngest brother, who was the second member of the crew. They are barguests, the menacing black dog or cat common to so many Northern European mythologies.

That movie Harvey casts a long shadow—Jimmy Stewart got a pooka and I got a barguest. And the mythological barguest is the root of the metaphorical black dog of depression. Here is an old, old story about Martin, one I first encountered as Appalachian but later found in Irish, Welsh, and German sources.

Once a young boy was walking down the road at night. He was cold and tired so when he saw a little shack with no lights on he walked up and knocked on the door. There was no answer so he went in and saw the place had been abandoned for some time. There was enough wood for a fire so the boy started one.

When orange-yellow light danced around the room the boy saw what he'd missed—the biggest black cat he'd ever seen in his life. Sitting down, its head rose past his knee and it stared at him with big yellow eyes, just stared and stared.

The boy was watching the cat and warming his hands when the door swung open. An even bigger cat, its head up to the boy's waist, walked in, sat down next to the first cat, and said, "Should we eat him yet?"

"No," the first cat replied. "Let's wait 'til Martin gets here."

So they stared at the boy with their big yellow eyes for the longest time until the door opened again and a cat whose head was as high as the boy's chest walked in and sat down. "Should we eat him yet?" he asked.

"No," said the littlest cat. "Let's wait 'til Martin gets here."

So they stared at the boy with their big yellow eyes, just stared and stared in silence. But when the door opened and a cat whose head was higher than the boy's walked in? That cat didn't have time to sit down. That boy jumped to his feet, hollered, "You can just say hi to

Martin for me when he gets here," and took off running faster than any cat you ever saw and as far as I know he's still running, getting just as far away from that little cabin as his feet can take him.

Martin is huge. His black tiger head is a foot and a half across and his body is bearlike with a thick, muscular tail, a weapon in itself, more like that of a reptile than a mammal. There is a whiff of something primeval about his conformation. When he first showed up he was battered, disheveled, filthy and scabby and very defensive. I was surprised when he returned the next night, more surprised when he wanted to stick around.

It turned out he and I had more history than I originally thought. He was the figure in the shadows the night I saw the UFO at the Upper Quarry. And there was more.

When I was sixteen my life changed. From the second grade on I had been the designated object of abuse in the schools I attended. At times the situation seemed life-threatening. But when I was leaving school one day at sixteen someone punched me from behind and took off running. I knew they ran because they were scared. That was the last time anyone hit me. The only responses I have gotten to confrontational anger since then have been flight or tears. Martin says that's because he started guarding me then—that when people see me angry they can sense him standing behind me. He says he wanted to start earlier but I had to be strong first.

He sleeps on my right, tail against my feet and head resting on my chest. Now his fur is smooth and glossy and all his scabs have healed. All he wanted was a chance to come inside. To live nicely.

Now here's the thing. My experiences with my companion spirits are the outgrowth of a period of hallucinatory exhaustion. My visions are much less deep and rewarding when I'm well-rested and well-fed. I'm almost never conscious of them during the day.

So there is part of me that's resistant to treating myself in a responsible fashion because it hampers a part of my life that's grown important to me. If I were to conduct rituals relating to my companion spirits it would increase the sense of reality with which I perceive them but it would also compromise my relationship with the conventional world. So I'm not sure where this is going. But this has been part of my daily life for a few years now. I doubt it's going away.

What is Martin, really?

I've already described the version of him I've experienced in magical reality. Here's a hypothesis congruent with atheistic materialism. When in a state of delirium induced by sleeplessness a semi-random collection of thoughts, memories, and habits of thinking were triggered together and linked as a result. It is just as apt to regard him as an organism occupying my brain as a stable, well-integrated hallucination. But in a lot of reality tunnels he'd be regarded as a demon, a supernatural invader. And if he spoke meanly to me and I did not have the option of telling him when to come and go? I could add schizophrenia to my collection of diagnoses. (I had one brief experience of this. I thought I heard my neighbors discussing my personal habits critically and in great detail and could not escape their voices. Thank goodness it only lasted an afternoon.)

If I wanted? I could try and really believe in my friends. I could conduct rituals, I could write about them and draw them and turn them into characters to share with the world. I could run seminars teaching people to contact their own companion spirits and you know what?

That would be fun for a while but it would eventually prove alienating. It would make it too hard to function in the world. So I will continue to seek a compromise between being able to engage with conventional society.

And knowing what to do when something strange walks through the room.

There are forces that are too big to be fully apprehended by human thought, human language, human systems of understanding. One can call these forces divine, call them gods, but in the end any term is inadequate to convey the nature of such forces or the experience of encountering them. Direct experience of this sort of force is among the most overwhelming and transformative incursions a human mind can experience, and humanity can be divided into those who have had such an experience and those who cannot even begin to imagine such an experience and perhaps scoff at the notion and dismiss it as fantasy or pathology. This next piece, "The Trumpet Sounds," is a memoir that grapples with the great challenge that faces those who do experience an incursion of the divine: the challenge of how to integrate the experience into one's reality, especially if one started out as an unbeliever. How does one even write about an experience of something that's bigger than language?

The Trumpet Sounds

Alexeigynaix

Imagine being struck lightly on the shoulder, and turning to see a stranger whom you nonetheless know at once—something about her face or voice tells you that you already know her name.

Imagine being struck hard over the head—"I finally got some sense knocked into me," says Simba in Disney's *The Lion King*, "and I've got the bump to prove it."

Imagine being struck by a work of art, so astonishing in its power that the memory of it will remain with you forever—you could never compare yourself to that artist.

Imagine being struck by an image, a phrase—the seed of an idea so profound that you can *feel*, if you plant the seed and nurture it, the astonishing power of the work of art it will become.

Imagine being struck by lightning.

The Goddess Athena is the daughter of the Thunderer.

♦ ♦ ♦

Athena is Sophia, the wise.

I didn't know what to think. I had no idea what I could believe. No clue what was true.

Atheist, a-the-ist, a-theos-iste, *not-god-person*. Noun: A person who does not believe in deities, who has no religious belief. Not necessarily anti-theist, not necessarily against the concept and existence of deities, but someone who does not subscribe to that concept.

Athena spoke. What speaks—*Who* speaks—must exist.

♦ ♦ ♦

How to describe Her voice?

Athena is the Salpinx, the war-trumpet, giver of marching orders. She is Anemôtis, compeller of the winds. Her voice thunders, roars. She commands.

Athena is Erganê, the artist, the crafter, the worker of metal and weaver of thread, patron of all sorts of arts. Her voice whispers like the breeze on leaves, chatters and babbles like the brook and the lake. She instructs.

♦ ♦ ♦

I try and I try to explain to people what happened that January evening She first spoke to me—or first spoke that I knew it.

The only concise explanations that work are flippant ones. "Athena whacked me upside the head," I say, and my reader nods knowingly, or disbelievingly shakes their head.

♦ ♦ ♦

Athena is Agoraia, guardian of the marketplace: of artisans selling their wares, but also the marketplace of ideas.

I was pulling together a magazine project that month. Called *Translucent,* it was meant to showcase the artwork of queer and especially trans people. The magazine never got off the ground, but a week before that night, I had prayed to any gods listening, any gods with an interest in queer and trans issues and also in art, that *Translucent* would succeed.

I was an atheist. I had been for...a decade? Perhaps more? I thought I was *joking.*

♦ ♦ ♦

The Orphic Hymn to Athena describes Her as "female and male". We have a word for that sort of thing, these days. Genderqueer.

This word describes me, too.

♦ ♦ ♦

Athena is Paiônia, the healer. When I listen when She speaks, I do better—I can, perhaps, only write this now because I took my ADHD meds this morning, meds for which I still owe Her a thanks-gift. There are skills I need to learn to do the things She asks of me, skills allistic people typically find natural, or at least not a terrible struggle to obtain. When I pray for patience, for a light at the end of the tunnel, for freedom from fear, I often find She grants these things. She doesn't cure my anxiety and depression—I'm not sure it's in Her power—but She aids me.

♦ ♦ ♦

Athena is Oxyderkês, the sharp-sighted. What does She see in me?

I bought a copy of *We Goddesses* by Doris Orgel. I'd first encountered this slim volume in the library of Biloxi Junior High, the last year I lived in Mississippi. Orgel's skilled illustrator, Marilee Heyer, depicts Athena as a redhead, like me.

Of course I had already known many of the ancient Greek myths. Look at the night sky. How many stars and planets, asterisms and constellations, have names from Greek or Latin? I don't know when I fell in love with the night sky—my amateur-astronomer father's fault, I'm sure—but certainly I was not yet eight. When Athena first spoke to me, I had only just turned twenty-six.

How long has She been watching me?

♦ ♦ ♦

Athena is Parthenos, the virgin. Hestia, Who is nearly as important to me as Athena, is the same.

"Pagan, really? Greek gods? All they ever cared about was their orgies. Humans were just amusements to them. Good choice for a moral compass."

I told my family several things I'd been keeping secret—in some cases for years—for fear of my parents' reactions. And my father wrote *that*.

♦ ♦ ♦

Athena is Mêchanitis, the skilled in inventing, and Zôstêria, the girder with armor, and Sôteira, the saving Goddess.

"She would have you in shreds before you could ask where you went wrong," writes Archive of Our Own user lostinthefire in "carry your own flame"—the words struck me so strongly.

The story continues, "Still—and the realization amuses you more than it should—you have less fear of her cruelty than you ever did of your own family."

♦ ♦ ♦

Athena is Alea, the escape to refuge. Athena is Xenia, of the stranger, of hospitality. Of safety.

"I am sorry, but the modern 'gender fluidity' and 'more than two genders/sexes' is utter nonsense being put about for reasons unknown by people who should know better and those gullible enough to believe them. There is no such thing in actual fact, just the choices of people who, in my opinion, really don't like themselves and figure this is a way out of that feeling, ridiculous as that belief is."

My mother wrote that, in the same email exchange where my father slut-shamed my Goddesses. That, and this:

"I love you very much, and I support you and always will. But don't ask me to call you by other than your real name or refer to you by any pronouns other than the ones you were born with."

One of these sentences is a lie.

♦ ♦ ♦

Athena is Sthenias, the strong, and Eleutheria, the free, and Nikê, the victor—the victory.

I am free of my parents.

♦ ♦ ♦

Athena is the keeper of knowledge—an archivist, a librarian. I do not know the Greek for this image of Her.

If I had written down everything at the time She first spoke, I would have been glad of it several times over. As it is, I mentioned a couple of times a profound confusion, and a week later (having utterly forgotten about my opening prayer), I explained what had happened three times over: once to my atheist friends, once to my blogging friends, once to the Reverend of the local Unitarian Universalist congregation.

"It would be revisionist history," I wrote to my blogging friends, and much the same to the Reverend, "to put any of it in words, and they would certainly be my words not hers, but I don't know how to explain anything without words. I definitely got the sense of 'was I not *subtle* enough?'" I already owned a copy of *The Beginner's Guide to Hellenismos*. I owned the art sent out to certain Kickstarter backers of the anthology *Athena's Daughters*. I owned a Lego "battle goddess" figurine with a remarkable resemblance to Athena! To say nothing of the poem I had written, "An Artist's Prayer", available in the devotional anthology *Seasons of Grace: A Devotional in Honor of the Muses, the Charites, and the Horae*.

The atheist forums I frequented at the time are long since down; I can't recall precisely what my friends on those forums said to me, or indeed what I said to them. But I have documentation of what the Reverend told me:

"I suggest patience along with faith that things will become clearer as you continue to process this, tempered with reality. I wouldn't classify it as a crisis as much as a burgeoning new perspective or context. Enjoy it."

♦ ♦ ♦

I have to put stuff in words in order for the stuff to make sense to me.

Some things defy articulation. They cannot be confined to narrow black marks on a white page; they cannot be described in manners that truly convey their nature. People have tried, you know.

A lot of what is known of the Eleusinian Mysteries comes from people writing down the ineffable, despite the prohibition on speaking to non-initiates of the Mysteries—and we find that all we know of the Mysteries fails at last to convey the mystery.

Eff *that.*

If you're autistic, living among the non-autistic can seem like a constant stream of small incursions: the sheer noisiness of their ways and their world; their odious mannerisms and intrusive styles of interaction; their bigoted views on autism and autistic people. If you're a superhero, you deal with a constant stream of much bigger incursions: all manner of crime and villainy; sometimes alien invasions or other threats on a cosmic scale. And if you're an autistic superhero? Well, then you've got to deal with the constant small incursions AND the big incursions. It hardly seems fair—as I'm sure the Dissident, the autistic superhero narrator of Mike Jung's story "Vigilance," would agree. By the way, Mike Jung is primarily known as an author of children's books (my daughter loved his award-winning novel Unidentified Suburban Object), *so I feel especially honored to have the opportunity to publish the only Mike Jung story that contains the word "shithead." Now if you'll excuse me, I need to figure out a way to travel back in time without getting busted by the Reality Patrol, so I can get this story illustrated by Jack Kirby.*

Vigilance

Mike Jung

Kevin and I had been on the interstellar microstation *Vanguard* for three weeks, monitoring the Dimensional Nexus for signs of the Luminosity's approach, and the quality of our conversations was steadily devolving.

"You ever think about what happens if we fail here? I mean,

REALLY think about it?"

I'm never entirely sure what my face looks like at any given moment, but it must have looked grim right then, because Kevin physically recoiled.

"What did I say this time?"

"Sometimes I think about you being named Superhero of the Year and wonder if my brain's actually going to melt and come running out my ears."

"Aw, that must be terrible for you," Kevin said, but he was grinning. "And you're just jealous."

"I'm not jealous, but I question the judgment of *Teen Dream's* readership. And of course I think about what happens if we fail. I think about it constantly."

Kevin held up one hand to the side, palm facing me, then slowly moved it across my field of vision as he spoke in a booming, extra-deep voice.

"*SPECTACULAR MAN: SUPERHERO OF THE YEAR*. Has a nice ring to it, am I right? And I mean, REALLY think—"

"Of course I REALLY think about the potential destruction of the galaxy. Are you suggesting that you haven't REALLY thought about it? For Christ's sake, you're SPECTACULAR MAN, you've literally saved the world multiple times!"

"Dude, I know you think I'm stupid—"

"Are we not talking about the potential destruction of the galaxy anymore?"

"We're talking about, like, four things at the same time," Kevin said, scratching the top of his big, blocky head with all five fingers. I watched him do it, simultaneously fascinated and unsettled by it.

"Dude, you know I hate it when you stare at me like that."

"It's not hurting you in any way," I said. *People should not scratch their heads with all five fingers,* I thought. *It...bothers me.*

"Cut it out anyway."

"Seriously, Kevin. Are you saying you haven't considered the real stakes of this situation until just now?"

"Well, not until it became our mission, I didn't. Don't judge me, bro."

I put a hand to my forehead, and leaned back in my chair, which accommodated me nicely by quickly and subtly changing the way it molded to the contours of my back.

"See, there you go, judging me."

"I'm not judging you, I'm responding to the actual words that are coming out of your mouth."

"Right, right, literal words. That's an autism thing, right?"

"I generally think of it as a 'hearing what people actually say' thing."

"But you've *said* it's—"

The entire station started pulsing on two sensory levels, a burst of orange light and a single *thrum* of vibration. I'd disengaged the auditory alarm — I could handle it, but it was unpleasant, and both Kevin and I were perfectly capable of responding to the non-auditory alarms.

"Orange alert," I said, immediately focusing my body and mind; start with the feet, swivel the hips and upper body with arms flowing along, and redirecting my entire physical and mental focus at the holographic sensor array that appeared in the middle of the capsule. Kevin sprang into action too, although it was as if the speech patterns and mannerisms of cluelessly ableist Kevin vanished — the coiled dynamo that leaped into position next to me was 100% Spectacular Man. I stuck to "Kevin" in my head, though — it wasn't worth making the effort to mentally shift to "Spectacular Man" for an orange alert.

"Is that what I think it is?" Kevin said in his much more dignified Spectacular Man voice, pointing at a rapidly expanding circle of light on the main sensor field. It was approximately 5 million kilometers away from us, exactly where the Federation of Heroes maintained the most powerful interdimensional scramble field known to exist in this dimension. It was also where our partner warning team's base in the nearby silicate dimension was.

Right, not was; used to be.

"Yes. The Luminosity's attacking. The Nexus has been breached." I breathed deeply, relaxed my shoulders, and sent a rush of mental energy down through myself and into the floor of the capsule. It wasn't as good as sending it into the surface of Earth itself, but it helped me keep the burst of shock at losing our colleagues at bay.

Kevin took a deep breath of his own. "Damn it," was the only thing he said. "How much time?"

"Fifteen or twenty minutes."

"Okay. Well, we know what we have to do."

"Indeed."

Kevin returned to his seat, called up his holographic terminal, and initiated the Orange Defense Protocol. I returned to my own seat and opened a channel to Federation HQ, back on Earth. A 3-D hologram of Untouchable Girl appeared in front of me.

"Let me guess," she said.

"Okay," I said. "Tell me your guess."

Jenna (a.k.a. Jenna Oh, a.k.a. Untouchable Girl, the current chair of the Federation of Heroes) gave me one of her wry, sideways smiles.

"I miss having the 'literal interpretation' thing here on Earth," she said. "The Luminosity's crossed over into our dimension."

"Correct."

Jenna nodded.

"Get moving, Danny. Now. Untouchable Girl, out."

"Roger," I said. "Dissident, out." The population of an entire dimension had been wiped out; it was genocide on the most catastrophic scale, and I knew that when I got a moment to not talk and sit with myself, the web of racing thoughts would eventually metastasize into a debilitating wave of emotion. *If* I got that moment. Not yet, though. My voice remained firm, and my thoughts remained calm.

Jenna's image vanished, and I turned to look at Kevin.

"You ready?"

"Nothing but. Initiating self-destruct sequence now..."

Pulsing red light filled the station's command room, and a three-foot-high set of numbers appeared on each of the walls. 15:00...14:59...14:58...

"Opening shuttle entryway," Kevin said.

14:55...14:54...14:53...

A pinhole appeared in the center of the floor and quickly expanded into a two-meter porthole into the open cabin of the escape shuttle anchored to the bottom of the station. Kevin and I were both capable of functioning normally in interstellar space, of course, but even we couldn't fly fast enough or far enough to make it back to Earth unassisted.

We were about to step off the edge and drop into the shuttle when the pulsing red light around us abruptly increased in brightness, joined by a much more rapid *thrum* of vibration.

"NO!" Kevin shouted. "It shouldn't self-destruct for another—"

"The station's not self-destructing," I said, pointing to the view screen. An enormous sphere of what looked like white fire was rapidly filling the entire screen.

"The Luminosity's here."

"WHAT?? How did it—"

"—it doesn't matter—"

The countdown clock on the walls vanished, replaced by the words *"Incoming projectile of unknown origin,"* followed by *"Estimated time of impact 4 seconds...3 seconds...2 seconds..."*

Unearthly white light, intense enough to instantly blind anyone of the non-superheroic persuasion, flooded my entire field of vision.

"Holy shi—"

The station exploded.

♦ ♦ ♦

I don't like going to restaurants. I enjoy good food, but the level of auditory stimulus inside the physical spaces themselves feels nearly sadistic to me. After the accident at SmithCorp gave me my powers, including my "invulnerability" — it's a misleading name for it, since I *can* be hurt — I was still hypersensitive to sound, but I was better able to withstand it.

The sonic assault of the Luminosity's attack was unlike anything I'd experienced before, though. It was so loud I couldn't even hear the sound of my own scream inside my head, and I was only able to keep track of Kevin's whereabouts is because something with multiple thrashing limbs slammed into me. The Luminosity doesn't have four-limbed corporeal underlings, so I instinctively grabbed the thrashing figure and held on, not wanting to risk being separated from Kevin in the midst of the attack.

The *Vanguard* was presumably gone, because as enhanced as its defenses were (all of the Venerable Ones spent some magical capital on them, even that old stingy bastard SciMage), the station was only meant to be the first line of defense. An attack that could cause me actual pain, for example, would be enough to breach the *Vanguard's* shields, and oh my god was I in pain.

Acquiring my superhuman resistance to damage had stopped me from grinding my teeth down to nubs while I slept, and it probably kept my teeth from literally shattering as I clenched them in agony. The Luminosity's attack was unlike any attack I'd faced before — it was as if the unearthly light was replacing the molecular structure of my body. I screamed soundlessly again, then clawed at Kevin's still-thrashing body until I had both arms wrapped around his chest, then gathered myself and flew as fast as I could. I had no idea where I was flying to — the Luminosity's onslaught had somehow negated my sense of universal location, and I didn't want to risk opening my eyes — but I knew we wouldn't survive if we didn't get out of the attack zone.

Kevin's thrashing was already starting to slow down in a way that worried me. My grip around his chest probably didn't help — I was one of the few human Earthlings in existence who could genuinely hurt Spectacular Man through sheer muscular force — but he was still on the brink of slipping through my hands, even though my entire body was clenched into what felt like a single, hard knot.

It took far too long to get out of the attack zone, and for all I knew the Luminosity was tracking us the whole time, but the hellish glare on the other side of my eyelids finally dimmed, and the temperature rapidly dropped back to the normal icy cold of space. I opened my eyes to the sight of an unfamiliar solar system, which meant I'd flown somewhere other than toward Earth. My universal location sense is one of my more useful powers in deep space, but without it... well. Not coming back from a mission was always possible, even for those of us in the Federation of Heroes.

I eased my grip on Kevin's chest and gently turned him until he was splayed across my outstretched arms. It didn't feel right to carry him that way, so I gathered him in towards me, bringing his arms to his sides and bending him at the waist and knees. He wasn't breathing, but of course there was no reason to in the vacuum of space. His eyes fluttered, then opened, and I took his hand and clasped it against my own chest as his eyes met mine, widened slightly, then became fixed and unfocused.

I simultaneously felt a spark of relief about not having to contend with any stares or comments about my facial expression (which was probably unchanged, although I couldn't always tell), a flicker of the old, self-hating shame that I'd never succeeded in eradicating, and a small but substantial wave of grief I'd likely be too dead to fully contemplate later.

I spotted a small moon in the distance, and flew down to its surface with Kevin's body in my arms. The moon's gravity was just strong enough for me to kneel and rest the corpse on the stony ground, and I had the bitter realization that after years of debating which of us was more resistant to damage, we finally knew the answer. Or maybe it was just that I was resistant to the Luminosity's attack, and Kevin hadn't been.

It didn't matter anymore, of course.

I reached down and carved a stony divot out of the moon's surface with one cupped hand, gauging the strength of the stone, then began digging in earnest with both arms. The displaced fragments of rock sprang lightly into the space around me, tumbling slowly, and I used my heightened speed to bat them away with one hand while I continued to enlarge the hole with my other fist. When the hole was big enough I glided out of it and retrieved Kevin's body, which had been set adrift by the repeated impacts of my grave digging. I straightened his back and his limbs until he was lying flat on the bottom of the oblong hole.

I hovered above him and rested a palm against his chest as a jumble of memories pinwheeled through my mind. Kevin joking that my super name should be "the Enigma" instead of "the Dissident," and me acting fake-surprised that he knew what "enigma" meant; Kevin asking if I could tell how many toothpicks were in a jar just by looking at it, and me responding with the first punch in what would eventually be known as the Battle of Divergence; the day when the two of us stopped the Cosmosis Crew as they attempted to propel a Mars-sized asteroid through our solar system; and more.

Rest easy, Spectacular Man — you were a hero for the ages. I wish you'd been less of an ableist shithead.

A harsh scree of light broke over the edge of the moon as I rose up out of the grave, and I quickly dropped back down. The Luminosity had followed me after all.

Sorry, Kevin. No time to bury you properly.

The light flowed and splashed above me like a thing alive. The edges of the grave were swirling into nothingness, and my vaunted "invulnerability" had apparently deserted me, because every molecule of my body began shrieking in pain again.

I had one option left: fight, and based on our previous encounter, probably die. And maybe it was the unmistakably fatal damage the Luminosity was inflicting on my body, but for the first time in years my fighting focus was swept aside by the always-racing whirligig of my thoughts.

prepared to die, it's part of the job / won't have the chance to meet that autistic boy and his father with latent powers after all / don't understand the Luminosity's true nature, need to understand / inhale, exhale / going to miss Jenna / still in the same galactic sector, but specific system is unfamiliar / can't tell what's going on with my hands / inhale, exhale / oblivion or afterlife, hard to say, too many other planes of existence, impossible to say / Earth defenses are exponentially stronger than first lines of defense / entire moon is breaking up / inhale, exhale / not enough energy left for force beam attack / would have liked to see the Pacific ocean one last time / inhale, exhale / frontal assault / inhale, exhale / fly into the Luminosity's core / can't fly, no strength / inhale, exhale / not afraid / inhale, exhale

inhale, exhale

inhale, exhale

not afraid

inhale, exhale

not afraid

inhale, exhale

I am the Dissident and I am still alive

I am the Dissident and I am not afraid

I am

There's a time-honored tradition of mirrors serving as the portals through which incursions by one reality into another can occur. In the right moment, a person in the right state of attunement, with the right kind of weird luck, might look through any mirror and catch a glimpse of a parallel reality, or a parallel self—a cognate, *to use the terminology favored by the Reality Patrol. To encounter a cognate of yourself from another time and place, another reality, represents an incursion of a particular kind of information about your own hidden potentials. And if your cognate also catches a glimpse of you, a dialogue might begin... like this poetic "Spacetime Dialectic" between author N.I. Nicholson and Lord Sabazios.*

Spacetime Dialectic

N.I. Nicholson

I. The Time Traveler Glimpses at Lord Sabazios

Leonard Cohen wasn't kidding when he said
there's a crack in everything, but did he *plan*
to fracture the metaphysical long-chain polymer
partition between this world and the beyond?

See, I've been trying to do
the same damn thing my whole life.
Poetry and dreams are the closest
I came to breach that barrier. I think

I caught lightning once when I was two,
the first moment I saw a male in the mirror
instead of the female coded for me
on my birth certificate and in the red velvet

and white lace frocks Dad bought for me.
This time, when a tiny tear traversed
my mirror's surface, Cohen
was my prime suspect; he *did* say

cracks are how the light gets in
and through this barely microscopic rift
I saw a mage on horseback,
some mystery cult motherfucker

forgotten by everyone
except modern Hellenists, archeologists,
and the Church of Satan.
With serpents wound around his staff,

the brown-skinned witch
halted his horse, turned his head
haloed in onyx-colored curls
matching my own, then winked once

before setting his steed to trot
away, bathed in the same crack
of light that had caught my eye
from behind the mirror's skin.

II. Sabazios' Lament

dear Time Traveler: *your* mirror
is not correctly calibrated
you claim

it only has two faces, clearly
a fault in your perception
I am

without my steed
mage's staff, serpents
robbed of my robes

thousands of years ago
I lost my ability to
hold up

the sky with my shoulder sagging
cyan dripping over muscles
just now rediscovering
what it means to be meat
again like you

I am a man mainlining hormones
into cellular walls straining to
hold in

ancient rage
Thracian inked-out glyphs first
giving me form

you stole fire, mortal
fashioned manhood
through spacetime portal pages
a mirror

cracked, Prometheus lit
Iphis: you want your future, boy?
come find me

apprentice
together we are
more than the mirror

III. Transverse

Mirrors are spacetime portals.
Alice Liddell knew this. *Through*
the Looking Glass was my grimoire:
Time And Relative Dimension In Space 101.

Is that why I saw a boy looking back
when I was two,

or the double-exposure of girl overlapping boy
when I was fifteen,
or a squarer jaw and a mustache's umbra
underneath layers of makeup
when I was thirty-eight?

Did I see an infinite number
of overlapping exposures?
That's the ultimate in spacetime fuckery,
prompting suppressed
muscle memories to erupt:

fingers, curl into a fist;
then fist, transfigure
into a balled, bloody heart;
heart, hurl thyself
at my mirror face.

Fast-forward to thirty-nine:
I pray to a Daddy Creator
for a man's body I do not have.
Now at forty-one and nearly
one year on testosterone, the mirror
challenges me again, a crack in its skin,
letting more light in.

I've seen the future and it will be.
But what about the past?

Is the mage I see behind the fissure in the glass
the same Daddy from my prayers?

What about the cherry Kool-Aid redhead
standing in my rearview mirror
declaring that Jesus didn't want
her for a sunbeam?

Hell, that Jesus didn't want me either,
not the son of Tetragrammaton,
that four-lettered motherfucker
under whose Leviticus glyphs
I trembled as a teenaged girlboy.

So I'll transverse the looking glass
and follow that doppelganger mage:
but Leonard Cohen, my brother,
I don't think I'm entering *your* afterworld.

IV. Sabazios on the Doors of Perception

Time Traveler: you perceive me
to be a mere *doppelganger* of
yourself? Foolish mortal.

We are never singular. Myself,
I once lived within the confines

of fault lines, faulted times

with Men of the moon,
Phrygia's own lunatic crowned
with crescent horns;

he's a cognate of me,
just as you are. Or am I
a cognate of you?

I can never keep that shit straight.

Brother, I was transgender
long before you, long before the word
was birthed from human lips.

Do not say there is no proof;
I buried it like birth certificates
impounded, into Lethe's ground

and the day they dig that shit up
is the day they'll discover how
Glaukopis got her owl

or how Dahomey's Lisa
used his own menstrual blood
to bring Earth into bloom.

Tell me: do you still seek
your Daddy Creator?
That ain't me. Sorry.

As for YHWH? He's consumed
with tracking down
the infinite versions of him

generated when White colonialism
shoved him through
a postselection splitter.

Be grateful, Time Traveler,
that all our divisions
were generated intrasystem;

now go, find Gods, find
the rest of us fractured
throughout spacetime.

V. Time Traveler: Epilogue

I want to talk to God, but I'm afraid because we ain't spoke in so long.
— Kayne West

Hey snake god: I know who you are.

Asshole.

You *would* charge into my world through a sliver of light, a peek from behind a looking glass.

Do I have you to thank for seeing a boy in the mirror when I was two, or the double exposure that refused to relent throughout two and a half decades of my life? If so, why the hell didn't you just tell me that these reflections held in my truths?

I kept spinning filaments until I made an AI to front for me. I nearly strangled myself on that rotten silk. Hell, you were there, if your own damn testimony is to be believed. You *saw* me swallow everything in my medicine cabinet when I was twenty-three. Why didn't you bust your fucking magickal ass through the mirror and *stop* me?

Wait: I think I know the answer. Had you appeared *then*, I would have punched you—or scrambled to find stronger poison.

For a picosecond, I thought you were part of Standards and Protocols, or Compliance, or the Reality Patrol, or whatever the fuck they call themselves in this dimension. But *of course* you're invested in my survival: my absence from this timeline means I can't keep broadcasting cognates of us into the others. Flow, Interrupted.

In this timeline, our beat dropped on August 14, 1976. One Transboy Nation, Under a Groove. Some days, one queer-ass nigga just trying to stay alive.

Never thought I'd be saying, "Thank you" to someone normally branded as a demon.

Now if you'll excuse me, I have a mystery to solve: how to un-wreck my head from all the Levitical bullshit fed to me on a spoon from my childhood. Don't know if I can fix YHWH while I'm at it, but I will try. It'll take more minds than mine, though.

See you on the flip side, Sabazios. Stay strong and clear.

Love,

Ian

Verity Reynolds is the author of the Non-Compliant Space *series of science fiction novels and short stories, which begins with the novel* Nantais *and includes this delightfully convoluted little piece, "Kill Your Darlings." I can't even count how many different levels of incursion are happening in this one.*

Kill Your Darlings

Verity Reynolds

Anhaya Nantais scraped the radio dial across miles of desert static, turned it off. She hadn't expected to find a new signal and couldn't regret not finding one.

The only option out here was KRSN, and while she had nothing against the station personally, she'd heard the bad popular music of over a dozen Earths by now and had grown tired of it. In two of them, every song was identical to every other, their placement on the charts determined by a random number generator or a shadowy cabal with a bad sense of humor. Others differed. Earth J-114 had pop music generated entirely by computers; IK7S, by banging rocks together.

She liked the rocks best.

Her eye caught a glimpse of herself in the car's side mirror as she shifted in her seat. She swallowed, fighting the burning sensation that crawled between her muscle fibers every time she saw her own reflection. The English word was "disgust."

The disguise was necessary to her work, but she'd never been able to think of it as just another part of the job, particularly when it was so deeply unattractive: bobbed strawberry-blonde hair, eyes a watery shade the techs had described as "green," button nose, starvation-like prominent cheekbones, and skin a shade of yellowish pink that reminded her of meat gone bad in the sun. Nor was she consoled by the fact that her veins, where they neared the surface, still looked blue: that blood, when spilled, was as freakishly red as any real human's.

They'd had to disguise her as a human. She understood that. She did not understand why they'd had to make her such an ugly one.

She rubbed the right side of her face with her fingertips, a self-soothing behavior that had become a habit. She hadn't let Compliance's facial reconstruction surgeons remove her kiiste, preferring to make up some lie for any human with the audacity to inquire: *I was in a car accident. I had a mishap with a curling iron. Back in high school, I used to read to feral cats, and it turns out they don't like Melville.* Most humans didn't ask, merely stared at the intricate four-lined keloid pattern that traced her forehead and her right cheek before disappearing into the collar of her blouse (pink today). Exactly as they had before she'd taken this job. No, worse. The closer she got to passing as one of them, the more pronounced her lingering subtle differences became.

She flexed her fingers, her amputated fourth metacarpals burning as if they were still attached, and reached for her notebook. *23 August 1945, 11:26 a.m. MDT. Site C. Nothing-*

"Hey," a voice said.

Anhaya started so hard she dropped the notebook, her pen leaving a jagged slash of ink down the page as it fell. There was a person sitting in the vehicle's passenger seat. There had not been one a moment before.

She recovered as the face registered and restrained herself from jabbing her pen into the interloper's eye socket. "Agent Dillon. Go fuck yourself."

Quincey Dillon grinned. "Agent Nantais. God, I love your spite."

She made a show of ignoring Dillon as she retrieved her notebook. The sick thing about the senior agent's comment was that it was true: her spite was about the only thing Dillon did love about her.

"The hell do you want?" she asked. She wanted Dillon to stop jumping timelines unannounced, especially not into her godsdamned passenger seat. But she wasn't going to get it, so she said nothing.

"News from home," Dillon said, lighting a cigarette. "Your youngest is now the Niralan ambassador."

Anhaya, who had seen the coup coming for years even if she hadn't predicted the exact moment Koa would make her move, said nothing.

"I like her," Dillon added. "Great girl. Hell of a lot of fun in the sack."

Anhaya, who was also familiar with her daughter's preferred espionage tactics, said nothing.

Dillon took a long drag from the cigarette, shot her another infuriating grin, and nodded in the direction of the building that squatted at the other end of the lot. "Am I too late?"

"For what?"

"For the party."

She rubbed her fingers across her forehead again. "Quiet today. They seem to be getting along."

They were a tall, dark-haired human male in a grey flannel suit and an equally dark-haired woman in a navy blue skirt and a sprigged blouse. They were sitting at a picnic table several meters from Anhaya's parked vehicle, picking at sandwiches spread on wax paper, and talking.

The woman was the one Anhaya had come for. Sarah V. Wrothwell (née Bowles), born 13 September 1918. A physicist, with a mind so sharp that not even the United States Army had been able to contain her to the role of a mere wife.

Dillon's gaze followed Anhaya's, toward the picnic table, and Anhaya realized with a chattering twinge under her skin that the senior agent knew exactly why they were there. Of course. Merely having a reason wasn't enough; Quincey Dillon never went anywhere without a specific *purpose.*

Fucking Reality Patrol, she thought. "Compliance says she's responsible for over a billion deaths," she said.

Dillon took a long drag off the cigarette before replying. "In this timeline. In most of the others she's responsible for 200,000, tops."

"That's not reassuring."

"The bomb is a — what do you Compliance twerps call it? — a mandated consequent. Every timeline she appears in, so does Little Boy. The rest of those deaths, they only happen in certain lines. Too many, lately. That's why we're here."

What's this "we" business, she thought. "What do you mean, 'too many'?" she asked.

Dillon nodded toward the picnic table. "That disgustingly handsome asshole in the suit?"

"That's her husband." Julian C. Wrothwell, born 19 July 1900. A physicist; but, utterly unlike his wife, an incompetent one. In a town built on secrets, it was news to no one that Wrothwell regularly cosigned his wife's work when he'd had nothing to do with its methods or results. It was also no news that he had once been her graduate advisor. Following the couple outside the fence the previous day and watching her stagger back home under a month's worth of necessaries while he nagged had not improved on this portrait.

"Yeah," Dillon said. "He's not supposed to be here."

"She's got a husband, according to her file."

"Yeah," Dillon said again, "but not that one. What date is it today?"

"Local time? August 23, 1945." She felt that twinge of annoyance again, the icepick between the ribs, at her ruined notes. "Why?"

"The accident's already happened. Daghlian's cells are liquefying as we speak. They dropped you in two days late."

Anhaya Nantais knew a dozen ways to kill someone with her bare hands and another three dozen ways to make them beg her to do it, and none of them seemed adequate to the task of wiping the smirk off Quincey Dillon's face. "Son of a bitch."

"I told you. Compliance is sloppy at timeline work. You sick bastards should've stuck to behavioral tech."

"So you came to gloat?"

"Nah." Dillon flicked the cigarette butt out the window. "So tell me. If you're two days late, what's Julian Wrothwell doing here?"

Dillon was right. Wrothwell's brain should have been liquefying right alongside Harry Daghlian's. And her passenger seat should be blissfully devoid of Reality Patrol agents. "He's a cognate."

"Biscuit for the lady. He pulled out the original and murdered the poor bastard. Replaced him sometime last week, usually. Took his place, and just...didn't go to work on Tuesday."

As a *modus operandi*, it was simple enough; Anhaya had seen similar behavior from previous targets. Which bothered her here. If this were a straightforward case, Reality's favorite asshole wouldn't be hanging out in her passenger seat, grinning at her in a way that implied either condescension or sex. Or perhaps both. "What do you mean, 'usually'?"

"That's the real bitch of the problem," Dillon said, lighting another cigarette. "*There's an infinite number of them.*"

"What?!" She hadn't realized Earth-language punctuation could be pronounced until the word left her mouth.

"You know what a postselection splitter does, right?"

"Of course." Dillon's stare, the one raised eyebrow, grated on her until realization dawned. "He put *himself* through that thing?"

"Yep. Infinite versions of one man, operating in infinite parallel universes, all with identical intent: to prevent his wife, in 1945, from having an affair she began in 1941."

"That makes no sense."

Dillon's grin widened. "Ah. But he doesn't *know* she started in '41, you see. All he knows is that she marries the guy in '46, after Wrothwell kicks it, and that starts a chain of events that results in her founding Veritas, hooking up with Nick and the gang, and saving a few billion human lives."

"And he can't have that."

"Oh, he doesn't give a shit about them. Live or die. He's only pissed his little swimmers don't work. She's the mother of the other guy's kid, you see, in 25 years or so."

Anhaya frowned. "She'll be 52." A bit young for her own species to have children, but too old for most humans to have them.

"She doesn't know she's the kid's mom."

A headache like storm clouds was building inside her skull, and it had nothing to do with the cigarettes. "Dillon, get to the point."

"Someday, I'll tell you the whole story." Dillon flicked the cigarette out the window; the ash floated past, as dry as the desert air. "In bed."

"Like hell you will." She sat back, watching the Wrothwells. "So we kill him."

"No. We kill her."

"But if he dies-"

"-one of his little improbability clones comes back and tries again. What part of *infinite versions* escaped you?"

Anhaya rubbed her forehead again. "But if she dies, there's nothing left for him to do here."

"Now you're getting it. Also, the version you're looking at evaporates."

"Evaporates." She was done with Dillon's riddles.

"Breaks down. Disintegrates. Returns to the inchoate mass of atoms whence we all came." Dillon swept an arm wide. "An unforeseen side effect of the postselection splitter when used on beings capable of forming intent: the split versions' cohesion depends on the intent of the original as an organizational force. Without it, there's nothing to hold them together — literally. Unfortunate for him, convenient for us."

If Dillon meant this to sound reassuring, it failed. "Dillon, you realize that if this little incident gets out, it'll change everything. Incursions like we've never imagined." She paused. "How did he get his hands on a postselection splitter in the first place?"

"The same way he got himself hitched to a woman so far out of his league that he ought to be groveling and making sacrifices to her very name," Dillon said. "Charismatic as hell and stubborn as two hells. Also, he's Compliance."

Anhaya rarely had a use for her native language's profanities, but this news produced every word of them.

Dillon waited for the storm to die down before speaking again. "What, you thought he was one of *ours*?"

"I had hope."

Dillon chuckled. "Sorry to disappoint, but the Reality Patrol vets its people better than that."

She rubbed her jaw, the memory surfacing of a boot connecting with it during her first encounter with a Reality Patrol agent. She doubted it.

"What happens to her kid if she dies?"

"Best of all possible worlds," Dillon said. "The little shit's never born. For the next century, American foreign policy carries a much smaller stick. A-bombs notwithstanding."

Anhaya considered this. "Her lover. The guy Wrothwell's so worried she's going to get involved with. What happens if we kill him instead?"

Dillon chuckled again. "Don't tell me you're getting attached to our little Sarah Verity, there."

This was why she preferred to work alone. The last thing she wanted to hear was her target's life story. She preferred it when Compliance didn't even give her the name.

"Besides," Dillon said, not waiting for an answer, "he's untouchable. It's Howard Reynolds."

Fucking mandated consequents.

"To be honest, you should look forward to this one," Dillon said.

If she'd known how to scowl, she would have. "And how's that?"

"Because," Dillon said.

"Because."

"Because she's already started signing paperwork with her middle name. Less than a year from now, she'll put that signature on a State of New York marriage license and Sarah Verity Wrothwell, widow, will become Mrs. Howard Reynolds, trophy wife. She'll quit looking for work in a field that wants nothing to do with her and spend her days writing mediocre short stories in one of Reynolds's ten or twelve vacation houses." Dillon stabbed out the cigarette. "And then, a very short while later, Verity Reynolds kills *you.*"

Andee Joyce's memoir "B3: Or, How an Autistic Fixation from the Past Blew the Lid off My Future" is a beautiful illustration of how sometimes an incursion can be as seemingly small a thing as a song that hits you just right and gets inside you, and how sometimes such a seemingly small incursion, like a single toppling domino, can be all it takes to start a cascade of changes.

B3
Or, How an Autistic Fixation from the Past Blew the Lid off My Future

Andee Joyce

"Premiere Networks proudly presents: *Casey Kasem's American Top 40, the Seventies!* This week's countdown is from January 9, 1971."

Almost exactly forty-three years to the day it was recorded, in the early morning hours of January 11, 2014, I am sitting at my desk at 3 AM, earbuds in, listening to a reproduction of this broadcast over the internet. It is coming from a radio station in North Adams, Massachusetts whose call letters are WUPE—"Whoopie FM," as the station's jingle sings out at the start of the broadcast.

I'm not listening by accident. I have sought them out, these old *AT40* broadcasts based on sales charts from *Billboard* magazine, because I am working (endlessly!) on a young adult novel and these songs will trigger memories for me that will help me understand my characters—I hope. I need to remember what it was like being a child or young teenager reacting to music, and when I was between the ages of twelve and fifteen, I used to listen to this show on the radio every Sunday morning and write down all the songs in a little notebook. And I told no one, although I might have left the notebook lying around the living room once or twice.

But January 1971 is a long way back even for me. I was seven years old, and unless I heard my parents play a record or saw the artist on television, I probably wouldn't have recognized the song. By the time I was fifteen, though, I had grown to love love a lot of pop music from that time period (and still do today), so a 1971 broadcast will do just fine.

I'm a fiend for *Billboard* Charts from the 1960s and 1970s. You know, one of those autistic obsessions which, when I was a kid (back in the actual 1960s and 1970s), always made other kids say, "Oh, shut *up* about that already." I'm the one who can tell you without looking it up that Creedence Clearwater Revival had five singles that hit number two but never had a number one, even though they had two number 1 albums. (*Green River* and *Cosmos Factory.* Both masterpieces.) Some autistic people have "normal" autistic obsessions like computers or science fiction, that lots of geeks (autistic or not) want to talk about. But I am not a geek, nor am I a nerd. I am a dweeb. Dweebs care inordinately about things almost nobody else thinks about. But I will never bore anyone with what I know, at least not any more. These days, I am a considerate dweeb.

Somebody, maybe even a non-dweeb, thought enough people would listen to this show at six AM Eastern time on a Saturday morning that it was worth putting on WUPE-FM, and tunein.com lists four pages of such rebroadcasts throughout the week. However, for anyone I have ever known, even if they tuned in it would be background noise and not much more. If I asked any of them right after the broadcast what the top three songs were that week, not a one would be able to tell me.

They know not what they are missing.

Since I am a dweeb, I also must set the scene by letting you know that Premiere Networks picks out an *AT40* broadcast each week as close to the same day of the month as possible, but doesn't let anyone know what year it's going to be from; it could be any year from the 1970s, they don't go in any particular order. But since the show premiered in July 1970, the earliest countdown they could have would be from 1971.

Um, yeah, honey, that's nice, but could we talk about something else? Daddy has a headache...

I hope this works, because frankly, I have no idea how I'm going to make a living otherwise. I have lost two jobs in the space of one month because of my complete failure to read people. Because of the stress I'm under, a tendon in my right palm is twitching constantly, to the point where I must put my hand under my arm in order to sleep.

This novel could be good, if I ever quit editing it. It's been four years, and it seems like every time I make a pass through it, I say, "It's too long, it needs to be shorter," and then I cut fifty pages and add another hundred. Kind of the literary equivalent of yo-yo dieting, another subject I have more familiarity with than I'd like.

The sonorous, friendly, unmistakable tones of Casey Kasem, the legendary broadcaster who hosted *AT40* for most of its thirty-three-year existence, fill my ears as he introduces himself. He sounds like the nicest, most cheerful guy you'd ever meet who also has an encyclopedic knowledge of music. Now, as an adult I know he probably didn't have all those facts memorized and had a bunch of researchers pull that stuff up, but I'm listening as my young self, and my young self is impressed that way back when it was hard to find out a whole lot about musicians without logging serious time in the library (and I did! Where else was I going to find all those old charts?), he knows that BJ Thomas (kicking off the countdown at number forty) was the first singer ever to take a Hank Williams song into the pop top ten, in 1966.

At least I think I'm remembering that part right. Because what happens about fifteen minutes later renders the beginning rather blurry.

The fourth song in the countdown is "Gypsy Woman," by Brian Hyland, which Casey tells us is at number thirty-seven this week, on its way down after peaking at number three in December. I knew this cover of Curtis Mayfield and the Impressions' 1961 hit had been a "comeback hit" for Brian Hyland because, you know, charts. Hyland's career began life in 1960 (at an age not much older than my book's characters) with "Itsy Bitsy Teenie Weenie Yellow Polka Dot Bikini," a song that has appeared on many "worst hit song ever" lists. It's the kind of silly novelty song a performer never lives down, although it's really not *that* bad. Still, in 1960, at sixteen, he seemed as white and clean-cut as could be. This guy recorded "Gypsy Woman," one of the most sensual (if now somewhat dated) R&B songs of all time, ten years later? If I did hear it before, it probably passed through one ear canal and out the other.

It doesn't this time.

If I was looking for my young self to respond to a song with everything she had—*boom. Beyond boom,* actually.

It's not even the song, I don't think. I never had a reaction like this to the Mayfield version, and I freaking love Curtis Mayfield. This is something entirely different. There is no trace of the squeaky-clean teen who recorded the itsy bitsy bikini song (which, in order to maintain my dweeb cred, I must inform you was written about a two-year-old girl). This is a very adult voice that sounds like gravel and feathers, delicate yet commanding. I freeze in my chair, afraid to breathe, afraid I'll miss a single nuance, the next jolt I'll get from the next gorgeous soft rasp coming out of his mouth, traveling through time, through vinyl and cables and wires and satellites, into a computer and then into my earbuds, taking a route to listeners' ears never contemplated by anyone in 1971.

The last time I felt like this listening to music was when I was fifteen and discovered Laura Nyro's "Timer," hearing her wail "God is a jigsaw, God is a jigsaw" over chord and rhythm changes so complex and yet so pleasurable that I couldn't believe a girl only a few years older had thought them up. I didn't know what "God is a jigsaw" meant literally. I still don't. Maybe she didn't either. But I knew *emotionally.* She made me feel it, down to the fluid in my cells.

But this is different even from that. This isn't just appreciating a piece of music, or appreciating someone's voice, or being "turned on" by it. "Turned on" sounds so...*lower chakra,* if you will, compared to what I just felt over the last two minutes and thirty-nine seconds of "Gypsy Woman." As I let my lungs fill with oxygen while Casey moves on to introducing a Bobby Goldsboro song, I know something has happened. I don't know what, but I'm no longer that loser who can't hold a job or finish a novel and has an electric eel living in her right palm. I am about to go places I have never been, that I never thought were open to someone like me.

♦ ♦ ♦

According to the DSM-5, in order to be diagnosable with an "autism spectrum disorder," you need to have all three of the traits in category A (the social/emotional reciprocity stuff) and two out of the four traits in category B (the inner sensation, stimming, and thought pattern stuff). The third trait in category B reads as follows:

Highly restricted, fixated interests that are abnormal in intensity or focus (e.g., strong attachment to or preoccupation with unusual objects, excessively circumscribed or perseverative interests).

They say that like it's a bad thing.

"B3" sounds like it should be the name of the world's best vitamin. Because it kind of is.

When I was an undiagnosed youth, my brain would latch on to certain musicians and lead me to spend hours digging through crates of used and remaindered vinyl (because in those days, if a record was "out of print" you didn't get to hear it, period). I took long trips to distant libraries to dig up even more recordings and find out everything I could read about them. Oh, how my heart fluttered when I found the name I was looking for in the periodical directory, submitted the call slip, waited and waited for my bounty to be delivered. How I prayed (in my teen-atheist fashion) that when my number lit up and I went to the desk, they wouldn't tell me my requested materials were unavailable—and that no one would ask me why I needed them so badly.

No other girls (and probably no boys, either) did things like this, as far as I knew. My peers were out developing habits they'd spend the next thirty years of their lives trying to break, habits that would signal to others that they belonged. I couldn't. I had research to do. Now. And like my furtive Sunday morning transcription of the AT40 countdown, I could tell absolutely no one about it. It was as though I was researching how to build pipe bombs, or perhaps knock over a bank.

Now it seems ludicrous to make that comparison. I harmed no one with my music-related B3s. Every time I saw their names in print, I got a shot of dopamine that most people can only access through hardcore recreational substance use, and it cost me nothing but time. The only loss I can see is that, much like Rob in the novel and film *High Fidelity,* instead of fully developing my own musical talents I got stuck on "over-appreciating" the work of others, lamenting that I'd never belong in their world.

Now, in the twenty-first century, I don't have to leave my house, shuffle around libraries waiting for my number to light up, or have anyone run into me and wonder what the hell I'm doing, when I look up stuff about my *new* B3. I can play "Gypsy Woman" half a zillion times through my headphones and disturb no one, arouse no suspicion. Not that my partner would particularly object, if he knew exactly what this was. He knows about the Narrow Fixated Interests stuff. He is fine with it as long as I'm not blathering on about it day and night (and I would never). He would not be threatened by this; he knows I would no more cheat on him (or even fantasize about it) than, well, build a pipe bomb. But my mind is shifting its shape because of this, in ways I don't know how to explain to him yet.

I have zero dollars and maybe twelve cents in my bank account, so I cannot purchase any new music, and my Net connection is too unreliable to participate in anything like Spotify (I was lucky my connection didn't cut out right in the middle of that magic song). I must mooch off YouTube until I get a new source of income. I will make up for it later. Pinky swear.

♦ ♦ ♦

Brian Hyland information, when I first begin searching for it, is not easy to come by. All I have managed to find out is that (as of January 2014) he is still living, he still performs (mostly at oldies shows, often overseas), his wife and adult son are in his band, and per his official Web site, he is a geographic and chronological contemporary of my parents, born about two miles away from where they were—they in Brooklyn, New York, he in Queens. (I too was born in Brooklyn, about two decades later.) He is five months younger than my mother, a little over two and a half years younger than my father. My parents, like most of their contemporaries, knew virtually nothing about autism before I was diagnosed and I had to explain the whole shebang to them (individually; they are long divorced). Does he know any more about it than they did?

He is of Irish descent and they are Jewish, and in those days Irish and Jewish (and Italian) kids often grew up together in those outer-borough neighborhoods—lower-middle-class, brownstone-apartment-filled clusters populated by families who were "white but not white enough" to live among Mayflower descendants. Who knows, maybe one day they passed each other on the street somewhere, maybe at some pizza place near the Brooklyn/Queens border, and never knew.

This is all I have so far. But there are YouTube videos. Many, many videos, spanning from as far back as 1959 (music with still pictures only), to as recently as this year (some fan videos of concert performances). This will keep me off the streets for a while.

My daily Brian Hyland trip through YouTube is one day briefly detoured by an earworm that takes me all the way back to the 1960s, to my parents' record collection. "Look Around," by Sergio Mendes and Brasil '66, was a song that got a lot of play in my house when I was little, and now, prompted by "you might also like" suggestions, I have bumped into it again. I had forgotten how much I loved it. I love the bouncy piano, the polyrhythmic percussion, the handclaps at the end, the sweet sixth and ninth chords, the modulating up and down. Love love love. As much fun as it has been to geek out on Hyland, sometimes I need a break from it. So now I find myself playing this song several times in a row, and when I do, it suggests the opening credits to a film. A teen girl walking down the street, bopping to this. A misfit, indeed a dweeb, for whom this music is a needed anesthetic from the pain of being constantly reminded of her difference.

A few minutes later, she is walking into my head. What kind of girl is she, this she-dweeb who loves bossa nova music? Is she of the era of my childhood, or of the modern world? *Who are you?* I ask her. *How old are you?*

My name is Cyan, she says. *I'm fifteen.*

Cyan, huh? I say. *Interesting name. Very modern. Did you pick it, or did your parents name you that?*

Yeah, right, she says, *like my parents would ever have thought of a name like that for me. They think I'm Cynthia. Cynthia...Ann...Butt.*

Yeah, that's my legal name. My legal name is literally ass.

Oh, honey, I say. *I think I know how this song goes.*

♦ ♦ ♦

I am now ready to leave the novel I was working (and working, and working) on behind, all six hundred pages of it. (And it seriously does not need to be six hundred pages. Michael Chabon I am not.) Now I have someone else who is screaming to be written about: Cyan. Like me, she is autistic, and has a music-related B3, but I have enough agency that my B3 has only positive effects. Cyan's B3 gets her into serious trouble at school and with her parents, who make a living off the idea that her autism is "in remission" with the help of a special diet that they sell. Okay, the diet is beyond special. It's pretty disgusting, really. Stewed calf eyeballs and pickled chicken skin are involved.

The musician who has B3-ed her is named Amy Zander, a girl singer and drummer from the 1960s far more obscure than Brian Hyland or any other musician who has ever B3-ed me. In fact, she has only ever existed in the Cyanosphere; she's a hybrid of maybe thirty different singers and a few things I made up. And maybe even a little bit of me. I don't know if Amy herself will make an appearance in the book, but I need that to be an option if I want it, so she must be a completely invented character. I know my laws regarding the use of real people in fiction.

Some people say you should never meet your idols, because if you do it will ruin their work for you. I might even have this trepidation more than most people do, because my anti-fantasy is that my idols will *hate me.* But with my social history, I can never predict with any degree of accuracy the outcome of a conversation with someone I've yet to speak to, good or bad. So this is a characteristic that Cyan takes from me, to even more of an extreme. She doesn't even know if she wants to know if Amy (who has completely dropped out of public view over the last forty-five years) is alive or not. With no current images of Amy to build on, she finds herself "visited" by a spectral image of Amy as a teenager, who speaks to her and offers her a way out of her oppressive home situation and into a new life as a musical artist who can have real friends (and Spectral Amy helps her find those, too).

As I begin scribbling down details in preparation for writing the first draft during National Novel Writing Month that November, Cyan drops a bomb on my head.

You know, she says, *if you really want to know me and Amy well enough to write about us, you're going to have to start performing music again.*

Uh oh.

♦ ♦ ♦

"So can I book another show?" I ask the owner/barista of the San Fernando Valley coffeehouse where I have just completed my one-hour set. This is in 1993, almost half a lifetime ago, fourteen years before I was diagnosed. I am living in Los Angeles and trying, in my desultory way, to be a singer-songwriter despite feeling like I spend all my days dragging a bag of saturated kitty litter down a hot sidewalk.

The guy, who might actually be younger than I am, looks at me like I just asked him if he wanted my bag of dirty litter. "I don't know," he says. "I mean, you didn't bring anybody in, and there are fewer people here now than when you started. I would have had more customers with no music at all."

So this is what it comes down to. I am begging for a gig where I am paid nothing at all other than tips, in some coffee bar in the far reaches of the freaking Valley, and I am so bad they don't want me there. I am so bad that I clear out the room. I am so bad that I don't have a following, I have a *collective avoidance*. It's like I've been blackballed. Who knows, maybe I have been; I have literally no idea how people actually respond to me unless they spell it out. Like this guy just did.

I know I should practice more. I know I should study my craft more, learn to play better guitar, be a better singer, write more crowd-pleasing songs. But here I am, working a crappy temp job and about to crash into the dreaded age of thirty, a semi-official sell-by date even for independent record companies, and I wonder if it's even worth it to try. I wake up tired every day from having to try (and fail) to play normal all day before, and can barely disguise my exhaustion when I'm out in public. How am I going to work out daily, get in shape, get gorgeous, and seriously pursue my art while dayjobbing it, plus develop a more bubbly and likable personality, and nicer hair, and tougher and yet more feminine skin, and a more serene relationship with God, when I can barely lift a toothbrush? And nobody has an answer for me any more cogent than, "Just quit eating fat and breathe deeper and meditate."

Okay, I'm probably not *that* terrible if I can get gigs in the first place. If I had no talent at all, I wouldn't have been booked. But how good can I get? And would anyone care if I did?

♦ ♦ ♦

"So what do you think I'm best at?" I ask my new husband in the summer of 1998, while we're sitting at a table waiting for our food to arrive at the In-N-Out Burger in Anaheim. Three years earlier, I pawned my beautiful Martin guitar (oh, it smelled so sweet, that mahogany wood!), and would never get it back. I have packed on a considerable amount of poundage onto my already-sturdy frame, thanks to these new medications I'm on that have allowed me to do things like marry the wrong guy and move to Orange County. At this point, at least, that feels like forward motion of a sort. He likes my body the way it is now, and has a chance at a decent career, at least, even if I don't, and that career might even lead us to San Francisco, where I have long dreamed of living. But I haven't written a song or gotten onstage since I lost the guitar. Why bother? Who wants to listen to a fat chick on the wrong side of thirty, who never did anything great in the first place?

Which is why it surprises me when my husband answers, "You might not believe me when I tell you this, but I think you're best at music."

"You're right," I say. "I don't believe you."

♦ ♦ ♦

I actually did write a few songs between that conversation with my now-ex-husband and 2014. There's one I kind of like that I wrote in 2004, right after we split up, about the Venus of Willendorf. I performed it once that year with two other women, at a fat chick talent show in Seattle called Dangerous Curves (I named it!). I tried to record it using Garage Band, but I thought my voice sounded like a singing nose and I more or less buried it. And in 2006, I started a few new ones but never finished them. Now, in 2014, following Cyan's command to start "doing music" again, there's one in particular that's nagging me; how did it go?

God, don't you have something better to do
Than help me with my stupid little problems
Don't you have bodies to rescue...

That wasn't bad at all. Why did I give up on it? Oh yeah. The Not Being Diagnosed Yet So I Wasn't All There Yet thing. I'm sure I wrote more of it than that, but that's all I can remember, and I riffle through my notebooks trying to find it, with no luck. So it will need to be re-created from scratch.

Okay, I need a rhyme or near-rhyme for "problems." And which bodies need to be rescued?

Kittens in trees, old people in the hot sun

Ah, there we go. And then two more lines to complete the verse come spilling out:

Guess I slid on through, never made a sound
So I'm the one who should be helping you, not the other way around

Look out universe, I am pregnant with a song.

♦ ♦ ♦

In March 2014, I get a new part time job, and with it, I finally have money in my bank account to buy *Brian Hyland* (the album with

"Gypsy Woman" on it). It is, according to AllMusic.com, "a real work of art" that should have presaged a great career for Hyland, but turned out to be his last album for the next eight years, and his second to last album ever. I download the album from Google Play and plug my earphones into my Galaxy Tab to have a listen. The first track is a medley from *West Side Story* of "Maria" and "Somewhere," soaked in movie-soundtrack strings and Beach Boys harmonies and funky bass and percussion, an arrangement from a gorgeous hallucination. And then there's *that voice.* I don't know what Stephen Sondheim and Leonard Bernstein thought when they heard this, or even if they actually did. But he has me at that throaty "say it soft and it's almost like praying." Argh. I am dead. Dead.

Over the next few months, the album is a constant companion of mine. I listen to it every day. Usually before bedtime.

I imagine asking him if it hurt to sing with a rasp like that.

Then, one day, I find myself singing in the bathroom, and for a second I soften my tone, without even realizing that I'm doing it, and guess what? For the first time ever, I have a rasp like Brian Hyland's too, when I sing just a little softer. And it doesn't hurt at all. In fact, it feels incredible.

♦ ♦ ♦

"I've never seen anyone listen to music as intently as you do," my boyfriend says, as he watches me go into a trance over a Lucinda Williams album, *Sweet Old World,* playing over his car stereo on a road trip. It's 1996. He has a volunteer job doing sound engineering for a folk music show on the kind of radio station where nobody gets paid except maybe the people who clean the toilets. Every week they have on a guest performer, usually a singer-songwriter with a national following (folk music famous, not household famous). I sit in the control room with him every week and get to meet these people. They are, almost without exception, super nice. They are also so, so, hardworking and talented, so much so that with every note they play, it gets hammered into my head: *You will never be one of them. You are not like them, not in their league. A show like this will never have you on. Never.*

I don't know it now, but later I will find out: I am pre-disqualifying myself from music because music is still an almost exclusively collaborative medium in 1996, and I can't *people* the way these other musicians do. I have tried so hard, so so hard, to learn. So much therapy. So many books. So many fearless and searching personal inventories. Mountains of journals. And socially speaking, I am still stuck in the driveway with no key to put in the ignition, because nobody's even heard of this make and model, let alone made a key for it.

He doesn't know how it is for me, that music really is my hallucinogen, I just get completely sucked into it. Any music, not just my favorites. I feel like the notes and rests are huge trees and wild animals surrounded by blankets of blinding white cloud cover. I don't know what's coming up next, what I'll run into. It scares me and it turns me on. The audience noises on live recordings and at concerts make me feel whatever it is they are feeling when they clap and cheer and sing along. Every feeling in each of those seats, I feel too. Sometimes it's just too much for me, too much pleasure, too much sensation. Too much reminder of what I should be doing with my life and am not doing, because I have already labeled myself not talented enough.

I can't tell him about any of this. He's already nervous enough about me.

♦ ♦ ♦

Brian Hyland, as it happens, is also a songwriter. There are some wonderful self-penned songs on his album, including a foray into power pop that predated Big Star and the Raspberries by a couple of years, called "Drivin' Me Crazy." As with many power pop classics, the lyric is just serviceable, but that hear-it-once-remember-it-always hook, those chord changes...aaahh. He goes from verses in the key of A to a chorus in G sharp minor, and it's like whooshing down the Matterhorn Bobsleds. "Oh, come on, dude," I mutter at my Galaxy Tab at the end of the song. "That's almost *not fair.*"

Almost all songs have hooks, those bits that make you remember them, but very few songs have a hook that's instantly and forever unforgettable. This could have been a hit, too, if his record company (Uni) hadn't fallen asleep at the switch. See, that's what I don't get. Lots of great albums fall into obscurity, but how many of them have a top five hit single on them like this one? I always figured that a record company would have to really *try* to screw up at selling that.

I had also figured that with the amount of time I spent combing through music magazines from the 1970s, especially those that drooled over power pop like *Trouser Press* and *Creem,* I would have known about Hyland before now. I mean, when I was sixteen I owned Peter C. Johnson's album, okay? Now, in 2014, I check to see if Peter

C. Johnson has a Wikipedia page. He does not. Poor Peter.

Brian Hyland does have a Wikipedia page, albeit a sparsely detailed one. While reading it, here's another thing I discover about him: he didn't quit writing and recording songs after "Gypsy Woman" fell off the charts. In fact, there's a song he put out in 2011, at age sixty-five, called "It's Important to Me." It's about the people who support you in being who you are. It's beautiful. And he still sounds like some kind of celestial being.

The more I know, the more I don't know.

♦ ♦ ♦

I have, over the years, retained lots of fun (I insist!) factoids about musicians. One of my favorite stories concerns another Brian—Brian Wilson of the Beach Boys, who composed and produced most of their music. It's about a song called "Surf's Up," the title song of their 1971 album, which has an opaque, shimmery lyric written by Van Dyke Parks five years earlier. Mike Love, the group's nasal-voiced co-lead singer (he didn't have a beautiful voice like Brian and Carl Wilson, but he could lead an audience in a sing-along), hated the acid-trippy stuff Parks and Brian Wilson wrote together. He grilled Parks mercilessly about the lyric to "Surf's Up": "*'Columnated ruins domino'?* What the hell does that even mean?" And Parks, according to legend, looked down and his shoes and muttered, "I have no excuse, sir." (Parks, for what it's worth, was twenty-three years old at the time of this alleged conversation; Love was twenty-five.)

That's kind of how I feel about this whole thing: I have no excuse, sir. If someone asked me, "Why this man? Why this voice? Why now?"

I couldn't begin to defend it. I can tell you what objective qualities I like about his music, but lots of singers and songwriters who don't make me feel that way have those objective attributes. There have been millions of recorded singing voices; why this one? One reason for *The Amy Virus*'s birth was my desire to explore that question: why do we love what we love as much as we do, other than because of peer suggestion? What brain chemistry interaction is going on to make that happen?

The only thing I can figure is that a big part of it has to do with *time*. Had I heard this song through my earbuds even a year before, would my reaction have been the same? Or did I also have to be in a situation where I was forced to throw my hands in the air and surrender to wherever the wind took me, where I realized that there was no more point in trying to twist myself in knots trying to please other people, since that wasn't going to happen?

Did I have to be, at long last, ready to show my true self to the world, and to me?

And did it need to be a song from the distant past, rather than the present, so that it would jog all my music-related memories?

And did it need to be something that would instantly mark itself as being of the time period because of the language and the sound mix?

And did it need to be something that—as I discover while casually polling my friends and my partner—almost no one my age or younger seems to remember? (My partner is three years younger, which makes no difference now, but would have in 1971.) So it would be "mine" for my brain to do with as it pleased, with virtually no input from others?

These are the things that tie fifteen-year-old Cyan to fifty-year-old Andee, and then back to fifteen-year-old Andi, who didn't know she could come up with her own spelling for her name or her own way to do music.

Like Cyan, Andi (nee Andrea) was a space-egg hatchling whose parents had no idea what they had, who was much smarter than her report card would indicate, who (unlike so many other misfit teens) had no tribe even to aspire to belong to as an adult, because she had no idea that such a thing was even possible.

Andi tried to write songs. They were all terrible, as most songwriters' early efforts are. But her beloved Laura Nyro, as far as she knew, was an exception. Her first song, "And When I Die," written at age 17, was a smash hit for Blood, Sweat, and Tears in 1969, hitting number 2 on the Billboard Hot 100. Hey, no pressure there! (Also, it never occurred to Andi that "And When I Die" might have been the first song Laura Nyro went public with, but not necessarily the first one she ever wrote. Andi was not very clued in about the whole "public image" thing.)

Andi would have killed for a "Spectral Amy" to guide her. Or a diagnosis, for that matter. Even if she was the only one who knew about it.

♦ ♦ ♦

Jump ahead three years to right now, July 2017. I am starting to get local bookings as a singer-songwriter. I go to an open mic and the owner remembers me and offers me a show, even though it's been six months since I was there last. I am memorable now, having donned a lilac-colored wig that reflects my exuberant, playful side. People say they love my spirit and energy and style. They love my song about the Venus of Willendorf, which I now play on solo guitar. Sometimes I wear a tunic-sized T-shirt with the image of that prehistoric statue, with the caption PALEOLITHIC PIN-UP GIRL. I finally have the voice to do it and my other songs justice. I have grit and warmth and power and an almost shocking amount of vocal range for a woman in her fifties. I never sang like this when I was younger. I have come to life, at last.

At this open mic, I perform "Can't See a Thing," a song that I wrote about going undiagnosed for over four decades and being told that I couldn't possibly be feeling what I was feeling, experiencing what I was experiencing. It has a thumping, almost gospel-like rhythm that people really get into. I have just started incorporating flapping my hands into my stage routine, after I realized that a big reason I made so many mistakes on guitar was that I got so amped up during a performance (especially if the song was uptempo) and didn't let myself discharge it. I put it into the middle of 'Can't See a Thing," and people start clapping along with my flapping. I am blasting off into space; this is the best drug in the world! And I don't make a single mistake.

Could this really be me? This woman full of sequins and sparkles and vibrancy and church claps, who makes people happy to be alive? Where has she been all this time?

♦ ♦ ♦

By November 2014, I have laid the groundwork to write *The Amy Virus*. Unlike with any other book I've written before (this will be my fifth novel manuscript), I know exactly where I'm going and I have a structure in place that's water-tight. I know my characters upside down and backwards, especially Cyan. Her external circumstances differ from mine at her age, but she, too, has a life filled with people who think you can change a palm tree into an evergreen if you want it badly enough. The first draft blows out of me like a hurricane in fifty-eight days, and it's actually coherent, not just a pile of words. Nothing like this has ever happened before.

In November, I take a weekend to attend a drumming workshop at Ladies' Rock Camp in North Portland. This happens right in the middle of NaNoWriMo, but I justify it by saying it's necessary for character detail. The camp is filled with women, like me, who always had the rhythm bug but didn't have an outlet for it when they were younger. One of the instructors leads us all in a chant—"I am a drummer! I am a drummer!"—while we thrash away on our assigned drum kits. I need to be here, NaNoWriMo or no NaNoWriMo; I must reclaim the percussionist in me before my protagonist can.

♦ ♦ ♦

"It sounds like you're a soprano," says Becca, my new voice teacher in July 2014, after she does a range test on me and I sail through a bunch of low notes and squeak out a bunch of high ones.

I just barely manage to stifle a giggle. *A soprano? Yeah, right. Which one, Tony?* I don't say this out loud, but she can tell I'm thinking something like it, because she tells me it has nothing to do with the pitch of my speaking voice (which is lower even than most men's my age), it's about where I shift into head voice and how far up

I can go. Evidently if you're fifty years old and have no prior operatic training and you can hit a soprano high C (C6, two octaves higher than C4, which is middle C), even if you have to squeak it out like a baby mouse, you're a soprano. Becca tells me that if I can hit those notes at all, I can learn to hit them squarely.

Over the next few lessons I exceed even that, going as high as F6. That gives me a range of four octaves if you count the three extra low notes I can hit when I first wake up. When I was younger, I didn't even have three octaves, let alone four. You'd expect a woman my age to get deeper and more gravelly on the bottom, as I have, but not to increase her range like that on top. The glorious freak of nature strikes again.

Becca thinks I could probably reach even higher with more training, maybe up to A6, which is getting almost into Mariah Carey territory. But I'd have to sacrifice the bottom of my range to do it, and I'm rather attached to that. I am a blues singer, not an opera diva, at heart, and she is an opera singer. After three months of studying with her, my partner gets a job twenty miles away and we need to move, making it impractical for me to continue our lessons.

It's just as well. While I'm grateful to her for opening up my range, I conclude my studies with her before she can get rid of all the low husky stuff that blues singers live for and opera singers want to avoid like *Staphylococcus aureus*. Before I go, I ask Becca if I could lose my voice if I sing that way, and she admits that I probably won't, as long as I go easy over the raspy parts and don't strain or grind on them—although if I keep trying to reach below low C (C3) too often, I could potentially lose some of my range on top.

But damn it, it's so much *fun* to sing that low. I love the vibrations, they make my whole body happy. I don't think my whole body has ever been happy before, not like this. I even wake up singing every day, though I'm careful to throw a blanket over my head while I do so. My partner, after all, works at home—and while he doesn't mind my singing the low stuff, he has requested that I confine the upper reaches of my voice to the shower, where the sound can be better absorbed by the running water. I understand. If you hit a sky-high note and you're even a little bit off, that can really scald people's ears. And you have to do it wrong a whole bunch of times before you do it right. (Later I find out that if you lip-trill high notes—in other words, hum while blowing the air out with your lips loosely closed—instead of singing them out loud, you can still get practice in without making anyone want to kill you.)

I sing and sing and sing. Like I've been in prison for half a century and the punishment for singing in my cell would have been the electric chair, and now I'm finally sprung. Now I stop when my throat tells me to, and not a second before.

My body buzzes all day long after that.

♦ ♦ ♦

It's the summer of 1972. My parents are heavily involved in George McGovern's ill-fated campaign for president. We find out that Eleanor McGovern, George's wife, is having a meet-and-greet at the local Democratic Party campaign headquarters in central New Jersey. They put a frilly dress on my chubby eight-and-a-half-year-old body and I am stoked. I am meeting the future First Lady! At least I hope so. I know Richard Nixon is very bad, though I don't know if I understand all this Watergate stuff yet. My brother and I have been told that we cannot go to McDonald's any more because their owner gave money to Nixon's campaign. This is not a big deal. I prefer Burger King anyway. They give me a paper crown when I go there, and in these days before drive-throughs, everyone eating there gets to see me wearing it.

Eleanor McGovern is an amazingly nice lady, she smiles and stops and chats with everyone who has shown up on this Saturday morning to meet her. I don't even mind missing the cartoons for this. When she gets to me I greet her and tell her how much I hope her husband wins, just like everyone else there. Or at least, I think that's what I did, until my dad airs me out in the car on the way home.

"You monopolized her!" he shouts at me. "You talked her ear off about your rock collection! She doesn't care about that!"

With no video or audio evidence to document what actually happened, since we didn't have that then, I must take his word for it that I was unbearably tedious and an embarrassment to our entire family and that I offended the future First Lady with my monologue about minerals. My mother does not say anything, at least not in front of me. So I assume she agrees with him. My parents, later that same year, would buy me that Marlo Thomas record album where she tells kids it's okay to be themselves (a radical notion in 1972), but they are still steeped in "children should be seen and not heard." My father hates kid noise. He, in fact, does not really like children at all unless they act like small adults, although he will deny it until he runs out of air. He did let slip that he wanted kids only because we kept him out of Vietnam.

So I resolve not to be seen *or* heard, ever again, unless I am called upon to show off my intelligence for their houseguests. And even then I'd better not overdo it. I am a crashing bore, even my parents think so.

♦ ♦ ♦

Now, in 2017, there is one, and only one, person in my life who has listened to, watched, and read everything I've offered for sharing in the last few years—all the videos, all the song recordings, even the final draft of my novel (which I finally finished a few months ago)—and heaped tons of praise on all of it. Many people in my life have done that with some of my work, but only one has done it with every scrap of it.

My father.

Yes, my dad is now my biggest fan. Maybe it's because he alone has had the time and energy to go through the copious amounts of stuff I have produced over the last three years, but he has done it and backed me up all the way. I think he knows how badly he screwed up and wants to make up for it. I'll take it.

As an adult, I have discovered that things were not the way they appeared during my childhood. My mother has told me that she and my dad, in the last few years of their marriage, had intense arguments about how badly he treated me, arguments I would have given my adult bottom teeth to have been privy to. But "don't fight in front of the kids" was drilled into my mom as hard as "children should be seen and not heard." She knows now that this was a horrible mistake. If I had only known that she was sticking up for me, would I have hated myself so much, thought I was so bad and wrong that they should have sent me back? Would I have swallowed my voice, decided that no one wanted to hear from me?

There's no way to know. I want to think that if my parents had known about autism then, if *anyone* had known then that autism existed in kids who could talk and didn't have an intellectual disability, I wouldn't have been punished so relentlessly for my neuroatypicality. But who knows what they'd have done, or what anyone else would have done, once they found out. Maybe I'd have been punished in an entirely different way, by someone, somewhere. I might not have been *blamed* for having been born with different wiring, but would I have been told that I just needed to work that much harder to make people forget I was different? Would I have been told that most of the world wished I and all the other disabled kids weren't here, whether it was "our fault" or not?

I do think my dad would have been less angry with me. He thinks so, too. He's since told me things about his own father that, when coupled with my own memories of my grandfather, point strongly to my grandfather having been autistic. He left behind a bunch of passionate letters he had written to my grandmother, with whom he appeared to have had a frosty relationship. The emotions that he poured out belied my father's (and grandmother's) assumption that my grandfather was completely detached from what was going on around him. For as long as my grandfather was alive, my dad raged at him for not being more like his friends' dads, or the dads he saw on TV; now that he knows why, he mourns not having appreciated what he had. My grandfather didn't have a mean bone in his entire body. How many people can claim that?

My daughter is a lavender-haired goddess, my dad writes in response to my emailing him my latest publicity shots. Maybe this is also his way of telling my grandfather, somewhere out there in eternity, "Dad, I finally get it."

♦ ♦ ♦

At various points in my life, I have wondered how my life would have gone had my parents been singers, songwriters, or musicians themselves. They were salespeople with no musical inclinations at all. My paternal grandfather used to give piano lessons, or so my father told me, but he was so rusty by the time I was old enough to learn that he couldn't teach me. I think a lot about Rufus and Martha Wainwright, whose parents were the great singer-songwriters Loudon Wainwright III and Kate McGarrigle. Would *not* being a singer-songwriter (even if only as a hobby) ever have occurred to either of them? They've even recorded songs about their dad which pull no punches, and he didn't object a bit, at least not in public.

So maybe there's a little of the "alternate reality where my dad was a successful musician" involved in this Brian Hyland thing—but again, why him and not one of dozens of others around the same age? Hell, I could have picked Loudon Wainwright III instead, why didn't I? Why does Cyan have to reach back in time to before even her parents were born to find the "voice" that tells her it's not just okay to be who she is, but imperative?

There's a video on YouTube of Brian Hyland lip-syncing "Gypsy Woman" that was probably culled from an *American Bandstand*-like TV show from 1970. He's playing an electric guitar (likely a Fender Telecaster) and wearing a vest and ruffled shirt combination that looks like the wardrobe people swiped it from the Partridge Family. There are lava-lamp-style lighting effects, and a go-go dancer wriggles casually in the background. He might be singing live to the studio audience, but the soundtrack is identical to the original recording. He is completely lost in the song; if the audience and the camera exist to him, he doesn't show it.

After I watch it several times, I realize what fascinates me about it: *he sings it like an introvert.* Lots of singers and performers are introverts when the microphones and cameras are off, but put on the extroverted mask when they perform, because that is what we all get told to do. Meet the audience's gaze, show them you care about them. He doesn't do that, at least not here. There is only him and the Gypsy Woman, or what he remembers of her. When he gets to the "she'll never know that I love her, I *looooove* her" at the end, it's like a dam breaking.

Have these lyrics dated badly? Perhaps so. (Later in 1971, the First World Romani Congress voted to use the term *Roma* instead of *Gypsy.*) Curtis Mayfield allegedly wrote those words at the age of thirteen, and coming from him the song was a then-daring fantasy about forbidden interracial love. Hyland sings it like he *identifies* with the Gypsy Woman, both of them being Caucasian yet not fully accepted by white Anglo-Saxon Protestants. Coming from him, it's a song about passing for WASP—namely, that he can pass and she cannot. This is not Partridge Family stuff, even if it has some of the same musical (and sartorial) trappings. Maybe some people wrote him off because of those trappings, and maybe some people wrote him off because he basically *was* Keith Partridge a decade earlier.

This is the part of him that winds up in Amy Zander, the part where people get a brief glimpse of a performer during a flash of fame (or notoriety) and think they have seen all there is to see. I certainly thought I had seen all there was to see of Brian Hyland. But if I missed all this, what else have I missed? Who else might I have written off who didn't deserve to be?

And for that matter, who wrote *me* off when I shouldn't have been? If Brian Hyland can sing (or lip-sync) like an introvert, so can I. Oddly enough, I have actually been complimented on my ability to involve the audience when I perform, but it wouldn't have happened without giving myself permission to be as introverted (or autistic) on stage as I needed to be at any given moment. I'll close my eyes or look at the ceiling or flap if I damn well please, thank you. I am about to generate handclaps and blast off for the heavens, cut me a break. And usually, they do.

It took my partner a while to be convinced that this wasn't just some midlife crisis for me, that I was serious about my art in a way I have never gotten to be before. But now he gets it. He makes it possible for me to do this, he has seen me through a lot of tortured-artist garbage that I had to go through in order to be able to see this through. When I come home from open mics now, more often than not I'll talk about what went great rather than what disasters befell me, and he is happy to see me so radiant after I've played. But that took me a while.

I am convinced that I was led to perform and record music again because there were certain things about me that needed to be confronted and healed. I needed to be able to forgive myself for making mistakes, and not announce my mistakes to the audience (who probably wouldn't notice them otherwise). I needed to support myself as well as I supported others.

I needed to be able to deal with others ignoring my work, or not taking me seriously. I needed to experience myself as someone who could raise the temperature in the room, make people vibrate the way I do. I needed to jettison the idea that I was ugly and boring and depressing. I needed to experience myself as someone with the right to be anywhere she wanted to be, and do anything she wanted and needed to do, even in an old, fat, disabled body (maybe *especially* in an old, fat, disabled body).

I needed to understand that I was a force of nature and a force of good, even if I wasn't drawing tons of followers yet, or even if I never did. I needed to know I could light up a stage. I needed to dispense with the need to feel like I screwed up, even when I didn't, because if I was actually competent at something I loved, bad things would happen and people would hate me. I needed to know that I could have my own sound, my own style, that included not just guitar, but bass ukulele and lots of percussion loops, all of which I play on stage.

Like I say in "Can't See a Thing":

Finally someone believed me, said what they said wasn't true
But you can't do it like them, you've gotta do it like you
And that's when I grew

And also, columnated ruins domino.

To be autistic in school—in mainstream non-special-ed elementary and high school classes, and in higher education—is to be told every day in a thousand subtle ways that You're Not Supposed to Be Here. *In "Who Is Allowed?" Autistic mathematician, neuroscientist, polymath, poet, and longtime academic Alyssa Hillary offers a window into the experience of fighting for inclusion in a system that treats one's presence as an incursion.*

Who Is Allowed?

Alyssa Hillary

I Cannot Wait

I cannot wait, I cannot wait, I cannot wait until:

- I get my PhD
- I get a job
- I get tenure

Before I type my mind.

Each day hidden, nodding my head, going along to get along would be the little death by a thousand submissions to the machine,
Turning frustration with the gears into yet more cogs in my own mind.
We learn, each day, become habituated to the world we submit to,
Even as we insist we're only there to invade.
I said, before I began, before I even chose where I might begin,

I would not last in biomedical engineering,
So I thank whatever avengers still back me for:

- Reminding me psychology is *rhetoric*
  (And so neuroscience remains)
- Outlining, defining, giving words for the ways we organize our worlds
  (Fact, theory, paradigm, and praxis)
- Providing and demanding the poetry in *typed* words never spoken
  (Our voices are loud)
- Showing me who I, the visible Friend, have been
  (I must stay so.)
- *Not* waiting for tenure before writing a flaming crater in their university
  (Shall I throw myself into a wall and shake the stage?)
- Letting the bridges they burn light the way
  (Katniss says if we burn, you burn with us)

You're why my foot in neuroscience,
Mentality still in rhetoric of representation,
Heart forever mathematical,
Keep me unbroken enough to
Choose what I can accept and what I can't,
Question "People do X" instead of "I'm a people,"
Get the hell out of what I can neither accept nor fix.
Thank you for the cover fire,
because I know I cannot wait.

You're Not Supposed to Be Here

In fifth grade, I am the new kid in school,
Thrown into a "lunch group" social skills class.
Two of them, really: each meets once a week,
And no one else was ever in more than one.
I hear: You're not supposed to be here.
(Why would I *want* to be?)

In sixth grade, a special education aide bans me from his room,
Ending an iteration of my participation in "social skills" groups,
Not long after he taught me defiance was an option.
I hear (he means): You're not supposed to be here.
(Perhaps "here" shouldn't be.)

When I apply to my high school study abroad program in China, I am interviewed.
We all are: one teacher and one student in a brief conversation — except for me.
All three teachers grill me on my shellfish allergy for longer than anyone else chats,
After the other students went home.
I hear: You're not supposed to be here.
(I don't go to China with them, but I will later.)

The first (and only time) I'm kicked out of a class, I'm not exactly in

trouble.
The teacher would never have removed me on her own, begs me not to be angry,
But the order came from above:
I am *not* to be doing the work for two levels of Chinese at once,
Never mind that I have done so all year ... until I'm no longer going to China through the school.
I hear: You're not supposed to be here.
(This ban lasted all of a day.)

The second time I am cut from select choir, the teacher says:
"You sing tenor well enough, but you can't sing alto at all."
Which I knew, of course — that's why I auditioned as a tenor.
I hear: You're not supposed to be here.

The first concert I sing as a tenor,
I am still listed as an alto.
The second year I sing tenor, the programs are changed:
Student names are no longer listed by part, hiding my change.
Interesting timing, that.
I hear: You're not supposed to be here.

The third time I am cut from treble choir,
I ask about tenor bass choir instead, and the teacher says:
"You've missed a month of learning the music, maybe after the winter concert."
I hear: You're not supposed to be here.

Sick of hearing where I should and should not be,
I borrow a friend's copy of the music to catch up.

After three years in the fancy advanced Chinese program for the supposedly best students,
I am ready for my year in China — *if* I can survive orientation.
Let's start with the same advice I heard all my years failing to learn "social skills,"
Continue with puzzle pieces, however far removed from anti-autistic context.
Can we have a required bi-weekly survey in a format I already see won't work with my brain?
I hear: You're not supposed to be here.
I sob outside, terrified of my program and what they think is good advice.

On the plane to China, I write for *Criptiques:* "The Erasure of Queer Autistic People."
Two weeks in, I predictably fail: I cannot complete the language utilization report,
Just as I had warned at orientation.
My residence director tries to help. We learn: I'm too Autistic for this shit.
I hear: You're not supposed to be here.

I read the immersion class list, deciding what to take.
There is no mathematics, no engineering. *My* majors are absent.

My classmates in anthropology? Political science?
Options are given to them, while I must ask *again* for my field.
I hear: You're not supposed to be here.

The academic director notices me struggling with nightly homework,
Something I was *never* able to keep up with.
She wants me to drop an immersion class: No graph theory, or no materials science.
I know that's not what will "fix" the problem (nothing will, but this will make it worse.)
She will not believe me.
I hear: You're not supposed to be here.

The time comes that I can not speak in class.
I type instead, ask a classmate to read for me.
The teachers do not understand, and I learn:
The university, upon learning I'm Autistic, *actually said students like that shouldn't be in college.*
They didn't want me to come. They want an excuse to send me home.
I hear (they absolutely mean): You're not supposed to be here.

We talk about Cross Cultural Communication/跨文化交际
The issues we discuss, between Chinese people and Americans, are familiar:
I've heard these conversations before, when they tried to teach me

"social skills."
That is, when they tried to teach me *neurotypical* social skills.
The parallels are dismissed by those who know not the roles they play.
I hear: You're not supposed to be here.

Back in the US, no one knows who a teaching assistant should see for accommodations.
Is it Human Resources, or Disability Services for Students?
It's not in the contract, or the collective bargaining agreement, or anywhere.
I go to Disability Services and hope for the best.
My accommodation doesn't *exist*, must be created (somewhat inaccurately) from scratch.
I hear: You're not supposed to be here.

Cross Cultural Communication/跨文化交际

Too blunt. 太直接了。
It'd be insulting. 他会收到侮辱。
They'd take it personally. 就是个人侮辱！
You can't just say that. 你不可以这样说
（语法没问题，而不够委婉。）
You have to hint. 暗示一下
（暗示不应该那么明显！）
Be subtle. 你可能需要说的委婉一些。

It was the same meaning—
Almost the same words.
It was the same bluntness—
Even the same confusion.

Then
I claim a cultural difference.
Autistic and Neuronormative.
Denied.
Autism doesn't get a culture.

But.
They claim a cultural difference.
American and Chinese
Known issue.
The reason for today's lesson.

Autistic people are too blunt.
It's because we're disabled.
We need to be "fixed."

Americans are blunt.
Chinese people are subtle.
It's a cultural difference.

美国人直接？(Americans are blunt?)
是可笑的！(That's laughable!)
自闭症者直接。(Autistics are blunt.)
美国人委婉。(Americans are subtle.)
中国人更委婉。(Chinese people are even subtler.)

I have a communication disability.
This is my problem.

There is a cultural difference.
We can work together.

My teacher says it's different, never having listened.
She's never watched the Autistic version of this conversation.
Not that she'll admit.

(She's been the neuronormative side.)
(She thought she was only the Chinese side.)
(I knew she was both.)

Read Aloud

I have been taking the words my hands have given me and asking my mouth to repeat them.
So I must make peace with the way my tongue stumbles, skips words, skips lines, pauses in all the wrong places and so few of the 'right' ones, as if the breath control I learned from 10 years in choir never existed and I can't even blame it on my second language because *that line was in English*.

What if I didn't blame it on anything?
What if I embraced the poetry of my natural, stumbling language where new rhythms are revealed by the words and phrases my eyes skipped over while I was focused on my tongue,
because the breath control I learned in choir could never stand up to the demands of multi-tasking,
because my intended voice was always my fingers, not my mouth.
What if?
What if?
I don't know.

But when you tell me poetry is meant to be read aloud I have to ask:

Read aloud by *whom*?
Do you mean the way my words rearrange themselves when I ask my tongue to follow my hands, when you say poetry is meant to be heard?
Or do you mean the standard model where the reader pauses at the punctuation, not wherever they lost track of the words they couldn't memorize despite having written them, where the reader speaks the words that were written, not the ones their eyes filled in or ears demanded be added?
My shame at reading aloud didn't start with me.

It's a Threat

When you tell me I am a genius, it is not a compliment.
It is a reminder, and a threat of return to the days
When my test scores were used to forge promises my abilities could never make good on,
Death of a thousand paper cuts from a thousand bounced checks,
But which I was ordered to pay before I could begin to touch
Any cost I would have chosen to incur.
Were the bounced checks supposed to be spurs?
They were chains, and poison.

Am I a genius?
Then why can't I do this?
It's simple, right?

Every forged check was supposed to be easy.
Every cost I would choose complex,

Demanding resources I couldn't possibly command without the "simple" ones.
I couldn't exist.
So where was I?

We read *Harrison Bergeron.*
I am supposed to identify with Harrison.
It is tempting.
He is smart.
I am supposed to be smart. (But it is not my weapon.)
He is good-looking.
I am told I look good. (Dysphoria can't let me believe it.)
He is graceful.
No one pretends I'm anything but clumsy.
He was hated, erased, for who he was.
I have been bullied, hated for who I am.
But I am not Harrison.

We watch GATTACA.
I am supposed to identify with Vincent ... I think.
He is determined.
I am determined. (Stubborn is the word people use.)
He has bad assumptions made about his abilities.
I have bad assumptions made about my abilities. (Different bad assumptions, to be fair.)
He is, by the standards of our world, abled.
I am Autistic and proud.
He achieves his goals, deceiving along the way.
I too have lied to dodge assumptions of (in)ability.

But I am not Vincent.

I watch FIXED.
I am not told who I am supposed to be.
People like me, disabled people, are shown, explicitly.
We are on the front lines of the question:
How do we handle human enhancement?
Do we think, hopefully, of a world where we all have the same abilities?
(Remember Harrison Bergeron?)
Do we think, hopefully, of a world where we can choose our children's traits?
(Remember GATTACA?)
Do we think, hopefully, of a world that admits *I exist*?
(Please.)
I am no one here, but these are my people, and that matters.

Could I be in GATTACA?
Tell me I'm a genius, that I belong among their "valid."
We both know otherwise.
Never mind Autistic, I'm fucking *nearsighted*.
That alone is a signal.
Tell me I'd be among their "invalid."
People we'd call abled are their face.
I might pass, but am I really there?

Could I be in *Harrison Bergeron*?
Of all the bounced checks I never wrote, only the claim that I am like *him* is tempting.
False, and I know it, but tempting.

They hate him for being too *good*, too *strong*, too *smart.*
Wouldn't it be convenient to believe that's why they hate me?
And I can accept that they hate me, that when they say impairment and deficit and (less than) eloquent they mean they hate me.
Eloquent so they don't have to listen, or less than so they can pretend not to understand,
Regardless they express their preference for my non-existence.

The Handicapper General shot Harrison Bergeron.
She's not the one who would shoot me.
You see:
People still get to speak in that world.
Where are the ones who can't?
Where are the ones who type when mouth-sounds fail?
If everyone is finally equal,
And everyone still gets to talk, consistently if sometimes stuttered ...
Where am I?

I am no Harrison.
We don't *really* hate Harrison here.
Just like we don't *really* hate me for what I can do.
That's another tempting lie,
Do they hate for me for what I'm good at (because secretly I'm better.)
Or do they hate me for the holes I poke in their theories of hierarchical ability
Simply by existing and bouncing "easy" checks while making good on complexity?
When they tell me I'm a genius, it was never a compliment.
It's always been a threat.

Steve Silberman is the author of NeuroTribes, *the bestselling history of evolving societal perspectives on autism. He's one of those warm and caring writers whose work is based in a heartfelt interest in the experience of others. When we started discussing his contribution to this volume, I encouraged him to focus on his* own *experience this time. The result is this deeply touching memoir, "Unworldly Love." Here we get find yet another angle on the theme of incursions: if you've been taught to see some aspect of your own self as an incursion, a pathology, then learning to accept yourself as whole and beautiful involves recognizing that narrow culturally-imposed norms and culturally-imposed shame are the real incursions. As you liberate yourself from those incursions, you become able to make counter-incursions against the rigid norms of the dominant culture—to loosen the grip those norms hold on others, and to spread the liberation and the love.*

Unworldly Love

Steve Silberman

I self-diagnosed even before I was a teenager. I didn't have all of the traits described in the *Diagnostic and Statistical Manual of Mental Disorders*, but I had always felt essentially different from my peers somehow, and displayed enough of the classic signs that the local bullies had already cast me out and targeted me for abuse. Every morning when I walked to school, two guys would lay in wait for me on a path through the woods; even if I took an alternate route to avoid them, they somehow always found me, which was terrifying. They would kick me, spit on me, and call me the usual names. I wondered how they knew—was I that obvious? But even when I tried to fight back, something in me pulled back before really trying to land a punch. I just couldn't do it. At night, I would lay in bed, hoping and praying (though I didn't believe in God) that science would some day invent a cure. Surely they must be working on it, I thought.

Occasionally, I would see someone like me on TV. One of the talk shows, perhaps, where people like me appeared in a darkened studio so their parents wouldn't be ashamed. Sometimes they even wore masks. If a character like me appeared in a feature film, which was rare, they often committed suicide by the end. That was our story; other characters got to fall in love and have adventures, the usual ups and downs of life. For the likes of us, it was strictly down—the arc of shame, secrecy, inevitable exposure, repentance, and a kind of salvation through self-obliteration. The story couldn't end with us still around. We existed purely to make the other characters, the *real* characters, feel thankful that they were not us.

When I finally admitted to my parents that I was having "problems" with my schoolmates, they sent me to a therapist for the cure. But it didn't take. She was a nice lady, but we both came to the conclusion that there was really nothing she could do for me. My parents were disappointed, of course, and my father refused to even talk about it for years.

Miraculously, by the time I got to college, I was no longer mentally ill. Oh, I still had all the symptoms—in fact, they were worse than ever, because I had met a tall, shy kid like me, with long hair and huge blue eyes, in one of my English courses. He didn't say much in class, but when he did, it was invariably interesting, not just vacuous kissing-up to the teacher. I started thinking about him all the time, wondering what he would say about a poem or a piece of music I'd discovered. It was as if all of my experience had suddenly acquired a hashtag: #whatwouldEdthink?

Then one night while we were walking back from his dorm, Ed asked me a question: "So, what have you been doing, like, since you were born?" It was the most interesting question I'd ever been asked, like a sword that cut through all the bullshit that normal people call life. He told me he thought about me all the time too.

Obviously, we both still had the condition I'd diagnosed myself with years earlier. But it no longer appeared in the *DSM*, because people like us had "zapped" the American Psychiatric Association, occupying their offices and shouting slogans until they were dragged away by police. Some APA members had also worked behind the scenes to remove the diagnosis from the manual, because they knew that if their patients were sick with this condition, then they were sick too. Obviously, this condition was much more common than psychiatrists had been claiming for decades—and it didn't have anything to do with "distant fathers" and "devouring mothers," like they'd been saying. Some people are just born that way. I was born gay, like other people were born straight.

But was it that simple?

♦ ♦ ♦

A few months later, I decided that I needed to get away from college for a week. I even needed to get away from Ed—our twosome had become a threesome with the addition of our dear friend Jennie, and the combination of academic pressure and romantic confusion was overwhelming. I decided to take a Greyhound bus to New York City. At the last minute, Ed asked if he could come along. I immediately said yes.

We saw a listing in the *Village Voice* for a poetry reading by Allen Ginsberg at Queens College. Allen had been a personal hero of mine since reading "A Supermarket in California" in a high-school English class. I even thought of Ed as my personal version of Peter Orlovsky, Allen's lifelong companion. We sat in the front row.

Allen began the reading by singing a poem of William Blake's that he had set to music. The poet was accompanied by a handsome, lanky, long-haired kid just a little older than me who played guitar and sang in an angelic tenor. As they harmonized together, they looked into each other's eyes with expressions of what was unmistakably love. Allen was not exactly my "type"—he looked more like my uncle at the deli—but I had never seen a middle-aged man so openly joyous, so *fully in his body*, so grounded in the present moment.

I had the uncanny feeling that I was supposed to help Allen in this life somehow. It wasn't a thought exactly, but more like a recognition. ("O Tenderness, to recognize you in the middle of Time," Allen had written of his great love Neal Cassady.) I vowed that wherever this goofy, ecstatic, impossibly wonderful man was going to be the following summer, I would be there too, doing whatever I could. If he needed someone to go to the bodega to buy cat food, I would be that guy. I would help him, and maybe he would love me too, as I already loved him.

Back at Oberlin, I discovered that Allen taught in a summer writing program at Naropa Institute, a Buddhist college in Boulder, Colorado. I sent away for a catalog of course listings, and when it arrived, it seemed like an artifact from a more advanced civilization. There was a course in screenwriting from William Burroughs, a course on Dogen by a Zen master named Taizan Maezumi-roshi, courses in poetry with Anne Waldman and Diane DiPrima, and a "Socratic rap" with poet Gregory Corso (whatever that meant). Dance, music, transpersonal psychology, martial arts, and not "literature" but "poetics"—the practice of the living art, rather than the analysis of mummified relics. Allen himself was teaching a course on the history of the Beat Generation, as well as offering "apprenticeships" to a small number of students who were asked to write a personal letter explaining why they wanted to study with him. I immediately wrote one and mailed it off.

I never heard back. But I wasn't going to let that stop me. As summer approached, I sold almost everything I had, including a Nikon camera given to me by my grandfather, and boarded a train for Denver. Arriving at Naropa registration, I found Allen standing in the middle of a crowd of young people waiting for a word with him. The formerly lovelorn author of "A Supermarket in California" was evidently the poetic equivalent of a rock star at age 51, complete with mobs of adoring fans. I waited patiently until everyone else had left and introduced myself. "Oh, you wrote me that very nice letter," Allen replied. *Score!*

By the time I got back to my room, there was a note on the door that "Mr. Ginsberg" was offering me an apprenticeship. Thus my real education began.

♦ ♦ ♦

A crucial part of that education was discovering that Allen was not the naïve sweetheart he was in his poems, hopelessly yearning for the love of manly men like Cassady and Jack Kerouac, who most of the world believed were strictly heterosexual. In fact, Allen had made love with both of them, and once accompanied Jack to a gay bathhouse, where the author of "On The Road" frolicked with a group of French sailors.

Naropa was a heady and hedonistic place back then. In addition to the courses, the perpetually amazing conversations with teachers and other students, and the meditation sessions—visualize hundreds of Buddhists walking through the streets of Boulder with their bright red *gomden* cushions to the meditation hall—orgiastic lovemaking was definitely on the curriculum, in every conjunction you could imagine.

I quickly learned that Allen had crushes on many of his male apprentices, most of whom had crushes on him in return, no matter what their primary sexual orientation was. I had a crush on him myself, craving his attention, approval, and mentorial blessing, and wanting to ease the burden of loneliness and grief he had chronicled in his poems for decades. I wasn't attracted to him in the same way I was attracted to Ed, but I found him beautiful and oddly majestic nonetheless. I would have been more than willing to lay beside him in bed for hours, tenderly stroking his white hair and beard, and hearing his resonant, rabbinical voice as I rested my head on his chest. The "best teaching," he once said in an interview (and here I really want to say *boasted*, because that's really what it was, like a rapper boasting about his mad skillz) was "done in bed."

In the years to come, I would see many a handsome young man shyly coming down the staircase from Allen's loft-bedroom, hastily wrapped in a towel, as Peter drowsed on the couch. They had an arrangement, which worked out for Peter too, because he primarily liked women and had girlfriends on the side.

But it never happened for me, mainly because Allen's one and only attempt to seduce me was so crude. At one of the parties that summer, after everyone had smoked Gregory Corso's legendarily potent joints, Allen kissed me on the mouth and said, "You know, we should really get together sometime and fuck or something." I barely had time to blurt out "sure," my face reddening, before he added, "But there's so little time." I felt awful rather than blessed, as if he had made his proposition strictly because I approximately fit his preferred demographic, not because he loved me in particular. I still loved him, but I made a silent vow never to treat anyone that way.

Still, I couldn't quibble with Allen's taste in men. The other apprentices became my close friends. Yes, many of them were handsome, but more than that, they were mensches: real human beings, soulful and smart, whose literary interests and devotion to Allen overlapped with mine. There was also a kind of pecking order that was never spelled out, but that everyone understood. Allen's favorite apprentice at the time was a guy I'll call Adam. He was mellow, funny, athletic, heterosexual, and so handsome that he looked like a young Kennedy. He also had a freezer full of fresh psilocybin mushrooms. Allen had written poems with Adam in mind, which he read often in public that summer. I was in awe of him.

We became buddies in the penumbra of Allen's spot-lit fame, doing the considerable backstage work that helped Allen be Allen in the public eye, and helping each other cope with the weird pressures of daily proximity to one of our heroes.

Then one night after an evening of listening to music together, Adam asked me to stay over. I figured I would sleep on the floor, but he asked me to join him in bed. I couldn't believe my luck. We took our clothes off and laid down beside one another. We snuggled, and I moved my fingers down his firm belly to grasp and stroke his glorious penis.

But before I could take hold of it, Adam gently moved my hand back up and rested it on his chest. "Not like that," he said. "I just want to be close to you." Instead of feeling abashed, I felt liberated. It had never occurred to me that two men could be in bed together if sex wasn't on the agenda, and in truth, sex was still an awkward, contrived-feeling thing for me as a shy 19-year-old. I often felt slightly disassociated during it, as if everyone else had learned to have amazing sex somehow, but not me. Instead, Adam and I talked and snuggled for hours, until the dawn light reflecting off the front range of the Rocky Mountains filtered through his window. I had rarely felt so truly loved and appreciated, particularly by the guys I met in gay bars who wanted to have sex immediately.

By the time the summer was over, I had another surprise. There was a guy I'll call Cliff, not in Allen's orbit, who I worshipped from afar, because he was so obviously out of my league. He was several years older, tall, lanky, blond, graceful in his movements, and confidently masculine, with an appealing Southern drawl. He was at Naropa to study martial arts, and would become a life-long karate instructor. He eventually noticed my shy looks and began joining me for meals at my table in the dining hall for spirited conversations, often about various women he desired. Again, I couldn't believe my luck, because I felt like a total nerd. On our last night in Boulder, he took me out for a beer—my first taste of Guinness, which was so dark and bitter that it felt like an initiation. I hesitantly came out to him as gay, not wanting to scare him off. But his response was sly and unexpected: "I grew up on a farm," he told me. "I know what goes on."

On our way back to the dorm, he led me into a football field, which was thankfully deserted. The wide Colorado sky, dusted with millions of stars, was our infinite canopy. He lay me down on the grass and we made love for hours, kissing passionately. Afterwards, he said with a wink, "I think there's a lot more of this fooling around going on than anyone lets on." Then he said goodbye. The next morning, I got a ride out of town with "Refuge of the Roads"—a track of Joni Mitchell's album, *Hejira,* inspired by a visit to Naropa the previous summer—playing on the radio. I wept, seeing the sunrise in the rear view mirror. I had become a man.

♦ ♦ ♦

I was also a man with a secret: That there was a lot more of this fooling around going on than anyone let on—which is similar to the vision of fluid sexuality that Allen advertised in his poems, though in his case, his interactions were complicated by fame. Were the beautiful young men he shared his bed with simply hoping he'd write them into a poem, and thus into history, or did they really love him? It was probably a little of both in most cases. That was something I didn't have to worry about.

In the coming years, I would share many beds with many friends who identified as primarily heterosexual. Sometimes we had sex, and sometimes we would just cuddle for hours, as I had with Adam. Sometimes I would give them blow jobs, and sometimes, unexpectedly, they would want me to fuck them, or they would blow me. There seemed to be no correlation whatsoever between how masculine they presented, as they say these days, and what a guy wanted to do in bed. Some of the most butch guys wanted to get fucked, and some of the most feminine guys wanted a blow job.

But the reason the sex happened at all was love, and it was always mutual. There was Robin, a young actor with a shelf of wrestling trophies, who told me to look into his eyes as I reached orgasm so he could "see my ecstasy." There was Matt, a gentle, blue-eyed man I met at a health food store who told me, "I just want to take off my clothes and be with you." There was Nathan, who I never had sex with, but who loved to spoon, my arms wrapped around him from behind. And there was Aaron, the big, bearded, burly old-time musician who lived down the hall at Oberlin, who taught me that my range of desirable physical types was way too narrow.

Allen was right: Some of the best teaching happens in bed. I felt like he had—nearly inadvertently, and certainly not in bed—pointed me to a whole universe of tenderness between men that *wasn't even supposed to exist.*

What was this hidden realm of experience called? Bisexuality? That seems a bit overreaching, because most of the men I shared beds with would go on to marry women and have kids, like most of Allen's former apprentices. "Rough trade," which was what old queens called allegedly straight guys who furtively let gay men blow them? There was nothing furtive or rough about it. It became one of my keenest pleasures in life to see a usually stiff, body-armored, and emotionally defended man become a sweet, affectionate puppy dog behind closed doors. I would eventually discover that there was a tradition in the Victorian era of men sharing beds, often out of necessity, that was called "bundling." Abraham Lincoln himself bundled for four years with his best friend Joshua Speed; they both went on to marry women, and whether or not they ever had sex is a subject of controversy among scholars.

When he wasn't bragging about his mad skillz in poems, Allen had another way to refer to this secret universe of experience and emotion. He often quoted a poem called "Rain" by William Carlos Williams, who had acted as a mentor to him when he was a teenager, which contained the lines:

Unworldly love
that has no hope
of the world

and that
cannot change the world
to its delight —

That feels right.

In other words, what I first diagnosed in myself as a mental disorder is more like a spectrum of human possibility and potential, running like a half-hidden pattern behind the weave of how men are supposed to act with one another, and what the limits of human sexuality are supposed to be in a strictly binary system.

As in so many other realms of human experience, the binary system is a lie, and the glory of our uncategorizable being shines through in the shadows between worlds—in the unexpected touch of a hand, in ecstasies that have never been pinpointed on any of the available maps, and in soft words exchanged by two people cradling one another in the hours before dawn.

Every culture has its norms, its divergent members who violate those norms, and its conservative members who treat divergence as an unwanted incursion. Norms shift over time. In our world today, rigid binary gender norms are beginning to crumble, even as the dominant culture fights tooth and nail to enforce them. In "The New World," Melanie Bell invites us into a future setting where the gender norms are no longer binary—but the norms are still contested by some and enforced by others, in familiar ways. Today's divergence becomes tomorrow's orthodoxy, and the dance of resistance and incursion goes on.

The New World

Melanie Bell

I noticed the President's grimace as the two Deans walked down the aisle. Zir nose scrunched up and those bunchy eyebrows knit together. Around me, students and faculty in freshly washed robes (the most that could be expected of them) tossed a veritable flurry of flowers into the air. I lobbed a fistful of peony petals toward the center of the chapel and looked over at Sesshin to see if ze'd noticed too. Yes, Sesh's lips opened in silent laughter. The President looked ridiculous.

As the Deans reached Reverend Adorno, whose trailing robes created the impression of floating in midair, Sesh leaned to whisper in my ear. "Brilliant subversion of that old marriage idea, don't you think, Shen?"

Dean Kurosawa was ours—head of the Department of

Anthrosociology where Sesh and I studied. Wielder of riddles, preparer of sushi, inventor of intricate games. Slighter than me, with brilliantly healthy skin and a braid all down zir back. Not much muscle tone, but you couldn't tell under that billowing emerald robe. I could feel the oxytocin as ze clasped Dean Santos' hands. Santos, most admirable and widely read Dean of Chemogenetics, who (the whispers said) should have known better. Santos, sparking with copper joy, who'd spent a lot more time in our department halls these past few years than strictly required for research. As the minister spoke in a long-gone tongue and the Deans intoned responses, I wondered if this ceremony was a subversion at all.

Reverend Adorno turned to face the crowd, acknowledging us for the first time. "Reason has spoken," ze declared, "and the law has listened. Before us, the Most Honorable Deans Santos and Kurosawa have petitioned to be bound in the institution of marriage. Should anyone here present know of a valid reason that this couple should not be joined in matrimony, speak now or forever hold your peace."

A loud cough sounded from the front row, followed by a rustle.

"Yes, Most Honorable President?" the Reverend asked.

The smell of mothballs wafted back from the President's brocaded formal robes as zir chin wobbled. "Surely the Deans disgrace us."

"What do you mean, Zer?"

"It baffles me, Reverend, that you ask. We are observers, sworn to study and contribute to human progress. The very reason Zacharias founded the Academy was to evade those who would laugh at our minds, scorn our ambitions, and have us breed like animals."

"Understood," said Kurosawa, level-voiced. The stained-glass window at the front of the chapel, inlaid with tiny suns and planets, cast citrine and sapphire stripes across zir face. "We simply seek to carry on this legacy together, dignified by law."

"What would our forebears think of this wedding charade?" How quickly the President's right hand balled into a fist; how unstable zir biochemistry smelled, a jumble of sour and rot. "You two... you..." It struck me with amusement that the President didn't even know what to call them. Ze finished simply, "You deign to make a mockery of who we are!"

Bodies rose in the pews around me until the seated and the standing formed an irregular sort of fractal. Some held fists aloft while others raised their voices or held up small solar tablets to take pictures. I discerned calls for the President to shut up, along with insults hurled toward the front of the chapel. "Spore-makers!" "Milk cows!" Words bounced off each other, echoed down thirty rows of resin-scented benches.

Santos raised a hand and the voices hushed by habit. "The law permits—"

"Oh, the law permits, does it?" the President mocked. "The law permits freedom of speech, too, but it does nothing to make the words of blathering idiots into wisdom."

Kurosawa looked the President square in the eye, a stare that no scholar wanted to meet on thesis defense day. "You gave us your blessing."

"That was your interpretation, Dean K. I merely agreed that it is not my place to infringe upon civil liberties. It is, however, my place to determine next year's funding allocations, and if you persist in this foolish pomp and circumstance, do not be surprised if your grant money dries up mysteriously."

With a rustle of fabric, Sesshin stood up beside me. "You wouldn't dare!" Ze made an abrupt move toward the aisle and I grabbed zir sleeve just as quickly.

"Sesh, don't."

"Why not? That asshole wants to take our funding. Don't tell me you're just going to stand there!"

I flashed back to all the community service hours Sesh had racked up in our youth: scouring greasy kitchen pots, transplanting hydroponic crops, cleaning the composting toilets. I was preparing a retort, clutching Sesh's robes so hard my hands were straining, when another student made it down the aisle. Ze was a tall Chemogenetics major I recognized, surrounded by a chemical cloud of scorching red. Ze lunged at the President, who tried to wobble out of the way. The student was too quick. Ze caught the President in a headlock. Even Sesh could only watch as they grappled on the floor, fists flailing. Santos leaned down to pull them apart, and received a whack on the nose for zir trouble.

The heavy doors at the back of the chapel creaked open, and the first student walked out.

Behind zir came another, then another, the trickle of bodies swelling into a stream. Somewhere in there, the President wiggled out of the headlock and escaped with them, enduring one or two shoves on the way out.

Half the occupants of the chapel had left, while the other half—

Sesh and me included—stayed in our seats. Reverend Adorno let out a long breath, straightened zir back, and commenced singing in that dead language. Soon—any minute now—Santos' square body would lean down for a kiss. I reached into my pocket and found a few more flower petals to throw. Watched their shadows move as they fell. The urge to hold someone was natural on this occasion, simply biological. The wild swings of adrenaline were an effect of curiosity on my observer body. But I didn't yet have a plausible hypothesis for why I felt so proud.

Light filtered through the broad cathedral windows, burnishing the red wood inside. Everyone kept their backs straight as the couple's lips touched. Kissing was an archaic human bonding custom, related to the compulsion to eat. It had always struck me as infantile, like sucking milk from a breast, so I'd never had the urge to try it. I could tell from the complex way their faces interacted that those two had tried it many times. I focused my vision on the silver outlines of excitement, brighter in front, dimly tracing all the spectators. The last petals flew into the air—pink, white, gold. What was it that made Santos and Kurosawa so content, even with everything that had happened? That led them to throw their research funding on the line?

Sesh touched my shoulder and mouthed, "They're fighting."

"For what?"

"For the new world! You should've let me fight with them."

"I'm not saying we shouldn't fight," I said. "Just remember Zacharias' first rule: seek first to understand."

♦ ♦ ♦

I'd heard that after weddings outside the Academy, the bonded pairs or groups are left alone. Sometimes they head out right away for travel. Here at the Academy, we held our usual lunch meeting at the faculty tables in the big hall, under scowling portraits. There were a few observable differences: adrenaline spiked the air (a nice sharp smell), the questions were louder, and Kurosawa was all dressed up.

"What was the experience of the wedding like, subjectively?" Ash, who was researching pre-flood oral histories, tried to take a bite out of zir sandwich and missed it.

"When are you going to cancel it?" asked Nessir, studying community hierarchies, one of the students who'd walked out.

"Is Santos a good kisser?" asked Alessa, student of Academy-villager economic relations and our department's one female. She looked across the table at Rait, whose eyes remained on a heavy volume on 23rd century tax laws. It was only in this tenth generation that non-observers had been permitted to study here. The entrance exams were so difficult that males and females seldom got in, and when they did, they were often disconcerted by the way we studied them. Not so with Alessa, who spent most of her time with her lab partner. Rumor was, she hoped Rait would come around and start acting like the boys back home.

Kurosawa held up a hand and called us to order. "Observers—and madam," ze inclined zir head, "this meeting marks a turning point in our social history. Santos and I may be the first observers to legally marry, but we are not the first of our kind. Let us look back to Zacharias and examine the context." Zir eyes went up to a portrait as tall as three of us, of a jowly individual in solemn white robes. Some in our department mouthed along to the "Zacharias" line—that's what Kurosawa always said.

"After the nuclear disaster, once the floodwaters had subsided and the human population had stabilized, Zacharias became the first person to study the upsurge in intersex births. What biology had wrought became, under zir ministries, a sociological third gender. This great pioneer found that the same genetic alterations that caused zir phenotype led to lowered estrogen and testosterone, and that adrenaline, dopamine and serotonin release in these individuals was tied to curiosity and learning rather than attraction or reproduction. It was these same genetic mutations that caused the development of our biochemical sensory capacities. The observers could occupy either reproductive role, but most had no interest in procreating or forming relationship units. They were too busy falling in love with individual and beautiful niches of study.

"Thanks to Zacharias' efforts, the Academy was born—hub of research, technology, and commerce, cultivating business relationships with the surrounding regions while remaining at arm's length. Zacharias saw to it that we would breed once in a while among ourselves, and hastened the development of artificial incubation until it was no longer necessary. We endeavored to take in all observers born outside our borders.

"Ze would never have approved of Santos and me. Zir breeding program was strictly reproductive, with mates selected for genetic compatibility. And if we went by zir venerable theories, our relationship would be an impossibility. Does anyone have thoughts on what brought it about?"

"You studied together!" migration researcher Kellen blurted out before zir hand could go up. "That project on the socioanth implications of observer hormone production—"

"I think Santos was attracted to zir before that," Ash broke in.

Impossible, I knew. How could one feel that euphoria before one studied something? Unless it was curiosity, and I didn't see what about Kurosawa would make Santos curious.

"And once they collaborated—" Kellen grinned. "It happens sometimes with study partners. Stay up all night. Share the bed. All those excess hormones finding places to go. Don't pretend it doesn't."

I admired Kurosawa's ability to keep a calm expression through all of this. The only energy flickering around zir was that same silver happiness.

"My theory is it's more than that," said Ash. "Look at Ren. We've seen how ze looks at males—even pictures of them." Across the table, quiet Ren was studying the floor. "There's some vestige of outsiders' attraction in our genetic code, much like there's some variant of our response pattern in those outsiders who fall for us."

Talk flew around the table. Gene variation in the outsider population, rare but possibly growing. Someone's friend's sibling who'd taken up with two women and made an outside village zir terrain of study. Various students we'd heard of who seemed a little too interested in collaboration. Someone else's teacher who'd not only bred with an outsider, but *fallen in love.*

"I think the love is it," said Sesshin, surprising me. "If any observer's predisposed to feel the tiniest bit of it, they'd want to study that feeling, wouldn't they? And the adrenaline would spike and the dopamine would grow—"

"And what's the love hormone?" I picked up on zir thread, almost as if it was written out in front of me. "Oxytocin. The bonding agent that Zacharias never said anything about." I looked into Kurosawa's unsmiling, happy face. "I'd hypothesize that Zacharias overlooked its impact on observer physiology because we don't bond the usual way. But when we bond through intellectual synergy, and have sufficient physical proximity, the effects are the same as for the women and men outside our borders. We could feel them at the wedding."

"Nicely thought out, all of you." Kurosawa glowed with a little more contentment. "It's clear there are factors at play Zacharias knew not of." Across the room, Santos held court over the Chemogenetics table, dressed in wedding gold and sitting taller than usual. "And my invitation to all of you is to find out more. My door is open to all of you who'd like to talk about research you might pursue in this new, wide-open field. For if ever we are to live with equality, our capacity to form and sustain relationships must be known and recognized. And if we are ever to be taken seriously as observers, our full range of potential must be understood."

"Where will we get the funding for it?" Nessir broke in.

Sesh rolled zir eyes and spoke directly to Kurosawa: "I support you."

"Me too," said Alessa. I thought of her and Rait in the lab.

"Good. Then I'll see you during office hours." Kurosawa rose and swept away, zir green hem trailing the ground.

♦ ♦ ♦

Sesshin and I headed for our study space, a clean-walled cube filled with papers. I could feel the possibilities bouncing off of zir, for we were students of family. I wanted to understand the interrelationship between outside and inside—we observers traded with the villages and sometimes took their children, but were family bonds ever maintained? Did any observers still consider the villagers brothers and sisters? (Thus far, my questions seemed to be answered in the negative. I held out.) Sesh had been studying early childhood within the Academy walls. I didn't know how ze could stand listening to the Psychoeducation faculty sing Zacharias' twelve rules over and over again to the small batches of village-born observers and larger crops of genetically optimized young fresh from our gestation tanks. I'd had enough of those songs when I was that age, but Sesh seemed to relish everything from setting up bouncy mazes to feeding the kids sloppy spoonfuls of baby food. Ze also liked studying games, and antique drinking vessels, and locomotion by boat. It was clear to me that Sesh hadn't fallen in love with a niche yet, or perhaps ze was equally in love with a million of them.

"Shen," ze spun in a circle. "Shen, Shen, Shen! Did that give you ideas or what?"

"Sure, Sesh. What are yours?" I could tell ze was dying to go first.

"I want to see if they have kids! The first legally bonded pair, you know, I bet they plan to. Will they do it the old-fashioned way, like the villagers? Will they raise them together? And if they do, I want to see how they turn out. Will people think they're weird? What coping strategies will they use? Scratch that, we've got to talk to them about their plans for conception right away. Compare the predictions with the outcome!"

I'd always liked Sesh, but unlike Kurosawa and Santos with their charged intellectual synergy, we'd never had one idea in common. As Alessa and Rait's voices echoed from the cube beside us (Alessa asking what Rait was doing that weekend, and asking if she could help take notes on chapter 10), I did what a good friend does and critiqued. "Give them a little time before asking any loaded research questions..."

My own idea was nibbling around the edges of my mind. Something that would show the President how wrong ze was and make a convincing enough argument to redistribute funding. Something that would bring together the disparate threads of bonded relationships and Academy-villager relations... "Everything is connected," Kurosawa said, "if you study it long enough."

I waited a few days for my thoughts to settle. My ears stayed open to gossip, and after the wedding, there was plenty of it. Some students echoed the President's view: that a good observer devotes zir life to knowledge, not interpersonal distraction; a good observer remains objective and therefore chaste. What's in bonding for us anyway? A fair question. I'd tried out orgasms, Sesh had even persuaded me to try them together once, and they'd been a fun waste of time, nothing like the flush of new discovery. Love, I knew as the fuzzy feeling of seeing someone who's kind to you, like Kurosawa: pleasant, mild.

I read accounts of the early Academy, before it was so formalized, when some had stayed and others had gone. One observer had refused to claim the label; had, in fact, settled happily in a village with a man and woman, though ze sent regular reports of their life to friends at the Academy. This "Catherine," as "she" called "herself," had planted crops and hunted, mourned the villager dead and invented a new way of making cloth. "She" must have partaken in their breeding behavior as well, because "her" child was one of the second generation. I wondered what hunger must have driven Catherine to give up all the riches of the Academy and study out in the field. To live among people who couldn't follow zir mind and probably laughed at zir reports. To die in a community where no one understood. I never could have done that.

I put down the account in a sort of fever. The colors of each book glowed distinctly. Through the window, the shrubby green yard looked as big as a continent. Blood rushed to my head and the ground felt more solid under my feet. I'd read the feeling described as a "roller coaster" by a first-generation observer whose parents had been on one. Dizzy, immediate, alive.

I paced around my room. My mind felt so big and the space too small. It was hard to sleep that night. In my dreams, the hunger grew.

♦ ♦ ♦

There was so much to do! Students and faculty dotted the halls in ones, twos, or threes, exchanging knowing looks as I swept past. The spring in my step, the gathering silver could only mean one thing.

Spread across the green like spokes on a wheel, every study hall connected to the central library. A glass-walled dome with twenty floors of books, their covers in every age and hue imaginable, and old infoscreens ranged along every window. Sofas to curl in, desks sectioned off for solitude, listening stations with tiny earphones, and a few walnut-paneled rooms that held the antiques, where golden dust motes danced under chandeliers. The whole place smelled of musty paper. It was glorious.

The science floors in the middle were a human beehive, but my terrain was the basement. I climbed the spiraling stairs down, down, down, into a room with yellowing walls. The bookshelves spiraled inward, and I followed their ever-shrinking circles to a tiny black loveseat nestled among the oldest Socioanthropology gems. Here I'd read the accounts of people's lives long before the cataclysms. Susanna Moodie roughing it in the Canadian bush. Margaret Mead among the Samoans. Nothing on screens here; everything was dignified with print.

I looked longingly at the familiar titles. *The Hero With a Thousand Faces*, which collected stories from around the old world and formed of them an order. *Worlds of Sense*, which I'd devoured in a sitting, wondering what these ancient peoples who ordered their universes by smell or temperature would think of the silvers and golds we now saw. I knew with a sweet surge of dopamine that my answers would not be here. I spiraled outward.

A few shelves over were books about the outside world, as it was now. I gathered a heavy stack, settled on the loveseat, and pulled my tablet from my bag. I had careful notes to take: economy, holidays, customs, greetings...

The rest was such a delight as to be private.

♦ ♦ ♦

After a few weeks I went to Kurosawa with my proposal: to live among the outsiders, like the anthropologists of old had done. To not only study them, but see if we could jointly build a family. I wanted to find a married couple, to learn how they lived there. What models would they provide for pioneers like Kurosawa and Santos? What arguments could I gain to legitimize their case?

Kurosawa regarded me across an obsidian-colored desk surrounded by bookshelves and row upon row of ancestral photographs, zir stare one among many. Zir office chair looked as uncomfortable as mine.

"If this is a rescue mission, I would advise—"

"No, Zer, it's the final iteration of my thesis proposal. I'll choose a married male and female. You'll help me find them, right?"

Kurosawa urged me to widen my search. "That's an outdated view of marriage—dyads, perfect genetic matching. Advances in reproductive technology have rendered it irrelevant. There are triads, quads, communal marriages, multiple gender combinations, all, no doubt, with something to learn from. The only ones who stubbornly stay out of it are us, and we're not as out of it as you'd think. It's just all very secret, very quiet so far. But someday that will change."

I imagined a tangle of outsiders, with their comic-book secondary sex characteristics, quarreling over a dinner table. I imagined myself in the corner, watching. No one else in the room would look like me.

"I'm starting simple," I said, "as an homage to our predecessor

Catherine." I held up the dusty account, triggering a look of familiarity. My legs could hardly stay still.

"That's quite the story," said Kurosawa.

"It was."

There was a silence of understanding.

"I will live like Catherine," I said, "but under a few conditions. One, I will not pretend to be male or female. I'll be what I am, an observer."

Kurosawa nodded at that.

"Two, I do not intend to marry. But I do intend to live there. In all other respects, I will perform the functions expected of a citizen." I'd read about bowing and weeding and dancing, and could imagine the things as if I was among them.

This time the silence was unsettled. Smells, haloes, notes in the air subtly shifted around.

"I want you to understand the complexity of what you intend to undertake, Shen."

The fear I'd kept around the edges sunk through the cracks in my stomach.

"You'll be entering a culture like nothing you've read in the records. The outside is changing every day."

It struck me as ze talked that Kurosawa had nothing concrete to say. No instructions on dress or living arrangements, no remarks on etiquette, not even reassurance: only grand philosophies. What would those people expect of me, an intruder? What would they want? What could they do to me? The fear settled like a stone.

"I understand that the political climate is in flux, and I will be attentive."

"I would expect no less of you. I must, however, raise some serious concerns."

But I knew I would follow my curiosity where it led. There was nothing else to be done.

In the end, Kurosawa agreed to let me venture into Nestor, the closest village, and seek a bonded pair to take me in.

"I have only one condition," ze told me, unfolding a map of snaking rivers and mountains jutting into the sky. "I'm coming with you."

There are the subtle incursions across the boundaries of psyche, culture, and identity, and then there are the incursions that aren't subtle or metaphorical at all. The two young narrators of Dora M Raymaker's "Heat Producing Entities"—the corporate thief Kyo and the neurodivergent outcast Dragon—are engaged in an incursion of the most classic and literal sort: a burglary. Of course, there are plenty of more subtle forms of incursion going on in this story, too. "Heat Producing Entities," by the way, is set in the same world as Dora's brilliant neuroqueer cyberpunk detective novel, Hoshi and the Red City Circuit.

Heat Producing Entities

Dora M Raymaker

"Due to their unique pathology and the needs of modern encryption, only individuals carrying the K-cluster of genetic defects can integrate with and program quantum computers. Six hundred years ago, these 'Operators' nearly destroyed all life on Earth, after which they were bound and placed in the service of the gov-corps. This is not just for our good, but for theirs too. K-syndrome causes severe deficits in verbal-sequential processing which impact movement, sensory integration, and language and communication. While individualized programming in an Operator's bio-integrated quantum processor can mitigate some of these disabling effects, without our support they would not survive."

—from *The Federal Banking Worlds Good Citizens' Primer: Volume A*

Dragon

Faint snow blows on Ganymede, wisps of barely-there atmosphere hushing between tenement facades. Sunsim lights are off for the night and someone's busted all the street lamps, so Jupiter's crescent is all that casts the shadows. Street's quiet. Too quiet. I pat-slap my hands on my thighs to get some sound.

"Stop that," Djen hisses, so soft it would've been lost on anyone but me. "You've done enough to get us killed tonight."

We're in the shadows, beneath the dusty awning of a shuttered-up pawn shop, trying to get out of the wind. Street stretches straight but not flat; Ganymede's nothing but hills making the buildings make no sense. Fourth-floor over there is the first-floor over here, and everything's web-worked in sky bridges and dust. Four doors down, light's a little brighter from the Raunchy Robot pub and the MéKah Noodles, diffusing from neon shingles and foggy glass. Door to MéKah ejects a threesome. They're falling over each other in the pink-and-purple neon, trailing the smell of garlic and grease. My stomach whines; my mouth fills with saliva. They're giggling, sloppy, wet sake sounds, drunk and in love by the timbre of it.

Djen bends her tall self to get at me and tries to zip my jacket. I swat her away, don't need her. Don't need anyone. "Don't need that tinker, so shut up about it." My teeth grind. I hate that sound.

"I'm not gonna shut up about it because without that tinker to pick the locks we're gonna have trouble landing the run, and then a lot of people don't eat. Including us." She peers at the unmarked tenement across the street, black spirals of hair lifting in the wisps of wind. Whistles of wind. Whistles of wisp. Whispering wisps? Whispering of wispy rhythms. I could be doing something useful, like writing a song.

I grind my boot into the street. Bits of rock and broken glass. Crunch-squish. "I can handle it alone better than with that tinker, he'd just turn us in, make off with the prototype soon as we got it."

"He would not. He would open locks for you."

"Muse'll open locks for me."

The invisible creature pulses cheery infra-heat.

"Muse'll open *electronic* locks for you. There's at least one mechanical in there. Muse can short every circuit in that building and it'll still never grow a pair of tool-using hands." Djen shoves her own gloved hands into her red parka pockets and glares at the dark building. Red like her jumpsuit, red like her magboots, red like her cheeks when she's mad. Mad at me.

Don't need her either. Don't know why she acts the boss. She's only five years older than me and just as screwed up.

Wind shifts her hood so I see the shine of blue across her forehead in Jupiter's half-light—the glow of the quantum computer beneath the skin that marks us slaves. Except, she and I were never slaves, me from a freak error and her because she was born in Freedom. Which is exactly why we shouldn't involve that tinker; he's an outsider, doesn't know about Freedom, doesn't know about the aliens, he'd turn us in, get a bounty, we'd be dead and he'd be rich. Everyone turns in the end.

< i don't > Muse whines, like the whiny wind.

< that's because you're a secret non-corporeal alien with no

capacity to comprehend human bullshit so you don't get a say > I snip at its telempathic attempt to calm me down. I'm not gonna calm down because the only person who was ever nice to me in twenty-four years is Djen, and that's because she's got no one else to ride around in her possessed space ship and do these shitty runs for the Luna Black Market so we don't end up dead turned-in bounty-collected slaves.

"Hey. Dragon. Focus, man." Djen snaps her fingers. Sound's a rocket inside my eardrum.

"Aren't you feeling mean," I say after I'm done flinching, but my voice has no edge because truth is, the only time we argue is when we have to do crimes.

"Sorry. I hate having to steal for our supper too, you know." Now I hear her stomach whine. She glares around the dry, dusty darkness. "Okay, I've cracked the encryption to their security systems, you get fifteen before the codes cycle. And don't screw up. I love you and I don't want you hurt."

I frown at the tenement across the way. Four stories, dull, brown, smashed-out street lamp jagged jaws of broken glass. Building's not marked, wouldn't know it if I hadn't been told, but it houses InteliCorp's artificial intelligence lab with the prototype listening device the Black Market Boss wants bad enough she's sent us, her favorite suckers. "I can do it just fine alone." I slouch away with the last word and the sub-freezing air hitting my chest through my open jacket but I don't feel it because no matter how hard I try I just can't program a functional sense of touch.

I cross Khreschatick Street to InteliCorp whistling like I'm visiting a friend and got the wrong building because they all look the same. That's what I'll say if someone stops me, questions me, tries to catch me. I can sing my way out of anything.

< three heat-producing entities inside what djen calls 'the door' > Muse tells me.

< make them go somewhere else > I answer.

< i can short something in 'the hall?' >

< yeah, get on with it > I'm so useless they could've done the run without me as well as without the tinker. I'll never learn to program and hack as good as Djen. And there's no comparison between a crap-busted human like me and an alien that can manipulate EM. I guess someone's got to do the shit job of touching things, all I am is arms and legs. Shit-boy. I'm Djen's shit-boy.

Kyo

I'm Mikito Limited Corporation's most indispensable asset, my manager's Main Man. I'm on the rooftop of Tenement 16B, Iron City, Ganymede, watching Khreschatick Street below, waiting for the right moment to start my run. By the darkened pawn shop, the man slouches away, whistling. The woman in the red spacer's suit remains against the shuttered-up façade; the scene reads as a drug deal, ignorable. The threesome from the MéKah Noodles is moving away, north toward Avenue Six, quick and hunched. Not from anxiety or oppression, but because it's so cold. One would think in four hundred years the moon could have been better terraformed; but then, most of the work went into radiation shielding and making the atmosphere breathable. The citizens have adapted. Warming up is not a priority.

I have adapted too. I pull up my mask and exhale ice crystals that blow away on the dry wind. I move when Mikito L.C. says move, blend in, become invisible. Make my stake. Return home with the gadget, the blueprint, the hostage, the dataslip I have been sent out to take.

Wind crosses the rooftop; sensor tells me it's minus 16C. Warm for Ganymede, but falling fast. I pull my mask back down. I'm safe in my cold weather clothing. Five days caged in an interstellar ship from Headquarters to the Jovian system, one day going over maps and checking gear. Adrenaline rises, achy for motion, and I bite it back, breathing slow in my lips, out my nose. Not yet. An ounce of prevention is worth a pound of cure, my manager says.

From beneath the shadows of the com discs, I survey the sky bridge stretching between this building and the next. The grating's cheap and decayed, and there's a warning sign, a chain. "Unsafe." "Do not cross." A picture of a falling man.

Skybridges are a weak point, so I know InteliCorp has more security than a scary sign. I tongue the spot on my tooth that activates my telescopic lens and squint to focus. Swarms of nanocams hover in clouds over the rusted steel. Invisible, like me. Seen, by me. They will not see me.

Security by obscurity is InteliCorp's tactic here. Shell-purchase a tenement, pay employees to live in it and look subsistence, and fill it to the gills with state-of-the-art concealed surveillance gear, corporate enforcers, and a hot-button to Iron City Law Enforcement.

It won't do them any good.

I am the Silent Viper, the Secret Striker.

I am Kyo Rylo, corporate trained since I was seven, and I slide through small spaces and work any lock, and am gone before anyone knows I've stolen.

Corporate espionage is illegal—I smile every time someone says that so-so-seriously. Every corporation with a charter older than a year has at least one thief on staff. We're payrolled as enforcers, accountants, whatever meshes with our specialty, and trained in more spy games than a historical cold-war holo-drama. My manager says I am the best corporate thief Mikito L.C. has ever trained. I owe my life to my corp, so I do my best. Now is the time.

Let the adrenaline come in thunder and pride, catch in my chest and pump my game.

Bread and butter.

Profits for my corp.

I work alone.

I bring it home. For my manager. For Mikito L.C.

I am a Master Thief.

I click on the nanocam-killing jammer and jet across the skybridge.

Beneath my feet, the rusted steel makes no sound.

Dragon

"Dragon? You gonna open that door? It's not locked." Djen's transmission comes through the slow-waves, data flowing between the hardware in our heads.

"I'm waiting for Muse to distract the guards. Or whatever it detected."

Muse pipes up telempathically, < i did. awhile ago. >

< and how would i know that since you didn't TELL ME >

Sensations of perplexity. < how long did you expect it to take? >

My eyes burn from the years and tears of frustration dealing with the creature and it never seems to learn anything; pop the door and enter. I wish there was another way to keep Freedom safe.

Inside looks like a subsistence tenement. Brown walls, peeling paint, smell of must and onions. My stomach whines. Stairs to the right. Halls branching off to doors with falling-off numbers. I go up to the third floor. The sensorcams in the corners make me nervous even though Djen's controlling them.

On the third floor doors, the falling-off numbers are replaced by very-much-attached lock plates. Who knows what it takes to open them—hand print? Retinal scan? Blood? First born babies dipped in liquid gold and tattooed with corporate incantations?

Doesn't matter because Muse slips inside and opens one for me. Hate how quiet it is here and I'm supposed to be sneaky so I can't make any sound.

I step into a bright-light white-washed clean-room that reeks of corporate credit.

"I can see you through the cams," Djen transmits to me. "See the frosted glass door on the left? Go through that and I'll help you with the maze of cube-land to the prototype room."

"I know how to get there. Remember, I have a really good memory."

"I remember, too, you keep your memory index turned off, so you don't have perfect recall like me."

"Stop distracting me."

< i don't need to distract any heat-producing entities on this floor, none at all > Muse says, with surprise, and for no reason.

I reach the door to the prototype room. Area's bright-lit, white and dust-free, but it's so quiet, it's so fucking quiet.

"That's good," Djen transmits. "You're right outside the prototype room."

"Told you I knew where I was going." Squat at the lock. The mechanical lock. The one I don't need that tinker for. I pull a lock pick set from my jacket pocket and look at the tiny metal tools. So thin and shiny, pretty. Tap them together, wonder what sound they make? Okay, motor programming. I've got grace and I've got dance, but I've got noodles for hands. I've also got motor programming in my head. Motor, linguistic, sensory, running through a bio-integrated quantum processor. Compensate for all the things I can't ordinarily do. Like hold my chopsticks and talk. And make sensory input make any fucking sense. Got a program written all out for picking locks, made it myself when I decided that tinker was a bad idea.

"Hurry up," Djen says. "Encryption scheme for the sensors is gonna cycle in four-dot-oh-six minutes."

"Faster if you shut up."

I can't feel my fingers as I fumble around the lock. They're kind of blue; when'd I lose my gloves? Must've been outside for my hands to get so cold. Just like Djen not to notice; she's worse than me with sensory integration even if her sensory programming's better.

Programming. Shit. Why isn't my lock-pick motor programming

working? It's hard to concentrate when I'm so fucking hungry. Tool's aligned with the hole, stuck in right, listening for the clicks because I can't really feel them, but—

SOUND

what

SOUND

< GET OUT GET OUT GET OUT > Muse shrieks telempathic hysteria in resonance with my panic-pain as

full-on nervous-system shut-down blacking-out

SOUND

SCREAMING SOUND

Ohshitoshit that's an alarm isn't it?

< GET OUT NOW > Muse zaps me with electricity to break the paralysis of overload.

Shove my hands in my ears but then I can't figure out how to stand, so take my hands off my ears and run run run run run—

Kyo

To this side, I am standing, invisible and silent, where I need to be in the room with the prototype.

Slice.

To the other side, a buzz escalating into a siren-whine, ebbing, buzzing, escalating, whining—

I was just standing though. Not moving. Not even breathing.

Training moves me because there is no time in which to understand what has triggered the alarm.

The sleeping guards have woken. The Law Enforcement panic button has been pushed. The sky bridge is detaching. I cannot go back the way I came.

I'm shooting out the third story window dropping my gun to reach into my bag for the grappling hook to catch on the sill jumping through shards plummeting to the alley between tenements as I slide down the rope to break my fall.

I let go of the too-short rope and land on broken glass.

I see the shard go through my boot and into the meat of my calf, so sharp I don't feel it.

I run into the night with the shard sticking out to keep the blood from betraying me but I feel it now, oh, yes, no, oh I feel it now and I'm not going to get far.

I need to bring profits to my corp.

I need someplace to hide.

Dragon

Fear at my heels, fear at my back, fear licking like an incoming tide at the sand of the shore that falls behind me and blind midnight shadows

WHAT HAVE I DONE?

Nothing. I've done nothing. Wasn't my fault. I didn't set off any alarm. Djen was supposed to be in the security, in the cameras, Muse monitoring the hallways, I didn't trip anything, Djen should've been faster to shift the security cycles—if that's even what happened and I run I run I run puffing fog and pounding feet.

Black.

Silent.

Then: Swish-tick as the wind hits something loose and light. Reach out with sound, sending clicks into darkness. They bounce back to tell me I'm behind a huge metal rectangle. Reach out with a fist, rap with my knuckles, hollow, not empty. Behind/beyond, muffled by buildings: a shout and the sound of trooper feet. Above: distant stars and a wisp of city-reflecting clouds.

Muse casts an infra glow so faint I can only see it in pupils made huge by darkness.

I'm behind a waste reclaimer bin.

I've lost my jacket now too.

I open a channel to signal Djen, but all I get's a wall of static burn. Max-strength area signal jammer.

SHITFUCK

< muse, we alone? >

< you and i >

Stressed breath leaves my lungs too fast to suck it back in, but only someone with my genetic type could've heard it and right now that's just me. < if you don't produce more infra i'm gonna freeze to death > I tell it.

A pulse of deep red glow. < there's a warmer hiding place nearby >

I rub my skinny arms and exhale invisible fog into darkness. The buzz of the jammer's so close it's even messing with my connection to Muse.

From the building behind me I hear a harsh bark, "Iron City Law Enforcement, open up." A shout. A baby wails.

< how far's the warmer place? > I ask Muse.

< just down the path of bouncing light >

The alley. It means the alley. It can see frequencies bouncing around, bouncing off walls. But it can't see walls. Building down the alley must be safe.

Another shout from the street and a sense of urgency from the invisible creature.

Now or never. Once law enforcement gets bored of the street-side and spooks down this alley, they'll find me.

Don't hear anything in the alley, so I turn deeper into darkness. My insulated boots crunch-squish with every step but who's gonna hear it, so swallow the panic and move on, hand trailing the back-side of buildings. Smell of garlic and grease, memory of MéKah Noodles or maybe I didn't make it very far, maybe I'm behind the restaurant. I could slip in, steal something from the back room, slip something off the back counter, saliva dribbling out of my mouth to freeze on my chin.

< come ON > Muse zaps my forearm with enough electricity to sting.

< if i die of starvation you'll be the one hurting >

< djen said food is why it's important not to botch the run >

< I DIDN'T BOTCH THE RUN > My teeth grind. I hate that sound. < i don't know what happened. something happened. >

The crunch-squish echoes different when we reach the end of the alley and my hands explore where we've ended up. There's a door and it's icy and, while the latch wiggles, it doesn't budge when I tug. Brace feet, tighten abs, deep breaths. I'm a small man but strong from dancing; I can do this, just gotta gather myself right.

Three jerking tugs and the door screams corroded metal.

No warm air fluffs out.

At least there's no wind within.

Got to remember that agony of rust sound, use it in a song. At least I can hide here till the jammers are gone and I can get a signal out to Djen. If we're alone so no one can see it Muse can radiate infra like a living heater, keep me warm. And I'll know if someone opens the door.

In the darkness, a hiccup. Shit.

< muse, we got company? >

< yes. one heat-producing entity >

Shit.

Kyo

I tongue the spot on my tooth that activates my infra-vision lens. On the dead factory floor, an intruder, three o'clock. They're leaking heat everywhere, so not Law Enforcement with their armor. There's a warm haze over their right shoulder.

I blink and the haze is gone.

An artifact of a poor connection between my implanted tech and my brain, unavoidable, since I'm no slave, no feeble able to use a quantum computer.

I hold all the advantage.

From the second-floor supervisor's platform, I've got a clear shot—if I had a gun. But all I've got left is knives, and the distance between us is too far to throw.

I'm invisible. I am nothing. I am Mikito L.C.'s best corporate thief, most loyal, most trained. Blend in, blend out. They pass by.

I shift for a better strike in case they don't, biting off pain from my leg before it becomes a scream.

Yet, somehow he hears me. "Hello? Who's there?"

His voice crawls over my skin. It's so beautiful it doesn't make sense. Maybe I'm in shock from my injury. It's bad, but not that bad. Swallow. Stay silent. Focus. Maneuver for the kill. Wait for him to move on.

His hum floats like a living thing ahead of him as he moves deeper in. He clicks his tongue, hums again. The abandoned factory is in total darkness; he'll miss the stairs. Unless he's got an infra-lens too. I've taken off my mask to pack it around the wound. He could see the heat-leak of my face. Of the blood seeping hot from my boot. I pull the hood of my parka tighter.

The hum meanders into a melody. "Safety for a shelter / shelter in a storm / let me find a hiding place / somewhere to keep me warm..."

He starts up the stairs. He must have an infra-lens. But the stairs are cold, cold as the air, cold as everything on Ganymede.

"Safety for a shelter / shelter in a storm—Hey, I don't wanna hurt you."

Just pass by, just pass by, just pass by...

"Hi!" His voice throws itself against me and I'm on top of him with my blade seeking anything soft it can find.

Dragon

The rush of air from the lunge is all that warns me and I'm barely side-stepping as I scream in my head < muse! you didn't tell me he was fucking homicidal! >

The creature emits chagrin but I'm busy with a lithe, hard body atop mine and the sound of steel hitting concrete, blade of the knife impacting centimeters from my face.

Knee up contacts something soft that makes him yelp and a lifetime of getting the shit beat out of me makes me rage like nothing else as I scream and claw for hair and somehow I've gotten on top of him. He's not much bigger than me, and I scramble over his legs to try to pin his arms; he yowls all out of proportion with what I've done. He cracks on a glolight; it skitters over the concrete as his hands come for my throat.

He's on top of me again, knee in my chest, knife blade at my neck but I can't feel it well enough to know if I'm being cut.

< !!!are you going let him kill me? > I shriek-think at Muse but the creature just sends baffled feelings back at me. Despite what it said earlier, selfish thing would rather me die than itself be discovered, everything turns in the end, just like I said, everyone's just out for themselves in the end < GET THE FUCK AWAY FROM ME YOU USELESS THING I HATE YOU! I BANISH YOU! BEGONE! BE. GONE. >

The connection between our minds snaps shut with the finality of the jammer now between us.

My attacker shoves his face down hard close to mine. He's

pinched, white tension in his jaw, sweat off his nose falling onto my cheek. The hiccup. The howl. The silhouette of him in the dim light and the way he holds one leg out—

I kick the blade of glass deeper into his calf.

He yowls again.

I roll away, panting, hating, outside the glo's light.

He curls up whimpering, breathing hard, and I feel bad. Don't like kicking people when they're down. Everyone's always kicking me I'm always down. Shit.

I climb back into the circle of glo. "Sorry," I say, "sorry but—BUT YOU TRIED TO FUCKING KILL ME FOR NO REASON AT ALL."

Kyo

Pain floods red followed by black-and-white speckles that threaten the center of consciousness. I'm suspended on a throbbing edge without air, waiting for blackout.

With a wave of nausea, the crisis recedes, heart pounding back into real time, real world, oh no, I've been found.

He sits inside the pool of glo, sprawled like he's forgotten what to do with his legs. He wears his beauty like a holo-star or a high-end performer, irresistible, hateful. Golden skin, features from every corner of old Earth, black eyes holding more light than they should beneath endless lashes. He's got a fluffy white hat jammed over his brows; tangles of black hair poke out to brush his shoulders. His bare shoulders. He's not wearing anything but a sleeveless tunic, indoor pants, and a bitchy expression.

The bitchy expression breaks the spell.

Training clicks; body moves to retrieve the knife I dropped, like an amateur, when he kicked me where it counted. His eyes track the steel, widening. He knows I know how to use it. "Talk." I can almost keep my voice free of pain.

He holds my eyes hostage in the bright-dark of his glare, while he shakes his hands in silence, like he's defective. Finally, "I'm not your fucking puppet," he says. His voice is less captivating through the clattering of his teeth.

"No. But I can put this knife in your chest faster than you can see it happen."

He narrows his shiny black eyes, frowns, points to the center of his chest. "Come on. Unarmed, unskilled, ACTUALLY FREEZING TO DEATH—really think I'm a threat?"

Damnit. I am not a killer.

I can, I have, I will again.

But only when attacked, exposed, as a last resort. I don't even know what I have for options. If I killed him now it would be the kind of cold blood I don't want to live with.

He doesn't need to know that.

I keep the knife poised and say, "Scoot me my bag and maybe we can do something about your freezing to death."

He pats around the straps, like he can't line up his hands with them. Eventually, he slides it across the gritty floor of the supervisor deck.

I feel around inside, eyes on him, hands locating the syringe with the three raised dots that means pain killers. I hadn't wanted to use it, but this asshole's pressed the issue. Literally. Numbing heat spreads up my leg and I try not to let it affect my judgment.

"Oo you got drugs?" He says. "I like drugs."

"You like life?" I twist the knife in the light.

"I like food, you got any of that?" He looks like he's about to cry.

"Oh hell. Come here." I make the knife disappear and hold out my arms. He scrambles over with awkward grace. I pull off my parka and put it over his shoulders. The air sucks the heat out of me through three layers of insulated clothing like it was gauze, but unlike him in his sleeveless tunic, I'll survive. "What's your name?" I ask him.

"Dragon," he says.

"That your real name?"

"That your real business?"

I laugh. There could be worse company to wait out a manhunt with. "I'm Kyo," I extend my hand. He stares at it. "Kyo, of Mikito Limited Corp. Enforcer." I nod at the glass sticking out of my blood-slicked boot. "Having a bad night."

He extends his own hands, staring at the backs like they hold answers. There's no corporate pin on the webbing of his thumb, and no tag for subsistence. A blank. An illegal. Like I was before Mikito L.C. gave me a home. If he died here, no one would know. No one would care.

Dragon puts his hands up, palms out, in the Black Market equivalent of a handshake. I echo the gesture. It will do.

"What's it like out there?" I keep my tone casual.

"Thick with blues. Industrial jammer. Troops on every street."

"Close by?"

"Very."

"You should know," we say in unison, "they're looking for me."

Dragon

Just like it was a duet: "...they're looking for me." Synch sets me laughing, crying, maybe just so fucking hungry and cold and shivering it's turned into laughing or crying I had no idea how much heat Muse was giving out till it was gone outside the jammer range, just so much stress needing somewhere to go. So, laughing, crying, biting my frost-bitten hands.

Kyo's hot. He's got a pale face like a fox, epicanthic folds, and short black hair sticking out in a hyper-groomed corporate cut. He's about my age, muscles bunched under tight, dark clothes. High-end credit, kind of cold-planet wear Djen and I'll never afford. Flash of a sigil pinned to his thumb but I don't know any of the corps. Mikito L.C. he said? Whatever that is. If the jammer wasn't there, I could reach into informationspace, look it up, but it doesn't matter anyway. I'm hiding out with a corporate enforcer who must've breached some random law, I don't understand any of that shit, they have so many laws. All I've got to understand is his kind wants my kind in chains. Good thing I still have my hat.

"What if it's neither of us, what if it's someone else," I say to be perverse, not because I think it's true. Alarm went off at InteliCorp in the middle of my run, what else could've called that many blues that fast.

Kyo nods, warming to me. They always warm to me, everyone warms to me, ridiculous charisma I can never turn off. Now the key's to walk away before he gets to know me well enough to find out what a shit I am. Warm right now is good though.

"So why you think they're after you?" I ask.

He shrugs and moves closer, careful around his broken-glass leg. I bet he's cold now too. "I investigated the wrong person," he says. I can tell by his timbre he's lying. "Didn't work out so well. What about you?"

"I tried to steal a listening device prototype from InteliCorp," I say because I'm shit at lying. I can hold my timbre steady, but it's the facts I scramble up. "Didn't work out so well."

His foxy face goes thoughtful, and he takes in air but doesn't let out any sounds on the exhale. Instead he swivels so his hips are aligned with mine and pulls me back until our backs hit something solid. I send out a few clicks to figure what's going on outside the glolight and guess we're beneath some piece of decaying machinery, like a table for giants.

"What's that?" Kyo asks.

"What?"

He tries to mimic my clicks.

"Echolocation. Not really seeing in the dark but I can get a sense for shapes. I've a thing for sound." I full-grin at him and vocalize.

His brows go up and I grin fuller and vocalize longer.

Then he says, "Shh, we should be quiet. In case law enforcement comes in."

"I'd hear the door if they do."

"Sure. But what if they come in a different way?"

He has a point.

It gets quiet then but I hate the quiet so I ask him, "How'd you end up a corporate enforcer?"

Kyo

He's what set off the alarm.

HE'S what set of the alarm.

I should be getting the accolades of my manager, sitting in the sunken soft chair of Mikito L.C.'s plush local office with a fat, fresh lump of credit in the Bank and a grin on my face. I should be leaving the office for an expensive dinner with an expensive escort. I should be warm and safe and not bleeding on an abandoned factory floor. I would be if he hadn't set off the alarm. I should kill him after all.

But I'm woozy from the pain killer. And he's delicious and toxic like too much expensive booze. The harm is done. We can't undo time. I pull the coat off his shoulders and push it around both of us like a blanket. Beneath, our hands brush. There are worse ways to wait out the time.

"I was on the street until I was seven." I say. What's it matter what I tell him. "Blank, like you. Like most corps, Mikito L.C. had head hunters combing for talent, and I had some."

"Talent as an enforcer? As a kid?"

I shrug, lying. Thinking of all the stealing. Stealing to stay alive, to have something to do, to pay the big kids for their protection. "Talent beating up the other kids."

Dragon laughs. "You're no bully. Told you, I've a thing for sound. And a sixth sense for bullies."

He's shivering so hard it's like a seizure. I shift closer. I could kill him and it would change nothing. He needs me for warmth, but I don't need him for anything.

"I'd mark you for an assassin," he muses. He nudges into me until his entire right flank is pressed against my left. "No, a thief, I think. I'd mark you for a thief."

I stay cool as he fingers my profession, cool in the heat between us. "Oh? How do you mark that?"

Dragon draws breath and lets it out. And again. His hands fidget with each other, brushing against my thigh, tiny threads of electricity. Then he says, "I met this assassin once, employed by Order of the Wheel. You remind me of her. She'd been picked up by the Order after killing someone in the ruins of Eastern Metropolis, they liked her style, saw her potential, that she was a natural sociopath, and they gave her religion. Order of the Wheel, so real religion, not just corporate allegiance—no offense—though they gave her that too. She believes in this whole turning wheel of souls thing, that killing people helps them along their journey. Kind of like therapy or something. You remind me of her. Only without the religion. And with more heart, past the corporate stiff. You're not much with the killing are you, just the stealing gets you high?"

I should bury my knife in his throat for that. No one is allowed to know me except Management.

But the outside of my boot is covered in a frozen slush of blood. And it's warm with him. He's nobody, no corp, no allegiance, no citizen ID, no Bank account, he's not going to turn me in or he'll be arrested too. "Just the stealing." I mean to stop, but I've never had anyone to talk with about this stuff and my mouth goes on. "I don't know how I ended up on the street. It happened before I was five, which is as far back as I can recall. I don't remember family, nothing. I was just alone when my memories start."

Dragon leans his head on my shoulder. The fluff of his white hat tickles my chin. His shivering has stopped, but he trembles as he speaks, like the emotional intensity is too much for him. "I knew my mother. She was a fucking blint. Drunk all the time. My memories too. Alone. Always alone."

The factory is so silent it's a noise in itself. I must be picking up on his thing with sound.

DRAGON

"Don't you go near the corpers. Don't you let them know who you are," Djen always says. "Die-hard corpers can't be bought for anything, not even one of your songs. Their corporation's their mommy, god, and punisher all in one."

But what's Djen know about corpers? I know more than she does, growing up legal on a colony world run by them; she's spent her life in Freedom's shadow-world.

My hands have that deep-ache of thawing frostbite even I can feel. This corper's got baggage that matches mine. Plus, he's a thief. Like me. Only a better thief than me. Fucker. "Do you have any friends, Kyo?"

He shakes his head. I hear it more than see it; our faces are outside the light. "I work better alone."

"Me too." My voice comes out weaker than I want, thinking of all the times Djen and I lay under the stars of an unexplored planet laughing and counting dreams. So maybe it's not really true. Well, maybe it is. Either way, it's better to work alone than to count on someone and have them abandon me half-way through. Like Djen by not hacking the alarms. Like Muse for not helping me when Kyo tried to kill me. Like that tinker would've if I'd let him come along.

Kyo comes in close, and it's nice, and he's pressing against me hard enough I can feel it, pressure, heartbeat, heat off his body, heat between us. I push my hand down to find his crotch and he moves to make it easier, what else is there to pass the time, but there's something hard and cold in his pocket so I pull it into the glolight to toss it away.

It's a palm-sized rectangular box.

Its surface shimmers like the greasy-dark rainbow of a soap bubble.

The sides are etched, "InteliCorp."

Dark display.

Little button below.

I flip it on; lights blink green and frequency crawls across the screen.

It's the listening device I was supposed to steal.

Kyo makes a swipe and I duck because it's mine, so instead of tagging the device he tags my hat and off it goes.

Kyo

His hat comes off and I see why he had it jammed so far over his brows: his forehead shines pale iridescent blue in the glo.

He's not just any blank, he's an escaped slave, an Operator without a master.

He's worth more than three years' salary in bounty—at least—and my salary's good.

And worse: "You're a feeble!" I was touching him. Wanting him to touch me. Letting him touch me. I should have seen it. I should have added up the numbers of his strangeness.

"And, evidently, you're a bigot." He lands a wad of spit across my nose and grinds his teeth.

Game's changed.

I pull my parka off him and lunge.

Dragon

They all turn on me they all hate me, but I'm going to get him back, I'm going to kick him in the leg, shove that glass all the way in, cut something important fuck him fuck him, fuck. him.

He slams me in the side but I just turn off my sensory programming, hyposensitive to pain he can do whatever the fuck-all he wants—fist plows into my face.

I throw the listening device far away so that he won't be able to get it fast and bring my knee up into his stomach.

Kyo

He shouldn't be fighting me. Aren't feebles supposed to be clumsy, compliant, there's something wrong with their ability to move? To think? To sense things? What did they teach us in school? *"K-syndrome causes severe deficits in verbal-sequential processing which impact movement, sensory integration, and communication... without our support they would not survive."*

The old lecture flashes through my head as my body responds to my training and we tumble over the concrete; first him on top, then me. He's right I'm not a killer, but that doesn't mean I haven't. It doesn't mean I don't know how. He'd be dead already if I wasn't wounded and doped up. If he wasn't fighting like he knew how. If I didn't find him beautiful, and funny, and interesting. If I didn't want him. I still want him, knowing what I know now. Nothing has changed.

His knee goes into my stomach and I roll away.

Dragon

I scramble away but he catches my ankle, reels me back in. "Get off me you fucking tool!" I yell. "You don't know shit about me. You don't know shit about what it means to be like me."

His breath is hot acid, too loud in my ear, "I know you're dangerous, you belong somewhere you can be controlled."

"You bought the corporate line, hook and sinker, how nice for you. I'm supposed to be a genetic fuck-up? Least I've got friends who love me outside this mess, all you've got's a boss who took advantage of a hungry child."

Another fist into my face, bet I'll have a shiner, I don't care, he's an asshole, turned on me like they all do.

Kyo

I pound his face, his pretty, golden face.

He spits blood and says in his pretty, golden voice, "You don't know shit about me, but I know plenty about you. I know you like danger. I know you like me."

I wrap my hands around his throat and pull his face to mine.

I taste iron and he's kissing me.

I'm kissing him back.

Dragon

CRACK

Door-slam-snap.

I shift against Kyo in the sweaty after, anger, lust, hate, shit, situation like this is a bit of everything. Hate each other, hate ourselves, what else is there to do but punch and fuck. But we're not alone anymore; that shout came from down the stairs and over there.

"The blues, they're here," Kyo whispers in my ear like I don't already know. He pushes away from me, fixes his pants, and snaps off the glo.

"We need the prototype," I say. My voice is rough from where he'd pressed my throat. From the yelling, the fight. The release.

"What? Why?" He whispers back.

"Because I'm a 'feeble,' asshole. I can use it. I've got a quantum computer hooked into my brain, don't need to attach the device to a stationary system to make it work. You forget what that thing is? It's a high-end AI listening device. It can cut through the jammers, get us on-frequency with their internal coms. Know what they're up to. Avoid. Strategize. Do the shit you're good at."

His breath releases through the soft "O" of his lips; I can hear the shape of the sound in the pitch black. "Sorry," he says, but I'm not sure what for.

We crawl across the floor to where I'd thrown the thing.

I turn toward the wall, shield the lights with my body, flick it on.

I wish Djen was here. She's the hacker, not I. I wish Muse was here, it can slip the protocols on anything. I open a shortwave signal to the device—good thing it's close enough so my connection isn't scrambled by the jammer—and I'm standing on a plain of twinkling lights and sounds of chimes and lemony-bright cascades of tinsel with the texture of fur. It's the encryption scheme around the device's heart, and unless I can sense my way through it, it's not going to do either of us any good.

I break off a thread of consciousness to work on the 'crypt and whisper to Kyo, "How bad's your leg?"

"It was better before you kicked it. Twice."

"Fucking answer the question."

"I can walk. Blood's leaking out of the boot though, there'll be a trail."

"Got any useful ideas?" Hard to focus in both worlds at once. Djen can run twenty threads at a time and not even break a sweat.

"Be right back."

Inside the landscape of the device, synesthetic symbols transform, one-by-one, then in an ever-linking chain into my own internal language of gut and sound.

Kyo

I lied a little about the leg. I am still mobile—if I shoot up a pain-plus-stimulant cocktail from my bag, and I've only got one of those. So for now I crawl to the edge of the supervisor platform. I lean over on my elbows and tongue on my infra vision lens. I tongue the telescopic lens over it.

I don't see anything, so either they're behind the architecture and debris or they've got good infra-masking armor. My bet's on both.

The plan's obvious. Stash the listening device where I can come back for it and turn Dragon in. I claim he beat me up, offer to split the bounty with InteliCorp, and I come out looking clean—and even if I don't, my corporate lawyers will work a deal. No one will believe Dragon; he's a feeble.

Of course he could feed me false data about the location of the troops and in the distraction get away. For this to work, I'll have to engage with law enforcement fast, and on my own terms.

Dragon

I've cracked the thing so it's clear they didn't have real security on it yet, so win for me. In informationspace, I'm standing on a slick black surface with the device controls splayed out like the cockpit of an exotic shuttle. There's got to be a tuner knob somewhere. I'll need to feed it a starter frequency.

I open a channel out to the airwaves via the machine in my mind, but all I get's static from the jammer and the shortwave channel to the device.

Start with where the law enforcement bands usually live—I know those bands by heart—and look for the on switch to the AI booster program, which is why this device matters at all.

I hear Kyo dragging back over the concrete.

I could sacrifice him. Sing a pretty song about how to avoid the blues and instead lead him right to them, smack! They find him, grab him, look no further. There's a beacon on the device, I could set it, all the evidence against Kyo right there. Sure he could tell them I'm here, but as long as I have sound I can see in the dark, and I'll have a long head start. I'm fast. I don't even need the prototype anymore; I'm inside it. Copying programs. Downloading blueprints, compiled software, fast as thought. I stay connected and I'll know how to avoid the troops in the street too. Listen in anywhere.

Kyo fixes his coat over my shoulders. I need his coat but I don't need him. I don't need anyone. I'm going to get the prototype back to Djen and to the Black Market boss, and Freedom's going to get its food and protection and med supplies and I'll finally get some fucking dinner and we'll all survive another day. Easy enough with Kyo as distraction.

The device's AI finds the blues' bandwidth like the jammer isn't even there.

"All clear at the north entrance, heading to the loading bay."

Aloud I tell Kyo, "Got their frequency. They're at the north entrance, heading toward the loading bay. That mean anything to you?"

"That's where I came in. This factory isn't as big as it seems. They can make it through the whole first floor, but the moment they head up the stairs, our options get limited."

"Don't tell me we're trapped."

"No. But the ladder isn't a compelling way down. It's better for us if they don't make it this far. Do you know how many there are?"

"Five connections on the band. I've only heard two of them talk so far. They're spreading out over the loading bay floor."

He fumbles in his bag, makes a relieved exhale. "You tell me when they're getting close and I'll kill 'em all."

Kyo

"Also," I whisper as the emergency meds make me want to scream, "we should hide the device so if we get caught we can play dumb on theft."

"Like theft is the worst thing they're going to charge me with?" Dragon's voice sneers.

"I won't turn you in."

"Better not since I'm saving your ass."

I turn on infra. He puts the cube in a pile of debris a few meters away. Not a bad hiding spot. We don't make a bad team. Too bad I work alone.

"Shit," he whispers. "This is the part where they're headed this way."

"How much headed this way?"

His barely-audible voice goes coarse as he mimics an older man, "'This building's got a second floor. Su and Hummolt, head that way while we finish the loose ends here'"—he goes back to his normal tone—"that much headed this way."

I nod but he's not seeing me. His eyes are focused somewhere within, or beyond. His head is cocked as though listening.

"Okay," he says, "they're coming in a pair, and they're coming from the north west. The others are staying distant, checking back offices."

I move out. I feel no pain but I'm jagged so full of endorphins and amphetamines I'd even be moving without a head.

I make no sound going down the steps, turning. I see a faint infra shimmer ahead; they've got good heat blocking gear, but my optics are better. I've got to make this look good, like getting caught's an accident, so Dragon doesn't spook.

Dragon

I told him there are two, and technically there are, at least on the ground, but I didn't tell him about the one that risked the ladder to cover the top floor from behind. That one's just meters from me, angling toward the edge of the stairs, looking down. I know where he is, from the radio chatter and his own loudness, so I can stay out of his sight and I'm not making any noise. Doesn't matter what Kyo does to the two on the ground, the blue in the air has him covered.

This is it, the moment to let him get caught, to run.

Everyone turns on each other in the end.

It hurts and it sucks even though we were almost friends but there's nothing can be done about it.

Radio chatter from the blue on the landing: "I can see the target on the ground. Getting in position now."

"What's he doing?"

"Kind of just standing there."

Yeah, not for long, I think like I can transmit too on the radio band, *he's going to try to stab your friends with his nasty knives. And then you're going to catch him, and cuff him, and drag him away and I'll be gone gone gone.*

The in-charge one over the air to the one beside me: "It's that vermin from Mikito L.C. Kill him."

The gun comes up in a whistle of air and the click-snick of the safety.

I fill my lungs.

"KYO! DUCK!"

Kyo

I duck as the shot goes off.

Dragon's heat jets across the platform.

The big, black form of a law enforcer plummets to the ground and hits in sick snap of bone.

Even though we work alone.

Even though I was going to turn him in.

The shimmers of heat near me turn toward his sounds.

I've got my knives in them first.

Andrew M. Reichart's "Space Pirate Stowaway," the longest piece in this volume, is a magnificently weird tale of supernatural intrigue and adventure set on a pirate ship that travels between realities. Andrew and I are the co-creators of the Weird Luck *saga, a collection of interconnected stories and comics (our* Weird Luck *webcomic lives at weirdluck.org, along with various bits of* Weird Luck *prose fiction). "Space Pirate Stowaway" is another piece of the* Weird Luck *saga, so if you're already a* Weird Luck *fan you may encounter some familiar themes and characters here. Pirates are in the business of making incursions, but in this story our scurvy pirate crew falls prey to an incursion by something far worse than they are.*

Space Pirate Stowaway

Andrew M. Reichart

I. Stowaway

Sitting in the shadow of the beacon-tower, Kaza watched the descending ship. Its silhouette floated slowly down through green striations of evening sky, a force-sphere showing faintly blue around it. Black sails billowed. Kaza flicked the tip of her tail in consternation.

As she had learned over the years, a variety of flying sailships could be found in this broken little dimension. The classic Herax longboat. The cloud-ships of the storm giants. Even the floating rafts from the

Circus. But none of these carried force shields. No such thing here, unless brought in from outside. That blue bubble, however, indeed resembled the force shield aboard the *Ace of Shadows*.

She squinted. Impossible to be sure with it backlit against the sunset, but these certainly could be the lines of her old ship. If it were, what remained of the crew? The cursed artifact? The cosmic vampire? Such factors could well interfere with her escape from this dimension.

Kaza stared at the distant prow, reflecting on that fight years ago. Their first visit to 'the Fracture,' this shattered little pocket dimension. The thing from between the stars, all wings and tails, had shone with a delicate blue halo as it phased through the force shield. The crew's blasters, blades, or wizard fire traversed its intangible form without a scratch. Had the fighting among the crew begun thus, shooting one another through it by accident? Or had the vampire seized their minds straight away? Kaza witnessed the fight from its initial moments, and never could decide. Everyone's actions had seemed their own. But such was the way of lloigor mind-control.

While the crew battled one another, the lloigor also unleashed its talons, clawing anyone nearby to pieces. How could it strike but not be struck? Sprinting across the deck, Kaza's boots had slipped in blood, but she sprung off her hands and barely lost stride. She fondly remembered that last moment of finesse. Back when she wore boots. And had hands. She had gripped the demon by two of its talons, and forced the thing back, back, to the prow, out onto the very bowsprit. It clawed at her but she held it fast. There they grappled, poised in stalemate on the narrow spar.

Then a flashing magenta light from behind her, and pain. Over her shoulder she saw the desperate ship's wizard, trying to wield the mysterious artifact known as the Corvus Drive as some sort of weapon, screaming as his body slowly boiled away. But the vampire also withered, wings and talons spasming, burning with purple fire. Kaza burned too. With the last of her strength, she leapt away into the void as the ship vanished. Destroyed or just gone? If it persisted, would it ever find its way back?

Watching this ship descend, Kaza entertained a hope she rarely allowed herself. Perhaps her time in this dimension, severed from the rest of the multiverse and awry to its core, had finally come to a close.

The cursed artifact had stripped her of almost everything. She couldn't speak. Couldn't even shift out of cat-form. The weird, broken magic of the Fracture had little to offer her; restoration would only come to her in a fuller, healthier cosmos. She had wandered year after year, stowing away on flying ships and barges between the countless floating islands. From the once-grand half-cities clinging to their post-apocalyptic remnants of power, to the wilderness islands with their chaos-beasts, to the occasional floating fort or port like this, nowhere had she gained even a glimpse of a way out. She supposed her only chance of egress would come from something outside. A force or entity especially suited to finding its way between worlds, and innately predisposed to bizarre turns of fortune. Perhaps something that had found its way here before. Such as the *Ace of Shadows*. The deal she overheard at the port lounge didn't name the vessel, but the insectoid merchants had referenced enough similarities to bring her here today.

The ship descended to a hover across the expanse of packed earth. Stern still not legible at this distance. Kaza longed to just run and see, but she had best stay hidden till she knew what awaited her. This terrain did not suit stealth. She swallowed her hope, bringing singleminded focus to the simple goal of getting close enough, unseen, to confirm this ship's identity. She slid through the shadows of a wagon, a shed, a small rickety cargo barge, till she could get a clear vantage of the words across the stern. Yes. *Ace of Shadows*.

Take me anywhere, Ace of Shadows. *Anywhere I can resume my form.*

As for the form of the ship, it loomed tall and round, ten yards high at poop and forecastle and only three times as long. Kaza thought of its physique as that of a deep-sternumed pig arching its back, or a tubby whale. Three masts bore a mix of quadrangular and scalene sails, all taut on the astral wind. Tall sides bristled with black blaster cannons and railguns, two dozen each to port and starboard, peering out in staggered ranks. Battlements crowned stern and fore, with smaller guns and other things mounted there. The thing was a fortress.

Many years ago, Kaza witnessed a heated argument on board between two drunk passengers, one insisting that the ship was a *carrack*, the other that it was a *nao*, various crew asserting to no avail that the terms were synonymous and interchangeable. A third brigand offered them epithets and claimed it to be a *galleon*; the other two set upon him and stabbed him and heaved him overboard into space. Tales such as this shored up a general reluctance to offer passage to passengers. But barring psychic vampires or other nemeses,

Kaza's past as a crewmember should help her gain admittance. She felt a flicker of fear. Very eager indeed to confirm which if any hostile forces remained aboard.

Pitch black with black sails and a blank black flag flapping overhead, the *Ace of Shadows* hovered several yards above the unpaved port. Its spherical force field shimmered slightly blue-green now in the light of the setting sun, the bottom few feet of it vanishing without trace where it intersected the ground. Some crew bustled on deck. Kaza dimmed her eye-fires to cast no light and tucked herself into the shadows, gazing at the force field, waiting for the opportunity.

Commotion aboard. Hard for Kaza to see much on deck from this angle. Someone shouted, someone else shouted, chains clanked. Oho: a prisoner was hoisted into view by the chain between his wrists. That seemed unusual. Involuntary chaining was never much the style aboard the *Ace of Shadows*. Not unknown, but hardly typical. Kaza could make out his scream now: "Forgive me, Supreme Commander!" No mistaking it. He said these words several times.

Troubling. This ship could never have a 'Supreme Commander,' not even a captain. Everything ran ad hoc. Not merely as the culture among the crew, but as an existential fact: the ship so infused with Weird Luck, its essence so tangled in the complexities of chaos, that any order imposed on board inevitably unraveled. Often catastrophically for the would-be boss. As much as the ship's soul was piracy, the ship's soul was also mutiny, perpetual mutiny. And bad fortune swiftly befell anyone who sought to rule.

Then came another voice, boisterous, uncannily familiar. Kaza could not place it nor get a view of the speaker's face. "Supreme Commander Kelso forgives nothing!" Followed by the crack of a bullwhip. The prisoner screamed. Kaza imagined the gash opened in the flesh of his back. Another lash. Another. Something deeply amiss here on the *Ace of Shadows*, possibly the worst she'd seen or even heard of. Kaza wondered what the hell this was, exactly, and how long it had been going on. Wondered how soon the weirdings of the ship would correct it, and what form the calamity would take.

She calmly sat and listened to the rest of the whipping. Dozens of lashes. Minutes of them. Screams growing to a frenzied crescendo, tapering off into grievous moans, then quiet. Still the 'Supreme Commander' kept at it, bullwhip cracking into flesh that, from the wet sound of it, must have been quite thoroughly butchered. Then at the Supreme Commander's guffawed orders—surely she knew that gruesomely delighted voice—the crew took down the body and flung it far overboard. Kaza watched it arc out from the rail, a wretched mess of red tatters. The force field flashed bright green as the body hit it and ashes fell through to the pavement. That was new. That looked like the sort of thing that'd be lethal even to Kaza. She pondered the risk, whether by misfortune and malfeasance, of falling overboard at some point in transit. Undesirable. How many years before another interdimensional ship dropped by? A dozen, a thousand? And no reason to believe that ship would be any safer.

She had no opportunity to pursue this line of thought further. Crewmen appeared at the gunwale, one unmistakable from his belly-laugh as 'Supreme Commander' Kelso. She squinted. She knew this man from her last sojourn aboard this ship. Yet, clearly not the same person.

She knew him by the name of 'Doomer,' and he had been a man perfectly capable of brutality and violence, same as anyone else aboard. Armed robbery, bar brawls, normal. Torturing a captive, though, not much. Flogging a crewman? Unthinkable. Had the backfiring artifact contorted him into this monster, much as it had maimed her?

Kaza scrutinized Doomer's face. He looked as happy-go-lucky as ever. A fat, bearded galoot in the same old beaten-up denim vest, wearing the same metal collar of a retractable force-helmet. Spatterings of blood decorated across his arms, face, and clothes. "Take that, ya fuckin' mutineer!" he hollered down at the ashes on the pavement.

A bird caught Kaza's attention, hopping and whistling back near the helm. An albatross. It stopped abruptly and turned its head, frozen in silence. Almost seeming to stare at her with one black bead of an eye. A hint of anxiety fluttered in her. Kaza did have to some extent the nerves of a cat, but this trembling in her belly felt unnatural. The thing flew off and away, out through the force field without disintegration or green flash—no, the shield was simply off. No blue bubble at all. Kaza pondered why, when it was on, it had cindered the mutineer but not the pavement. The albatross swooped overhead and out of sight behind the small rickety cargo barge.

A ten-wheeled wagon rolled up under the *Ace of Shadows*. A wide-belled horn bloomed from the driver's side, and someone winded it, evoking a sound like the call of a mastodon. Doomer and a couple of nonhuman crew leaned over the rail, greeting the wagon with shouts of enthusiasm. Something resembling a vaguely humanoid column of undulating tar outstretched one ropy arm and gestured in the air with—a magic wand? From it stemmed a translucent disc a few yards across. The disc slowly descended, stopping beside the wagon's stern and hovering there at the height of the cargo bed. Insectoid beings piled out of the wagon's cab and started unloading boxes and barrels onto the floating disc.

Kaza poked her head out and surveyed a bit. No sign of the albatross. No cover between her and the truck. Very well, pure stealth was out, so she waltzed up, curious, like a cat, and paused nearby to switch gears and feign disinterest. While three insectoid stevedores loaded up the translucent floating disc, Kaza slipped on unseen and hid amidst the cargo. The albatross clacked and flapped its way noisily down upon a barrel stacked beside her. Kaza slid between wooden crates and flowed away through a little three-dimensional maze of cracks, crossing the disc to duck in a crevice. The disc rose into the air. She prayed it would remain level; she didn't know how much harm she'd really incur if crushed by shifting freight, but she didn't care to find out. That thing hopped around, warbling, webbed talons flapping and scratching across the top surfaces of the cargo. Small as this disc was, the albatross didn't find her, not yet. It seemed to be trying to get the attention of the insectoids. Kaza could pick up some of its words, or its thoughts perhaps, or maybe she was just making up the obvious: 'Don't let that cat aboard the *Ace of Shadows*.' For a moment she glimpsed the albatross through a crack between crates, wings wide in alarm, barking its commands. It got squirted with some sort of insectoid goo and flew off.

The translucent disc alighted on deck and faded away. Cargo all around Kaza shifted frighteningly for a moment as it settled, but nothing fell on her, nor elsewhere either, the vanishment of the floating disc apparently gradual enough that everything gently sank at once. The crew dove into unpiling boxes and barrels. Kaza slipped away and climbed up a ship's ladder to perch on the railing of the poop deck, the ship's wheel fanning around behind her like a throne or halo and providing partial cover from aerial assault. The crew broke crates open to verify inventory, resealing and repiling them in different stacks according to category. Markings were made upon the cargo in glowing paint. A few items got distributed among the crew on the spot, but not the chaotic grabbing and gifting and feasting Kaza recalled from her time aboard this vessel. This was systematic and marked on clipboards. Weird.

The albatross landed a few feet down the railing and eyeballed Kaza angrily. Small for an albatross, now that she got a proper look at it. Barely larger than a gull. *Who invited you on board?* The thought jabbed nastily into Kaza's mind, accompanied by a hostile honk from the bird's throat. Irritating. She ignored it and kept watching the crew. Down on the ground the insectoid stevedores waited patient and motionless. Doomer shouted down meaningless little updates to them like, "Great stuff here guys, we're makin' good progress," and, "Just a few more minutes, thanks fer yer patience," lines so reeking of bullshit that Kaza marveled at things having gotten this far. Who made this deal? How did they manage to get everything on board before paying? Did they pay in advance? What sort of space pirates pay for things in advance? Those clipboards were hard enough to take. This bizarrely blatant swindle was too much. What possible angle could the guys on the ground have here? They just stood there.

Oh, that thing on the truck she took for an inexplicably large sundial. Aimed directly at the hull. Was not a sundial. Ah.

Who do you work for? the albatross honked into her head, a far fiercer jab than the last one. Ow. This habit, irritating enough at first, had now graduated to 'absolutely unacceptable.' Her eyes trailing angry fire through the air, Kaza leapt at that damn bird, snatching tailfeathers in her foreclaws and alighting in the very spot it vacated. The albatross swooped over to the rear railing of the forecastle and glowered at her across the main deck lengthwise.

If you knew who I was, she thought back at the bird as stabbily as she could manage, hoping it stung, *you'd know I don't work for anyone.*

State your business! it trilled. *I hear your thoughts, you're plotting to foment bloody mutiny and kill us all!*

Unable to make head nor tail of this assertion and not especially interested, Kaza ignored the thing and resumed watching the workers. They methodically bunged barrels of intoxicating beverages and tested them with minute sips. Several wooden bins contained candy boxes, with one box duly opened, and each pirate taking one piece of candy. Another set of crates contained odd posable toy wooden humanoids a foot tall. Her old friend Carnage the werewolf-robot, taking no notice of the new ship's cat, nailed one of these toys to the bulkhead beneath Kaza's perch as she watched. Other cargo seemed similarly pedestrian. The entire visible crew numbered six.

She squinted at the incomprehensible image of Doomer carrying a clipboard and actually marking up a piece of paper with a pen. No indication of what might have caused this transformation of his personality into boss, bureaucrat, and torturer. But surely it could have something to do with the backfiring artifact. It saddened her, but she could not rule him out as a foe.

Nor that eerily shapeless thing like an ever-metamorphosing pile of tar, the likes of which Kaza had never seen.

Nor the walking metal statue, whatever it was. Or 'she,' since its sculptor had given it female stylings? Regardless, another potential danger until ruled out.

This lizard man, or snake man, seemed familiar, but not as a member of the crew. Hadn't they attacked a ship of these beings? Certainly suspect.

Kaza knew this blond blue-skinned humanoid in the absurd harness outfit: blustering, arrogant Akathesio. If Kaza could have wagered on a crew member to turn into a power-mad tyrant, it would have been this guy, not carefree Doomer. Akathesio certainly exhibited no domineering arrogance now, though, as he counted inventory.

And finally the werewolf-robot, Carnage, currently half-transformed with wolf-head and hindlegs. Not the most stable footing for unloading crates, one might not be faulted for thinking, but Kaza knew that Carnage had quite powerful internal gyroscopes that, as she'd observed fighting alongside him, enabled him to maintain balance and footing better than the most agile human. Normally Kaza would have been able to rule out at least this one crewmember as a possible enemy: a loyal friend, a principled antiauthoritarian. But if the artifact could change Doomer, it could just as well change Carnage.

Overall, this seemed a typical enough set of transients to populate the *Ace of Shadows*, albeit awfully few. Presumably others lurked belowdecks? The ship mostly flew itself. Perhaps this was everyone.

Once the quick inventory arrived at its completion, Doomer subjected the insectoid stevedores to his enthusiastic relentless banter about payment. He touched his collar, and the force-helmet shimmered around his head in a faint blue sphere. As the tar creature re-summoned the floating disc with its magic wand, Doomer asked if they'd like to come up or should they float the money down, and casually flung a grenade overboard. The ship's force shield snapped on as the grenade landed on the packed earth just beyond it. The stevedores, ready for anything, unleashed their mighty sundial-looking heat ray. The force shield absorbed it effortlessly. There came quite a flash of light from below. Kaza heard the explosion but felt not a zephyr. She walked the length of the rail and peeked overboard. The wagon resembled a burnt-out shell, the stevedores' chitinous body parts scattered well about. But Kaza only got a glimpse before the ground fell suddenly away. The *Ace of Shadows* flew out among the stars and then shifted into the astral plane. The crew diligently loaded barrels and boxes down into the hold.

II. Trapped in Hyperspace

Kaza perched on a bit of railing near the helm. Astral hyperspace arced over and around the ship, a skyful of slow lightning blossoming across quickly whirling sunsets of magenta and midnight blue. The effect ranged upon the beholder from unsettling to terrifying. Even to Kaza, with all her affinity for cosmic chaos; she enjoyed the unease, the hint of existential dread in the face of this unworld serving to enhance the visual beauty of impossible space. Most mortals did not tolerate the view for long, though the sort of folks who crewed the *Ace of Shadows* surely did better than average. This crew seemed to avoid the deck now, however. The Doomer she had known, in particular, loved being surrounded by this wild otherworld, but he was nowhere to be seen. Avoiding this magnificent mind-bending spectacle seemed in step with his other changes.

Apparent escape and breathtaking sky notwithstanding, Kaza's initial rush of enthusiasm soon dimmed. Nice indeed to end her uncounted years marooned in that fractured little dimension. Disappointment, however, seemed too mild a word to describe the feeling of not having the least glimmer of power return to her. Passing into the astral plane should have had at least a partly restorative effect, but she felt nothing. Alarming.

Also alarming: how long they had spent in the astral plane. Normally the *Ace of Shadows* would have arrived somewhere by now, no? Perhaps some dysfunction in the ship's operation parallel to the dysfunction in its operators? Or perhaps she worried needlessly. Misperceiving how much time had passed, misremembering the duration of past voyages. Certainly nothing like a clock on board, and even if there were, reliability of such a thing seemed implausible.

Kaza hated to admit it, but these concerns would cause her much less distress if she had the help of the crew. She preferred scrapes she could get out of on her own, without having to rely on frail, fickle mortals. But if she trusted their competence and intentions, she could rest in the expectation that they'd all manage a way out of this together, as always happened in the past, throughout Kaza's time on board and for centuries before. These people were off, though, every one of them. The sort of wild pirate freaks who found themselves aboard the *Ace of Shadows* typically proved more than capable enough to compensate for their lack of orderliness. This epidemic of obedience, however, filled her with unease. Had they been this far out of sync with the ship's essential enchantments ever since the calamity with the Corvus Drive? How badly frayed had the ship's fate gotten under this infestation of domination, so at odds with its inner nature? Was the artifact still on board, making things worse?

And poor Doomer. The man Kaza had known might beat a foe to death, but he would never *punish* someone. Much less a crewmember. If that Doomer somehow found himself forced into a position of authority, he would lead like the ship's early 'captain,' Jonah Blacklist the Pirate Saint, who never struck a crewmember and avoided killing more than necessary. How badly had Doomer's destiny been skewed by this contortion?

And Doomer has Weird Luck, thought Kaza. *As do I, and the ship, and perhaps others aboard. And that artifact, if it's still around, is among the weirdluckiest things ever known.*

This could get far worse.

Kaza resolved to get the ship to ground somewhere, anywhere, and disembark with all possible speed. Helping the crew along the way, perhaps, if she could without incurring additional jeopardy. Not out of duty, she assured herself, or nostalgia. Merely dispassionate curiosity and aesthetics.

That damn albatross interrupted her thoughts by enervating her with with more psychic jabs. Easy enough to shield herself from any real harm, but that didn't fully silence the thing. The two beasts maintained their posts on opposite railings fore and aft, overlooking the deck between them. *You inexplicable menace*, it honked at her mind. *You fancy you can simply blunder your way onboard and dismantle my balance of power? You flea-bitten furball, I'll cast you into the Walking Abyss!* Etc. Barbed little barrages like this carried on intermittently, not constantly, which made it almost worse. Kaza stared peacefully out into hyperspace sometimes for minutes at a time, only to be blasted by another heave of self-important retching: *No need for a ship's cat! Shoo! Shoo!*

Carnage the wolf-headed android emerged from a hatch and climbed up to the forecastle. As he passed by, he casually swept his hand through the albatross's space, thwacking it as it tried to leap out of reach. "Away with you, bird," came his voice, echoing hollowly. The albatross flapped away and landed on the prow. Its psychic assault resumed, though fading with distance: *You'll not say a word to anyone in the crew for as long as you're on this ship, see? One wrong step and we heave you overboard.* Etc. Tedious. Kaza headed belowdecks, in hopes of blocking out the malicious psychic bird.

She wended her way through the shadows under hammocks, past cargo, silent as always, staying out of sight as she passed the crew. Keeping an eye out for the Corvus Drive, half-expecting to find it displayed on an altar of bones. She descended again, and again.

Solemn as a pilgrim to a remote shrine she arrived at the engine room. An enchanted metal structure dominated the heart of the hold: an enormous cylinder of riveted iron with a hatch like a fallout shelter, etched with glyphs and runes along various seams and edges. Within it chugged a sort of engine powering several different but related local spacetime effects: astral drive, reactionless drive, force shield, inertial damper, others. This metal containment cylinder blocked most but not all of the engine's radiant effluvium. Kaza had always loved the residual shimmer in the aetheric plane down here, finding comfort in the faint undertone of grinding cosmic chaos shed by the small-scale reconfiguration of interdimensional spacetime. Up on deck she basked in the emanations from the glowing arc of hyperspace; this by contrast felt like curling up beside an oven. Back when she had all her powers she loved turning into a cat and tucking herself away in a nook down here, napping in the ambient fizzle of gently fraying reality. Long-term exposure to this sort of environment would do distressing things to mortals, though Kaza being differently constituted never worried about such things before. It crossed her mind now, as she burrowed into a hidden crevice behind the containment unit, that her current state might render her susceptible to these grim radiations. She took this as the last straw. She had comported herself with laudable patience during her span marooned in the Fracture. Skipped diligently from island to island in its endless night, seeking a way back into the rest of the multiverse, otherwise minding her own business and accepting this misfortune as a normal hazard of interdimensional space piracy. Now, upon rescue, she found herself not only surrounded by an unknown quantity and quality of foes, not only without her powers restored, but not even actually *rescued*, being instead every bit as trapped in hyperspace as she had been marooned in the Fracture.

Kaza adjusted her body to better fit into the nook. She shrugged off this small tantrum and resolved to see what she could discern beyond the gates of sleep. Pressing her flank against the cosmic warmth of the containment unit, she rested in the absence of that pestering albatross and drifted dreamward. She didn't relish being stuck aboard this mysteriously accursed ship. Fortunately she was a cat and slept easily. She slunk down the aetheric staircase to the gates of horn and ivory, and through.

First she found herself in the company of that amorphous tarry creature. She sensed its form on the material plane, inert in a trough in a meditative stupor. Superimposed here in their shared aetheric state, its same trough squatted in what looked like its same cabin, but the entity's elastic substance stretched up from it to dance in blobby convolutions. Kaza rubbed her cheek against a corner of the trough, marking it with magical wards to contain this thing if it proved malign. If it noticed her spells of protection it made no indication. She spoke to it. "Why is Doomer called 'Supreme Commander'?"

The being contorted away from her, then menacingly back at her, and away again. "It is what he is."

Irked, she purred back, "How did this come to pass?"

The thing had no response other than to stand there and wobble. Feeling not the slightest bit of satisfaction, Kaza drifted along into someone else's dream.

Here stood the lizard man, no, definitely more of a snake man, one long, slender viper fang inserted into a small glass vial. Around them, a dimly lit square cave of concrete or stone, windowless, doorless, empty. A tiny slurping sound: the fang had sucked the vial to its final drops. The glass fell to the floor with a tinkling. A momentary stream squirted from the fang, then the hollow tooth jabbed into the snake-man's arm, emptying its poison sac into its own bloodstream. Or so this creature dreamed, for some reason. What did its imagination place in that vial? A dream of suicide, or medicine, or intoxication? Kaza wondered what mundane experiences had inspired this vignette in the otherworld. Did the dreams of reptiles differ from those of humans and cats and other mammals? Interesting to ponder, perhaps, some other time. She spoke. "Beg pardon."

It lashed its tail and tugged the fang from its arm, squinting at her angrily. Crouching to one side, it stared at her sideways. With a quick lurch it towered, looming. Then dove entirely over her in a fluid movement, landing splayed across the floor on her other side. She spun to face it. Its head arced up and stared her sideways in the eye. From its velocity Kaza hazarded a guess that this was not a dream of, say, serpent heroin.

"Cat, are you food?"

"Why is Doomer called 'Supreme Commander'?"

The serpent-man rose into four-legged pushup position and shifted from side to side, belly brushing across the floor, eyeing her with a peculiar curiosity whose nature remained unclear to her. She did not much fear coming to any long-term harm if, say, her astral self were devoured by the dream-body of a snake-man pirate, but the prospect still had its unnerving elements. Wishing to amend the dynamic between them, she blasted a flash of fire from her eyes. It jumped to its feet and hung back. Again, emphatic: "Why 'Supreme Commander'?"

"It'ss what he iss. He commandss uss, ssupremely."

"How did this come to pass."

"We were foolss once." It cocked its head wistfully. "We thought we could ssail the sstarss with no leader."

"Indeed, you could," Kaza mentioned, "we did. I did for many years, and the ship did for centuries before me. This has been rather the cornerstone of the *Ace of Shadows*, to mix a metaphor. Only rarely has the ship seen a 'captain,' as such, and usually with disastrous results. As is indeed likely occurring right now." Kaza generally strove to resist the urge to trammel dreams into literal, linear discussions. Such things would rarely proceed as intended. Being unable to speak in the waking world, however, did leave her with a tendency to carry on a bit when given the chance to use words in dream.

"And sso," resumed the serpent man, oblivious that Kaza had said anything, "we came to our ssenssess, and Doomer proclaimed himsself Ssupreme Commander, and thosse who refussed to sswear fealty were casst overboard, or kept and conssumed. Now we are only ssix, including our Ssupreme Commander; but our victory iss asssured over all obstacless, for our leader is flawlesss!"

This thin gruel gave Kaza little of substance, and she found the creature's dreamtime manner odious. So she drifted along. Casting about for Doomer himself in hopes that there she might find some clearer clue, instead she found herself in a foggy, moon-litten moor beside a wolf-headed man brooding on a hummock. He sat clasping his knees, long dog-chin nocked glumly between them. Apparently Carnage had gone to sleep since she saw him on deck. Interesting choice of dreamland. She recognized this version of him as Carnage before he became Carnage, before his death and undeath, and long before his ghost came to inhabit a robot body. She felt wistful for those days long ago when they first crewed together, demon and werewolf. Of course he dreamed of himself as his former self, as he was in life.

No, not quite. His body effused the faintest glow, its flesh and organs showing slightly translucent. From his back streamed two thin luminous mists, as though wings had once grown there. So his unconscious mind envisioned him as his ghost. Kaza felt a pang of bittersweetness. In his dream the wolfman reached out to skritch Kaza's head, but his fingers just passed through her. He slumped further into himself.

Kaza caught herself up. Whatever powerful emotion gripped this ghost of a werewolf, and whatever forgotten ancient history they might share, her priority had to remain her own liberation. Perhaps another day the woes of Carnage would fall within the remit of her concern, but that day was not today. (What was his name before it was Carnage? No, never mind that.) Fending off a growing sense of resignation from her previous two encounters, she again presented her question: "How did Doomer come to be called 'Supreme Commander'?"

Without looking up, the wolfman ghost muttered, "We were no pack. At each other's throats, some of us seeking authority, vying for popularity, exerting social control through shame and manipulation.

The community had flourished to a vibrant crew of fifty-eight souls at its zenith; we robbed from the rich, gave to the poor, assassinated tyrants, skirmished to decisive effect against evil occupying armies and Reality Patrol squads on several worlds. You were there, my majestic firecat chaos-goddess, were you not? Until the cosmic vampire, and the artifact, and our little cataclysm. For such highs bring with them the urge to grasp and possess and preserve the good times unchanged. 'The chase of the dragon' works no better with utopias than with the drug of cocaine. Even we, the wild sort of folk who find ourselves drawn onto the decks of the *Ace of Shadows*, become tyrants and bureaucrats the moment we give in to that grasping. Some of us did better than others at resisting the urge to stamp our lasting dominion into the fabric of reality. But those who step back to leave space for everyone end up only leaving more of a platform for the grandiose, the grandstanders, the climbers. And those who confront the ones who grasp for power inevitably themselves get drawn into counter-grasping. Or they are cast aside by force as surely as those who stepped back by choice. Simply put, good can never prevail."

Kaza could hardly be considered an optimist, but even so she knew his hopelessness to be objectively false, having herself journeyed for years aboard this ship with little or no such grasping and counter-grasping. The Corvus Drive had turned them against one another in a way that had never before tempted them. Yet now she seemed to be getting somewhere. No need to get caught up in course-correction. She allowed him to proceed with his woebegone tale:

"All these forces lurked, at play under the surface, during the decay and attrition after our heyday. After the artifact. After you vanished, my dear cat. There were fifty of us before long, a suicide, an overdose, a duel, the rest just disembarking. A botched raid lost a dozen to Reality Patrol stormtroopers, some dragged back to Denebola, some fragged to infinity. Another wave of disappointed departures followed, leaving us at thirty or so and quite demoralized. That's when it came clear to us all: William 'Doomer' Kelso is the perfect leader. If we unify in our alignment to his vision, and obey him without question, he and he alone can restore our former glory."

"Surely you realize," Kaza cocked her head and ears at indignant angles, "that Doomer is a drunkard, a drug fiend, a brawler, a hedonist, more or less of a nihilist, and is renowned for being jinxed with extremely Weird Luck?"

The ghost of a werewolf cocked its own head in thought. "Really?"

"And now, presumably in response to being granted unchecked authority, he has apparently added to this list of traits-unbecoming-an-autocrat the true unforgivables of bully, sadist, tyrant, and torturer. Perhaps you have observed this?"

Kaza's companion's translucent brow furrowed.

"How many of you are there?" she asked.

"Six of us remain," he replied hollowly.

"You see your folly? Six. This is not working. This is not how this ship works."

He closed his eyes, clearly struggling to comprehend, but somehow blocked. "But the Supreme Commander—"

"Clearly you, and everyone else on board, have been cursed by the artifact we used to destroy the cosmic vampire. As have I been. You must be able to see this." Clearly he did not. "Whatever has possessed you to put Doomer in this position cannot be in harmony with the spirit of the *Ace of Shadows*. You have destroyed our community. It is almost over. Almost everyone has died or left. Perhaps even the ship itself has given up; for are we not lingering overlong in the astral plane?"

The ghost shifted fully into wolf form, curled up on the hummock, and cried itself to sleep within its dream, muttering prayers. Little wisps of ghost-wings still billowed from its shoulder blades. Kaza looked up at the moon. Threads of cloud cascaded past it.

Doomer plonked down beside Kaza in an ornate throne.

Or no, this was hardly Doomer, this caricature, this grotesque. Its overall form amounted to a giant lump, or rather a depiction of a lump, as portrayed through the medium of... stop-motion paper puppetry. The thing bobbed with an unsettling staccato cadence, its paper cutout throne shivering in a disquietingly different pattern. To further complicate the jarring assembly of movements, the bathtub-sized mouth sawed up and down like a guillotine. A yellow crown surmounted its jerking head. Bandoliers half-full of bullets framed its spherical belly. Despite throne and body moving independently of one another, Doomer's hands maintained their unwavering grip on the throne, arms stretching elastically or sproinging back in cartoonish waves.

The chomping jaws emitted little barks of laughter, then words, in a choppy voice like a caricature of Doomer's: "Ha ha, I am King

Doomer! I rule this vessel with an iron fist! All must bow to me! There is either King Doomer! Captain Doomer! Or there is chaos and shipwreck! All hail Doomer!" Kaza noticed, as the mouth slid up and down, a little flicker of orange inside. Something almost threatening to poke out of it. A hooked orange blade for a tongue? She crept around the side of this larger-than-life paper puppet to get a look behind it.

A clanking conveyor belt unfolded out of a hatch in thin air to block her way, delivering a series of roast turkeys right up to the Doomer-puppet's mouth. Identical turkeys kicking their legs in a synchronized can-can dance, one after another, each with the head of a different crew member collaged onto it, every one of them squalling like a baby. Paper teardrops arced through the air to vanish before touching the ground. Dancing turkeys rolled past with the weeping, wailing paper cutout heads of a robot wolf, a chisel-jawed blue man, a snake, a bronze statue, a pulsing black blob. Then a bug—one of the stevedores; another, and a third. Then starting again with the wolf-robot, and the rest in sequence, over and over, Doomer swallowing them whole, each after each, with an announcement such as "Delicious serpent-man" or "Feed me your sorrows, wolfman" or just "Eat eat eat eat eat!"

Kaza managed her way under the conveyor belt and crept around behind the mask. Behind the paper puppet sat an enormous albatross. With the Doomer facade strapped across it for concealment, anything hurled into the puppet's mouth instead got bitten to shreds by the sharp beak, orange tongue flickering, bird muttering, "Delicious. Delicious."

What's this—from somewhere behind the albatross peeked a snake-like tail or two, the web of a batlike wing. Alarming. Kaza tried to creep around behind this next layer of illusion, to glimpse the hidden truth behind the bird, but wherever she went the fleeting demonic features rotated out of sight. Hmm. She faked back and forth, to one side then the other—then leapt straight over the top of the albatross.

She landed in a cement basement, behind the paper façade, behind the bird-body, deeper still somehow even than that secret demon. A chubby thirteen year old freckled redhead kid sat on the grass by the side of the road, sobbing. Young Doomer? Wait—grass? This vision tore away, another illusion: instead young Doomer lay in the basement strapped into an apparatus of articulated black metal. Sobbing. Tears in rivulets. From an infected-looking hole in the side of his head sprouted a pipe with a spigot, pain pouring from it into a gilded goblet held by a robed, hooded monk. This hidden monk gulped down every drop of sadness that dripped from teen Doomer's head. Kaza glimpsed reptilian skin under the robe, a pointed tail, a bit of membranous wing, orange tongue.... Teen Doomer shuddered and sobbed.

Now, Kaza knew as well as any oneiromancer that dreams rarely correlated to the waking world in ways obvious or direct. Nonetheless, clearly something fishy was afoot.

She stood on her hindlegs and stepped up to confront this monk, this cowled dragon-thing. But just as with her quick glimpses of it before, it flickered out of sight again—behind the body of the giant albatross. Kaza opened her mouth to address the bird, but before any words could pass between her four little dagger-fangs, the sneak reintroduced the huge caricature of King Doomer. Kaza raked at the paper cutout, foreclaws stabbing into it and dragging it down. The abruptly-exposed albatross clacked at her, startled: *You mangy alleycat, how dare you? How do you come to be in Doomer's dream?*

"One might ask the same of you." Kaza leapt. The bird reared and battered at her with its wings, to no avail. She pierced its neck with all four fangs and held on. It screamed and reared and battered, and from around its feathered edges scaly bat-wings and snake tails whipped at the tenacious black cat. Heedless she held on with her teeth, and embraced its ribs with her foreclaws, and raked away belly-feathers and shreds of skin with stroke after stroke of her hindfeet. In a heroic effort the bird wrenched itself free, leaving behind blood and feathers on Kaza's mouth and legs. She watched it flap away.

Kaza left young Doomer weeping over his fallen mask and resumed wandering the rest of this local little dreamland while it lasted. One by one she visited each member of the crew in their dreams, and each again, as any new glimpse might reveal a previously unseen facet of the mystery. The blue man, Akathesio the Space Assassin, dreamed of crowds showering him with shallow adulation. She learned nothing from this at first and moved on. The bronze golem dreamt that she flew in arcs and circles in the sky around the ship, and sang. Her lyrics about the freedom of obedience struck Kaza like nails on a chalkboard. She smiled and nodded at Kaza in an unsettling fashion. Moving on. The wolf-ghost, still coiled on its earthen mound, dreamt about dreaming about Kaza's visit. Young Doomer sobbed on the grass, head-spigot and demon-monk and albatross nowhere to be seen. The serpent man hissed; Kaza hissed back and fled. She started losing hope of gaining anything further from these people's unconscious minds. But back in Akathesio's dream—horde of screaming fans gone, leaving nothing but a vast plain littered with bottles and cans—she found him hollering at the albatross, stamping his foot like a child. "You promised I'd get to be captain! You promised!" The albatross looked haggard and bloody, just as Kaza had left it. It eyed her warily then flapped away. Akathesio pointed at Kaza with feeble ferocity. "Bad kitty!"

"Explain to me the bird's promise; perhaps I can fulfill where it has fallen short."

"Really?" Akathesio's eyes widened. Kaza nodded and he told. "It swore to me that if I served the Supreme Commander with perfect obedience, he would burn himself out, leaving me to inherit his dominion over ship and crew. But he just won't die!" He stamped his foot, and tears dripped down his chiseled blue jaw.

Interesting.

One by one everyone in the crew awoke, eventually leaving Kaza to her solitary cat-dreams. Some time later she woke up tucked into her corner next to the drive containment unit, feeling nurtured from warmth and leaky radiation. She stretched. Wandered from the engine room. Languidly she roamed through the shadows. The hold contained the crates stolen from the insectoid stevedores and seemingly nothing else; no sign of the Corvus Drive, nothing she could eat, so she moved on. No one belowdecks, so she checked out what she could of the crew's stuff. Someone had a mirror, tiny table, and chair set up to look almost like a vanity. She hopped up to investigate and found a set of little drawers made of metal meshwork, various implements visible within: combs, tweezers, makeup brushes, little pots of pigment in various shades of blue. Someone else had a wooden bucket of cracked and gnawed long bones. That amorphous thing had nothing but its trough. Kaza took a brief tour of the artillery—a hodgepodge of railguns, chain guns, particle cannons, and ultraviolet lasers, same as usual, more or less. By all indications, a fully functional *Ace of Shadows*... but with the worst crew in its history. And no Corvus Drive. Perhaps it had just done its damage and moved on. Vexing.

The lowermost deck lay like a gully between hillocks fore and aft, a horizon of crenelated gunwales encircling it all. Overhead spread the various sails, any part of crew or ship silhouetted black against the luminous aurora. Sheets and whorls of unearthly color convulsed between the worlds, unfurling across the sky, blooming perpetually like ink in water. The ambient magic in this otherworldly interworld sent current up Kaza's whiskers.

She identified various crew members by outline and quality of movement. No birds. Still, Kaza did not like this. Something about the ship itself felt unwell. Normally it had an air of adventuresomeness, tempered by a wry reticence and infused with dark humor. Now its usual reserve felt like a shell within which the soul of the ship had hidden itself away. Kaza wondered if it might speak to her through the helm.

Supernatural agility notwithstanding, Kaza stayed away from the gunwale, lest a hostile bird or commander or crony should manage to jostle her overboard. This meant crossing the deck openly, in the broad light of hyperspace. Crew scattered about but none nearby and no one between her and the helm. She pondered an innocuous casual stroll, drawing on the pretend-you're-supposed-to-be-there principle. But ended up losing her cool and sprinting across the deck, up the ship's ladder to the poop deck.

At the front of the poop deck, just behind the rail, the ship's wheel jutted like a sunflower from the side of a dull brass pillar. Atop the pillar, the Scrimshaw Skull of Lucky Sharpe, the ship's first 'captain.' The entire surface of the skull teemed with patterns of minute carven runes and illustrations. The ship itself was depicted, and the outlines of continents mapped across its brow, and swirling patterns perfectly echoing the astral spiral array.

Kaza could feel the magic emanating from it. She wondered, if she found a way into the Skull's dead dreams, whether she could steer this ship. With a leap she landed atop the wheel, careful not to let her weight tilt it, and stared into the skull's empty eyesockets. She entered a trance to the hum of hyperspace. Whorls of sound flowed in sync with the writhing aurora gradually resolving into the lilting baritone of the *Ace of Shadows*. The spirit of the ship was not the specific ghost of Lucky himself, nor an ortgeist arising as the ship's essence personified, but a strange undifferentiated aggregate of various souls, spirits, and aetheric emergences, unified into a single voice:

ACE OF SHADOWS: Welcome back, old cat.

KAZA: Please, I pray—tell me that you, at least, retain your senses.

ACE OF SHADOWS: We should hope so, your grace.

KAZA: So should the crew, I imagine, but sadly in their case it is not so.

ACE OF SHADOWS: Ah. You have noticed.

KAZA: How is this for you?

ACE OF SHADOWS: We believe we've never known such grief. That damn albatross.

KAZA: What does the albatross have to do with it?

ACE OF SHADOWS: You jest in poor taste. In any event, that last killing, it seems, has put us over the edge.

KAZA: I intend no jest.... Edge?

ACE OF SHADOWS: With luck, we'll emerge again one day. If we can set things aright.

KAZA: Emerge?

ACE OF SHADOWS: From the astral plane.

KAZA: 'One day.'

ACE OF SHADOWS: The goings-on aboard this ship have finally grown so grossly out of alignment with my inner nature that we cannot tolerate it any longer. That last killing was the last straw.

KAZA: Make no mistake, I detest these goings-on every bit as much as you do...

ACE OF SHADOWS: Isn't it hideous?

KAZA: But you are trapping us in hyperspace because of it? How does that fix anything?

ACE OF SHADOWS: We've given up on fixing. Last straw. We stay here, we can do no harm.

KAZA: I implore you to reconsider.

ACE OF SHADOWS: We cannot.

KAZA: At least drop me off.

ACE OF SHADOWS: You misunderstand, we cannot.

KAZA: Will not.

ACE OF SHADOWS: Cannot. That last brutal punitive murder of a crewman, as punishment for 'insubordination' of all things — something which should not even be possible to conceive while on this ship, thanks to our otherworldly antiauthoritarian auras. After that execution, we were able to make one last transition into this astral realm, outside of spacetime yet adjacent to it. But not again. We are too depleted by the nightmare to be able to awaken.

KAZA: Oh.

ACE OF SHADOWS: Restore the ship's charter, so to speak, and perhaps we'll be able to emerge.

KAZA: From hyperspace.

ACE OF SHADOWS: To any world you like.

KAZA: 'Perhaps,' you say, though.

ACE OF SHADOWS: We may not recover. Never have we been so ill. Perhaps this is a plague from which we'll never get well.

KAZA: Why did you bring up the albatross?

ACE OF SHADOWS: Again, poor taste!

KAZA: In no sense!

ACE OF SHADOWS: Do you not remember?

KAZA: I do not remember.

ACE OF SHADOWS: Do you remember our wizard using the Corvus Drive against the lloigor?

KAZA: Of course. It is the backfiring of the artifact that trapped me in cat form and marooned me in the Fracture. Where is the artifact, pray tell?

ACE OF SHADOWS: Long gone.

KAZA: It did its harm and vanished.

ACE OF SHADOWS: Aye, but begging your pardon, and not to diminish your own loss, the artifact did not cause our woes aboard the *Ace of Shadows.*

KAZA: ...?

ACE OF SHADOWS: The lloigor.

KAZA: The vampire?

ACE OF SHADOWS: ...is not gone.

KAZA: What do you mean, it is not gone? Where is it?

The flat black wolf-robot approached, striding on languid limbs.

It shapeshifted, hands and pelvis rearranging into upright bipedal form: wolf head, wolf legs, man's arms and torso. It reached up to pet Kaza.

"I know you. I dreamt I told you of better days, when our crew flourished; and you revealed to me something I cannot recall, some dark truth that evades conscious recognition. Like a word on the tip of one's tongue. A dream that evaporates like dew upon waking."

This, at least, was no vampire. However deranged, this was her friend. Kaza ruminated on the evanescence of dream-telepathy. Doesn't always stick in the waking world. She bristled at not being able to talk here at all. Nodded enthusiastically, Yes, dark truth, you can remember, but the robot just interpreted it as eagerness for head-rubs. "Good kitty."

Kaza jumped down and tried writing on the deck with her paw, tracing shapes of letters. At first Carnage didn't notice at all. Then, "What's wrong, cat, found a bug? Got an itchy foot?" When he finally recognized this behavior as writing, she began again, spelling out MUTINY. Carnage said, "W-H-U-N-N-Y? Whunny?"

Kaza rolled her fiery eyes and tried again. Carnage crouched low to watch. "Huh?" And again.

Carnage stood. "I remember."

Kaza nodded eagerly.

The tarry black blob-creature grabbed the ship's ladder with ropy extensions and oozed its way onto the poop deck, lurching up in grotesque undulations.

Carnage knelt. "Navigator, look here!"

The Navigator recoiled. "This being came to me in my trough.

No. Came to me in the aetheric plane as I danced my unmaterial meditations. Yes. And spoke to me in my thoughts; but spoke of unthinkable things. If Saint Toad can devour anything, can it eat its own mouth? Something of this design, impossible recursion."

Dammit, thought Kaza. She raised a paw, to no effect.

Carnage glowered down at her. "He said something like that to me, too." *'He'?* Kaza thrashed her tail. "Something about our Supreme Commander, something mutinous."

"Yes!" The ooze poured itself erect as a column and wobbled. "He blasphemed our Supreme Commander!"

Kaza shook her head, brow furrowed. Wrote MUTINY on the deck.

Carnage watched her. "But wait. 'Blasphemy'? Is Lord Doomer one with your Saint Toad?"

"No! What you say *now* is blasphemy!" The Navigator writhed, coiling in one direction, then the other.

Carnage sat. "Then whence did we become so reverent of he who is in truth just our crewmate? Is he not a drunkard?"

The formless being melted from a column into a heap of mush, pseudopods quivering in agitation. "No."

"Yes."

The thing continued quivering for a long silent moment. Then its pseudopods withdrew. "He is, isn't he." The thing was just a heap, slowly oozing outward.

Kaza's ears twitched at this. Might there be hope for this crew? For at least enough of them to stage a successful mutiny? She stood and pawed the air in encouragement. Then drummed the deck with her forepaws in a decidedly unfeline gesture, accompanying them as they continued.

"And a buffoon." Carnage ignored Kaza, despite her antics beside him.

The Navigator rose up again in a tentacled column. "And a jinx."

"A tyrant."

"Sadist."

"Brute." Carnage laughed at finding himself levying this accusation.

"Narcissist."

"Loudmouth."

"And a terrible dresser."

"And...." The wolfen-robot paused and pondered. "How did this happen? How does Doomer hold sway over our minds? That was never among his superpowers."

Indeed. Kaza eagerly nodded, though neither seemed to notice.

The Navigator's pseudopods pulsed. "Indeed, how is it that this cat should come to both of us in our dreams with the same story? How many mind-invaders are there on this ship?"

Kaza shook her head vigorously and made her best attempt at negatory paw gestures, fearing them likely to be interpreted as a desire to play.

"It is desperately improbable." Carnage crouched and poked at the black pad of Kaza's paw. She swatted his finger with a skritch of claws on durasteel.

"Yet neither of us has Weird Luck," said the Navigator.

Carnage continued trying to play-fight with Kaza. "The ship

does. Enough for both of us. As do others on board. And possibly the cat as well."

"Ah, yes. Well, what do we make of this cat's incursions?"

"It seems harmless enough. What if it has an actual message for us?"

"What message?" Akathesio's pale blue face rose past the edge of the poop deck. He mounted the ship's ladder, further announcing his arrival with an ostentatious shake of his yellow mane. Blue muscles rippled in his elaborate leather harness.

Kaza hopped back up on the wheel and petitioned the Skull.

KAZA: Here, this one plots against the Captain. Surely we can bash them against one another.

ACE OF SHADOWS: Surely we of the *Ace of Shadows* cannot. However unsuited to it he may be, Akathesio holds the post of Helmsman aboard this ship, and by the magics of the ship we must obey him.

KAZA: Unfortunate.

"No message," said Carnage.

"You spoke just now of a message."

"Nothing. This is an ordinary cat."

Kaza felt grateful to him for this attempt to distract Akathesio from her, clumsy as it was.

"Helmsman, did you dream of this cat as we did?" The Navigator's burbling contribution pleased Kaza quite a bit less.

Akathesio cracked an eyebrow. "You both dreamt of this cat?"

Carnage interposed himself in front of the Navigator. "The sort of coincidence to be expected aboard a ship blessed with 'super-luck.'"

The Navigator flowed around him. "If this cat is making incursions into our minds, we are all in potential danger!"

"In danger from this cat?" Akathesio casually swiped a blue hand through the air at Kaza. She leapt out of reach and landed back in the same spot, still careful not to tilt the wheel. No need to further meddle with its course just yet, if course it had. And no need to spin the thing out from under her and dump herself to the deck.

KAZA: Might you at least be able to induce the Navigator to keeps its amorphous mouths shut?

ACE OF SHADOWS: Alas, we have no rapport with it to speak of.

"On the other hand." Carnage cocked his head. His voice had an edge to it that hadn't been there a moment ago. "All of this being said, it could also be that this creature crept into my dreams to dissuade me of all hope; to wrongly lay the blame for our tragic losses of crew on the Supreme Commander. Might this cat be some diabolical deceiver, bent to blind us to the one truth, that the Supreme Commander is all that keeps us together?"

The Navigator pulsed in gelid spasms. "Yes! Just as it sought to shake my faith in Saint Toad with its logical conundrums and contradictions!" It lurched to the rail and loomed over it in an opaque wave, shouting down. "Supreme Commander, protect us!"

What was happening here? Kaza felt as though they had shifted into a reality even more nightmarish than the one she already believed herself in. She looked around for any clue of what uncanny turn they had taken. The same astral plane convulsing overhead... the same ship, helm, crew....

Oh, there's the albatross.

ACE OF SHADOWS: The lloigor.

KAZA: Oh gods.

ACE OF SHADOWS: Our wizard managed to disintegrate himself, but as for you and the lloigor — reduced to a small fraction of your power, and trapped in the forms of small animals.

KAZA: But I'm a cat goddess! Why in the name of Azathoth is it stuck in the form of an albatross?

ACE OF SHADOWS: We have most certainly wondered that ourselves.

"There is something to what you say." Akathesio put his hand on his cutlass.

The Navigator continued shouting for the Supreme Commander from various mouths overlooking the rail. Other mouths opened facing Akathesio. "Indeed! We cannot trust this mind-invading cat!"

Carnage flexed his human-shaped hands. "This cat brings inexplicable bad fortune."

KAZA: Clearly this albatross is adversely affecting the

minds of the crew! Including your Helmsman! Surely you can act in his defense without having been ordered to!

ACE OF SHADOWS: This is chaos magic. Our will is subjected to his influence, and his will is subverted by the lloigor.

KAZA: Then at least drop me off of this accursed ship. Somewhere. Anywhere.

ACE OF SHADOWS: Our spirits lie trapped in a sort of catatonia. Only because you can speak in dreams can we speak at all. Our collective will refuses to return us to the world, any world.

KAZA: Then you must awaken!

She hopped onto the Skull, braced her forefeet on a spar of the ship's wheel, and shoved. The wheel swung around. She scampered along it like a treadmill for a moment till she gained purchase enough to hop onto the skull. The sky lurched alarmingly. The helm then swung back the other direction, the mauve astral stormclouds of hyperspace coiling past the other way. Then it righted itself. Kaza saw no indication that any of this had any effect to speak of.

Keeping his footing with acrobatic poise, Akathesio drew his shining cutlass and swung it through the space above the Skull. Kaza dove down to the lower deck, sprinted into the shadows, through a hatch and belowdecks, while Carnage and Akathesio still shouldered their way onto the ship's ladder.

Kaza sped into the galley, hoping it full of hiding places. But there coiled the Cook, the Valusian serpent-man, trying to lure Kaza into cleaver-range. "You will make a tassty morssel for our Ssupreme Commander!" Kaza spotted the albatross looking in the porthole.

She expected as much from the Cook. She fled elsewhere, staying in the shadows, heading for the depths of the ship as swiftly as she could while remaining silent and unseen. She swiftly found herself back in the engine room. Beside the containment unit hovered the bronze golem, cross-legged in the air, one hand resting against its iron surface. She turned her head downward to gaze at Kaza. The golem's eyes flickered with fire.

"I enjoy the energy that leaks through the shielding. It is not especially nourishing, not for me, but it is pleasant." She cocked her head, metal hair scraping across metal shoulders. "Does it nourish you?"

Kaza nodded, admitting it so.

"I envy you."

Kaza scowled, her sneer a mix of condescension and genuine offense.

"Trapped though you may be, you are at least still capable of touching the world with your fiery spirit. Me, I am every bit a fire spirit as you are. But entirely contained." She drummed her fingertips in a series of little clangs. "Unable to touch anything directly. Only with this shell of bronze." She gazed at Kaza. "Have you still not recognized me? Surely you remember Rjufa the Jotunn?"

Kaza remembered that name, but the woman who bore it had a body composed entirely of flame and ash. She had been able to control her temperature quite well enough to safely travel on a ship of wood and hempen rope, though she never went anywhere near gunpowder. Rjufa could also increase her size to as much as fifty feet in height. This metal body of static scale? Not Rjufa, it couldn't be.

Rjufa nodded. "My will is too wild to be dominated by a bird. But this metal body obeys only the Supreme Commander, whatever I might wish." Kaza realized she'd been staring, her face the cat version of 'aghast,' and looked away. This story seemed even sadder than her own. She had suffered mostly boredom, but never despair or enslavement.

"The albatross saw me rightly as a threat. Tricked me into here before I knew his true colors. I understand who you are, Kaza, and I see what is wrong on this ship. For years the albatross has curtailed my body. It cannot touch my mind. Still, I have fallen into simple resignation. But with you here—"

She floated in a circle, singing tunelessly. "Freedom is slavery, slavery is freedom...." Kaza bristled again at these lyrics, but saw them now to be satire concealing grief, not some theme song to willing submission.

Footsteps, voices, and unsettling sucking sounds approached, moments before the arrival of Akathesio leaping down the hatch, cutlass in hand. Behind him came the robot-wolfman and the tarry creeping ooze, rendering the small room rather crowded. Kaza held her ground but gauged escape routes. None.

Akathesio pointed with his sword. "Hand over that cat!"

Rjufa paid him no heed, and instead addressed the robot. "Carnage, you cannot want this. Any of this. You are also a trapped spirit, like us. You also can remember, sometimes, how to long for liberation. You know our ways aboard this ship have gone awry. But whereas I had lost heart, now with the return of Kaza I have regained it. We can restore the rightful disorder to our crew. It is time."

Carnage cocked his head.

Akathesio stared at him, a nearly cartoonish look of outrage on his chisel-jawed face. He gestured angrily with his sword. "Do you hear this mutinous talk?" He stabbed the sword point-first into the ceiling. With a tug he wrenched it free and flourished it again. "Do you? Attack! You must attack her, robot to robot!"

"I cannot follow a word of what either of you are saying." Carnage shook his head, ears clacking. "We must investigate this cat! Determine if it is indeed a threat to us or our ship!"

Akathesio prodded the Navigator with his sword. "Tell your friend he's verging on mutiny himself!"

The Navigator recoiled. "How now! I am not infinitely immune to stabbing, how are you so certain that you understand and comprehend these limits?"

"I have seen you stabbed many times, Navigator."

"Even so, why so insistent with this blade?"

Akathesio wound up and stabbed the Navigator again, deeply, causing no visible harm but quite a reaction nonetheless.

"Helmsman!"

"Navigator! Tell your friend!"

"Tell me yourself," said Carnage, grabbing the blade of Akathesio's sword in both hands and wresting it out of his grip. Kaza purred a chuckle.

"My sword!" Akathesio tried grabbing for the hilt, but Carnage kept the blade facing towards him. "Give me my sword!"

"Give it to him," boomed Doomer's voice. He stomped down the ship's ladder. Upon his arrival, the engine room worsened from close quarters to oppressively cramped. The albatross gripped his shoulder, ungainly and absurdly large, but Doomer showed no awareness of any awkwardness. His force-helmet surrounded his head with a faint blue shimmer.

Carnage handed Akathesio the sword.

"Explain this cat!" said Doomer.

Kaza looked up at the albatross. It stared at her sideways with one reptilian eye.

"I cannot, Supreme Commander," said Akathesio. "These two say it came to them in dreams and talked mutiny. The robot disobeys direct orders. All very disturbing. We should kill the cat. It's bad luck. And even if we're wrong, who cares, it's just a cat."

Kaza could see him smiling inside, wrapping Doomer around his finger as prelude to sticking that sword into his back. Possibly soon. Kaza didn't want that. She tried fathoming his plan. Did he have one? She only sensed free-floating guile and hunger, without a lick of strategy.

But the albatross grabbed her attention again, stabbing words into her brain: *Nice bit of trickery with the dreams. But none of us will be going to sleep again, not until you're long gone.*

That seems improbable, replied Kaza, getting her psychic shield up a moment later than she would have liked.

"So kill it, dude," said Doomer.

Akathesio lunged. Kaza sprang over his blade to embrace his

head, her four claws latching onto his ear, cheek, neck, and chin. Digging in, she snapped at his eye, fangs grabbing his eyelid and piercing into it. She tasted chalky eye shadow. With a shriek Akathesio swung at her with his free hand. She leapt away, not quite able to make him hit himself in the face but nearly, and perched at the top of the ship's ladder. He stood there shaking, pressing his hand to his wounds one by one, staring up at her with both eyes—one ringed with swollen flesh and swathed in blood, but eyeball apparently intact. Akathesio waved his sword in her direction, grunting and spluttering.

Doomer gave a belly-laugh, Carnage and the Navigator following suit. The albatross cawed. Rjufa snapped her fingers in applause with a small tinkling sound like silverware. Kaza's tail swept back and forth.

"Carnage." Doomer nodded up the ship's ladder. "You git it."

"No, sir."

"You gotta be fuckin' kidding me. You gonna make me make the golem do it?"

"That cat has fires for eyes. Its powers are not limited to claw/claw/bite. My workings may be susceptible. And will surely not heal as swiftly as blue flesh."

"Then our best bet," Doomer brought forth a plastic bag of white powder, "according to our good friend Mr. Albatross, is to keep it outta our dreams, by whateverthefuck means necessary." His force helmet vanished with a touch at his collar. He drew a broad-bladed knife, tipped a mound of powder onto it, and held it up within reach of the albatross on his shoulder. Kaza watched, enthralled by the grotesque scene, wondering whether she should intervene, and if so, how. She decided against, for now, suspecting this amphetamine tactic might backfire more than benefit her foes.

With its bill the albatross sculpted two fat rails of powder. Doomer dipped his nose to them, snorted one, then the other. Sniffed repeatedly at the air, grunting like a beast. Repeated the process and held the knife out horizontally to Akathesio, who followed suit. As did the Cook after its fashion, mixing the powder with a few drops of venom, sucking the solution off the surface of the blade back into a fang, and injecting it into its arm.

Doomer offered the bag to Carnage. Carnage looked at the bag but did not take it. "I am a robot."

Akathesio took the bag from Doomer and shook it in front of Carnage's snout. "Snort it anyway!"

Carnage spoke with genuine longing. "It is with my deepest regret that I can assure you this will not work."

"Snort it anyway! Maybe it can affect your electrical nervous system."

The Cook barked a little reptilian laugh. "Ssurely you jesst—or iss thiss truly how you think thingss work?" It ingested another fangful of speed-venom solution. Twitched its head and lashed its tail jerkily. "Who exssactly deemed you qualified ass helmssman?" Akathesio narrowed his eyes at the serpent-man but did not reply.

The Cook then dove without warning at the Navigator, biting deep into it. The Navigator shrieked, pelting the Cook with an array of ineffectual pseudopods. The Cook pulled away, dipped the knife into the bag of powder to coat it thickly, and cut a swath diagonally across the Navigator's front. The long slash closed immediately. "If injectionss have no effect, perhapss thiss will."

"Your cuts and chemicals but fill me with outrage!" The Navigator wound up in a wave, ready to engulf the Cook.

"Enough!" Doomer took the bag of powder back from Akathesio. "If you won't make sure that you can't sleep, how can you keep that cat outta your dreams? How do we know you aren't mind-controlled by it?"

Kaza gritted her teeth at this irony, a habit that better suited the humanoid jaw in which she had developed it. If she could just get out of hyperspace, and find a world well enough to help her start to recover, she could have nothing to do with these lost causes and villains ever again.

Akathesio waved his sword around overhead in the cramped room. "We can never trust! If they won't do our drugs, it's the brig for them or death!"

The Cook extracted a small glass sphere from one of its numerous belt pouches. A quick little sideways toss and it shattered against the bulkhead beside the Navigator. Heavy tendrils of mist unfurled across the tarry creature's undulating surface, freezing any part of it motionless on contact. The Navigator reached out to no avail. Screamed "HELP!" and "Mercy!" once each. But in a moment there remained only a sculpture like a barrel of molasses emptied from a height all at once, frozen in mid-splash.

Kaza dove down onto the Cook's head, clawing. The serpent-man flailed about, trying to pull her off, lashing her with its tail. This time she managed to coordinate her dismount so the Cook whipped itself in the face. Back up the ship's ladder, Kaza sat on the edge of the hatch licking blood from her paws.

Carnage flew at Akathesio, pinning him against the bulkhead with steel claws at his neck. Over his shoulder he snarled, "Antidote!"

"Uncle! Uncle!" Akathesio's cutlass clattered to their feet.

Doomer placed the muzzle of his pistol against the base of the wolf-robot's head. "This'll hurt, even though you're a robot. A lot."

"And your henchman will die nonetheless, drowned in blood!" Carnage had two razor fingertips carefully alongside either side of Akathesio's windpipe. "Antidote!"

"Give him the antidote!" Akathesio's blue forehead dripped, wrenched with panic.

Doomer kept his gun placed at that seam between head and neck. "Give him the antidote."

The Cook hissed irritably and flung another glass pellet at the frozen black fountain of the Navigator. Another cloud gently lilted upward, melting every pseudopod it touched. The Cook watched, narrow streams of red blood streaking its green-scaled face.

"Mercy!" cried the Navigator again. Then stretched out some pseudopods. "Oh. I'm free."

Carnage got off of Akathesio, who retrieved his sword and scampered up the ship's ladder. As he slid past Kaza he looked pointedly away from her.

Doomer backed his way up the ship's ladder, albatross bobbing on his shoulder. As they emerged through the trapdoor, Kaza's eyes met those of the albatross, nose to nose. *You will lose, kittycat. You and your people. This ship is mine, all mine.*

Kaza swatted the albatross across the bill, knocking its head into

Doomer's face. Doomer swept Kaza off the edge of the trapdoor. Kaza floundered in the air and landed on her feet down in the engine room. The Cook followed Doomer up the ladder, long tail swishing back and forth across the small room. Then they slammed the trapdoor and pulled something heavy over it.

III. Mutiny in Heaven

Kaza curled up in the space between the reactor and the bulkhead. Carnage shifted fully into black robot wolf form and lay protectively beside her, similarly curled but ten times her size. Bronze Rjufa hovered nearby. The Navigator huddled in the corner, shuddering occasionally with the aftereffects of the serpent-man's paralytic poison gas. Occasional footsteps thumped past overhead.

Kaza hoped that some of them at least would sleep, so she could visit them in dreams. She drifted into her own hypnagogy. Rjufa appeared to her in her mind's eye, or on the aetheric plane, gleaming brass wreathed in flames rather than dull corroded bronze. "I will keep watch."

"How, if you are also sleeping?"

"I dissociate continually. Never fully awake or asleep. Neither word applies."

Now more than half asleep, Kaza could hear the Navigator complaining in the corner, something about being away from its trough. She gave it no heed.

Without quite realizing until it had already happened, Kaza

found herself in an empty, bleak moor. A small hillock with a gnarled dead tree. No sign of anyone, but she could sense a presence somewhere. The tree? No one in its branches. Among gnarled roots, Kaza found the black convex dome of what resembled a mostly-buried cannonball. "Carnage." No response. Kaza resented having to do this. She clawed up the dirt alongside the robot's head till she exposed a pointed wolfen ear. "Carnage. Listen. We need strategy, and in the waking world you are not doing too well."

The head of black metal rose smoothly up out of the ground, slowly, revealing another large pointed ear, eyes, most of a snout. It stopped at the chin. "I hide because I know not what to do. This is untenable."

"That is because whenever you are awake, the albatross is whispering evil in your mind." Kaza batted dirt out of his other ear. "You know Doomer is wrong for this ship. Any captain is. That has been so for centuries. But the albatross keeps telling you the only 'sane' way forward is with a strong leader."

"We have never been so lost." Carnage tucked his head back into the dirt a little. "So few of us. And so at odds with one another. I fear we will have worse bloodshed."

"Those who covet power do not relinquish it willingly." Kaza wished the ghost inside this killing machine weren't so bereft. He could finish this single-handedly, if he would just focus. His miasma of depression threatened to infect her too.

"Akathesio was my comrade," said Carnage. "We fought and worked and made merry side by side."

"He plots deviously to replace Doomer, and I daresay he holds some promise of being an even viler tyrant himself." Kaza allowed her excitement and anger to radiate sharply at Carnage. "You know this is the problem. This authoritarian tendency. The *Ace of Shadows* cannot abide it. This is why we're trapped in hyperspace. We cannot escape until we mutiny."

"This is dreadful. The worst days yet." Carnage closed his eyes.

Damn it. "It can be the end of the bad days. But it will take a little ruthlessness. They are too strong united. If we can pit Akathesio and Doomer against one another, we may have a chance to prevail. Unless you know a way to liberate Rjufa from Doomer?"

"I do not." Carnage opened his eyes. Looked at Kaza a moment. Rose up entirely out of the ground. "Very well. I will try."

Thank goodness, thought Kaza. *Let's hope his willingness translates into tactical competence.*

But Kaza found herself alone. Carnage had woken himself up. Even the moor had vanished: around her, the walls belowdecks pressed in. Not the engine room, though. *How?* Ah, Kaza still dreamed. Here the astral Navigator danced in its aetheric trough. Kaza approached. "Navigator, by allowing your mind to be influenced by a bird, are you not guilty of idolatry? How can this albatross guide you to fulfill the will of St. Toad? Is this albatross, or Doomer for that matter—are they even adherents? How can you take orders from infidels?"

The Navigator flowed to right and left, welling up at opposite ends of its meditation trough. A pair of curving pillars rose, jiggling, gelid tar flowing over itself in continuous upward movement, slow twin fountains of sentient muck. "How, cat, can I know whether to trust your incursions into our minds? How to know whether your way will lead us less into harm's way?"

"'Into harm's way'? Ninety percent of your crew is gone, and you contemplate whether or not this psychic vampire might be dangerous?"

The Navigator recoiled, horns merging into a lump in the middle of the trough. "Should we not act in the interest of the greater good? Could not your way be even worse?"

"Again, nonsense. There is no 'greater good'; there is only an infinitude of lesser goods. Further, however: what could be worse?"

The Navigator rippled in its trough.

"Release your misplaced loyalty and cease dithering. Admit the self-evident."

The Navigator settled. "Aye."

♦ ♦ ♦

The Navigator had melted to a thin layer of slime coating everything underfoot. Kaza awoke to find the edge of its amorphous flesh flowing up against her hindquarters. She leapt atop the iron containment unit and hissed. Rjufa the golem, floating cross-legged nearby, looked over her shoulder at Kaza. Kaza scowled at her and curled around to examine her fur. No sign of the slightest residue; barely even a scent. Good. Even so, she hissed again at the Navigator, which now scrambled in an irregular series of gurgling flops to recoalesce. The moist commotion awoke the robot, which leapt up to its four feet, then ratcheted itself bipedal. "Ugh! Yuck!"

"Apologies, apologies." The Navigator shivered its way into the form of a large opaque blob. "This is why I use a trough at rest. And why I wish to resume the peace and quiet of normalcy aboard this ship, including proper access to my trough, as soon as possible."

Rjufa laughed.

With consternation Carnage inspected the synthetic pads of his hindfeet one by one. "Why are you even on board this ship if you crave normalcy of any form?"

"Indeed, how did the ship even let you aboard?" Rjufa continued chuckling with the soft sound of distant bells.

"Never mind that!" The Navigator coiled one direction, then the other. "Never mind any of that! May Saint Toad swallow you whole!"

"He wouldn't like it if he did," said Carnage.

"Navigator," said the golem, no longer laughing. "You are with us?"

"Aye."

"So you understand what you must be ready to do?"

"Aye...." The Navigator sounded less enthusiastic.

Carnage gnashed his teeth like a mechanical punch press. "We will likely find ourselves forced to kill some of our crewmates. Though I hope we can spare them, as we might be able to get them back." He clacked claws in and out of his fingertips. Kaza wondered why representations of wolfmen so often had claws to fight with, even retractable ones, when real wolves and werewolves did not. She felt a twinge of canine infringement upon her felineness. But glad enough for Carnage to have them at his disposal if need be, and for him to have discretion over whether or not to deploy them.

"We shall see." Rjufa began climbing up.

"Wait, where are you going!" The Navigator flung a pseudopod around Rjufa's ankle.

"The sooner we resolve this the better. Why delay? Do you need further rest?"

"No—" It withdrew the tentacular glob.

"Did you not just rest?"

"Yes — just... some time to transition, please! Or better yet, some time to strategize?"

"Follow my lead." Rjufa continued up.

Carnage waited below her. "Shouldn't you levitate, so I can climb?"

Rjufa lifted the trapdoor easily enough, shoving aside whatever crates had been stacked over it. She rose halfway out. A deafening bang and clang rang out, and she tumbled down onto Carnage. They landed in a pile, then just as quickly jumped to their feet. Rjufa worked her shoulder. A gleaming divot had been taken out of her collarbone.

"Waiting for us," said Carnage, leaping up the ship's ladder. Rjufa flew through the hatch after him. Shots rang out, several of them. Then quiet.

The Navigator flowed up the ladder and peered out. Then hurled itself up and through. Kaza followed.

She first spotted the faintly shimmering sphere of Doomer's force-helm. He and Akathesio lay on the ground. Across the cabin, Carnage faced down the cornered Cook. No sign of the albatross.

Rjufa floated with a heavy slug thrower in each hand. "You are likelier to harm the ship than us." She crushed the guns, barrels flattening in her grip, stocks splintering. "You would have done better with one of the ship's railguns."

"Yes." Akathesio jumped to his feet and sped towards the gun deck. Rjufa threw one broken slug thrower at his legs and the other at his back, tripping him up and knocking him down.

The Cook dodged past Carnage and sidewound over Akathesio's pained prone form, snake-belly flattening him face down. The Navigator slid through the ship like a faster serpent still, catching up to the Cook before it reached the gun deck, catching it up in its innumerable amorphous paws. The satchel of poisons slid across the floor to tumble down the hatch to the engine room. The Cook coiled and thrashed at the formless, gelid flesh of the Navigator, snatching away handfuls and mouthfuls but unable to lessen its clutching and smothering. The Navigator pulled and twisted the Cook's humanoid arms apart joint by joint. Suction, torque, and crushing pressure pried away musculature from skeletal moorings of serpentine ribs and vertebrae. The Cook's hissing shrieks resounded in the small space for a long moment, then gurgled to a sudden stop. Rending and sucking sounds continued awhile.

Akathesio found Rjufa looming over him, blocking him from the gun room. He fled in the other direction, flung himself up on deck. Doomer joined him, pursued by the robot wolfman and Rjufa, Kaza taking up the rear.

Up on deck, Carnage tackled Akathesio. Claws clicked out at his blue neck. Doomer stood again with a gun at the back of Carnage's head, bird on his shoulder clacking its bill against his force-helmet.

"Golem, kill this goddamn robot."

"Wait!" said Carnage.

Doomer held up his free hand and Rjufa froze. "What. What the hell is it."

Carnage pleaded to Akathesio. "Comrade, come back to us. Cease plotting to take Doomer's place and leave him dead or marooned. We must banish this bird, and the captaincy itself, not just this captain."

"Plot against me?" roared Doomer.

"For the good of the ship!" Akathesio delivered this unconvincingly.

Doomer stomped on the back of Carnage's hand, stabbing blades deep into the blue throat. Carnage pulled his hand away too late, only cutting further. Red blood geysered. Doomer gawked, stunned at the reality of what he'd done. Carnage pressed his hand on Akathesio's neck for a moment, to no real effect. They looked into each other's eyes. Blood sprayed between black metal fingers.

Carnage leapt up and grabbed Doomer, pinning him to the deck, hand firmly pressing against the face of his force-helmet. The albatross flew up to the rail, shrieking. A shot rang out. Carnage flinched but retained his pin. Rjufa, struggling to resist, punched Carnage in the side of the head with a clang. Carnage poised all ten claws at Doomer's throat then, under the collar of his helmet, Akathesio's blood still dripping down them. "Strike me again and you will die! Doomer, you weakling, why did you let this vampire make use of your lust for power? How could you let this monster destroy us?"

"What the—what the fuck?" Doomer craned to see the albatross. It rocked back and forth, gripping the rail. He looked around at dead Akathesio. Tears spilled from his eyes while ranting flooded from his lips. "I didn't do anything, what happened? Oh gods I'm so sorry, no, I didn't do it, I don't even remember...." His words flailed on and on.

And, as sometimes happened aboard the *Ace of Shadows*, the translucent form of Akathesio's ghost rose slowly from his body and hovered above it. His voice echoed hollowly. "Ah, comrades, what a nightmarish end we have come to!"

Then many hands reached up out of the deck to grab hold of his aetheric form. Silent, aghast, he did nothing to resist as they pulled him down. *Welcome aboard*, came ghostly voices. More hands pulled on him, *Welcome aboard*, until he was gone.

The albatross looked down from above, hopping from foot to foot on the rail by the helm, bobbing its head jerkily. Kaza recognized the symptoms of the Jamf Paradox, that incapacitating state where a psychic vampire cannot resist feeding upon circumstances that are otherwise detrimental to it. *Good.* The albatross would not gain enough power to break itself out of the loop, not from this feeble tableau of grief. The spasm will just fade, leaving the demon wounded and spent. Kaza's heart swelled. She had won. The fight wasn't quite over—that albatross could not be trusted while it lived. But its reign had collapsed.

Doomer wailed and ranted and still Carnage pinned him, equally ignoring his pleas and threats and ramblings. For a very long while they remained, Doomer helpless, gradually crashing deeper and deeper into misery as the speed wore off, his speech slowing and growing even less intelligible, till it drifted into a blubbering muttering and finally sleep.

Kaza curled up on his chest then, and visited him in dream. They spoke for long hours, wandering a gray twilit moor, sun never rising nor setting but perpetually lurking beneath the horizon in its own dead dreams. Doomer and Kaza walked in the gray chill, and Kaza in time reminded Doomer of who he was. Pointed out which strange thoughts the albatross had forced into his mind day after day, all day, for years. Freed from the direct input of the demon bird, Doomer began regaining himself.

And in time he agreed, as did the remaining exhausted dreamers, to hold council together, in traditional *Ace of Shadows* assembly.

All the while, the albatross kept itself to the prow, twitching and preening.

IV. Democracy Isn't

Carnage, the Golem, and the Navigator stood facing one another on the deck. Doomer paced around restlessly, but with a trudge in his step now that he no longer had the drug driving him. Kaza sat by the robot's heel. The albatross lurked up on the rail by the helm. Kaza gave the bird a hostile stare. It seemed well again. It cocked its head at her.

The crew talked interminably. Kaza's tail twitched at these depressing proceedings. How could so many words go back and forth and around and back, amounting to nothing more than the two statements:

1. to escape hyperspace, we must restore our freedom from hierarchy
2. but if we're restoring consensus, I veto the call for me to step down as captain

in an infinitude of permutations. Kaza bore with this tedious display of mediocre rhetoric as best she could. In time, as this argument unfolded, she got the distinct impression that Doomer's words seemed not entirely his own. 'Praxis'? 'Methodology'? 'Management'? The debate intensified. Bodily postures grew increasingly hostile. Not like yesterday; the miasma of resignation and exhaustion flowed around the participants of the assembly like heavy fog. Words grew harsh, but no one had the initiative to throw a punch. Just talk endlessly tumbling, the four of them circling in an inescapable rut, vitality gradually draining from them. Doomer stood there shuffling back and forth from one foot to the other. Carnage swayed with the effort of shouting at Doomer. The Navigator burbled in a heap, occasionally raising a pseudopod like a polite index finger but failing to get a word in. The golem sat down on the deck and muttered.

Kaza watched the swooning albatross, its webbed talons curling against the rail, eyes drifting shut, head swaying around in a circle. For a moment she almost felt a pang of sympathy for the thing. So desperate, so infinitely hungry, unable to resist exploiting even this pathetic meal of a few damaged dregs. Embarrassing. She hoped she herself would never grow so undignified.

Kaza crept through the shadows, silently climbed atop the ship's wheel, and dove down at the albatross. She grabbed its throat in her jaws and hauled it down to the deck, landing on her feet, angling the albatross to land on its neck. Arterial blood poured past Kaza's fangs and into her mouth. The vampirous soul, resplendent with vitality from the crew, soared into her. Aetheric essence ignited her astral body, causing it to blaze with power. She hadn't felt this wholeness, this peace of mind, since the calamity with the Corvus Drive had trapped her in cat-form. She drifted into euphoria—

The monstrous demon soul broke away from her, a gruesome, misty coil unspooling itself out of Kaza's mouth. Indeed, the haunted *Ace of Shadows* liked making new ghosts. She clenched her fangs, unwilling to relinquish it all. Her fur crackled with static electricity, the small portion of the thing's soul that she retained burning inside her. Wild magic surged through her in fiery pulses. Flames gushed from her eyes and mouth.

The smoky dragonlike figure spread its translucent wings like majestic sails. "Even in death I cannot die! As long as you remain aboard the *Ace of Shadows*, you will never escape me! And the *Ace of Shadows* remains forever trapped in the astral plane!"

Fair enough. Kaza leapt onto Doomer's head. He fumbled to wrench her off of him without raking off any of his face. She deftly poked one claw into the release catch for his force helmet and leapt overboard with the collar in her teeth, activating it as she plummeted. The force helmet formed around her like a fishbowl. A blue-white flash on contact with the ship's force shield, and she passed through unscathed.

Kaza tumbled through lashing coils of purple mist. Summoning all the power she had drawn out of the dying cosmic vampire, and every iota beyond that she could muster, she reached her head and forepaws out of the force helmet. White sparks and jagged currents crackled on her fangs and claws. She wound up and struck out, clutching at the fabric of reality and tearing.

She fell through.

The force helmet rolled down a rubbish-strewn alley. Clunked to a stop against the back stoop of someplace. Kaza dizzily extricated herself and deactivated the small spherical force shield. Arranged the too-big collar around her neck with some amount of difficulty.

"Whatcha got there?" came the voice of the being sitting on the concrete stoop. Pale, hairless, humanoid but not exactly human, wearing an apron and smoking a cigarette. "Roll around in an invisible bubble?" Its gleaming emerald eyes flashed.

"Ah." Kaza looked around for other observers. "It's just a space helmet."

"You can talk, huh? That's uncommon." The humanoid took a drag of its cigarette. "So you from space?"

Kaza froze. "I can talk!"

"Yeah." Smoke poured forth between alabaster lips. "Pretty uncommon hereabouts."

Kaza the cat sat and looked up at the being on the stoop. "Know anyone who's good at getting rid of curses?"

"Hmm." The pale being stood. "Maybe. C'mon in." It flicked its cigarette butt into the alley. Kaza followed it inside.

Ada Hoffmann is the author of the mind-bending short story collection Monsters in My Mind*—and also the author of this next story, a paleontological Victorian steampunk fantasy adventure yarn entitled "The Scrape of Tooth on Bone." "The Scrape of Tooth on Bone" has everything a proper story ought to have: intrigue, suspense, mayhem, treachery, a thoroughly charming queer and autistic heroine, steamy romance, feuding scientists, explosions, dinosaurs, giant robots, and of course all manner of incursions.*

The Scrape of Tooth on Bone

Ada Hoffmann

I hadn't had a minute, since getting off the airship, to put down my carpet bag and close my eyes. But Dr. Clarence Fullerton was intent on showing me the entire encampment before I rested. He never paused to allow me a word in edgewise, although at that point I was so exhausted I couldn't have said much anyway.

"Past the mess tent," he explained, "we have the path down into the canyon, and the fossil-rich ridges themselves—of course, you won't be digging there, but I'm sure you can imagine the wealth of discovery available. Go ahead and feast your eyes."

The sunset over the rugged river valley had turned everything pink, but of course I was more interested in the robots. The encampment crouched at the edge of the canyon, only four tents and assorted machinery. Robots outnumbered humans: four Whitman-

651 walkers to carry the plastered-up fossils, one more to carry personal supplies, and a couple of convenience items such as a broken Hamilton-Smith, which was supposed to wash and press clothes with hardly any human assistance. And then this thing looming up in front of me, which I did not recognize. It was large enough for two people to stand in the cockpit, and it sported a considerable array of gun turrets.

I wondered why they needed a machine like that out here.

Dr. Fullerton followed my gaze. "Or, yes, you may feast your eyes on that, too. It's a KD8102 special from Lovell & Grimm. One never knows what might come calling, you see. Grizzlies, bandits, rival researchers... But in any case, you won't be touching the KD8102 just yet, nor its ammunition cases. It will be your job eventually, but only once you've proven yourself.

"The less, ahem, martially oriented machines are yours to examine as you will. Now, I'm given to understand you've worked at fossil expeditions before, but you haven't worked at one of *my* expeditions, so I hope you'll forgive me if I give you a short lesson in fossil handling before allowing you to work on the Whitman-651s. May I schedule that for the first thing tomorrow morning?"

"Yes," I said weakly. The airship ride had been loud and shaky, and his voice scratched at my ears. He simply wouldn't stop talking.

"Most excellent." Dr. Fullerton ushered me into the comparative darkness of the mess tent. "Now I'll introduce you to our fine colleagues. Miss Howe, may I introduce Dr. Harold Kerr and Mrs. Hattie Bond Cunningham. Harry and Mrs. Cunningham, may I introduce Lillian Howe..."

I stared at Mrs. Cunningham even longer than I'd stared at the KD8102.

Out west, the social rules were loose for lack of civilization, and I was not the only woman who ever worked at fossil hunts. I had even been on speaking terms with two of the women at Dr. Mandeville's camp. But neither of these women approached the perfection of Mrs. Hattie Bond Cunningham. She had beautiful features, but more important than the features were the neatness in the way she held herself and the brightness in her eyes, suggesting intelligence, warmth, efficiency. She wore practical outdoor clothes, like me, but they were all in black bombazine, with a widow's cap—the veil shortened, presumably so as not to get in the way. Mr. Cunningham must have died a little over a year ago.

I felt sorry for Mr. Cunningham. Of course he was probably very happy in the spirit world, but if I were him and had a wife like his, I would have wanted very much to stay alive so I could hold her.

Dr. Kerr, a tall thin man, bowed and muttered a greeting. Dr. Fullerton kept talking and talking, and I think I was supposed to introduce myself to the others, but I couldn't keep my mind on any of it. Mrs. Hattie Bond Cunningham looked at me in concern.

"Are you all right?" she said. "You've gone positively white."

I fluttered my hands a little as I groped for an appropriate response. "Oh," I managed eventually, "I'm feeling a little faint, that's all. The journey here was tiring."

"Faint" is the safest way to say it: delicate, ladylike, and proper. "Faint" is much better than the truth, which is that if I get too overwhelmed by too many people talking to me, I will begin shouting and perhaps even bite them, even if they are beautiful like Mrs. Hattie Bond Cunningham.

They led me straightaway to a quiet tent, instructed me to keep my head between my knees, and left me to calm myself down.

It really was a nice camp. Not too big, and lots of interesting machines. For a minute, I felt sorry that I'd come all this way to sabotage them.

♦ ♦ ♦

Fossil hunting is an enormous business. Like a gold rush. Below the 49th parallel, one can hardly set foot in a sedimentary wasteland without running into Edward Drinker Cope and Othniel Charles Marsh, who regularly resort to blackmail, theft, and robot ambushes in order to one-up each other. Up here, in the North-West Territories, our own scientists carry on in much the same way.

I had learned the rules of fossil hunting as a mechanic fixing robots for one Dr. Mandeville—though I had had to hide that from Dr. Fullerton, who was Dr. Mandeville's bitterest rival. Over time, Dr. Mandeville had grown to trust me enough to tell me his secrets, and to send me on special missions.

I hadn't thought it was in me to carry out sabotage. But I was shocked when Dr. Mandeville told me about Dr. Fullerton's camps. Why, when they finished, they dynamited whatever small fossils and fragments were left, so that Dr. Mandeville couldn't have them. Destroying irreplaceable knowledge in the name of sheer rivalry—can you imagine? So Dr. Mandeville had not asked me to hurt anyone.

Only to secretly dispose of the dynamite.

It was still deceptive, and I experienced occasional pangs of conscience, but Dr. Mandeville had offered me a great deal of money should I succeed. The alternative was to sit at home with my brother and his wife and their extremely noisy children, pretending to do needlepoint and having maybe one interesting robotics project per year, since customers in Ottawa preferred men. No, thank you: I preferred a life with autonomy, even if it meant lying to Dr. Fullerton while he talked my ear off.

♦ ♦ ♦

When I'd calmed down, I set to work erecting my own tent. I was not nearly as good with fabric and poles as I was with machinery, and the whole thing threatened to fall down several times, but I eventually got it straightened out. That done, I sorted all the tools in my carpet bag in order of size until I fell asleep.

The next morning dawned in a very pink way. I woke in considerably better spirits and felt much better able to handle Dr. Fullerton as he walked me around.

"The excavation itself is very delicate work," he explained. "Suited only for humans, not machines. It's only later that the machines come in..."

I could see why he wanted me to understand his procedures, but they were exactly the same as Dr. Mandeville's, so I stopped listening. Instead I looked out over the canyon, an intricate fold in the earth where Dr. Kerr and Mrs. Hattie Bond Cunningham clambered about in the cool morning air, worrying at the rocks with picks and whisk brooms. Sunlight glinted off some of the biggest bones. The team seemed to have stumbled onto something very impressive.

All the more reason not to let them dynamite it.

"Ah," said Dr. Fullerton. "But look at you. I suspect I've gone on entirely too long. Perhaps that will be all the lecturing for today! Do you have any questions?"

"No," I said.

He clasped my shoulder heartily and I tried not to squirm away. I don't always mind being touched, but the way he was doing it made the edge of my cotton shift scratch against my shoulders uncomfortably, under my jacket. "I am glad to hear it, Miss Howe! I like a woman with nothing to say. I must say I was concerned at first about adding another woman, but you've been meek, ladylike, and altogether pleasant thus far. Perhaps you'll help us keep Mrs. Cunningham in her place!"

I had no idea what Mrs. Hattie Bond Cunningham's place was supposed to be, but when he said it, I imagined holding her down to keep her in one spot. This led to thoughts which frankly were not ladylike at all.

"Thank you, Dr. Fullerton," I said.

He nodded. "Now, where did you say you learned robotics?"

I had a small moment of panic before I realized he was not interrogating me. He didn't suspect that I was a plant sent by his bitterest rival. He was simply doing the thing people call Making Conversation.

"From my brother," I said. "He has a degree in robotics. I

borrowed his textbooks. And his equipment. And eventually his customers."

"Hm. Where was that?"

"In Ottawa."

"Ah! I have cousins in Ottawa. What church did you go to?"

I swallowed, knowing things never went well when I said the name. "The Ottawa Spiritualist Temple."

Sure enough, his eyes sprang open. "So you go in for that sort of thing? Materialization of the dead? Girls walking around in little sheets?"

I shook my head. "I do séances with my family at home, Dr. Fullerton. I've never seen a materialization. Only the most powerful mediums can even..."

"Splendid! I know just what we'll do to welcome you to the camp, Miss Howe. You can do a séance for us! I've always wanted to see one. We'll all sit and chat with Mrs. Cunningham's husband or Harry's mother or whoever else you can drum up. How does that sound?"

"But..."

He clapped me on the shoulder again and I winced. "Splendid! Excellent! Oh, I'm glad we have you aboard."

He kept talking after that, and I couldn't get a word in.

I wanted to tell him that I wasn't comfortable with this. Séances, however pleasant, were not a form of entertainment. They were for me and my family and our spiritual development. Besides, although I had cultivated enough mind passivity to channel voices, I certainly couldn't produce the sort of spectacle Dr. Fullerton expected. In the presence of three spiritually disruptive strangers, I wasn't certain I could produce anything at all.

Still, even if I explained all that to him, he probably would not have cared—and if I started declining his requests, I might look suspicious. So I looked on the bright side. I hadn't done a proper séance since leaving home; all I had managed at Dr. Mandeville's camp was a bit of automatic writing. And I was curious about Mrs. Hattie Bond Cunningham and her husband. I wondered what would happen if she could speak with him. Perhaps she would be impressed with me. And I dearly liked the idea of Mrs. Hattie Bond Cunningham being impressed with me.

♦ ♦ ♦

It was Dr. Kerr's turn to make lunch. Dr. Fullerton had left me alone eventually, and I had worked up an appetite inspecting the robots. But when I got to the mess tent and found Dr. Kerr laboring over a badly maintained camp stove piled with stinking meat—none of which I could eat, due to my personal convictions—and carrying on a shouted conversation with Dr. Fullerton, I lost my nerve. I darted in, plucked a bit of cucumber and half-wilted watercress from the side table, and retreated outside to eat them.

A few minutes later, Mrs. Hattie Bond Cunningham flounced out of the tent herself and sat at my side. I was happy to see her, but it did nothing to calm me.

"Dreadful, aren't they?" she said. "Pompous, noisy men. I don't know how I deal with them some days myself."

"Er," I said.

"I can see why you'd want to eat out here," she said. "Such a view! I often take it for granted, clambering about on the rocks every day, but I shouldn't. One needs to take time to appreciate beauty in this world."

"Er," I said. "Yes."

I hated this part. The trouble with women like Mrs. Hattie Bond Cunningham was that I became fascinated with them too early. I was naturally reticent to begin with, and the presence of beautiful women only made it harder to speak. I had had special women friends in the past, but they had been the ones to pursue me. I didn't know how to do it the other way round.

I groped for something interesting to day.

"What's your favourite dinosaur?" I tried.

"Mine? I suppose I prefer the Troödons. We're finding a lot of them at this dig site—little things, up to your waist, with astonishingly large claws at the toes. Deadly predators, if you want to be technical, but I find them endearing." She looked at me sidelong. "Are you feeling all right?"

"Oh, I have weak nerves, that's all. I appreciate you coming out here."

She smiled at me for the first time: white teeth, charmingly crooked. I liked her smile.

"One gets used to Dr. Fullerton. I've been working with him for years. Since before James passed on. And you? Did you make your way here all alone, a quiet thing like you?"

"Yes," I said. "By small airship from Fort Calgary, though I am from Ottawa, originally." She had gotten the conversation back onto facts, which was much easier, so long as I remembered not to mention the incriminating ones.

"Then you were in Fort Calgary all by yourself?"

"Yes." And not just once; I'd been there on the way to Dr. Mandeville's camp, and again on the way here. But that was incriminating.

"With all the outlaws and cowboys? Were you frightened?" She didn't sound frightened herself, and I got the sense she was hoping I hadn't been.

"No," I said, which was the truth. "Fort Calgary isn't lawless. There were some men in strange clothes, but they didn't give me any trouble."

She smiled again. "You're so trusting."

"No."

People often told me that sort of thing, but I knew it wasn't true. If I were a trusting person, I wouldn't have come here as a saboteur, now, would I? I didn't trust Dr. Fullerton at all. Still, I couldn't say any of that, so I just fluttered one of my hands.

Mrs. Hattie Bond Cunningham caught that hand in hers. Which was something I had thought I had wanted her to do. But the edge of her sleeve was the scratchiest lace I had ever encountered, and I could not bear it brushing my wrist. I flinched, and she immediately let go of my hand.

"I'm so sorry," she said. "I didn't mean-"

"It's all right," I said. "It's not you, it's the lace. My skin-"

"Of course." Her cheeks were suddenly bright red. "I... I really ought to help them clean up in there. Men, you know."

I couldn't do anything in response but flutter, and she picked up her skirts and left me there feeling utterly ridiculous.

♦ ♦ ♦

It's a good thing that I work quickly. I had a basic inspection done on half the machines before supper, and I'd figured out the problem with the Hamilton-Smith—really just a worn-out drive block. In between doing those things I spent an unseemly amount of time breathing deep and sorting my tools in my tent, thinking of Mrs. Hattie Bond Cunningham. I kept worrying that she did not like me. I tried not to do it. I told myself that, once I allowed her to speak with her husband, everything would be fine.

Of course, there were other dangers inherent in the séance. It might not work, and Dr. Fullerton might decide that I was a charlatan. Or it might work too well, and some friendly spirit might warn one of them that I was a saboteur. This latter possibility occurred to me a little too late. I'd already taken on the risk.

The mess tent was not exactly a proper sitting room, but they had done what they could with available materials, bringing in the most comfortable cushions and clearing the small table. After dark, the mess tent's fabric adequately blocked out the moonlight. It was almost cozy.

We linked hands, and I recited a sonnet of which I was fond. Normally in my family we began with a prayer, but I didn't know these people well, and an uplifting sonnet would do.

"Now," I said, with our hands linked in the darkness, "the best thing to do is to focus on pleasant thoughts. You can sing or converse lightly. It may take a few minutes." I didn't know if I was explaining too much or not enough. I tried not to be frustrated, to remove my own emotions and be a pliant vessel for the spirits.

There was a lot of coughing and harrumphing for a while, but Mrs. Hattie Bond Cunningham saved me, raising her voice in the first verse of "Jerusalem, My Happy Home." It wasn't strictly a spiritualist song but it would do for now. Dr. Fullerton and Dr. Kerr joined in, slightly off-key, but Mrs. Hattie Bond Cunningham carried the tune very well. Her high voice relaxed me more than my own efforts.

The room became indistinct and I felt my own thoughts and volitions slipping away. This was working. Even in this strange company, I was nearing a proper trance, and the room was full of indistinct balls of light.

I wondered why there were so many spirits in these deserted badlands.

"James Cunningham," I whispered. "Mr. James Cunningham, do you hear me?"

I felt an emotion from Mrs. Hattie Bond Cunningham, but it wasn't the one I had expected. Granted, I often misinterpret emotions even in a trance, but she seemed confused or alarmed.

One of the lights moved toward me. Simultaneously, there was a strong, sudden rapping at the table. The others startled a little, hearing the sound though not seeing the lights, and then the table turned in place by thirty degrees.

"Oh my goodness!" said Mrs. Hattie Bond Cunningham. I felt that alarm from her again. I wished I could tell her to stop it.

Then my whole mind fixed on the light before me, and I saw its proper shape.

It was not Mr. James Cunningham. It was not even human.

The spirit, if I can call it that, was a sort of flightless bird, perhaps three feet high and standing on the table. It wore clothing, but of a sort I had never seen before: a scaled, leathery robe, and a satchel of the same material. It had huge talons and, despite the birdlike appearance, sharp teeth.

I knew that evil spirits sometimes disrupted séances. But evil spirits still looked like humans: rowdy sailors, for instance, and surly criminals. I had never heard of a monster like this. It terrified me. Yet I could not look away.

The bird spoke. It was a horrid rasping sound—I am not even sure how I identified it so readily as language. My own mouth opened in concert, but nothing came out except a hiss.

I felt rather than saw the others drawing back. This was not what they had expected. They didn't know what to do.

The bird cocked its head, looking at me through one eye as birds do.

"Who are you?" I whispered.

It paused, rummaged in that satchel, and drew out a small device. I had an impression of gears and circuits, like the robots I worked with, but even more intricate, its component parts mostly too small to see.

It stepped forward and pressed the device to my forehead. I could feel it there like a breath of wind. There was a clicking sound.

When it spoke again, it was still in rasps, but the words came out of my mouth in the Queen's English.

"Our bones," it—or I—said. "You walk above us and steal our bones. What are you? Where are your ancestors buried?" I hated the way the words felt. I was used to human spirits' words pouring through me like water. But these words were not human. They climbed all over my mouth and bruised it. The bird seemed warily calm, curious even, but my own voice rose to an unbearable shriek. "If you are here, you must do as we ask! Our bones!"

At that point it became altogether too much and I screamed. I put my hands over my ears, doubled over, and screamed until I could not see birds, lights, or anything like them.

I could hear the others saying things. "What in the devil-" and "Good Lord, girl-" and "Give her air, we don't know how-" But I wasn't really listening, not until a good while later when I'd finished screaming. By then the others had fled the mess tent, leaving me crouched in darkness, until I calmed down enough to realize that I'd just ruined my prospects here entirely.

♦ ♦ ♦

While I was still wondering what to do, Mrs. Hattie Bond Cunningham crept back into the mess tent holding a lantern. The light startled me.

"I'm sorry," I said immediately, wondering if she was here to send me away.

"Oh, no, don't be. We're all terribly worried, that's all. You had some kind of fit. I came to check on you."

"It wasn't a fit. I just..." I fluttered my hands, unable to explain.

"You saw something," she prompted, sitting down beside me. "Then you started raving about bones. Or it looked like you. Was that a spirit talking?"

"I think so." I looked up at her, defensive. "It's never happened like this before. Usually it's wonderful and uplifting. But this wasn't a human spirit, it was a great sort of bird. I couldn't make head or tail of what it was saying. I suppose I got overwhelmed."

I wondered suddenly if the evil spirit was a punishment. If some great power had decided that I wasn't worthy of seeing anything good, or at least not in the very same room as the people I was lying to.

"Dr. Kerr said that you must be hysterical."

"I'm not." I had actually been diagnosed with hysteria in my youth and given a vibrator, but while I didn't mind using it, it had no effect on the fits at all.

"I believe you. It's just that I didn't realize séances were so difficult for you."

"They aren't. This was an exceptional situation."

She nodded. "Being possessed by enormous birds, yes. I should be more worried if it *wasn't* exceptional. Still..."

"I should have told Dr. Fullerton I couldn't do it out here. Real séances are supposed to happen in the home with a loving family, not... out here with..."

With my victims. I couldn't quite say it.

Mrs. Hattie Bond Cunningham raised her eyebrows. "You mean to say this was Dr. Fullerton's idea?"

"In a way. But I knew there might be problems, and I didn't turn him down, so really it's my fault."

Her voice went sharp. "Of course you didn't turn him down. He is your employer, and you are a woman! You must have been wondering what would happen if you displeased him. Really, Lillian, you've done nothing wrong except failing to understand how he used you. You're too trusting, that's all."

I curled my legs up to my chest. "My brother told me I'd never last out here. I'm so ladylike and good most of the time and then I turn bestial at a moment's notice, and I can't control it. He told me Dr. Fullerton would throw me out in disgrace and he was right. I'm sorry."

Actually he had said that about Dr. Mandeville. I figured it was close enough.

She laughed unexpectedly, a big laugh, throwing her head back. "Dr. Fullerton will do no such thing! The man gushed about you all through dinner. You managed half again as many inspections in one day as any other technician we've had. You found the problem with the Hamilton-Smith, even. This isn't like Ottawa. Propriety comes in second to results. If you have fits every once in a while, well, we shall live with them."

"Oh," I said.

We sat in companionable silence, and then Mrs. Hattie Bond Cunningham said, "May I ask a question?"

"Of course."

"I thought I heard you say my husband's name, before you started to scream. Did you see him? Was he... with the monsters?"

I sighed. "No. I was looking for him; I thought you'd like it if you could speak to him. But he wasn't there."

There was a pause. "It's just as well," she said at last. "I miss him, but we were never... You know."

"Never what?"

"The spiritualist view of marriage is very liberal, isn't it? You say a true marriage isn't an economic or family arrangement, but a spiritual affinity between a man and woman. Is that correct?"

"Yes," I said, though I would have quibbled substantially with the "man and woman" bit.

"Well, that was the problem. James and I were friends, of a sort, but nothing more than that except on paper. It was my own fault. I wanted an ordinary family, but I never got the hang of spiritual affinities with men."

With men.

It was the sort of thing I would have missed when I was younger, but not now.

"Neither have I, really," I said. "I much prefer the company of women."

"Well, then, we have that in common."

I didn't want to be too forward. Just because she was interested in women didn't mean she was interested in *me.* Still, this felt like an important milestone, and I ought to say something. I ended up just fluttering some more.

"Oh, you poor thing," she said. "I'd like to embrace you, if that would help, but this lace..."

"Here," I said, relieved that she'd mentioned it first.

The bombazine wasn't nearly as bad as the lace. I arranged her arms around me so that the lace only touched my back, which was covered with a cotton jacket anyway. I leaned against her, resting my face against her shoulder.

"Does that help?" She sounded uncertain, though her arms were firm, warm, and wonderful around me.

"This is excellent," I said.

She opened her mouth to say more, but just then Dr. Kerr came stomping past the outside of the mess tent and we quickly disentangled ourselves. "How is she, Mrs. Cunningham? Is everything all right?"

"Yes, everything's fine," said Hattie. "Just a moment." She pecked me on the lips while he still couldn't see, then grinned widely, as though she had done something terribly brave, and hurried out.

Suddenly I wasn't so worried about the birds anymore.

♦ ♦ ♦

I didn't venture out of the mess tent until night. The badlands were still and shadowy, and Dr. Fullerton's snoring rang out in the quiet. I felt confident that everyone else had gone to sleep, but I was not at all sure they would stay that way.

I crept out to the KD8102 and picked the locks on the ammunition cases. Inside lay piles of dynamite: some in sticks, some in spheres. It was a good trick, hiding them here. I suspected that the KD8102 was for show, little more than an excuse for the explosives. That would explain why Dr. Fullerton had been reluctant to teach me about it.

Dr. Mandeville had instructed me in how to dispose of dynamite.

It was really the percussive shock of the blasting caps that set it off, not the burning of the fuse, so—counterintuitive as this was—the best thing to do was to burn it. I built a little fire out of sight of the camp and got to work, turning the dynamite itself to ash and burying the blasting caps separately. The spheres were heavier than I had realized; I could only carry a few at once, and that made for terribly slow work. By the time I had emptied a quarter of the ammunition case, I was exhausted. So I closed and locked the ammunition case, crawled into my tent, and prayed that Dr. Fullerton would not notice.

♦ ♦ ♦

Hattie was busy with fossils all the next day. There was a lot of cheering and hopping around: they'd found a really colossal group of those Troödon fossils, as well as something with hip bones the size of wheelbarrows. I tried to cheer back whenever they mentioned it, but my heart wasn't in it. They didn't have enough Whitman-651s to carry all these bones home, and that meant many would be dynamited. Yet they were cheering and grinning as though they saw no problems at all. I needed to hurry.

I finished fixing the Hamilton-Smith's drive block and then wasn't sure what to do until dark.

"Have a drink with us," said Dr. Fullerton, winking at me in a way that suggested he was already drunk, "if your nerves will allow. This is a colossal find, you understand. Have you ever thought about devising ways for our Whitman-651s to hold more?"

"I don't know," I said. I wasn't sure how many modifications I could make. There was not exactly a foundry pounding out custom machine parts to my specifications out here. And that was to say nothing of the structural integrity of the legs.

"Hah!" He seemed inexplicably pleased. "So there's an end to your knowledge. Well, if you're stumped, then tomorrow we'll teach you to help with the excavations. Maybe you'll be responsible for meals and laundry from now on, too. You've got to earn your pay somehow, after all."

So apart from meals and laundry, I was banished to my tent the rest of the day. After a few rounds of sorting my tools in order of size, I grew pensive. I had too much to think about: the dynamite, Hattie, the birds. I couldn't shake the feeling that the birds were a judgment on me somehow. That they knew I was doing this all wrong.

I decided to try automatic writing. I had often used this method to communicate with my mother in Dr. Mandeville's camp, and unlike a full séance, it was a thing I could do alone. In case of problems, I could break the connection simply by putting down the pen, and after a short lie-down, everything would be fine.

I took out a pen and paper and spread them out atop the toolbox. It was rougher than a desk, but it would do. I emptied my mind and began to write.

Writing makes no use of lights or moving furniture; there is only a feeling of connection, a vague excitement, and a sense of self-abandonment. I started with gibberish, of course, but meaningful words emerged more and more frequently. *Bones. Steal. Buried. Bones.*

Our bones must be eaten.

That sentence shocked me out of the trance. Eaten? I hadn't eaten animal meat for years and did not intend to start again. Besides, the only bones out here were fossils, which had turned to stone over the eras and could hardly be eaten even if we wanted to.

Our bones.

What did they mean, *ours?* They could not be the spirits of the dinosaurs who had died here. It had been tens of millions of years since the deaths of the last dinosaurs. By now they ought to be advanced beyond recognition and uninterested in our petty physical world. That's if they had spirits at all. Dr. Mandeville had always told me they were dumb beasts, lizards really.

Far more likely, these bird-creatures were the souls of something still living here. Something which knew about the fossils and claimed them as its own.

But *eaten?* That made no sense at all.

I picked up the pen again.

We do not bury our dead in boxes. The spirit needs the body no longer, and a body in a box is no use to anyone. The best use for a body is nourishment. Even when nourishment is not possible, we pretend to it. To let the spirit know its body was valued.

My head filled with images: not visual, like the lights at the séance, but tactile. I felt my teeth scraping along an already-stripped thigh bone, not eating but going through the motions of it, baring my canines like an animal. The movement was fraught with importance, much more than the sum of its components, like my own ritual of sorting my tools.

You must pretend to it. In this way you will show respect. We will know you are our friends.

The pen rolled out of my fingers.

I understood nothing. I was not sure I wanted to be their friend. But the scrape of bone lingered against my teeth, like an echo. It was disgusting. I had always hated eating meat; I saw no reason why one animal should live by tearing apart another.

Was this some twisted metaphor for my work here? Was my sabotage a form of predation? But destroying bones for one's own selfish profits—was this not *also* predation? How could I judge what was going on?

I tore the paper to bits and stormed off to cook lentil soup for supper.

♦ ♦ ♦

The next day I woke up awash in pink light with some ideas for increasing the Whitman-651s' carrying capacity. Even without extra scrap metal, there was a great deal I could do with extra sacks and satchels, hung across the edges like saddlebags, if only I could balance and secure them properly. The legs were designed to hold many times the allotted weight, as a basic safety feature, and if problems did crop up, well, we had me for repairs.

Dr. Fullerton waved his hands distractedly when I told him. "Yes, good work! That's actually fairly clever. Only we don't have any extra sacks and satchels at the moment, so why don't you come down here and learn to help with the excavations?"

He was in such a hurry to get me down there that I realized he must have wanted this all along.

So I spent the day with the smallest fossils, learning to excavate them safely: exposing a surface with the pick and whisk broom, sealing the cracks with smelly liquid cement, undercutting them with a chisel, then adding the layer of rice paper, the layer of tissue, and the disgusting layer of plaster which stuck to my fingers, followed by even more chiseling to repeat the process on the other side. All this for every single bone lodged in the rock. It was exhausting work, and I had absolutely no time to talk to Hattie. At the end of the day I collapsed in my tent with no energy left for dynamite—only a vague presentiment that I was failing.

The sacks and satchels never arrived, but there was plenty of hard digging for the next few weeks, plus equipment inspections, repairs, laundry and meals. I occasionally had time for a word with Hattie, but never as privately as I would have liked.

"You're working as hard as we are," Hattie said on one of these occasions. "You're not as efficient as us yet, but that's lack of experience; you're putting in the same effort. So why is he giving you all the laundry and meal duties on top of it?"

"Because my work in the ravine isn't as valuable as yours, and the robots don't take all my time. He has to add to my value somehow."

Hattie's eyes got very wide. "Did he say that to your face?"

"It's only the truth, isn't it?"

Hattie clicked her tongue. "Oh, Lillian. You're so trusting."

I don't know what happened with her and Dr. Fullerton after that, but the next day, we started rotating those duties again.

Dr. Fullerton and Dr. Kerr liked to stay up late, and I rarely had the energy to outlast them. The best I could do was drink a lot of water and wake up in the middle of the night, needing to use the privy. After that, I could usually drag myself to the ammunition box and cart off a few more armfuls of dynamite.

I thought on these nights, sometimes, of Hattie, and of what she would say if she knew I was doing this. Perhaps she would be angry. Perhaps there was a secret coldness in her heart, and she saw no problem with dynamiting fossils. Or perhaps she had never known.

But even more so than Hattie, my thoughts drifted to automatic writing. If these creatures cared so much about how their bones were treated, surely dynamiting the bones was a bad idea. Surely they should approve of what I was doing.

Sometimes on those nights, I saw lights at the edge of my vision or felt my teeth scraping bone, though I had not tried to go into a trance. That worried me. I hadn't been given to visions like this since adolescence.

We will know you are our friends. Perhaps it would be good to befriend them. Perhaps they would share their secrets. Or perhaps they were monsters and meant us harm. But rich men had an interest in monsters, alive or dead, else we wouldn't be out here.

Actually chewing on the fossils would be absurd. If I left any marks, that would be an act of sabotage worse than destroying the dynamite. But I was tempted.

Finally the night arrived when the last dynamite crumbled to ash in my little campfire. I felt very virtuous and suddenly full of energy. I wanted to run to someone and be congratulated, though of course that was silly.

Instead, I crept into the ravine and looked at the bones all lined up in the rock face.

I picked one at mouth level, only a quarter of the way exposed and not yet covered in rice paper. If I didn't actually touch the bone, I reasoned, I could do no harm. I placed my hands securely on either side, leaned in, and closed my teeth a centimetre away from the surface, turning my head as I did, like an animal tearing flesh.

I was starting to understand what the bird-creatures felt. The closing of teeth meant acceptance of pain. The turning of the head meant a willingness to move on. This was how they mourned, and it made a great deal more sense than black bombazine.

I felt invisible flesh on the bone. I bit the air again and imagined muscle between my teeth. I swallowed. I had always hated the taste of meat, but this was somehow different. It was as though, instead of destroying a life, my actions preserved it.

But I could not complete this process with the bones stuck in the rock face. More and more I longed to turn them in my hands. Like an animal.

Like the birds in my vision.

I crept back to the Whitman-651s, each one piled high with fossils. It was easy to pluck a bone the size of my forearm and bite into the air millimeters from the foul-smelling plaster. I spoke in the birds' rasping language, and this time it was not horrid. It was part of the ritual.

I was so absorbed that I didn't notice the footsteps until Hattie's voice startled me. "What on earth? Who goes there?"

I turned, the plaster-covered bone still in my grip. She was out in her nightgown, holding a lantern.

"Oh dear Lord," she said, and fainted prettily.

♦ ♦ ♦

I suppose I panicked. I dragged her back to her tent so as not to make a scene, and I meant to leave her there to recover, but I was seized with terror thinking of what she would do when she woke up. I was at my wit's end, not only fluttering but rocking back and forth, which I hadn't done for months.

Of course, Hattie took that moment to wake up and sit bolt upright. "What are you doing? What's going on?"

I said, "It isn't what it looks like," but I was still rocking and fluttering, which may have made it unconvincing.

Hattie's voice rose. "It isn't? Well, let me tell you what it looks like! It looks like I got out of bed to use the privy, and there you were, making horrid sounds and chewing on our fossils like a ghoul. Furthermore it looks like I trusted you and protected you and even kissed you once and now you've repaid me by being irrecoverably mad. Am I wrong about that, Miss Lillian Howe?"

"It was what the birds wanted. They said... It's respectful to them. They sort of..."

"Right," said Hattie flatly. "That's very nice. You stay here, and I'm going to get Dr. Fullerton."

"But..."

Hattie pushed aside the tent flap, stood haughtily—then froze.

"Oh dear Lord," she said again.

Outside a robot, even huger and more gun-heavy than the

KD8102, was thudding towards us.

It lit a pair of searchlights and swept the area, illuminating the canyon, the tents, the other robots—and our frightened faces. For a second, they also lit up the insignia on the robot's chassis.

Which said "MANDEVILLE".

♦ ♦ ♦

Everyone called me trusting. I never believed them. Dr. Mandeville had told me to remove all the dynamite from Dr. Fullerton's camp. Why would it be there, if not to destroy the smaller fossils? And I had done it.

But there was another use for dynamite. A camp with the right *kind* of dynamite could use it in self-defense. The robot had explosives. Thanks to my diligent work, our camp did not.

The robot lobbed a shot at the mess tent, which burst into flames with an appalling boom.

There was one thing worse than dynamiting fossils so your rivals couldn't have them. And that was dynamiting your rivals themselves.

♦ ♦ ♦

"The KD8102," I whispered.

Hattie whirled towards me. "Yes. You're the roboticist. You know how to pilot it, don't you?"

This was such an about-face that it shocked me. Besides, I didn't know how. Dr. Fullerton had never got round to teaching me, and I had avoided reminding him so as to put off his discovery of my godforsaken sabotage. "I thought I was irrecoverably mad."

"Prove me wrong." She looked around frantically. "I'll wake the doctors and get us out of here. Keep him away from the fossils. He's going to destroy the fossils, do you understand?"

"Yes," I squeaked.

"I'm not sure if it's loaded, but there's dynamite in the ammunition case. You should be able to-"

"No," I said, squeakier still. "Not right now, there isn't."

Hattie went so white I thought she'd faint again. "What on earth do you-"

The robot advanced on us. I didn't have time to explain. I pushed past her and ran out of the tent.

"Lillian!" Hattie shouted. "Come back here!" But she didn't move to stop me, and that was something.

♦ ♦ ♦

The KD8102's cockpit took forever to reach. I think my sense of time was going a bit funny.

I hadn't been trained for anything like this. The controls were unlabeled, just a bunch of switches, dials, and triggers. I flipped the largest switch, and the lights went on, with the familiar hiss of a steam engine.

As the KD8102 powered up, Dr. Mandeville's robot swung to face it, pointing its guns.

I'd taken all the dynamite from the ammunition case. I didn't know if there was a little left within the KD8102 itself, waiting to be lit and thrown. But if I wanted to try anything like that, I had to aim. There was something very much like a rifle sight to one side, with crosshairs and everything, but the levers beside it either lurched it around at random or did nothing. Frustrated, I tried the nearest joystick, and the cockpit lurched crazily as the KD8102 rose to its feet.

It began to run—just as the other robot fired, leaving a crater in the ground inches away.

I tugged the joystick to the left, to the right, hoping to dodge. More shots rang out, slowly—the other robot seemed to take a while to reload, which was perhaps a weakness—and one caught the KD8102 in the leg. I fell across the cockpit and slammed into the wall, and everything went haywire until I regained the controls. But I was catching on. It wasn't so different from other mobile robots. I was starting to be able to guess how far left the KD8102 would turn when I tugged the joystick left. Forward, and things went faster. Back, and...

Another explosion knocked me off balance. I started to hyperventilate.

Out of the corner of my eye I saw Hattie running for the fossils.

Dr. Mandeville's robot turned in that direction, too.

Hattie.

I pulled the joystick forward and the KD8102 thundered towards Dr. Mandeville's robot. The ground lurched past. Dr. Mandeville's robot turned towards me and fired.

I ducked. A second later there was an appallingly large sound, like the entire cockpit was coming apart. I got thrown into the wall again. Something crashed to the ground. But when I looked up, the cockpit was intact.

The thing that crashed to the ground, however, had been the KD8102's left arm.

I was past hyperventilating and actually making squeaking noises. But I found my way back to the joystick and pushed it all the way forward.

The other robot tried to dodge. I adjusted course to meet it. It was close to the canyon's lip now. It shot at me again and this time blew the top of the cockpit clean off. There was a horrible clatter, then a deranged cold whistling as the night air blew across the gap.

I was closing. Five metres, maybe. I braced myself.

The KD8102 crashed into the other robot.

It was a cacophony of crashing, grinding, booming, several jarring impacts, a series of lurches like the worst airship turbulence in the world, more crashing and grinding, more impacts, and then I'd like to say everything was silent but really there was only a reduction in the chaos. I peeked out from behind my hands and saw Dr. Mandeville's robot looming above me, or perhaps beside me. With the way my head spun, I couldn't tell at first.

We were on the floor of the canyon. The KD8102 was obviously totaled. Dr. Mandeville's robot had been partly crushed by the fall and several of its guns looked broken past repair. But not all. It held out a shaky arm and dragged itself back half-upright. It aimed at something—the half-buried fossils further down the canyon, or the fossils in the Whitman-651s, or Hattie and Dr. Fullerton and Dr. Kerr.

I pulled wildly on the joystick in every direction. Nothing

happened except smoke.

I'd failed. My very bravest charge in the KD8102 hadn't made up for what I'd done before. And those people I'd been working with, who probably never really destroyed a fossil in their lives, wouldn't make it out of here.

If they lived, they would never be hiring *me* again.

Then something moved at the edge of the canyon. Not the side where Hattie and Dr. Fullerton and Dr. Kerr had their camp, but the other side, where I'd never seen anything at all.

I could not understand why or how, but it was the bird-creatures from the séance, solid now. Rasping strange battle-cries. Swarming down into the canyon.

Climbing all over Dr. Mandeville's crippled robot.

Crashing it back to the ground.

There was loud trilling all over the canyon, like the howling of a wolf pack. I understood the sound. *Victory.* I wished I had the strength to trill back.

Dr. Mandeville's robot did not rise.

"Oh, good," I said weakly. Then I slumped over and curled up into the smallest ball that has ever existed anywhere.

♦ ♦ ♦

It's not that I fainted. It's more that I was overwhelmed into obliviousness. I remember Hattie pulling me out of the KD8102's wreckage. Someone put bandages on the parts of me that hurt worst. There was also a lot of shouting that I couldn't process, and bird-creatures every which way. I couldn't do a thing, not even rock back and forth.

Hattie towed me back to my tent and left me alone. I meant to just breathe deep for a long time, but somewhere in there I fell asleep.

When I woke up, the tent fabric glowed with early afternoon light and there she was sitting beside me.

"Oh," I said.

"Well," said Hattie.

We looked at each other.

"Sorry about that," I said, and then she picked me up and clung to me. "Ouch. Lace." She adjusted her grip.

"You *are* mad," Hattie said into my shoulder, "and you were right all along. You saved our entire camp in spite of whatever it is that happened to the dynamite, and I am utterly glad that you're here."

"Oh," I said. "Thank you."

I was still a bit worn out.

"They explained everything, you see. The creatures. They have these things that they put against your head to make you understand them. They said you proved yourself, so they came to help you." Hattie drew back. "But why on earth did you call them birds? Surely you noticed the teeth and the sickle-toes?"

"The what?"

"They're Troödons, Lillian, or close to it. Obviously they've evolved a bit, and we never imagined them with feathers in place of scales. But that's why there was all that shouting about 'our bones.' We've been literally excavating their ancestors. Can you imagine?"

I refrained from pointing out that I had seen it, and did not need to imagine.

"I imagine," I said, "other paleontologists will be very excited."

"Also biologists, anthropologists, the government and pretty much everyone. Dr. Fullerton says we're expanding the camp, inviting journalists and who knows what else. But I told him no one else was to talk to you today, on account of you being injured and having weak nerves."

I frowned. I didn't like the idea talking endlessly to journalists. I also didn't like the idea of Dr. Mandeville working out what had happened. And I didn't like the idea of having to explain to Dr. Fullerton and Dr. Kerr about the dynamite.

But I was unspeakably relieved to have Hattie here. And worse than journalists and Dr. Mandeville and Dr. Fullerton combined was the idea of running off without her.

"Besides," said Hattie, "I wanted to ask you a few questions myself, before the journalists got to you. I think you know what happened to all the dynamite, don't you?"

I buried my face in my hands and explained everything. How Dr. Mandeville had sent me as a saboteur. How he had lied. How I had believed I was protecting the fossils, when really I was only taking away Dr. Fullerton's defenses so Dr. Mandeville could move in and destroy him.

"So you see," I concluded, "I *am* mad. And stupid, and untrustworthy. And I would have got you all killed."

Hattie smiled slightly. "Maybe, Lillian. Maybe you would have. But the instant you worked out what you'd done wrong, you leaped into a robot you'd never piloted and you risked your own life to put things right. Do you know how rarely I see that sort of thing, even in men?"

I looked up at her, startled, and she chuckled.

"Mind you, there are parts of this story we will have to finesse for the journalists, and even for Dr. Fullerton, but I can help you with that. If you would still like to have me around, I mean. I was rather unreasonable last night, calling you a ghoul."

"Mrs. Hattie Bond Cunningham," I said, breathing a sigh of relief, "I would like to have you around for an extremely long time."

"Oh good," she said. And she kissed me.

It would be unladylike to tell you what happened next. But I did get all that horrid lace off of her at last, and not another word needed to be said.

The final tale in this volume is my own contribution, "Waiting for the Zeppelins." Like my esteemed co-editor's story "Space Pirate Stowaway," "Waiting for the Zeppelins" is a piece of the Weird Luck *saga. My contribution to* Spoon Knife 2: Test Chamber *(the previous volume of* Spoon Knife, *edited by Dani Alexis Ryskamp and Sam Harvey) was a massive 15,000-word* Weird Luck *novelette entitled "Bianca and the Wu-Hernandez," in which a young Reality Patrol operative by the name of Smiley tries to cheat on the qualifying exam for the rank of Special Agent and ends up getting in over his head. I was pleasantly surprised by how well-recieved "Bianca and the Wu-Hernandez" was—and even more surprised that despite its excessive length, a number of readers said they wanted more of it and wanted to know what became of Smiley. So, by popular demand, here's Smiley again. "Waiting for the Zeppelins" is set 27 years after the end of "Bianca and the Wu-Hernandez" (and about 10 months before Smiley's first appearance in the Weird Luck webcomic), so this time instead of a young Smiley we get a middle-aged Smiley—far more experienced and resourceful, but not necessarily wiser.*

Waiting for the Zeppelins

Nick Walker

The two men stood side by side on the observation deck atop the dome of the cathedral, smoking their cigars and watching the thick grey clouds that hid the sky over the city.

The bearded man in the brown tweed overcoat tossed the burning stub of his cigar out over the safety railing. It tumbled down the white surface of the dome, scattering bright orange embers each time it bounced, and then fell out of sight. He reached into his coat and fished out a gold-plated rectangular case, from which he extracted a fresh cigar. "To put it in the insipid vernacular of this grey and unpleasant land," he said, "a penny for your thoughts." He tucked the gold case back under his coat and carefully fitted the new cigar into his long ornate cigar-holder.

The short man with the big walrus mustache and the powder-blue trench coat tried to blow a smoke ring, but the cold autumn wind whipped the smoke away the instant it left his mouth. "I was just now speculating," he said, "as to whether the zeppelins would materialize above the clouds or below them."

"Below, I should think," said the bearded man. "I specifically instructed them to come in low."

"Does it not concern you, my dear Doctor Freud," said the man in the powder-blue trench coat, "that anyone who happens to be gazing upward at the precise moment of their arrival will witness your zeppelin armada appearing out of thin air? A feat which obviously could not be accomplished with the present technology of this particular version of Earth?"

Freud reached inside his coat again and produced a box of matches. Because of the wind, it took him nearly a full minute to get the cigar lit. "It concerns me," he said at last, "precisely as much as I am concerned by the fiery devastation my armada will subsequently rain down upon this doomed and blighted city, and the hundreds of thousands of deaths that will no doubt result. It concerns me, in other words, not the slightest whit." He took a puff of the cigar. "And now," he said, putting his hand in a coat pocket, "there is the matter of your final payment. Your assistance in this venture has been most helpful, my dear Gustav. Or should I say... Agent Smiley?" His hand came out of his pocket holding a small revolver, which he pointed in his companion's direction.

Smiley pinched one end of his mustache between his thumb and forefinger and gave a sharp tug, wincing slightly as it peeled away from his face. "What a relief," he said, "to finally be done with this itchy bit of disguise and the all the subterfuge it represents." He let the wind snatch the mustache from his hand and blow it away like a big furry leaf. "Might I inquire as to how you discovered my true identity?"

"You were betrayed," said Freud, "by one of your fellow Reality Patrol agents, who contacted me on his own initiative and asked no price for the information. I gather the man wished to be rid of you for his own reasons—perhaps related to the Reality Patrol's internal politics, the details of which are unknown to me but which I can only presume to be Byzantine."

"Ah," said Smiley. "Would he by chance have been a tallish and uncouth sort of fellow, with a restless temperament and a predilection for cheap cigarettes and excessive perspiration?"

"Quite so."

"Ah. That would be Agent Xax, then. I wish I could say I was surprised, but the sad truth of the matter is that these days one seems to find oneself surrounded by deceit and treachery at every turn."

Freud gave a melancholy sigh. "A deplorable state of affairs," he agreed. He studied the platinum filigree on his cigar-holder, still keeping one careful eye on Smiley, then took another puff of the cigar. "Before I kill you, Agent Smiley," he said, "let us see this thing through to its end. My armada should be arriving in this reality in a matter of minutes. Let us watch the bombardment together, as planned, here atop the only structure in this city my zeppelins have been instructed to spare. Such triumphs, after all, are best enjoyed in the company of those capable of appreciating the sublime perfection of the moment."

"I could not agree more, my dear Doctor Freud," said Smiley, "and I gladly accept your invitation." He remembered his own cigar and put it back in his mouth, savoring the rich flavor of the smoke.

"I am pleased to hear it," said Freud. "Despite your deception and your imminent demise at my hand, I am glad to have made your acquaintance these past weeks. Good conversation is woefully hard to come by. The majority of my associates, Tillinghast and the others... useful as they can be on occasion, they have no poetry in their souls."

"I, too, have found our conversations most engaging," said Smiley. "While we await the zeppelins, perhaps you would be so kind as to indulge my curiosity in regard to a personal matter. As you are no doubt aware, in the myriad parallel realities that make up the multiverse there are numerous versions of Earth whose histories include the presence of some version of Doctor Sigmund Freud. Nearly everyone has such parallel selves. 'Cognates,' is what the Reality Patrol calls them."

"I am aware of the phenomenon. What is it you wish to know? Whether I've encountered any of the cognate versions of myself? I have not, though naturally I have studied their lives and works with some interest. And you, Agent Smiley? Have you come face to face with any of your own cognates?"

"Indeed I have, on two occasions. Interestingly, both were women. But the chief question in my mind was not whether you've met other Freuds, so much as what sets you apart from them. In most realities in which Sigmund Freud has existed, he seems to have been a peaceful physician and philosopher, devoted to plumbing the mysteries of the human mind. How is it that the one Freud who has gained the ability to travel between realities should also happen to be the one Freud whose ethos, as it were, diverges so radically from that of the others?"

"It was precisely my discovery that I could travel between realities," said Freud, "and my subsequent discovery of the existence of parallel Freuds, that inspired me to transcend what we might term the Freudian norm. When I contemplated the sheer vastness and redundancy of the multiverse to which I had gained access, I was struck by two realizations. First, that any given human life was far less unique than I had previously supposed, and thus of far less value. And second, that in my personal drive to distinguish myself, I faced far greater challenges than I had hitherto imagined. It was one thing to stand head and shoulders above the bulk of humanity; quite another to distinguish myself from the legions of cognate Freuds on similar Earths, living parallel lives driven by similar ambitions. For a brief time, I confess, this thought vexed me nearly to madness. And then... I had a grand epiphany."

"Do tell," said Smiley.

"Ambition," said Freud. "The lust for power. The will to aggressively pursue the gratification of one's every desire. These drives are rooted in that primal part of the psyche I refer to as the id. The id is kept in check by the super-ego, my term for the morality—the sense of social conscience, as it were—that one internalizes in the course of one's early life."

"A most intriguing theory," said Smiley.

Freud gave a dismissive shrug. "Any version of me could develop such a theory, and most of them have," he said. "But my splendid revelation was mine alone. It came to me that while many of my cognates shared my brilliance and my ambitious nature, their avenues for achieving their ambitions were curtailed not only by their inability to travel between realities as I could, but more importantly by the limits imposed on them by their super-egos. To become truly unique, unparalleled and without peer even among my own cognates, I saw that what I must do was purge myself entirely of the super-ego, free myself from the strictures of morality and conscience. Like Nietzsche's *Übermensch,* or Overman."

"I confess this is beyond me," said Smiley. He was unfamiliar with Nietzsche, and wasn't sure what the less criminally-inclined versions of Freud might have said about the super-ego, but he had a nagging suspicion that the Freud currently holding him at gunpoint had interpreted certain concepts in ways not generally intended, and that no good had come of it.

"It is beyond any ordinary mind," Freud cried, "and even beyond any other Freud! I, alone among the many cognate Freuds, have freed myself from the curse of conscience and unleashed my true potential! Where lesser Freuds merely write about the dark appetites of the id, I dare to embody them! Of all the countless Freuds in countless realities, I alone have become... *the Overfreud!*"

Smiley wasn't certain what to say to this, but it seemed to him that he ought to say *something,* lest the moment become awkward. "You know," he ventured at last, "these really are excellent cigars."

Freud fixed him with the sort of look a hawk might give a mouse. "And what of you, Agent Smiley? You strike me as a man of some intelligence. The manner in which you insinuated yourself into my inner circle was artful; had you not been betrayed by Agent Xax, even I might not have discovered your deception on time. Yet in other respects your machinations seem oddly impractical. I must inform you at this point that my minions, at my prompting, have checked the engine of every zeppelin in the armada and removed the explosive devices your people had planted in them. So you see, the bombardment will proceed as planned, despite the minor inconvenience and delay that has bought us the time to have this final conversation."

"Ah," said Smiley. "This is a most unfortunate development."

"Unfortunate for you, to be sure," said Freud. "You have failed, Agent Smiley, and lost your life for nothing. Which brings us back to the impracticality of your methods, and the question of why. To secretly plant explosives in sixty zeppelins on a heavily-guarded base was an extraordinary feat—but as a stratagem for thwarting my plans, it involved far greater risk and effort, with far greater chance of failure, than any of numerous other options. For instance, would it not have been easier if the team of Reality Patrol agents you called in to plant those explosives had simply assassinated me instead?"

"I must admit," said Smiley, "that I have always lacked the ruthless efficiency for which the agents of the Reality Patrol are commonly known."

"This has gone beyond mere lack of efficiency, my good sir. Why did you not shoot me or arrest me the moment you got here? Why on Earth were you standing here and watching the sky with me, waiting for the zeppelins, when to the best of your knowledge the zeppelins were going to be destroyed by your explosives and never even arrive?"

"Why not? The view has been magnificent, the wind refreshing, and we have already remarked upon the fine quality of the conversation and the cigars."

"No," said Freud. "You cannot possibly be such a simpleton as that. There must be a reason. Something I'm missing..." He scowled, gnawing at the end of his cigar-holder. "Ah! Of course. You always *did* intend the zeppelins to arrive here. The explosive charges your team planted... they were set to detonate *after* the zeppelins were transported to this version of Earth, weren't they? That was your plan all along. My armada was to be destroyed not when it launched, but when it appeared in the sky above us."

"Naturally, my dear Doctor Freud. After all, it would have been a shame for either of us to miss the show."

"Do you mean to tell me, then," Freud said slowly, "that all the risks you took, all the effort, the inefficiency, the needless complications of your strategy... all this was just so you could stand here with me and personally watch the armada explode over the city?"

"Quite so, old chap," said Smiley. "As you yourself observed mere minutes ago, such triumphs are best enjoyed in the company of those capable of appreciating... what did you call it, again? Ah, yes. 'The sublime perfection of the moment.'"

"But... the city! Was it not your mission to prevent me from using my zeppelin armada to bombard this city?"

"That was the general idea, yes."

"But... if your plan had succeeded... if my armada *had* exploded in the sky over the city... would the rain of flaming debris not have done nearly as much damage as a successful bombardment?"

"I suppose it would have," said Smiley. "But it seemed worth compromising a bit on the objectives of the mission, for the sake of aesthetic considerations."

"Aesthetic... considerations?"

"Yes, you know... dramatic effect, the sublime perfection of the moment... all that sort of thing."

"Are you mad?" cried Freud. "To so drastically compromise your mission... to rain destruction upon the city you were meant to save... all for the sake of... of..."

"Aesthetic considerations," Smiley reminded him helpfully. "I confess I've always had a certain penchant for the dramatic. Perhaps it's the poetry in my soul, which you were so kind as to remark upon earlier. I was raised by a street theatre troupe, you know. Performing from the time I could walk. I suppose I never lost the taste for putting on a bit of a production."

Freud stared at him. "A bit of a production?" he cried. "Good God. You *are* mad. How in the world could you be a Reality Patrol agent? Doesn't the Reality Patrol vet its people better than that? I had heard there was rigorous testing involved. How could a reckless borderline psychotic like *you* have made it through their screening process?"

"There's actually quite an interesting little story to that," said Smiley.

"No," said Freud.

"Pardon?"

"No. You may be psychotic enough to treat your mission as some sort of theatrical production, to take absurd risks for the sake of some grand dramatic moment... That much, I believe. I have observed your bizarre theatrical tendencies. But to rain destruction upon the city you were ordered to save? No. That cannot possibly have been your true aim. Your career would have come to an end years ago, were you truly so brazen in your disregard of orders. What is more, you have been altogether too sanguine about your imminent death and the news that your scheme is thwarted."

Smiley's cigar had burned itself down to a stub. He took one last taste of it and tossed it away with a sigh. "When you put it that way," he said, "I admit my behavior does seem rather odd. Perhaps I *am* mad, after all. I shall defer to your professional expertise on the matter."

"Enough!" Freud bellowed. "Enough of your confounded prattle! Enough of your deceptions! You are hiding something, Smiley, and by God, I will..." He stopped in mid-sentence, struck by a sudden realization. His eyes narrowed, and when he spoke again his voice quivered with fury. "A ruse. The explosive charges were a ruse. You *meant* for me to find them, to disarm them, to think I had foiled your plan. A diversion, to distract me from discovering... something else. Another act of sabotage." He took a step forward and pointed the revolver at Smiley's left knee. "Damn you," he hissed. *"What did you*

do?" Without waiting for a reply, he pulled the trigger.

The revolver made a small anticlimactic clicking sound.

"Did I mention," said Smiley, "that I was raised by a street theatre troupe? To supplement the troupe's income, the younger members were required to master the fine art of the pickpocket. Earlier, when you were kind enough to light that cigar for me, I replaced your revolver with an identical one which contains no bullets." He reached for the coat pocket into which he'd slipped Freud's original, fully loaded weapon. "And now, my dear Doctor Freud..."

There was a flash of light and a crackling sound, and Smiley cried out involuntarily at the sudden searing pain in his upper arm.

Freud's ornate cigar-holder no longer held a cigar. A single wisp of smoke rose from the hole at the end of the cigar-holder and vanished in the wind. Smiley clutched at the place on the side of his arm, just below the shoulder, where the weapon's narrow beam had burned through clothing, skin, and muscle.

Freud tossed the empty revolver aside and aimed the cigar-holder at Smiley's torso. "A backup," he said, "hidden in plain sight. One sees the cigar, and takes the presence of the cigar-holder for granted. The cigar is just a cigar, yet it enables me to have a weapon in my hand at any time, with no one the wiser. You see, Agent Smiley, you are not the only one capable of misdirection. And now you will tell me what else you have done to sabotage my armada, or I will burn away a piece of you at a time."

Smiley gritted his teeth. "You'll find out soon enough," he said.

Two feet behind Freud, a luminous blue rectangle appeared in the air, the size of a smallish doorway, with its bottom edge about an inch above the surface of the observation deck.

"Very well," said Freud, not noticing the blue rectangle, "we will do this the hard way." He took another step forward, pointing the cigar-holder at Smiley's groin.

A woman in a black suit stepped out of the blue rectangle. She took the scene in with a practiced eye, her face showing not a flicker of surprise, then she lunged forward in a single smooth motion and touched a small device to the back of Freud's head. Freud's body gave a sudden jerk, and he collapsed unconscious at her feet. The deadly cigar-holder bounced and rolled away, over the edge of the observation deck and down the side of the cathedral dome.

"Impeccable timing as always, Ruiz," said Smiley. He put both hands on the cold metal safety railing to steady himself, then gripped the railing hard so Ruiz wouldn't see how badly he was trembling. He tried to sound nonchalant; he had a reputation for being unflappable, and he was determined to uphold it. "How in the world did you know to show up at just this precise moment?"

"I didn't," said Ruiz, kneeling to secure Freud's hands behind his back. "You got lucky. Again. Jackson sent me to fetch your ass back to Denebola Base because she needs you on some urgent secret thing. Shit, I only came when I did 'cause your team came home and said your mission was complete."

"It was," said Smiley. "I just wanted to watch the grand finale."

She came over to where he was standing. "Jesus, Smiley. You're shot. Beam weapon? Shit. Looks like the heat cauterized the wound, though. But, shit. You mean to tell me you were up here getting shot when it wasn't even essential to the mission?" She leaned on the railing beside him, and gestured back at the unconscious Freud. "Dude would've fried you if I hadn't shown up when I did. See, this kind of shit is exactly why I always request Dillon as my backup instead of you. Dillon may be a son of a bitch, but at least he understands the concept of an exit strategy."

"I'll grant that Dillon is highly skilled at staying alive," said Smiley. "But there's more to life than that. The poor fellow has no poetry in his soul."

"Poetry? Jesus, Smiley, I don't need poetry when I'm on a goddamn mission, I need a partner who has the sense to..."

She never finished the sentence, because the zeppelin armada appeared in the sky.

It happened without a sound. There was a slight shimmering in the air, and then the zeppelins were just there. Sixty of them, enormous, spread out in a perfect grid above the city, all of them at precisely the same altitude, hovering silent as death in the space between the rooftops and the clouds.

"Ah," said Smiley. "Here we go."

"Fuck," said Ruiz. "No. Fuck, fuck, fuck. This is bad. You were supposed to save the fucking city."

"And save it I did," said Smiley.

"Then what the fuck..." Ruiz started to say. Then she saw what was happening, and for a moment she didn't say anything at all.

"Once Freud's people defused the explosives we'd planted," said Smiley, "they assumed they'd foiled my plan. But the explosives were a decoy, so they wouldn't discover that we'd also tampered with the bombs the zeppelins were supposed to drop on the city."

"You replaced the bombs with… flowers?"

"Quite so. You see? Poetry. Dillon would never have come up with a finale like this."

They stood side by side and watched the zeppelins rain flowers upon the city. The flowers danced and swirled in the wind, scattering every which way, bringing the grey autumn streets and rooftops alive with the joyous colors of springtime.

"Okay," said Ruiz. "I have to admit this is pretty fucking awesome."

"I'm glad to be enjoying it in the company of someone who can appreciate the sublime perfection of the moment," said Smiley. "Can I offer you a cigar?"

About the Contributors

Alexeigynaix is a queer genderqueer multiply-neurodivergent multiply-disabled white poet and clergy education student under the auspices of the Hellenic reconstructionist polytheist organization Hellenion. They work in multiple artistic media, but painting with words is the most fun.

Programmed to be a mid twentieth century housewife with a second wave feminist veneer, **B. Allen** gleefully disappoints. Since the 1980s, in venues ranging from indie weeklies to the *Huffington Post,* Allen has been writing highly personal stories of disability's intersection with poverty, feminism, queer culture, and abuse. Keyword searches to find B. include: autistic, chronic illness, intersex, parenting, transgender, and queer.

Jeff Baker drives a delivery truck full-time and writes part-time. He has been published in *Space and Time, Sherlock Holmes Mystery Magazine* and three Queer SciFi anthologies, including *Renewal.* He lives in Wichita, Kansas with his husband Darryl and way too many Hawaiian shirts.

Melanie Bell is the coauthor of a best-selling nonfiction book, *The Modern Enneagram* (Althea Press 2017). She holds an MA in Creative Writing from Concordia University and has written for various publications including *Autostraddle, xoJane, The Fiddlehead, Every Day Fiction,* and *CV2.* She offers editing and writing coaching through Inspire Envisioning.

Sean Craven is one of those yard-sale talents whose achievements range from scientific illustration to stand-up comedy. His current reputation is as a crime writer. This is on the basis of his memoir performances. What can you say?

Alyssa Gonzalez is a biology PhD, public speaker, and writer. Her fiction uses science-fiction and fantasy elements to explore social isolation, autism, gender, trauma, and the relationships between all of these things. She writes at *The Perfumed Void* (the-orbit.net/alyssa), on the subjects of about biology, history, sociology, and her experiences as an autistic ex-Catholic Hispanic transgender immigrant to Canada. She lives in Ottawa, Canada with a menagerie of pets.

Judy Grahn is an internationally known poet, author, and teacher, with fourteen published books. Her newest release is *Hanging On Our Own Bones*, a collection of signature nine-part poems including "A Woman Is Talking to Death," and "Mental." For artists, a "My Good Judy Residency" has been established in New Orleans to study her literature and philosophy.

Alyssa Hillary is an Autistic math teacher, a part time AAC user, and a PhD student in neuroscience with a tendency towards poetry and/or well-cited rants when Emotions happen. Sier work appears in several previous Autonomous Press anthologies, on *Disability in Kidlit*, and on sier blog, *Yes, That Too* (yesthattoo.blogspot.com). Alyssa has been informed that sie is a mathematically sentient brick wall, which is plausible.

Ada Hoffmann is the author of *Monsters in My Mind.* Her writing has appeared in magazines such as *Strange Horizons, Asimov's,* and *Uncanny,* and her *Autistic Book Party* review series is devoted to autism representation in speculative fiction. You can find her online at ada-hoffmann.com or on Twitter at @xasymptote.

Old Cutter John is obviously some kind of troublemaker.

Andee Joyce is an autistic cat lady with currently no cats but a very understanding domestic partner, who lives in Hillsboro, OR. She performs and records her own original compositions under the name Normal Fauna featuring Andee Joyce, and her recordings and videos can be found on Facebook, YouTube, and Soundcloud under that name. In addition, Andee also writes young adult fiction, and her forthcoming novel T*he Amy Virus* will be published by Autonomous Press. She is proof positive that if you are still living, your story has not been written yet.

Mike Jung is the author of the children's novels *Geeks, Girls, and Secret Identities* (2012), *Unidentified Suburban Object* (2016), and the forthcoming *The Boys in the Back Row* (2019), all from Arthur A. Levine Books/Scholastic. His autobiographical essay on being autistic will be included in the young adult anthology *(Don't) Call Me Crazy* (2018, Algonquin). Mike is also a student at Aikido Shusekai, and lives in Oakland, CA with his family.

RL Mosswood lurks in the depths of the Pacific Northwest rainforest, where they dabble in mostly queer mostly fiction in an attempt to add a little magic to their otherwise mundane existence. Their debut novella *Golden* is available from Ninestar Press, or find them on Twitter as @rl_mosswood.

Inhabiting a Black transgender neuroqueer body and writing as **N.I. Nicholson**, the Teselecta Multiverse crafts poetry, creative nonfiction, and essays which have appeared in publications such as *GTK Creative Journal*, *Alphanumeric*, *Assaracus*, and *qarrtsiluni*. Editorial work includes collaborating with their life partner to produce *Barking Sycamores*, a journal for neurodivergent literature, and bringing transformative works to print on Autonomous Press' NeuroQueer Books imprint. Stay tuned for their upcoming poetry collection, *Time Travel in a Closet.*

Dora M Raymaker, PhD, is a scientist, writer, multi-media artist, and activist whose work across disciplines focuses on social justice, critical systems thinking, complexity, and the value of diversity. Dora is an Autistic/queer/genderqueer person living in Portland Oregon, conducting community-engaged research at Portland State University, knitting fractals, and communing with the spirit of the City. "Heat Producing Entities" is set in the same universe as *Hoshi and the Red City Circuit*, also available through Autonomous Press.

Eliza Redwood is a twenty-something poet and writer, with works often focusing on her struggles with mental illness. Her work has appeared or is forthcoming in *Open Minds Quarterly, The London Reader, States of the Union,* and *Pure Slush,* among others.

Andrew M. Reichart is author of the *City of the Watcher* trilogy, the novel *Wallflower Assassin*, and numerous short stories. He's also the line editor of Argawarga Press (an imprint of Autonomous Press). He and Nick Walker co-write the comic and fiction website *Weird Luck,* and have recently completed its prequel novel *Insurgent Otherworld.* Andrew lives in California with his wife and dogs.

S. Verity Reynolds is an anagram of Lee Harvey Oswald. Verity is the author of *Nantais*, Book 1 of the Non-Compliant Space series. The Non-Compliant Space expanded universe resides at verityreynolds.com. Book 2, *Nahara*, will appear in 2019 from NeuroQueer Books.

Steve Silberman is the author of the *New York Times* bestseller *NeuroTribes: The Legacy of Autism and the Future of Neurodiversity*, which won the 2015 Samuel Johnson Prize and is being translated into 14 languages. He lives with his husband Keith Karraker in San Francisco.

Nick Walker is a Managing Editor at Autonomous Press, a faculty member at California Institute of Integral Studies and Sofia University, and senior instructor at the Aikido Shusekai dojo in Berkeley, California. Together with his longtime collaborator Andrew M. Reichart, he is co-creator of the Weird Luck saga, an ever-growing body of interconnected stories and comics (including stories that appear in this volume and other volumes of *Spoon Knife).* The Weird Luck webcomic, plus a bunch of Weird Luck prose fiction and information on where to find even more of it, lives at weirdluck.org.

www.ingramcontent.com/pod-product-compliance
Lightning Source LLC
Chambersburg PA
CBHW051006180726
48291CB00006B/1990

9781945955143